"Eason resumes her Lake City Heroes series with a propulsive game of cat and mouse between a fire marshal and an arsonist who's eerily familiar with her past. . . . The result is a thrill ride worth taking."

Publishers Weekly on *Serial Burn*

"A fast-paced thrill of a ride from start to finish."

Library Journal on *Target Acquired*

"Lynette has another hit on her hands. *Target Acquired* grabs hold with nonstop action."

Dani Pettrey, bestselling author of *Two Seconds Too Late*, on *Target Acquired*

"Eason skillfully metes out details of the families' backstories, adding depth to a zippy plot."

Publishers Weekly on *Target Acquired*

"Lynette Eason at her best. Smart plotting, action-packed suspense, well-developed characters, and sweet romance. . . . I devoured it in one sitting."

Reading Is My Superpower on *Double Take*

"Eason's first book in her Lake City Heroes series grabs you and doesn't let you go."

Booklist on *Double Take*

"I thoroughly enjoyed the characters, the banter, and the suspense."

Jaime Jo Wright, ECPA bestselling author, on *Double Take*

"*Double Take* is phenomenal and had my heart racing from the moment I started reading. Brilliant plot. Incredible story."

Kimberley Woodhouse, bestselling and award-winning author

FINAL
APPROACH

BOOKS BY LYNETTE EASON

WOMEN OF JUSTICE

Too Close to Home

Don't Look Back

A Killer Among Us

DEADLY REUNIONS

When the Smoke Clears

When a Heart Stops

When a Secret Kills

HIDDEN IDENTITY

No One to Trust

Nowhere to Turn

No Place to Hide

ELITE GUARDIANS

Always Watching

Without Warning

Moving Target

Chasing Secrets

BLUE JUSTICE

Oath of Honor

Called to Protect

Code of Valor

Vow of Justice

Protecting Tanner Hollow

DANGER NEVER SLEEPS

Collateral Damage

Acceptable Risk

Active Defense

Hostile Intent

EXTREME MEASURES

Life Flight

Crossfire

Critical Threat

Countdown

LAKE CITY HEROES

Double Take

Target Acquired

Serial Burn

Final Approach

LAKE CITY HEROES • 4

FINAL APPROACH

LYNETTE EASON

Revell

a division of Baker Publishing Group
Grand Rapids, Michigan

Published by Revell
a division of Baker Publishing Group
Grand Rapids, Michigan
RevellBooks.com

Printed in the United States of America

Library of Congress Cataloging-in-Publication Data
Names: Eason, Lynette, author.
Title: Final approach / Lynette Eason.
Description: Grand Rapids, Michigan : Revell, a division of Baker Publishing
    Group, 2025. | Series: Lake City Heroes ; 4
Identifiers: LCCN 2024053863 | ISBN 9780800741228 (paperback) | ISBN
    9780800747060 (casebound) | ISBN 9781493450565 (ebook)
Subjects: LCGFT: Christian fiction. | Thrillers (Fiction) | Novels.
Classification: LCC PS3605.A79 F56 2025 | DDC 813/.6—dc23/eng/20241122
LC record available at https://lccn.loc.gov/2024053863

Cover image: Rekha Garton / Arcangel
Cover design: Ervin Serrano

Emojis are from the open-source library OpenMoji (https://openmoji.org/) under the Creative Commons license CC BY-SA 4.0 (https://creativecommons.org/licenses /by-sa/4.0/legalcode).

Baker Publishing Group publications use paper produced from sustainable forestry practices and postconsumer waste whenever possible.

25 26 27 28 29 30 31   7 6 5 4 3 2 1

Dedicated to Jesus.
I love you more than I have words to express.
Thank you for letting me do what I do.
May I do it for your glory, honor, and praise. Always.

ONE

Air Marshal Kristine Duncan leaned back in her seat, her eyes skimming over the sunrise outside the Airbus 319's window. Minutes ago, they left the Lake City, North Carolina, airport and had just leveled out at cruising altitude after a smooth climb. When the Lake City field office opened a little over two years ago, she'd taken the offered position without hesitation. Moving away from Asheville had been a good thing. In many ways.

The hum of the aircraft was a familiar comfort, but it was a smaller craft than she usually flew, with only one aisle and three seats on either side. She and her friends were about halfway back in the main cabin. Not her favorite seat, but she wasn't complaining.

This was her last flight as an on-duty air marshal for the next two weeks. Vacation with fun and sun was on the horizon. She went through her usual flight check, scanning the passengers and the luggage being brought on board and noting those traveling with her.

Lainie Cross had already fallen asleep in the middle seat, her head tilted slightly to the left. How the woman could sleep like that was beyond her. In the window seat, Jesslyn fiddled with her new camera. The excitement on her normally reserved features made Kristine smile. She'd just gotten into photography, and her husband, Nathan

9

Carlisle, had purchased the Canon R5 Mark II for her birthday along with two very nice lenses. Kristine couldn't help wondering how much that had set him back. Detective Tate Cooper and his wife, Stephanie, had settled in two rows up and had their heads together, talking quietly.

"I can't believe we're actually doing this," Jesslyn said, leaning forward, her voice low. "How long have we been planning this? Six months? It felt like six years to get to this point." She had her red hair pulled into a casual ponytail with a few stray tendrils curling around her temples. A smattering of freckles crossed her nose and fanned out over her cheeks. "Ten days at an all-inclusive resort in Key West, snorkeling, scuba diving, parasailing—"

"I'm not parasailing," Kristine said. "No way."

Jesslyn raised a brow at her. "But you love to fly."

"In a plane. With a skilled pilot—or two. Or frankly, myself flying. With safety protocols in place. Not at the end of a rope attached to a boat with a driver who may or may not know what he's doing."

"Could be a she."

"Exactly. And neither of them may know what they're doing."

Jesslyn laughed. "You're still taking flying lessons?"

"I am. It makes me feel like I have more control."

"You've been doing that forever. Don't you have your license yet?"

"Just have to take the test." Her heart pounded at the thought.

"And when are you doing that?"

"I don't know." The truth was, she'd been putting it off ever since she'd had an issue with her first attempt. Something she'd not shared with anyone for a multitude of reasons.

Her tone must have conveyed her desire to terminate the subject because Jesslyn went back to her camera with only a raised brow.

Kristine looked over her right shoulder and across the aisle to see Kenzie King and Cole Garrison engrossed in a travel guide, plotting their adventures—and probably their wedding—while James, Lainie's husband, was lost in the latest bestselling thriller by Kate Angelo. Kristine drew in a deep breath, taking in the atmosphere of anticipation and relaxation. It was a hard-earned break from their often hectic lives. With the exception of Lainie, who was a physician's assistant, they were all in some form of law enforcement, and the last couple of years had been chaotic. Thankfully, the last six months had been "quiet." Or at least "normal" for them and their occupations.

Her gaze drifted across the aisle and back one row, where a man sat immersed in his notes. FBI Special Agent Andrew Ross. Smart, dedicated, and definitely too handsome for anyone's good. His blond hair was slightly long, but not long enough to hide his green eyes from her. His five o'clock shadow was making an attractive appearance on his usually clean-shaven features. She and Andrew had known each other for a while now, but it was only lately that they'd acknowledged they wanted to get to know each other even more. She had to admit spending time with Andrew on a sandy Key West beach sounded like an amazing adventure. If she could just get past her fear. She'd avoided romantic entanglements most of her life simply because she was afraid that would entail giving up a lot of control over her life. She cleared her throat and pushed the thoughts aside, wishing she could dump her baggage once and for all.

Maybe one day. Her friends who were all pairing up at the speed of light didn't seem to have her issues and were offering her hope that maybe her perceptions of romantic relationships were wrong. That she wouldn't be giving up control of her life but sharing it. It was a nice thought, she just wasn't sure it was realistic.

Andrew looked up and caught her gaze. His soft smile stole the breath from her lungs. And then there was that. Every. Single. Time. She forced herself to smile back before returning her gaze to the other passengers, studying the ones she could see. All seemed well as, thankfully, it usually was. So why were her nerves itching?

"Come on, Kristine." Jesslyn reached across the still-dozing Lainie and nudged Kristine's arm. "Relax."

"I'm trying," she said. "Seriously. It's hard, though." She forced her features into a serious expression. "But keep your camera ready.

Nathan may decide to cut loose and dance down the aisle or something."

Jesslyn smirked and Kristine laughed. That was about as likely as below-zero temps in the Keys.

The laugh felt good. It was a bubble of normalcy in the midst of a tension Kristine couldn't shake off. She glanced around the cabin, her trained eyes scanning the other passengers once more. Most were absorbed in their own worlds. Sleeping, chatting with seatmates, reading, snacking, and trying hard to keep restless children occupied.

Once she connected to the plane's Wi-Fi, she sent a text to her brother and sister.

> On the way to Key West. I'm looking forward to the vacation, but wish the three of us could have some time together. Look at the calendar for next year and pick a date, okay? Take care and talk soon.

Emily and Ethan were twins and were six years younger than her thirty-two years. She'd been looking after them since their mother's death sixteen years ago and loved them fiercely.

When she looked up, one man five rows ahead, sitting in the aisle seat to her right, caught her attention. He seemed on edge, his movements rigid, jerky. She'd noticed him as they boarded, but he settled down, so she just decided to keep an eye on him. It appeared his restlessness had returned, though, and Kristine narrowed her eyes. Nervous flier? Personal problems? Or something more?

Or nothing?

The aircraft jolted, and a brief but rocky turbulence silenced the occupants. Kristine gripped the armrest, her body tensing. The captain's voice came over the speaker. "Sorry about that, folks. Hit a little pocket there. We're back to cruising smoothly, so go back to your book or your movie and we'll be on the ground in about an hour and a half."

Kristine relaxed. She wasn't usually jumpy. She flew all the time, but today . . . there was just . . . something.

Lainie, now wide awake, quirked a brow at her. "You okay?"

"Yeah. Yes, of course." Again, the turbulence was nothing major. It happened.

The uneasy passenger stood up. Looked around. Then headed to the back restroom. Kristine shifted so she could watch for his return. At the ten-minute mark, she was about to ask Amanda or Jeffrey, the two flight attendants, to go check on him. Just as she started to rise, the man exited the lavatory and passed Kristine to take his seat again. Andrew rose and walked to the front of the plane, slipping around Amanda in first class, and went into the lavatory. Kristine caught Amanda's eye as she moved into the main cabin. Jeffrey was at the tail of the plane. Amanda raised a brow and nodded in the direction of the man who'd captured Kristine's attention.

Kristine gave a subtle nod back.

Amanda moved toward him, her smile friendly and professional. The passenger jumped to his feet again, his hand diving into his jacket as he stepped into the aisle.

Kristine reached under her jacket to release the snap holding her SIG in its holster. She'd intervene only if the cockpit was threatened. Andrew and Nathan were FBI. They had their weapons and would handle it to that point.

Amanda stopped next to him. "Sir, please sit back down," she said, her voice calm but firm. "Everything is fine. If you'll just put your seat belt on—"

"Stay back!" He pulled out a makeshift knife and held it to the neck of the person in the aisle seat next to him.

Amanda let out a startled yelp and stumbled back.

"Unbuckle or I'll slit your throat," he told the passenger.

She obeyed and he pulled the woman to her feet. Her shocked whimpers reached Kristine's ears even over the eruption of the panicked, screaming passengers.

Nathan rose, pulling his gun. "FBI," he said. "Drop your weapon. Now."

"I'm getting in the cockpit," he shouted. "Open the cockpit!" His words were directed at Amanda.

A threat to the cockpit. That was Kristine's cue. She pulled her gun and stood. "Everyone, stay calm!" The command in her voice stilled most of the people. "I'm an air marshal," she said. "Sir, you need to drop the knife now." The cockpit had a keypad code that only certain people knew. Amanda was one of those people. Kristine threw a look at Nathan. If he had a clear shot he'd take it, but right now, he didn't. No one did.

"I got your back," Jesslyn murmured. "We all do." Jesslyn was a fire marshal, but she was also trained law enforcement.

Kenzie was also on her feet. A detective with the Lake City Police Department, Kenzie was a member of the SWAT team along with Cole and James, who also stood ready to assist. They wouldn't have their weapons on them, but they were still powerful backup.

The man's gaze flicked around the cabin, his desperation clear. "This plane is not going to Key West! I need the captain to fly it to another destination where I plan to disappear. Let me in the cockpit. Now!"

Disappear? Hmm . . . maybe. She wasn't sure she believed that.

Kristine kept her focus on him and moved into the aisle toward him. If she could get close enough, she could take him down, but firing at him with a hostage in front of him wasn't an option at the moment. "We can talk about this," she said. "No one needs to get hurt."

Andrew stepped out of the lavatory, his eyes bouncing between Kristine and the hijacker, who had his back to Andrew. It took him a nanosecond to read the situation. She shot him a quick glance and he gave a subtle nod indicating his readiness to help. His hand went to his weapon. Would he have a shot?

No. Amanda had just moved between Andrew and the hijacker. He frowned and shook his head. No shot.

Passengers whispered prayers, some crying, as the hijacker's hand trembled.

In a flash of movement, a man across the aisle lunged at the hijacker. The cabin erupted into chaos as the assailant, caught off guard, plunged the homemade weapon into his hostage's shoulder.

The wounded woman's scream echoed through the cabin and she went to the floor—and left the knife in the hijacker's hand. He swung the blade and caught his attacker across a raised forearm. Blood spurted and the man screamed and fell back. Another passenger jumped up to help him. "I'm a nurse," she said.

Andrew rushed at the hijacker and Kristine looked for an opening. Anywhere she could put a bullet in the man, but he twisted and slipped away from Andrew. Quick as a blink, he had his weapon against another woman's throat. "He shouldn't have done that! He shouldn't have . . . I didn't . . . She's . . ." He turned his attention to his new captive. "Get your seat belt off and stand up or I'll cut you too!"

Lainie rushed to help the fallen woman while James looked like he wanted to protest, but he clamped his mouth shut.

"Now!" The assailant's scream propelled the passenger to her feet. He pressed the knife against her skin, nicking it. A trickle of blood slid down and disappeared into the collar of her T-shirt. She squeezed her eyes shut but made no sound.

Kristine edged toward the assailant while motioning to Andrew to go to the left. He nodded his understanding and moved in accordance.

The hijacker swung the knife in front of him, keeping everyone at bay, then pressed the weapon once more against the neck of his hostage. "Stay away. I need in the cockpit. Someone open the cockpit door now or I'll—I'll slice her open! I will."

The woman bit her lip. Kristine caught her gaze and tried to convey she needed to remain calm. The woman stayed quiet, but her fear was a tangible thing.

Kristine didn't blame her.

Andrew moved in sync with Kristine, edging closer to the hijacker.

Slow, calculated steps. Each second stretched into an eternity while her mind raced, planning her next move. She had to end this before anyone else got hurt. Her mother's death flashed in her mind. Had her mom been as afraid as this hostage? Kristine could see the woman's tremors from her position in the aisle, but she was trying to be brave, to be strong.

"Sir," Kristine said, "no one can open the cockpit. You know that."

His eyes swept the sea of passengers. Some who were on their feet. He was looking for someone. His gaze locked on one of the passengers and tears trickled down his ashen cheeks.

"Th-then she dies!"

"No!" Kristine held out a hand. "Wait. Tell me. Once you get the cockpit door open, what do you plan to do?"

"Take control and fly where I want to go." His eyes flickered, and Kristine had a bad feeling he wasn't telling the truth.

"You can fly a plane?" She would play along for now.

He snorted. "Of course not. The pilot will."

Andrew had settled into an empty seat so when the man swiveled his head to look in his direction, Andrew looked like any other passenger. When the guy turned his attention back to Kristine, she caught Andrew's movement from the corner of her eye. He stood and moved closer. Nathan was ready to act as well. James, Kenzie, and Cole were waiting for her signal, but right now, no one had a clear way to stop this man without possibly hurting someone else.

The hijacker held the knife out in front of him once more, briefly removing it from the woman's throat. "Stop moving!"

Kristine froze and he swept the knife back beneath the woman's chin.

"I'm sorry. I have to do this. It's time."

TIME FOR WHAT? Andrew wondered.

"Time for what?" Kristine said.

"Time to do what I ask," the guy said.

Kristine took another step forward. "Where do you want to go? What's your plan?"

He shoved the knife toward her. "Stop!" Then back to his victim's throat. "It's not your business. All I need is to talk to the captain. I'll tell him where to go."

"What's your name?"

"It doesn't matter. Stop moving!" The knife swept out and back one more time.

Kristine stopped. "What are you going to do?" She took one more small step toward him.

Come on, shift and give me a clear shot. Andrew silently willed the man to move. But he was being surprisingly clever in his positioning.

"Hey! Put it down!" The yell came from several rows back in the main cabin.

Kristine shot a glance over her shoulder and Andrew caught movement in his peripheral vision. A passenger from the back raced up the aisle to tackle another passenger. Kristine's attention momentarily shifted to the commotion.

The man holding the other passenger on the floor of the plane looked up. "He was heading toward you! I had to stop him!"

"Stay there," Kristine ordered. "Both of you!"

She took another step toward the attacker, who swung the weapon out toward her. "Stop moving! I'm not playing with you!"

Before he could pull the knife back toward his hostage, Andrew moved fast, coming up from behind. He jammed his left arm over the attacker's right forearm, shoved the woman away, then grabbed the guy's wrist with his free hand. He twisted the captured arm down and back. The man screamed and struggled, but his one-armed fight was no match for Andrew's vise-like grip.

Kristine lunged in and snapped a cuff around the extended wrist while Andrew finally put enough pressure on the hijacker's other wrist that he released the weapon. It clunked to the floor. Nathan swooped in to snag it with a gloved hand, Andrew cuffed the defeated man's other wrist, and then it was over.

Then the clapping started. Passenger by passenger until the plane was filled with thunderous applause by those who weren't capturing the moment on their phones.

Ugh.

"I'll stay with him," Kristine said. "You call it in."

He nodded and got on his phone.

Lainie had the plane's first aid kit and had put it to good use to help the woman who'd been stabbed.

"How is she?" Kristine asked.

"Fortunate. Her name is Bri. I've cleaned and bandaged it as best I could, but she needs stitches and pain meds. Thankfully, the blade went in just above her collarbone, and while painful, I don't think it went deep enough to cut anything major. Jugular is intact and she's breathing great." Lainie smiled at the woman, who blinked up at them from her position on the floor. She patted the woman's non-wounded shoulder. "You're going to be fine, Bri."

"Thank you," Bri whispered, then closed her eyes.

"I was going to take a look at the other woman, but when I started to go to her, she waved me off."

Kristine patted her friend's shoulder. "Thanks."

Thirty minutes later, they touched back down on the Lake City tarmac and rolled to a stop at the gate. The prisoner sat still and silent, chin touching his chest, refusing to talk or look at anyone.

As soon as the door was opened, Andrew hauled the sullen man to his feet, and he and the others escorted him into the hands of waiting FBI agents. He'd be taken to the Lake City County Detention Center where Andrew and Nathan would head to question him. He could only hope the guy was in a more talkative mood than he'd been once detained.

Andrew stood on the tarmac and gripped the bag holding the weapon. He marveled at the creative piece of "art." Sturdy wire cut into pieces fashioned into a blade and held together with superglue.

Then superglued to the end of a toothbrush. Everything that fashioned the "knife" was allowed in a carry-on or could be purchased in the airport after going through security. Except for the wire and the superglue. So how had those two items made it through security?

"Unbelievable," he muttered. He couldn't wait to search the guy's bag.

"That's the weapon?" Kristine asked.

He turned. As always, her beauty threatened to unnerve him. He cleared his throat and ordered himself to focus. "Yes. It's clever, I'll give him that." Nathan and the others joined them.

"Who is he?" Nathan asked.

Andrew held up a black leather wallet. "ID says Marcus Brown. Forty-seven years old. Lives in Lake City." They walked into the terminal. "You ready to go talk to him? I had a friend drop off a car for me."

"Great minds think alike," Nathan said. "I'll see you there."

Lainie oversaw the transport of her patient and the other two wounded passengers to the waiting ambulances and said goodbye to the others.

Andrew glanced at his phone. His mother had texted him.

I saw the news. Are you all right?

He tapped,

> I'm fine, Mom. Back in Lake City, but fine. I'll fill
> you in soon. Let Felix and Carson know pls.

She sent him a thumbs-up and a heart, and he tucked his phone back into his pocket. His brothers would be messaging any moment now. Instead of waiting for them to do so, he sent them a text on the family loop.

> I'm fine. Busy wrapping things up. Will text or call
> later. Love you all.

His brother Carson was thirty-three years old and an architect in Atlanta, Georgia. He was older than Andrew by twenty-three months. Felix, their younger brother at twenty-nine years old, was a professional photographer, high in demand in the wedding and family portrait industry. He worked out of Greenville, South Carolina, and was married, with two girls. Andrew found it rather odd his parents tended to land where he was and not with their grandchildren, but he was glad whatever their reasons were. He climbed into the Bucar and headed for the detention center.

TWO

Kristine made it to the detention center about five seconds ahead of Andrew and Nathan. The press was already camped out front, waiting to swoop in like a pack of vultures on fresh carrion. Scavenging for any pieces of story they could peck out.

"Kristine! Kristine!" The female voice stopped her, and Kristine turned to see her sister, Emily, among the reporters desperate for anything she'd toss in their direction. Emily shoved her way to the front of the pack, not caring one bit about the glares and unkind words hurled at her.

Kristine walked over to her and hugged her.

"You're okay?" Emily asked. "Really okay?"

"As you can see, I'm fine."

"I was so worried. So stinking scared. I . . ." She choked on her words. Her strawberry blond hair—an exact match in color to Kristine's—fell around her shoulders in waves and gentle curls. Emily's green eyes were narrowed and her remembered fear shone clear.

Kristine hugged her one more time. "Come on inside with me." Emily followed her, Nathan, and Andrew into the building. Kristine looked at the men. "Can you give me five minutes?"

"Of course," Andrew said.

They nodded to Emily and headed down the hallway to the interrogation room.

Kristine turned to her sister. "I'm fine. Truly. I texted Dad to let him know too."

"He's the one who called me. You could have texted us all at the same time."

"I knew he'd let you know. And I wasn't sure you didn't know already."

Emily sniffed, swiped a tear, then dug her pen and notebook from her purse. "Well, now that you mention it . . ."

Kristine huffed a short laugh. "No, sorry. I've got nothing to say."

"Come on, I'm your sister. Give me the exclusive."

"It's an ongoing investigation. *No one* gets an exclusive. Not even my reporter sister. Sorry."

Emily sighed. "I won't push."

"It's nice to have one family member who won't," Kristine muttered.

"Just ignore whatever Dad says. You know he's going to give you a hard time."

"I know. I've got to go. Stay here and we'll talk when I'm finished."

Emily nodded and Kristine headed down the hallway. She couldn't help thinking about her family dynamics, though.

She wanted to call her dad old-fashioned, but even that wasn't exactly accurate. He'd been a strict disciplinarian, sparking defiance and rebellion in all of his children. Only their mother's calm influence had softened his rough edges. But once she was gone . . .

Kristine shoved thoughts of her father from her mind and focused on the situation. While she wouldn't be an active participant in the investigation—her job was done as soon as Brown was released into FBI custody—she'd be following this one very closely if the guys would agree.

She caught up with Nathan and Andrew. "Are you guys okay with me being in there?"

Andrew shrugged. "Fine with me."

Nathan nodded. "You'll have some good observations and questions we may not think of."

"Thanks. Anyone find his wife?" she asked.

"Not yet. Ready?"

"Ready." As the three of them entered the interrogation room, she stared at the man who'd just endangered a plane full of people. And for what?

Andrew sat in the chair opposite the silent prisoner, who refused to look up. "All right, Mr. Brown," Andrew said, "we'd like to hear your story."

The words were soft, compassionate, curious. Kristine had never worked a case with Andrew or Nathan, so she was interested in their approach.

Nathan started to say something and Andrew shook his head. Nathan snapped his lips shut, leaned a shoulder against the wall, and crossed his arms.

Mr. Brown didn't move.

Kristine followed Nathan's example and stayed silent. But she really wanted to know why she was here and not almost to Key West.

"Mr. Brown?" Andrew pushed. "I have a feeling you didn't want to hijack that plane today. I'd really like to know what compelled you to do so."

Now the man lifted his head and looked Andrew in the eyes. "It's Marcus."

"All right, Marcus. I'm listening."

"I'm dying."

Kristine raised a brow, then bit her lip. Sometimes it was better to stay silent than prompt the suspect to keep talking.

"If you mean you're literally dying, then I'm sorry to hear that," Andrew said.

"That's what I mean." A pause. "Why are you being so nice to me?" Marcus blurted, his brown eyes confused, brow furrowed. "I just did something I never would have thought I'd do. Ever. And I did it for money. You should be yelling at me, beating me to a pulp, whatever. But you shouldn't be nice to me."

"You did it to pay for medical bills?" Nathan asked.

Marcus slumped and shook his head. "To leave for my family." He sighed and dropped his chin to his chest once more. "I was diagnosed about ten weeks ago. We're broke. Once I'm gone, my family will have nothing."

"What about your wife?" Andrew asked. "She can't work?"

"She cleans hotel rooms. We have six kids, a mortgage, and no family. We both grew up in the foster system, and while we've worked hard and built a good life, it's still a hard one with both of us employed. There's no way she can support them by herself." Tears tracked his cheeks. "We wanted better for them," he choked out. "So when a man approached and asked me if I wanted to earn some money, but it would require great sacrifice, I said yes."

"Who?" Kristine asked. She glanced at Andrew, who gave a slight nod.

He looked at her. "I don't know. It's not like he gave me his name. Just handed me an envelope with fifty thousand dollars in it and said there was another one of those envelopes for my family if I did what he wanted me to do. But there were all of you law enforcement people on the plane." He laughed without humor. "Of course there would be a whole SWAT team on there." He glanced at Kristine. "And an air marshal." He heaved a sigh, then coughed. And coughed. His face turned red and he finally wheezed to a strangled croak.

Kristine rose. "I'll get medical help."

But he raised a hand, and she paused. When he caught his breath, he shook his head. "It passes," he finally managed to say. "Although it's taking longer and longer. Back to the fact that there was an entire police force on the flight—I should have known."

"Just a few of us are from SWAT," Andrew said with a straight face, "but you met this guy who paid you in person?"

"Yes."

"So you can work with a sketch artist and give us a description."

"Not really. He kept a baseball cap on, wore sunglasses and a surgical mask." He swallowed. "I know I'm in trouble, but I didn't think I'd survive."

"Why not?"

He shrugged.

"What exactly were you supposed to do once you got into the cockpit?"

"Demand the pilot take me to a different airport."

Andrew exchanged a look with Kristine, and Nathan leaned forward. "Which one?"

"He said it didn't matter, we just couldn't land in Key West."

"Okay. What did he say to do when you landed wherever you planned to land?"

"He didn't say to do anything. Just that I would know when I got there." He coughed again, another strangled fit that Kristine wasn't sure he'd recover from. Once again, she almost went for help, but the fit passed. Shame coated his features. "The truth is," he rasped, "I wanted the plane to crash. Then it would be done. I would be free of this miserable life and my family wouldn't have to watch me die. It would just be done."

Along with everyone else on the plane.

"And you were okay with killing all those innocent people on the plane with you?" Andrew asked as though reading her thoughts.

Marcus closed his eyes and shook his head. "No," he whispered, "I wasn't okay with it."

Kristine suppressed a shudder. But he would have done it. If she and the others hadn't been there, he might have succeeded. He was thin and looked tired—and the cough was scary—but she wouldn't have any idea he was actually dying if he hadn't said so. "How long have you been given?"

"They refused to give me a time. Could be a couple of days, could be a couple more weeks without treatment. I did the first two rounds of chemo, but I'm not doing any more treatments."

She blinked. "Not that it's any of my business, but may I ask why not?"

"The doctors say the cancer is too far advanced and I'd only be prolonging my life for a couple of months. What's the point in doing that? Also, my wife's mother died a horrible death with chemo and . . ." He waved a hand. "As a child, watching her go through that left an impression. It nearly killed my wife. Left her with a horrible fear of losing someone that way again. I won't put her through it." He pursed his lips. "She doesn't know I'm terminal. She just knows I've been fatigued and lost weight and was sick for a while . . ." He shuddered. "Anyway, I just wanted to leave her the money. To make her life easier when I'm gone. I left her a note explaining everything. I'm sure she's read it by now." He heaved a sigh and released a sob. "I've really messed up, haven't I?"

To say the least. Kristine had so many questions but couldn't stop the compassion and sympathy flowing through her. He'd made wrong choices for the right reasons, she supposed.

Not that it mattered in the legal sense. Assuming he was being truthful about his medical condition, he'd spend the rest of his limited days behind bars, then cuffed to a hospital bed. His poor family.

Andrew and Nathan exchanged a look. They felt for the guy, too, but needed to get the rest of the story from him.

She slid a tissue box toward him, and he mopped up his face, getting control of the crying. "Sorry. I'm sorry. I'm sorry for it all."

A little too late, but she kept that thought to herself.

"We need to know about the man who hired you," Nathan said. "Can you think of anything about him that stood out? A tattoo? The way he spoke? An accent, any kind of physical mark above the mask?"

"Um, no, but he told me part of the deal was that I needed to get this tattoo." He rolled up his sleeve and a three-headed snake coiled to strike popped off his skin in 3D. It looked real enough that Kristine wanted to step back. She hated snakes.

She hated what the tattoo represented even more. She looked at Nathan and Andrew. "The Serpentine Network."

Andrew's jaw tightened. "They're behind this?" He looked at Marcus. "Are you a part of that gang?"

"Gang? No way. Why?"

Andrew nodded to the tattoo. "That's their symbol. This is their way of taking credit for the hijacking?"

"Maybe."

Kristine narrowed her eyes and looked at the man, whose gaze was pinging among the three of them. He was truly confused.

So was she. "I've got to admit, this is a new one for me." She glanced at the men. "You ever heard of something like this?"

Andrew shrugged. "I've heard of some crazy stuff, but a gang putting a non-gang member on a plane and forcing them to hijack it? That's not gang work, that's terrorism. And while gangs often spread terror, I've not come across anything like this before."

And a gang certainly wasn't going to pay someone to do it.

"You were looking at someone," Kristine said to Marcus. "One of the passengers. Who was it?"

Marcus fidgeted, shifting his feet and raising his still-bound hands to rub his nose. "Um . . ."

"Look, Marcus," she said. "Planes are grounded, people's lives have been disrupted because we can't let anyone else go anywhere until we know if you were working alone."

"But I was," he blurted.

"And yet we can't take your word for it. We've been all over your social media history—of which you have very little—and your background check is clean. None of this adds up to you doing what we all know you did."

The man dropped his gaze and a tear leaked down his cheek. "I know. No one else is involved. I swear." He swallowed hard. "At least not that I know of. It's possible the guy could have found other schmucks like me." He swiped the tear with the back of his hand.

"Exactly," Andrew said. "Now talk. You want us to tell the judge you cooperated or not? Who were you looking at on the plane?"

Marcus shifted, a tic pulsing in his forehead. "I . . . I can't tell you that."

The man's surge of fear was obvious and Kristine frowned. "Why not?"

"I failed. He'll know I failed, and my family . . ."

"We can protect your family," Andrew said. "But only if you tell us everything."

For a moment, the man looked at his shaking hands clasped together and resting on the table. "You'll make sure they're safe?"

"Yes. I'll send someone over there right now," Nathan said. He reached for his phone and held it until Marcus nodded.

"I was told the passenger in 29C would be watching me, and if I chickened out, he would call the person who hired me and tell him. And that he would not only go get the money from my wife, but he would kill her and my children too." The last words came out in a whisper and the tears tracked his cheeks again. "I had no idea what I was getting into when I agreed to all of this. If I could go back and say no, I would."

But he couldn't.

Nathan headed for the door. "I'll be right back. I'm going to make a few calls."

Kristine nodded. He was going to make arrangements for protection for the Browns and to track down the passenger who'd been in that seat. She pulled Andrew to the corner of the room out of earshot of Marcus. "This is all off. Marcus isn't terrorist or gang material."

"And yet, he did this."

"He did. You worked in the gang unit for a while, right? I don't suppose you have an informant inside the Serpentine Network."

He shot her a tight smile. "I think I can come up with someone."

AFTER THEY GOT MARCUS settled in his cell, under surveillance considering his state of mind and desire to die, Andrew climbed into his Bucar and rolled Kristine's question around in his head. Could he come up with someone inside the Serpentine Network? Yeah. He could. He just didn't want to. A year and a half ago, he'd walked away from the gang unit, requested a transfer, and never looked back.

Much. At least not when he was conscious. His dreams sometimes snuck up on him, taking him back to that day when he'd gotten an innocent man killed. He winced and really considered what he was about to do. By reconnecting with Hank, another FBI agent and buddy who'd been undercover with the gang a very long time, he could totally re-expose himself to the network. It was a long shot, possibly, but not impossible. But what choice did he have? With a prayer for protection—for both him and Hank—he sent a coded text to his buddy, then stuffed the phone in his back pocket. Hank would call when he could, and if anyone else saw the text, nothing about it *should* set off any alarms. It was the same message they'd used when Andrew was under with him. Before his world went haywire.

But dwelling on the past didn't do anyone any good. Besides, he had more pleasant things to think about.

Like Kristine. What was it about her that he liked so much?

That was easy.

Everything. From her strawberry blond hair to her gray eyes to the three freckles on the bridge of her nose. He also liked the fact that she was kind, smart, had a rather dry sense of humor. And the list went on. But getting involved with her? He wasn't sure that was smart. He'd avoided any kind of serious romantic entanglement for the past several years. First, because of his job. Working undercover, he'd had no desire to bring a woman into that life—because of the danger and because it just wasn't fair to do that to someone. Now that his life wasn't one big lie, he could potentially be interested in someone. And he was. But . . . there was that word. *But.* He still wasn't sure it was fair to do that to her. He came with baggage—and a hit on his head. If Showbiz, the head of the gang he'd been under with, ever found him, he'd kill him and anyone Andrew cared about.

He walked into the Airbnb he'd found at the last minute now that he wasn't going to Key West and shut off his heavy thoughts. He locked the door behind him and pulled in a deep breath. That first hit of a new place smell always made him grimace, but he'd get used to it. He always did. He set his keys and laptop case on a table in the kitchen, then walked across the living area to crank up the air-conditioning, pull the drapes shut, and turn on the floor lamp. He could admit he was disappointed he wasn't in Florida sitting on the beach with Kristine, getting to know her better. But should he want that? He had baggage. Then again, who didn't, right?

But still, he'd trusted in a woman's love before, and when the going got tough, she got going. Walked away without a look back over her shoulder. So much for supporting him when his life went black. But something told him Kristine would be different if he was brave enough to trust her.

"Stop it," he muttered out loud. He could second-guess pursuing a relationship with Kristine all night. Even list the pros and cons. There would be more pros, but the cons would probably carry more weight.

He sighed and glanced around the rest of the place. Sofa, television, gas log fireplace, which he flipped on, coffee table, and a recliner that looked like a good spot for naps. He carried his bag into the bedroom and tossed it onto the bed. The place would serve the purpose. Hopefully he wouldn't be here too long.

His home was a small functional apartment in Asheville near the Bureau's branch off Patton Avenue, but for the duration of this case, he'd be working out of Lake City. His parents had moved here after Andrew had been assigned to Asheville. While they liked being close, they preferred a small town to the bigger city.

He smiled and shook his head. No one had been more surprised than he when they'd decided it would be fun to live in North Carolina, because none of their grandchildren were here. They'd opened up a bookstore off South Spruce Street that had a nice-sized apartment above it. No surprise there. They'd owned a bookstore for as long as he'd been alive. It hadn't always been the case, but his parents were now wealthy, living off investments and inherited family money, following their dreams, their whims . . . and occasionally, one of their offspring.

While he was a child and even a teen, his parents had worked every day in the bookstore, with his mother leaving in time to pick him and his siblings up from school, take them to all their afternoon activities, then have dinner on the table in the evening. Weekends were sports, church, and abbreviated bookstore hours. It had been a great childhood, and they all liked each other as adults.

With him in town for who knew how long, they'd offered to have him live with them and use the spare bedroom. He was tempted, but his job didn't always have the best schedule, and he didn't want to risk disturbing them should he be called out in the wee hours of the morning. He frowned. His cousin Corey was supposed to be moving in with them at some point as well. Definitely a sore spot. And Andrew wasn't interested in being in the same state with the guy, much less the same living space. He'd warned his parents, but his mother was adamant. His mind flashed to the conversation with her just a few days ago.

"He said he needs a place to stay," she'd said. "He also said he's not asking for money, just a bed until he can find a job."

"Okay." Weird, but okay. Corey had always been the troubled kid in the family. Drugs, gambling, alcohol. If there was trouble, Corey found it. He managed to shorten his prison sentence by agreeing to rehab. Then and now, he *always* needed money. "Are you considering it?"

"Well, yes, of course. He's my sister's son. What if it were you? I'd hope she'd take you in."

"I'm not sure that's wise, Mom." It definitely wasn't wise, but she'd held her ground.

Now, he took his angst about the situation to God. *I'm going to need your help with this, Lord. Like seriously. You know Corey and you know this isn't a good idea.* He grimaced. He probably shouldn't be telling God what was and wasn't a good idea. *I'm sorry, Lord, I'm just worried about this whole thing and need you to give me wisdom in how to deal with it.*

His phone buzzed with a text from Nathan.

Meet at the Cornerstone Café. We'll grab some food while the officers pick up Erik Leary. Dude from 29C. Then we ask him questions on a full stomach.

Andrew voice-texted back.

Throwing my stuff in the Airbnb. Be on the way in about five minutes.

He glanced at his phone. Still no word from Hank.

Fifteen minutes later, he walked into the restaurant and made his way to the table in the left corner. Nathan looked up from his menu. "All settled?"

"I think so. It's a nice place. I'll be fine."

"You can always stay with me."

"Not gonna happen. You're planning a big move. What does Jesslyn think about y'all leaving Lake City? You haven't really said."

A soft smile curved his partner's lips at his wife's name. "She said she can be a fire marshal anywhere. And if there aren't any positions available when we find out where I'll be, then she'll volunteer until something opens up." He rubbed his chin and shrugged. "She said now that she'd put her family's killer behind bars, she could finally focus on something else and doesn't mind taking the time to figure out what that is. In addition to me, of course."

Andrew chuckled. "Of course." He met his friend's gaze. "She's a keeper." He opened his menu, then shut it. He knew what he wanted.

"She is. Kristine should be here in a bit. She had to run home for something but said to order for her."

"Let me guess, cheesecake."

"Yup."

Kristine lived about five minutes from the restaurant when she was in town. She had a townhome she rented from her father and always frowned when the subject of who she rented from came up.

"How's it going collecting all the phone footage of the hijacking?" Andrew asked. "You get an update yet?"

All the phones from the passengers had been taken as evidence. The footage would be downloaded and the phones returned, but it took time.

Nathan shook his head. "Haven't heard a thing."

Kristine finally entered and slid in the booth next to Andrew. He watched her from the corner of his eye. She liked salads. And chocolate. And cheesecake. Especially chocolate cheesecake. "Emily okay?" he asked.

"Yes. She wanted a scoop on the hijacking, but when she realized I wasn't talking, she agreed to drop it. For now. I told her when the press conference would be and she plans to go to that. Then she wanted to borrow my big suitcase. She's going on a cruise tomorrow with some of her friends from college. They all agreed not to lose touch after graduation and to take a week out of each year to reconnect and have fun."

"Nice," Andrew said.

"Isn't it? Imagine that. Being able to go on vacation as planned."

Nathan snorted. "Yeah, imagine that."

"We'll get there soon," Andrew said.

Kristine pulled in a deep breath and let it out slowly. "But we're *not* there, we're *here*, and I'm *starving*." She took a big bite out of the mountain-sized piece of chocolate cheesecake the waitress had set in front of her, closing her eyes as she relished the bite.

A bit of cheesecake clung to her bottom lip and Andrew cleared his throat, forcing himself not to imagine what it might be like to have the right to kiss that away.

All righty then. He snagged a napkin and passed it to her. "You've got . . . right here." He pointed to his lip.

She met his gaze and took the napkin, then swiped her lips. He looked away. What was it about her that wanted to smash through every romantic defense mechanism he'd built over the last couple of years?

Nathan laughed. "So, let me guess, the salad cancels out the calories in the cheesecake?"

"Exactly," she said and took another bite.

"Are you going to eat that whole thing?" Andrew asked.

"Why? You want a bite?"

"More than just about anything."

Nathan laughed and Kristine snickered while she pushed the plate in front of him. He swiped a large bite, and the sugary cocoa explosion was definitely something to be savored. "Wow. That never gets old."

"Right?"

Nathan's phone buzzed and then Andrew's.

They both got the same message. Erik Leary was at the jail awaiting interrogation. He passed the word to Kristine.

All joking aside, they finished their meals in record time, paid, and headed out the door.

THREE

Kristine was tired. The day had started early with an adrenaline rush of excitement about the trip and ten days of sun and sand. Then there'd been the adrenaline spike triggered by taking down a hijacker. As for the motive behind the attempt, Kristine wasn't sure. Yes, Marcus's motive was crystal clear. But if he was telling the truth about the person who hired him—and she thought he was—then that was murky.

Terrorist plot or weird gang thing or . . . ?

And why the tattoo?

She didn't know, but they'd figure it out eventually.

She pulled into the detention center once again, parked, and walked inside. Andrew and Nathan were waiting just inside the glass doors.

"What's the background on this guy?" she asked. "You get that information yet?"

Andrew nodded. "Married, father of three, deacon in his church, volunteers with his wife at the homeless shelter once a month. And more. But absolutely no obvious connection to the hijacker and nothing to indicate he's involved in this."

She frowned. "And yet . . . *this*."

"Yes."

Nathan shook his head. "Something is very wonky. Nothing about this is adding up."

"Anything else?"

"Nope. He's waiting on us. Ready?"

"Ready." Once again, she followed them back to an interrogation room where Erik Leary sat. He had his hands loosely clasped on the table, but one leg jiggled. His green eyes bounced among the three of them much like Marcus Brown's had.

"What is this? No one would tell me anything." He paused and gasped. "Wait a minute. I know you three. You were all on the plane today. What's going on?"

Andrew took the lead and sat in the chair opposite Mr. Leary. "Do you know a man by the name of Marcus Brown?"

"No."

No hesitation, no blinking, nothing. Either this man did not know the name Marcus Brown or he was an excellent liar. Kristine had no idea which was true.

Andrew nodded. "He's the man who hijacked the plane we were on this morning."

Now the man blinked. "And that was terrifying, but I still don't understand why I'm here." His eyes widened and he gaped for a fraction of a second. "Wait. Surely you don't think I had something to do with that."

"We're not sure. You were seated in 29C and the hijacker identified you as an accomplice of the man who hired him."

"An accomp—what?" Mr. Leary sputtered and finally managed, "Why would he say that? That's not true!" He shuddered. "I thought we were going to *die*. I would never . . . no." He shook his head. "Please tell me you don't believe that," he whispered.

Nathan sighed. "Look, we're just in the initial stages of the investigation and you were specifically identified by the hijacker as someone involved."

"But I wasn't. At all."

Kristine found herself believing Mr. Erik Leary even while she cautioned herself to be careful. Some people were excellent liars.

"I don't understand why he would do that." He raked a hand over his head. "I don't know what to tell you. If you're going to arrest me, do it and let me call my lawyer. Otherwise, I'd like to go home. It's been a day to say the least and I just want to be with my family. The family I wasn't sure I was going to see again this side of heaven."

"Was that your original seat? Or was it changed?"

"It was my original seat."

"Did you make the reservation online? Through a travel agent? Phone call?"

"Um, online."

"What devices did you have with you?"

The man scratched his nose. "Um, my laptop, my iPad, and my phone."

Kristine, Nathan, and Andrew exchanged glances, then Andrew nodded. "We have no evidence to hold you so you're free to go, but if you think of anything, even if it's so small you think it's not important, will you get in touch with us?" He slid his card across the table.

Mr. Leary nodded. "Of course."

Nathan led him out of the room and Andrew looked at her. "We'll do our due diligence, but my gut says he wasn't involved."

"My gut agrees with yours, but I've also run into some really good liars. Once we eliminate him based on solid evidence, then I'll trust my gut."

"Same."

Kristine pursed her lips. "If he made that reservation online and chose that seat, how did the person organizing this whole thing decide to choose that particular seat? And why? There's no way he could have known who would be sitting there. Could he?"

"Not unless he—or she—has access to the booking system."

Now that was a thought.

Agents were questioning the other passengers one by one, asking if any of them switched from their original seats and why, but no other suspects had come to light. And no software security breaches had been reported.

Andrew sighed and shook his head. "Someone went to a lot of

trouble to try and send that plane somewhere else. The question is, why?"

HANK GALLAGHER finally texted him back while he was studying the crime board they'd set up in the office. At the top of the pyramid was Marcus Brown. A dry-erase marker line connected him to Erik Leary. Another line led to the big question mark labeled "mastermind."

Other agents were delving into Brown's and Leary's backgrounds and bank accounts. They questioned friends and family and went through every bit of passengers' cell phone footage. And more.

For now, Andrew and Nathan would focus on the Serpentine Network. Dread pooled in his belly at the thought of having to revisit those dark days and face the guilt that he managed to dodge except when he slept. Finally, he pulled in a ragged breath and looked at the text once more.

I can FaceTime in 30.

Asking Hank to make contact put the man at risk—and himself as well as he was still persona non grata with the Serpentine Network. The sting he'd been a part of had left more than one gang member dead. Including the leader's son. If they ever found out where he was, he was a dead man. Not that they knew who he was or would even recognize him if they saw him. But Andrew didn't feel like he had a choice. Not if he was going to do his job like he needed to. *God, I need your help. I thought I'd put the past behind me, but if I'm this torn up about talking to Hank again, I can see we've got some work to do. Please help me deal with this, keep me from delving into places I don't need to go.* He paused. *Or if I do need to go there, then meet me there.* His throat was tight and tears had pooled without him realizing it.

When his phone rang, he hesitated a fraction of a moment to make sure he could talk and to press the moisture from his eyes. Then he tapped the screen to pull up Hank's face. The forty-five-year-old undercover agent had leathery features, gang tats across his left cheek, and a scar that split that tattoo down the middle to disappear beneath the collar of his black T-shirt. "How are you, man?" Hank asked.

"Doing okay." *Liar, liar, pants on fire.* "How 'bout you?"

"Doing all right. But for real. How are you?"

Andrew swallowed, not wanting to visit that time in his past in spite of his prayer for help. "I'm dealing. Trying to move on."

"Dude, you're not anywhere near South Carolina, are you?"

"No."

"Good, 'cause Showbiz is still calling for your head." Showbiz. The leader of the Serpentine Network and the father of one killed thanks to Andrew's information on another bust. The bust that had blown his cover. The plan had been to pull in Showbiz's son, Paddy, to question him and turn him against his father. Unfortunately, the guy had been killed, but not before he'd seen Andrew and gotten off a text to his father that Andrew was a fed. A four-word text that changed his life. *"Warning Drew a fed."* Hank had the flu at the time—the only reason his cover had stayed intact and no one had ever connected him and Hank. Andrew had gone home, shaved his beard and mustache, cut his long hair, gotten the tat on the side of his neck and down his arm laser removed, and now looked like a completely different person.

"I know," Andrew said, "but we don't have time to delve into that. The longer we talk, the riskier it is for you." He couldn't fathom yet another death on his conscience.

"Tell me what you need."

"You heard about the hijacking?"

"Of course. It's all over the news."

"The guy has an SN tat on his arm."

Hank fell silent. "I haven't heard anything about a plan to hijack a plane. If I had, I would have found a way to warn someone."

"Yeah, I know, but can you do some digging? See if the SN is involved in any way?"

"Why do I get the feeling you don't really think they are?"

"I don't know, Hank. Call it a gut feeling. The tat was new. He was told to get it two weeks ago. His family was threatened, and he fully believed the person who paid him would kill them if he backed out. Everything he says rings true, but I gotta cover all my bases. If the SN is involved . . ."

"Right. I'll sniff around, see what I can find out."

Andrew paused. "Be careful, man. Please."

"Absolutely." A pause. "I miss you, dude. It's not the same here without knowing you're nearby."

"I know you got another good partner."

"Not as good as you. Gotta go."

Hank hung up and Andrew looked up to see Nathan studying the board. "Thoughts?" Andrew asked.

Nathan rubbed his chin, his brow furrowed. "I agree with you. Something's off."

"But what?"

"No idea. Hopefully something will break soon."

"Anyone sitting on Leary's house?"

"Of course. Just for the next twenty-four hours. He went straight home and hugged his wife and kids." Andrew raised a brow and Nathan shrugged. "The agent said the blinds were up. Had a good look at the reunion and said it was all he could do not to cry at how touching it was."

Andrew sighed. "Okay, then what about—"

"Hey, guys," Kristine said, walking over to their area.

Andrew sat a little straighter, and Nathan dropped his chin to cover a smirk that Andrew caught. He ignored his partner. "Hey, what's up?"

"I just finished going over everything once more and making sure my report wasn't missing anything. I've done all I can do, so I'm going to go home, unpack, and grab some sleep. It's been a long day."

Understatement of the year.

"You learn anything new?" Kristine asked.

"Not a thing," Nathan said.

"Then I'm out of here."

Andrew started to offer to walk her out, but his phone buzzed with an incoming call from his mother. He couldn't put her off any longer. To Kristine, he said, "See you tomorrow?"

"Bright and early."

She gave a mini-salute that included Nathan, did a one-eighty, and headed for the exit while Andrew tapped the screen to answer the call. "Hey there. What's up?"

"Thank you for texting that you were okay."

"Of course. I knew you'd see it on the news and know it was my plane." His family had all the itinerary details.

"I know you're busy so I won't keep you, but . . ." A sigh.

Andrew frowned. "What is it?"

"Your cousin, Corey."

His shoulders tensed. "What about him?"

"He's . . . here."

"Here where? Already?"

"Yes. He stopped in the store this morning."

"Look, Mom, I mean, I'm all for taking care of family, you know that, but Corey can't be trusted."

"I know, hon, but someone has to try and help him."

It didn't sound like she was trying to guilt him into volunteering, but he still hesitated. "All right, what can I do?" he finally said.

He'd already taken a lot of vacation days to meet real estate agents, look at properties, and help them find the perfect spot for the bookstore. He even put in time to run it while they ran errands necessary for setting up a life in a new town and a few doctor appointments. But that was months ago.

"Do you have time for dinner next Friday?" she asked. "That's when I'll have his room ready, and I thought it would be nice for all of us to sit down as a family and discuss . . . things."

"Things?"

"Expectations. Boundaries."

"Ah." Andrew ran a hand over his chin. "All right. Let me check my calendar and get back with you. I think I can."

"Thanks, Son. We appreciate it."

"Sure thing. Talk to you later."

He hung up and walked to the window. Kristine was long gone, but he couldn't help wishing his phone hadn't rung right at the moment she was leaving. Wishing they were in the Keys where they should be. But no . . .

Nathan walked over to nudge him with his shoulder. "Do you remember what you told me about Jesslyn when I was acting like a lovesick puppy?"

He remembered. "Nope, not at all."

Nathan chuckled. "I believe the words you used were something like, 'Ask her out, man.'"

They were. "Zip it."

Nathan laughed.

FOUR

Kristine walked through the door of her townhome and stopped with a gasp. "What are you doing here?"

Her father rose from the couch and faced her. He was a tall man, just a hair over six feet, with dark hair and gray eyes. Many women found him handsome—especially when he turned on the charm. "I needed to see for myself that you were okay."

"I'm fine, so, again, what are you doing here?"

"Well, it seems to me it's time to quit this foolishness you call a job and help run the agency."

She sighed. He had to start in as soon as she walked in the door? At least he'd led with making sure she was all right. "Dad, just because you enjoy being a private investigator doesn't mean I would. That's not what I want to do with my life."

"You could have died today! The plane was hijacked! You need to quit now before—" He clenched his jaw and raked a hand through his thinning hair. He'd gone from zero to sixty with his demands. Just like when she'd been a child, terrified to set him off, then a teen who didn't care. Then an adult who cared but refused to be controlled.

It was all she could do not to tell him to get out. She loved the man, but this conversation seemed to be the only one they had anymore. She was beyond sick of his telling her what she should do, what she *needed* to do. How to live her life. He'd done that ever since she could remember. More so since her mother's death. And yet, in spite of his tendency to want to control her, she knew where his fear was coming from, so she bit her tongue. "I'm not Mom. Just because she died in a plane hijacking doesn't mean I will."

"But you could!"

"Yes! Yes I could." She sucked in a deep breath and controlled her tone. "And I could get hit by a car crossing the street. Or slip and fall in the shower, hitting my head, or . . ." She waved a hand. *Or stroke out while arguing with a difficult parent.* "Please, Dad. Stop with this. I can't take much more of it. You can't just show up like this. It's not right."

"I'm your landlord."

"I know. For another six months, then you'll need to find another tenant. We've talked about this." She'd hoped renting this town-home from him would pacify him, give him the sense that he had a semblance of control over her. She saw now that it was a mistake. A huge one. But she wouldn't break the two-year lease agreement he'd made her sign. Six months. She'd survive. Maybe.

"Stop trying to distract me. My point is, your job is dangerous!"

"Life is dangerous," she said, her voice low. She refused to yell or lose her cool again. "That's why you're smart and take precautions while doing what could potentially be a dangerous job. But the local fast-food worker puts their life on the line every day as well. Not to mention teachers and doctors and nurses and police officers, paramedics, *private investigators*. Dad, drop it. Please. I'm not changing careers."

He groaned and grabbed his hair with one hand while he paced to the fireplace and back. "Do you want to get married one day?" he finally asked.

She blinked. "Yes. Maybe. Eventually. I'm not in a hurry." Although, at the age of thirty-two, she supposed most would think she should be. "What's that got to do with anything?" She finally walked into the kitchen and set her backpack on the counter. Looked like he might be staying a while. "And I thought we agreed you'd only use my key in the event of an emergency."

"I'd say you almost getting killed qualifies."

"I didn't almost get killed. Wasn't anywhere near getting killed." Not that there hadn't been a few harrowing moments. "Back to the marriage comment. Where are you going with that?" She opened her freezer to search for a nonexpired microwavable meal.

"Just that if you get married and have kids and you tell them that their grandmother died when a hijacker took down the plane she was a flight attendant for, then every time you walk out the door, they're going to be terrified you won't walk back in it."

Kristine froze. Then she shut the door and turned to face her father. "Always have to go for shock value, don't you? And for the record, why do you think I would even tell them? There'd be no reason for them to know until they were older and started to ask questions. Then my husband and I would figure out a nontraumatic way to explain it. And why am I even discussing this with you? You just crossed a line. You can leave now."

He met her gaze and swallowed hard. Tears welled and dripped down his cheeks. "I'm sorry, Krissy," he whispered. "I'm just terrified I'm going to lose you."

She didn't know if the tears and soft words were real or manipulation but decided to give him the benefit of the doubt. It had been a hard day. Apparently for both of them.

In an uncharacteristic move, she went to him, wrapped her arms around his waist, and laid her head on his shoulder. He stiffened, then sighed and held her for a moment. He wasn't a hugger, never had been, but for some reason, she felt compelled to push it. After a few seconds, she pulled back and cupped his face in her hands. She couldn't let him leave mad. She just . . . couldn't. "Listen to me very closely. There's more than one way to lose someone." She'd had enough of his control-freak antics to last her well into eternity. But she wouldn't let him leave with cross words between them.

He sighed, closed his eyes, and nodded. "Ten-four." He hesitated.

"Before I go, you know your sister is leaving tomorrow for that trip with her friends. Have you looked into them?"

"Who? Her friends? No. Why?"

"I did. They're troublemakers. You need to tell her she needs to stay home and find some new friends."

Kristine refused to close her eyes and groan. "Dad—"

"I know, I know. I'm just saying, hanging out with the likes of them is an invitation to trouble. I don't want her going with them."

"Like the rest of us, you don't get a say in what she does and doesn't do anymore. We're all adults." She searched for the words that would be firm but not harsh. "Dad, you and Mom worked hard for every penny you had. We never saw you guys have fun or do anything but work."

"Because we didn't have the money to do anything fun."

She ignored his sharp tone. "I'm just saying, Emily, Ethan, and I have all worked hard to get where we are today. If we want to have a little fun, then don't begrudge us that. We've earned it."

"I don't begrudge it," he said. "But money is hard to come by. Spending it on elaborate vacations is risky. You might need that money someday. You never know when an emergency will come along."

"Like Mom's death?"

He closed his eyes. "Yeah. It just about broke me. Mentally, physically, financially. You know how hard it is to make ends meet as a single father of three kids?"

"I don't, but I can imagine. And we made it. You have three amazing offspring. Why don't you trust us to do what's best for us?"

He rubbed his mouth. "It's just hard."

"I know. But here's the thing. Emily's a good person. She's a journalist with a great job. I doubt her friends are the troublemakers you've said they are. I'm not saying they're perfect, but honestly, if Emily wants to hang out with who you consider troublemakers, that's her choice." A part of Kristine was concerned about what her father found out in all of his snooping, but still . . . she refused to interfere in her sister's life like that. Emily would be livid.

"But—"

"No buts, Dad. Stop it. You have to stop this." He'd always been controlling, but it was like he'd ramped up the efforts over the last few months.

Anger zipped across his face, and for a moment, a spark of fear flipped Kristine's stomach. In her teen years, that look came before he'd yelled or thrown something. She steeled her spine. She was a federal agent and knew how to defend herself if it came to it. Then the expression faded, but he looked like he wanted to argue more. Instead, he finally said, "I have a long drive home and I want to go to the gym. I'll talk to you later."

She wouldn't classify the hour drive to Asheville as *long*, but whatever. "Sounds good. Be careful." He worked out on a regular basis and was in excellent shape. She was glad he took care of himself physically. She just wished he would also pay such close attention to his mental health. But she wasn't about to mention it. That would set him off again, and she didn't have the bandwidth for the discussion-slash-argument that would ensue.

At the door, he stopped and looked back, his eyes unreadable. "I love you, Krissy-girl, and your siblings. More than any of you will ever know or understand. Everything I do is with you three in mind. I just want what's best for you all."

"I know, Dad. You just need to work on better ways of expressing that."

"Right." He hesitated, then left, and she locked the door behind him, resisting the urge to bang her head on it. But she didn't need the literal headache *that* would bring, so she walked back into the den, kicked off her shoes, and picked up the remote. Had she really thought she might have to defend herself against her father?

Yes, she really had.

Shoving off that depressing thought, she got the opening credits rolling for *The Maltese Falcon*, then pulled up the food delivery app on her phone. She ordered a burger, fries, and two pieces of cheesecake. It would arrive in about an hour. She didn't even care that she'd already had a slice earlier. Most of it would wind up in the fridge for later. But not all.

The memories rolled over her. Working in high school so she could pay for her graduation stuff, working to pay for her car and insurance and cell phone. Work and school had been her life because her father always claimed to be broke. And she supposed he was. Like he said, trying to support three kids on a cop's salary . . . well, yeah. He was probably broke.

She sighed.

Her dad told her he loved her all the time. The words didn't mean much to her other than to make her question them. Did he really love her and her siblings, or did he simply use those words like he did everything else, as a way of trying to control them?

She just didn't know and she was too weary of trying to figure it out.

With a sigh, she snagged her work laptop, pulled up the report she'd submitted, and went back over every detail. Had she gotten it all? Emotions had been high at the time. She could have forgotten something.

Two hours later, she set the computer and her leftovers aside. She hadn't forgotten anything. Her phone buzzed with a text from her younger brother, Ethan.

Glad you're okay. Good job staying alive. Talk soon.

Short, simple, and to the point. That was Ethan. She smiled. He'd graduated from law school last year and was knee-deep working for one of the largest firms in New York. His dream was to make a lot of money and stay as far away from their father as he possibly could.

Even Emily didn't have much to do with the man.

Kristine didn't know why she allowed her father in her life as much as she did. Other than guilt due to the fact that she was responsible for his widower status.

She swallowed hard at that thought. Her mother's death never should have happened. At least not the way it did. If her father knew—

But he didn't and she wanted to keep it that way. Telling him would only hurt him. And she'd done enough of that.

With a groan, she surged to her feet and tossed the remote on the couch, then carried her leftovers to the fridge. She took a quick inventory and made a mental note to go to the grocery store tomorrow.

She shut the refrigerator door and walked back to the laptop.

Why had Marcus been put on *that* plane? Her plane. Coincidence?

She looked up the TSA agents working security. Every single one. Ran backgrounds on them.

Twenty minutes into her search, she got a hit. Colleen Pearson. She had a recent DUI. More digging turned up medical debts and a home in foreclosure.

She tapped her lips, then texted the information to Andrew and Nathan.

> I have no idea if there's a connection, but someone let Marcus Brown through security with a fairly large amount of superglue even though it was in a jewelry making kit. It still should have been flagged. I think we need to take a hard look at this agent. Could have been simple oversight. Or not.

Andrew answered her immediately.

> We'll have her picked up first thing in the morning and see if we can get footage of which line he went through.

Perfect. Now, she could sleep. Maybe.

FIVE

Kristine woke Saturday morning, her mind going straight to the hijacking, the Serpentine Network, and Andrew Ross.

Most especially, Andrew Ross. She'd been looking forward to the Florida trip in part because she wanted to get to know the quiet FBI agent without the interference of work or family demands. Against her better judgment, she was intrigued by him. And she could tell he was interested as well. But the thought of getting involved with someone while her father was so unpredictable with his behavior, well . . . she was probably better off not risking it. Even though she found herself thinking Andrew might be worth the risk.

But for now, it wasn't to be. She sighed and fixed her coffee, then grabbed a blueberry bagel and topped it with cream cheese. She carried it with her Bible tucked under her arm to the small patio off the back of her townhome, not bothered one bit by the chill in the early morning air. The sun was barely creeping up over the horizon, the world was still, and all was well for this brief moment. All too soon, reality would intrude, but she'd soak in this part of her day as long as she could. *God, thank you that I'm safe. Thank you for your goodness that no one died on that plane yesterday. Thank you for it all. I'm truly grateful.* She sighed. "Can we talk about my dad for a minute? I don't understand him, God, and I really need your help to keep my patience and my cool with him." Sometimes praying out loud even when she was by herself helped her feel more connected to the Lord. "He's getting more and more demanding. Controlling. And I don't know what to do about it except leave it in your hands. Be with Emily and Ethan and let them keep their hearts and eyes on you."

Her phone rang, interrupting the prayer. Her supervisor. She raised a brow and swiped the screen. "Hello?"

"Kristine, how are you this morning?"

She frowned. He sounded odd. "I'm fine. Recovering from yesterday and processing, of course. Do you need me to come in?"

"No. Er . . . that's why I was calling. I wanted to do this in person, but I'm getting ready to get on a plane to head out of town."

"All right." He had her full attention. "What's going on?"

"The woman from the hijacking yesterday, Brianne Anderson . . ."

"Yes. She's okay, right?"

"She's recovering, but, Kristine, I'm sorry to tell you this, she and her family are bringing charges against you. Saying you didn't do your job and she was unnecessarily hurt in the incident."

A bolt of lightning couldn't have shocked her more. "I'm sorry. What?"

He sighed. "I know. I don't believe it. But for now, until the investigation proves otherwise, you're on leave."

She opened her mouth, but nothing came out.

"Kristine?"

She cleared her throat. "I'm here."

"Don't let this get you down. I don't think it'll take too long to prove otherwise. We've got all the video footage we're still going through and the accounts of all of the law enforcement there."

"But they're my friends, sir. People could say they're not exactly objective and . . ."

"I know, but we're still getting the passenger statements, so like I said, don't let this get to you. Enjoy your time off. Go flying and finish getting your license. Stay busy, but don't put too much stock in the accusations. They probably just want a settlement."

"Right." She pulled in a ragged breath, then let it out slowly. "Okay. Thanks for letting me know."

"Of course. We'll talk soon."

She hung up and sat still for a moment. "Okay, God, that was kind of out of left field. You know I didn't do anything wrong. What are we going to do about this?"

She was going to leave it in his hands as best she could and pray her supervisor was right in his belief that she would be exonerated. *"Go flying and finish getting your license."*

"Ugh." With no appetite, she finished her breakfast, then checked in with Andrew and Nathan to see if they'd made any headway in the case. She left out the conversation with her boss. No need to bring that up until she knew more. Her phone pinged with a text from Andrew.

> Colleen Pearson is being brought in. Marcus Brown went through her line. Nathan and I are heading over to talk to Brown's wife. If you want to join us, I'll send you the address. Then we're heading to the detention center to talk to Pearson.

> I don't have a flight for the next two weeks thanks to my vacation days, so absolutely.

She could probably rectify that, but for the moment, she'd let it ride.

> I'd love to be involved as much as possible even though it's not my role to investigate.

> I think we can work with that.

He sent her the location. She finished the last of her coffee, then went to get ready. As she pulled her hair into a ponytail, her phone chimed with another text. Nathan.

> Late to the party, but I'll be there.

52

Thirty minutes later, she slowed to a stop outside the single-story home with the faded black shutters and peeling white paint. Nathan and Andrew were just climbing out of their respective vehicles. The house was in the roughest part of Lake City, situated across the street from a large trailer park.

Weeds had invaded what little grass there was, and the place looked deserted. Kristine frowned. "There's nothing to indicate a family of eight lives here," she said, walking over to the men. "Much less six kids."

"That house can't be more than a thousand, twelve hundred square feet," Nathan said.

"That's a tight squeeze," Kristine muttered. But people did it all the time. Better than living on the streets. "How is it that the media hasn't invaded yet?"

"I don't know, but it won't be much longer before they figure out who's who and where he lives. We'll need to put a police presence here or reporters will make their lives even more unbearable." He shook his head.

The door opened before they had a chance to approach. A young man about thirteen years old stepped out. He planted his hands on his hips and studied them with serious eyes. "You the feds?"

"What gave us away?" Andrew asked with a small smile.

The teen didn't return it. "If you don't know, that's sad." Uncertainty flickered through the bravado. "Did my dad really do it?"

Kristine bit her lip and heard a muted sigh come from Andrew. "He did," he said. "I'm sorry."

"Yeah. Me too." He swallowed hard, then cleared his throat. "I suppose you're here to talk to my mom?"

Nathan nodded. "She around?"

"Sleeping. She took some of my dad's migraine medicine and is snoozing pretty hard."

Kristine stepped forward. "Hey there, I'm Kristine. I'm so sorry about all of this."

His lips twisted and he sniffed. "Thanks."

"What's your name?"

"Jacob."

"I know this is hard to think about, but looking back, did you have any idea anything was wrong? That something was going on with your dad?" She kept her tone soft, hoping her compassion would reach him.

The kid hesitated. "Yeah. I just wasn't sure what it was."

"Can you tell us more? What tipped you off?"

He shrugged. "Dad's been acting weird. Not himself. He's been sad. Angry. Snappy. Some nights I hear him pacing." A tear leaked out and the teen swiped it away. "I don't understand why he did what he did. That's not him. He's a great dad. We may be poor, but he loves us and—" He shook his head. "I don't understand. Did you ask him why he did it?"

"We did," Kristine said. "But we think your mother needs to be the one to explain."

His jaw hardened, then he sighed. "Fine. When can I go see him?"

"We'll have to work that out for you," Nathan said. "We just need a little time to gather all the information we can."

"Right." Jacob shoved his hands in the front pockets of his well-worn jeans.

"Jacob," Andrew said, "did your dad have any visitors over the last few weeks?"

"Here? At the house?" He shook his head, then snorted. "If he was going to meet someone to plan a hijacking, it wouldn't be here. Too many ears." He crossed his bony arms and rocked back on his heels. His mannerisms and his eyes were older than they should be.

Andrew ran a hand over his chin. "Of course. Good observation."

"He'd go to Mike's." When he said the name of the restaurant, his expression softened for a brief moment before his features morphed back into a worried frown. Kristine shot a glance at Andrew and thought he noticed it too.

"The café on South Main?" Andrew asked.

"Yeah. He always takes one of us there on the weekend. We take

54

turns. But that's his favorite place and he'd probably meet someone there. Assuming he was meeting someone."

"Okay, thank you."

Jacob shrugged. "My dad would have to be forced to do what he did. Did someone threaten him?" His eyes widened. "Or us?"

Kristine blinked at the astute observation but kept her mouth shut.

Nathan let out a slow breath. "Why would you say that?"

"Because it's the only thing that makes sense." He raised a brow, looking much older than his thirteen years. "I'm right, aren't I?"

"Look, Jacob, we really can't talk about it, but just know that we're going to get to the bottom of it and one day you'll know the truth about the whole thing. Deal?"

"I guess."

Andrew nodded to Kristine. "Do you mind if Air Marshal Duncan tries to wake your mother?"

Jacob hesitated, then shrugged again. "Help yourself."

Kristine walked past them and into the living area of the house. The first thing she noticed was how clean it smelled. The second thing was the emptiness. She turned to Jacob, who'd followed her inside. "Where are the other kids?"

"Farmed out to neighbors and church people. It's amazing how many people offer to do something good so they can have a front-row seat to all the drama."

"A little young to be so cynical, aren't you?"

He snorted. "None of those people offered to lift a finger to help before. Why now?"

"Guilt? Realization that they'd failed and wanted to make up for it?"

"You believe what you want. I'll believe what I know is true." He swept past her and pointed down the short hallway off the living area. "Last room on the left. I don't think you'll have trouble finding it."

"Do you have any coffee?" she asked.

He hesitated, then nodded. "I think there's some left. Dad's the coffee drinker. Mom can't stand the stuff. If you're wanting her to drink it to help wake her up, good luck." He walked into the tiny kitchen and turned on the coffee maker.

"Well, we can try, right?"

"I guess."

"You get it ready and I'll wake her up." The guys were still outside, and through the storm door she could see them talking. Waiting on her. Not wanting to push too hard and shut Mrs. Brown down completely. Assuming she could get her up and coherent. Kristine knocked on the closed door.

No answer.

The blessed smell of strong coffee reached her. She knocked again. "Mrs. Brown? It's Kristine Duncan. I'm a federal agent. May I come in?"

Still no answer.

She tried the knob and it twisted beneath her palm. She opened the door and stuck her head inside. Mrs. Brown lay curled in a fetal position, eyes shut, face pale. Almost translucent. Her left shoulder rose and fell with each breath, but the delay between breaths worried Kristine. It seemed like her breathing was much too slow to be normal. She stepped to the bed and gave the woman a light shake. "Mrs. Brown?"

Nothing.

Kristine gave her a harder nudge.

Still nothing.

She felt her pulse, and while it was there, it was definitely too slow. She pulled out her phone and dialed 911.

"What's your emergency?"

Kristine rattled off the situation and turned to find Jacob in the doorway staring at her, eyes wide with fear. "Go get the other two agents," she told him.

"She OD'd?" His voice trembled.

She met his gaze. "I don't know what happened, but the ambulance is on the way. She's breathing and she has a pulse. All good things. Do you know what she took?"

"I'll get the bottle." He went into the bathroom across the hall, returned with the bottle, then ran toward the kitchen, yelling over his shoulder, "I'll get the other feds."

"Tell them to bring Narcan!"

Nathan and Andrew joined her, matching frowns and concern on their faces while Jacob hovered in the background, tears tracking his cheeks.

"What'd she take?" Andrew asked, pressing the Narcan into her hand.

"Percocet. It's an opioid-based drug." She passed him the bottle and continued to monitor the woman's breathing. It was still there—slow, but there. "The Narcan will help counteract that and I'm trained to administer it." She did so and waited. Sometimes it took a couple of minutes for the person to regain consciousness.

"Come on," Nathan whispered. "Wake up."

"Call CPS," she said, keeping her voice low. "They're going to have to get involved in this."

Andrew left the room.

"Suicide attempt?" Nathan asked, too low for Jacob to hear.

"Only she can tell us that."

"Mom?" Jacob asked, coming closer. He looked at Kristine. "Is she going to be okay?"

She glanced at his hands twisting in front of him and walked over to take them in her own. "Your mom is getting the best help she can and you've done a great job assisting. In fact, can you grab me a cold wet washcloth?"

"Yeah." He ran from the room.

Kristine heard the sirens in the distance and checked the woman's pulse once more. It was still slow, but faster than before. Jacob was back with the dripping cloth, and she used it to touch various pulse points on the woman's body.

Still, she didn't stir, but at least she was breathing easier. The

57

paramedics arrived and Kristine showed them the bottle. "Percocet 2.5mg/325mg. One to two tablets every six hours. Filled yesterday." The prescription came with ten tablets. There were four left. But how many were in there before the woman swallowed her dose? "She could have taken up to six pills," she said. "One dose of Narcan administered. You may need to do another."

"Got it."

"Dad took a couple of the pills," Jacob said from the door. Kristine hadn't seen him. "I know because I got him two before he left yesterday. He has migraines and sometimes that's the only thing that will help him."

"That's helpful, thank you." Kristine turned toward the paramedics as they started working on the woman, giving her more drugs to counteract the overdose. "Could be up to four."

"Got it."

The second dose did the trick. It didn't take long for Mrs. Brown to gasp. Her eyes opened and for a moment, she simply lay there. Blinked, then frowned. "What's . . . what?" She lifted a hand, then dropped it.

The nearest paramedic leaned in. "Mrs. Brown, how are you feeling?"

"Um . . . I don't know. Weird."

"How many Percocet pills did you take?"

She stared at him and the man repeated himself. "Three. I think. Maybe four? I needed to sleep so bad. I got the kids taken care of and . . ." Her eyes teared up. "I just wanted to escape for a little bit," she whispered.

An alarm went off and a paramedic moved in. "Her oxygen is dropping. We need to get her to the hospital."

They swept out the door and Andrew joined her. "CPS is here."

"Already? That was fast."

"The social worker, Billy Freeman, was close by doing a home visit with another family. Dropped everything and came right over."

"I'm not leaving her!" Jacob's shout carried right to them.

Kristine and Andrew made their way outside to find the teen gripping the gurney that held his mother, preventing the paramedics from lifting her into the ambulance.

Billy placed a hand on Jacob's shoulder. "I'll make sure you're updated every step of the way."

"No, I'm going with her. I can't leave her."

Kristine stepped forward. "Jacob, let her go. She needs to get help now. You don't want to keep her from getting that. We'll work out the details of you going to be with her while the doctors are with her."

He locked his gaze on hers. "Promise?"

"Yeah."

He let his hand fall away, and the woman was immediately loaded up and headed toward the hospital.

Seconds after the ambulance disappeared, a sharp crack sounded and the dirt in front of her spit in all directions.

AT THE FIRST SHOT, Andrew grabbed Jacob and yanked him behind the nearest Bucar. The kid shook, trembling from head to toe, but didn't make a sound. Two more bullets followed the first and then it was quiet. "Stay here," he said. "You got it?"

Jacob nodded, eyes wide with fear and bewilderment. "Yeah. I'll stay here. Where are you going?"

"To see if I can find the shooter."

"Be careful," the kid whispered.

With a light squeeze to the teen's shoulder, Andrew rose to look around. Kristine stood next to the other Bucar, and Nathan was just hauling himself up off the ground. The social worker rose and positioned himself slightly behind Kristine, his eyes bouncing from one person to the next. His gaze landed on Jacob and relief filled his features.

As Andrew passed them all, he motioned for Nathan to follow

him, then aimed himself in the direction the bullets had come from. Nathan fell into step beside him. They crossed the road and hurried through the trailer park's main entrance. The homes were lined up one after the other. About twenty on one side and twenty on the other. A dirt road ran between the rows.

"I'll take this side," he said to Nathan.

"I got this one."

They scanned each row one by one, looking for anything that might indicate a shooter had just fired three bullets from that area.

They arrived at the end without seeing a single person. No doubt they'd all hunkered down at the sound of the gunshots. Nathan holstered his weapon and planted his hands on his hips. "He's either hiding out in one of the homes or he's long gone."

"My guess is gone, but we need reinforcements to knock on doors." He put in the call for backup with the local PD. Once they arrived, Nathan and Andrew headed back to the scene to find local officers there along with the crime scene unit.

Kristine was speaking with Garrett Harder, the CSU lead on this scene. Everything was under control at the moment. Except . . . where was Jacob?

He scanned the area once more and saw the social worker had the kid in the back of his car. Andrew loped over to it and knocked on the window. The glass slid down. "You taking him to the hospital?"

"Yes. I promised I would."

"Okay, good. Thank you." The man nodded and Andrew gave Jacob a small wave, said a quick prayer for his protection and his mother's recovery, then checked his phone. He needed to talk to Hank. Had someone discovered Hank had talked to Andrew and sent a gang member to take him out? He wasn't quite sold on that idea, simply because he was still alive. The Serpentine Network shooters didn't miss.

Then again . . . who knew? Only Hank would be able to answer that question.

He walked back to find Kristine and Nathan in conversation

about the next steps to take. They arranged protection for the family. Mrs. Brown would have it in the hospital. After Kristine got the information from her, a police officer would be dispatched to each home where the kids were staying. Andrew didn't think it was completely necessary, but it's what would be done for the next couple of days. They'd revisit the threat after that.

They still needed to talk to the TSA agent, who was now sitting in an interrogation room. Mrs. Brown—who might very well be unquestionable for the next several hours—was the one who could wait. He sighed. "Let's talk to Colleen Pearson," he said.

Kristine nodded. "I'll meet you there."

A short time later, they once again found themselves in the detention center headed down the hallway toward the interrogation room. Kristine pointed to the room with the one-way mirror and Andrew nodded. As she'd pointed out, she wasn't an official investigator for this case. Her part was done. She'd protected the plane and the passengers. But she had the time to give feedback on the investigation, and frankly, he was glad to have her perspective. He might have to request that she be a consultant for the FBI specifically for this case so she could continue to be involved. Air marshals did not investigate, but her instincts were good and she had a lot to offer. He sent a text to his SAC with a request to make that happen. He received a thumbs-up in response.

Colleen Pearson was scared. That was Andrew's first impression when he sat down across from her. Well, who wouldn't be? A fine tremor ran through her clasped hands, and her pulse fluttered visibly in her throat.

Nathan leaned against the wall near the door and nodded for Andrew to take the lead. After Andrew ran through the preliminaries, he leaned forward. "Ms. Pearson, you've declined to have your lawyer present. I recommend that you reconsider."

"I don't need to. I'm guilty. I'll own it."

"Guilty of what?"

"Letting that man through my security line at the airport. Marcus

Brown." She ran a hand over her lips and swallowed hard. "I had no idea he was going to hijack the plane. I thought it was drugs."

"Care to start at the beginning?"

She sighed. "Right. The beginning. Which beginning? The beginning of the day my life fell apart when my husband announced he was having an affair and wanted a divorce? Or . . ." She shrugged. "The beginning of my stupid spiral four weeks ago when the divorce was final and I made the very bad decision to toast the occasion by getting drunk and then getting behind the wheel?"

"We know about all of that. And truly, we're sorry for it." He paused. "You know, we all make the occasional bad decision. Unfortunately, some of those have terrible consequences. Yours affected you and no one else. Thankfully no one died because of it."

She nodded. "But they could have."

"Yeah. They could have." He refused to let his mind go back to that day almost two years ago when his decision had cost an innocent man's life. He cleared his throat. "So, Marcus Brown."

"A man contacted me—"

"How?"

"He called my cell phone. Said he knew all about my DUI, my financial hardships."

"Did you see him? Meet him in person?" Nathan asked.

"No, it was just that phone call. He told me to go out to my mailbox. There was an envelope with ten thousand dollars in it as well as a picture of a man. He said if I wasn't willing to follow through with his request, then to leave the money where I found it and walk away. If I took it and tried to steal from him, he'd kill me." She pressed a hand to her forehead and closed her eyes for a moment. "I took the money and did what he asked."

"Which was?"

She sighed and dropped her hand back to the table. "Let Marcus Brown through security without question." She frowned. "I was looking for drugs. I didn't see any, so I felt relief more than anything else."

"Did you notice an overabundance of glue? Jewelry glue, to be specific."

She frowned harder. "Yeah, I did. And normally, I would have flagged it, but frankly, I just thought he was taking the kit home to his kid. Like I said, I was relieved I wasn't letting drugs through." Her eyes bounced between Andrew and Nathan. "But you asked about the glue. What about it? What'd he do?"

"Used it to make a knife out of wire and a toothbrush."

Her mouth dropped open into a perfect oval. Then she snapped her lips shut. "And that's what he used to hijack the plane," she whispered.

"Yeah."

"I didn't know. I never imagined . . ." She shook her head. "When I didn't find the drugs, I thought the guy must have changed his mind. I was so glad but worried too. Terrified really."

"That the guy who left the money would come looking for it?"

"Yes, of course. But I did as he'd asked, so . . . I don't know. I guess I thought that was it. If the guy—Marcus Brown—didn't do what he was supposed to, then that was between him and the guy who hired us. But then the officers showed up at my house and I knew there was more to it." She shuddered.

"You haven't paid the money to stop the foreclosure."

She shook her head. "I . . . couldn't. I've been trying to figure out how to give it back, but the number that called me is out of service. I assume it was a burner. I don't know what to do with the money. I can't spend it. I'm so ashamed." She buried her face in her hands and wept.

Andrew let her cry and rubbed his nose as he thought. Then checked his phone. Still no word from Hank. When she calmed down and had mopped up her face, he asked, "Are you familiar with the Serpentine Network?"

She blinked. "The gang? Of course. Why?"

"Do you see many of them getting on planes?"

"Yeah, sometimes. Probably more than we actually identify. Not all of them have their tats on display. But even if we do pinpoint someone, unless the person is on the TSA watch list or the No Fly List or contraband is found on his person during the screening, we don't have a valid reason to keep them off the flight." She picked at a ragged fingernail and shook her head. "You know as well as I do that gang membership alone isn't sufficient legal justification to detain a person. We'd need a warrant for their arrest. Or proof they're a member of a terrorist organization."

"And yet you took a bribe to let Mr. Brown through your line."

She bit off another fingernail. "I honestly wasn't sure if I could do it when it came down to it, but when all he had was a jewelry case and more glue than would normally be allowed, yeah, I let him through."

"He'd switched it out for superglue. And he could have killed a plane full of people because of it."

"Yes," she said, closing her eyes and dropping her chin to her chest, "yes, he could have."

Andrew and Nathan stepped out of the room, arranged for Colleen to be taken into custody, then Andrew checked his phone once more. A message from Hank had finally arrived. He translated the simple coded checking-on-you message into the time and place Hank wanted to meet, then frowned. Meeting Hank again would be dangerous. The man could drop off the gang's radar for only so long. And so often. An in-person this soon wasn't safe. Andrew texted his friend that very caution.

Hank insisted, giving the time and place.

Also, bring me a new phone, will you?

Andrew raked a hand down his face, promised he'd be there with the phone, and tucked his own device away. His next order of business was to meet his cousin before Friday to get the details of why the man was really in town.

Nathan walked over. "You all right?"

"Family stuff. The never-ending family stuff."

"I know all about that."

"How's Eli doing?" Nathan's brother had been on suicide watch for a while but seemed to be doing much better now that the brothers were getting along.

Nathan smiled. "Driving me nuts with all of his ideas for helping his patients. Seriously, the guy never shuts up." His eyes softened. "But it's a good thing. I'll listen for as long as I need to."

"He's blessed to have you as a brother," Andrew said, thinking of his own siblings who he rarely saw. The nieces who were growing up faster than he could believe. A pang twisted inside him. He wished things were different, but he'd chosen this job for all the right reasons. He just hadn't thought how it would come between him and his family. And the woman he'd once thought himself in love with.

At least his parents were nearby for the time being.

Nathan nudged him. "Lunch?"

"Definitely. Where's Kristine?"

"Still in the room."

Andrew stuck his head in and found her on the phone. "Right," she was saying, "got it. Thanks."

She hung up and looked at him. "You probably have the same message on your phones that I just got. Marcus Brown died in custody about thirty minutes ago."

SIX

While Nathan and Andrew debated their options as far as the investigation was concerned, Kristine tucked away her concerns about the suspension, walked into the break room of the detention center, and checked on Emily and Ethan via text. Their responses were immediate. Emily was finishing up some last-minute packing, excited about her upcoming cruise, and Ethan was headed into an important meeting. She told them both she loved them, then debated about texting her dad. She decided against it. While he was being quiet, she wouldn't rock the boat.

Her rumbling stomach signaled the blueberry bagel had long ago been digested and it was time to find something to eat. She walked over to the guys. "I need food."

Andrew raised a brow. "Real food or cheesecake?"

"Cheesecake is real food, thank you very much." She bit the inside of her lip, then frowned. "What are you going to do now that Marcus Brown is dead?"

"Take what he gave us and pray it's enough. We still have Colleen Pearson's testimony. We're still digging through everything in Marcus Brown's life and hoping something will turn up that will clue us in to who was behind all this."

"But why open fire on his home?" Kristine asked. "That's just weird."

"Unless it was a warning."

"A warning about what? He's already told you everything."

"Or so we thought. Now I wonder if it was a warning for him to stay quiet or his family would die."

"Well," she said, then sighed. "We might not ever find out."

"We'll find out."

She raised a brow at the certainty in his tone. "All righty then."

He chuckled, then shot her a grim smile. "I just can't see not finding the person—or people—responsible. I'm meeting a contact tonight to discuss the Serpentine Network's possible involvement—" His phone buzzed, and he glanced at the screen with a sigh. "And on that note, cancel lunch for me. I have a family errand I need to run. Catch up with you later?"

"Of course. Everything okay with the family?"

"Headed to find out." He left, and Nathan did the same with a small salute.

Kristine debated making a visit to the hospital. Technically, she wasn't investigating, but what harm would it do to visit a woman who had to be drowning in grief?

She hurried to her car, swept through a drive-through, and ate the burger and fries before she turned into the hospital parking lot. She wanted cheesecake, but at least she wasn't hungry anymore.

Five minutes later, she found Tabitha Brown sitting up in bed, sipping from a straw. Most of the remains of her lunch had been pushed to the side and she looked up at Kristine's entrance. Recognition flared. "You were at my house."

Kristine introduced herself. "How are you feeling?"

"Dumb. Thank you for getting me help. I didn't realize . . ." She rubbed her eyes with both hands, then dropped them into her lap. "I just wanted to forget for a couple of hours. I made sure the children were taken care of and just . . ."

"Took too many pills."

"Yes. Not to kill myself or anything, only to sleep. I just wanted my mind to shut off for a little while. Definitely not permanently."

"Understandable."

Tears flowed and she swiped at them with her napkin. "They told me Marcus is dead," she whispered.

"Yes. I'm so very sorry."

"I am too. He . . ." She shook her head. "We were both dumb."

"No," Kristine said, "not dumb. Never dumb. Not that it's an excuse, but sometimes life can be overwhelming, and desperation can lead to bad decisions."

"Yeah, but people don't hijack planes because life is hard." The bitterness echoed in the room, and she clamped her lips shut and closed her eyes for a moment.

When she opened them, Kristine motioned to the empty chair, wondering why there wasn't a friend or relative in it. "Do you mind?"

"No. Of course not." She eyed Kristine from under her lashes. "I'm really not a weak person."

"I didn't think you were. You've been hit with some massive things here. The hijacking, your husband's death, this hospital stay . . ."

"Yeah, the list goes on, doesn't it?" She shuddered, then pulled in a breath. I didn't try to kill myself in spite of what it might look like. Life is hard right now, but it's never been very easy. Not this hard, but never easy. I will push on and do what I have to do. For my kids."

The words were soft. But firm. And Kristine believed them. "You and your kids *will* get through this."

"Yes. We will. I'll make sure of it."

"May I ask you some questions about Marcus?" To satisfy her curiosity, not because she was officially investigating. But if she happened to learn something helpful . . .

Tears pooled once again and dripped down Tabitha's cheeks. "Marcus," she whispered. "He called me last night. They let him. He was in the prison's medical clinic and sounded terrible. They were getting ready to transfer him to the hospital. *This* hospital. I was afraid he'd die with my last words of anger in his mind, so I told him

I forgave him, that if he'd fight to live, I'd help him fight everything else." She sniffed and used the sheet to wipe the moisture away, as the napkin was now shredded.

"I'm so glad those were your last words." Kristine struggled to get the phrase out as past memories and angry shouts echoed through her mind. *"I hate you! Why don't you just leave and don't bother coming home because I'm never speaking to you again!"*

"Kristine, you don't mean that—"

"I mean it. Every word. I thought you would understand, that you would fight for me. Obviously I was wrong."

"It was hard when all I wanted to do was yell at him," Tabitha said, interrupting Kristine's memories, "but it's been him and me against the world for almost twenty years now. We met in foster care, aged out together, and vowed we'd never be separated again until death." She choked on a sob, pressed her fingers to her lips, and swallowed hard. The tears stopped as though someone flipped a switch. "He told me not to cry over him, but I can't seem to honor that."

"That's a lot, Mrs. Brown. I'm so sorry." That might explain the empty chair.

"It's Tabitha." She picked at the sheet, then used a corner to swipe her face again. She hesitated and shook her head. "I actually thought he was cheating on me."

"Why?"

"Because he'd disappear all the time. Wasn't where he said he'd be, didn't answer the phone when I called. I just . . . couldn't imagine it, but it was all just a one-eighty from his behavior. It was so weird. I asked him if he was going to leave me and he broke down crying. Said he'd never leave me if it was his choice. Well, now I know he wasn't cheating, he was going to the doctor's and . . . planning a hijacking." More tears fell. "I feel so alone."

"You're not alone," Kristine said. "I know it's hard, but you're not alone. You have all those people helping with your kids. People who would probably visit if you'd let them."

"Maybe." She sniffed and a shuddering sigh escaped her. "You know, that's why we wanted so many kids. So none of them would ever have to feel alone. We taught them that you might fight and disagree, but family is always there for one another and always loves you."

That just about broke her heart. She didn't bother to tell Tabitha that she had two siblings and often felt more alone than she could possibly describe. That if it hadn't been for her friend group, she'd be floundering. "I know I keep saying it, but I'm so sorry. I really am."

"I can't believe this is my reality," she whispered. "I said I'd push on and do what I have to do, but honestly, I have no idea how we'll survive without him." She blew her nose and gasped. "What's today?"

Kristine told her and the woman groaned. "They're supposed to turn the power off today. I forgot to go by and make the payment. That's just great." She closed her eyes and sighed while a tear slid down her temple.

"We'll figure it out and get the power turned back on so you don't have to go home to a dark and cold house, but for now, what about the money he got from the man who hired him?"

"Well, I can't keep it, can I? I mean, even if I could find it, I wouldn't feel right taking it."

"No, you won't be able to keep it. And what do you mean, even if you could find it?"

"I don't know where it is. He never told me." She scrunched the sheet in her fist. "He hijacks a stinking plane for money and then doesn't tell me where he hid it." She scoffed—a hard sound that echoed in the room—then shook her head. "How dumb is that?"

"Would he have hidden it in the house?"

She frowned. "I can't imagine where. You've seen the size of my home. And with six kids? There are no hiding places."

But desperate people often came up with surprising solutions to problems.

"But maybe he did," Tabitha said. "I mean, it's not in our account." She picked up her phone and waved it. "Trust me, I looked. But there's no other place he *would* put it. Not at work for sure."

"So, if it's not in the bank and you don't think he would leave it at his job site, then the house is really the only option, right?"

"Yes, I guess, but I don't know where to even start looking." She sighed and raked a hand over her head. "I don't even care right now, to be honest. If I have to stay here—and I think I do because some psychiatrist came by to talk to me—I want my brush and my favorite pillow and the book on my nightstand."

"Would you like me to go get those things for you?"

The woman bit her lip and hesitated. "Are you sure you wouldn't mind?"

"I don't mind at all." It wasn't like she didn't have time on her hands with the investigation into her role in the hijacking situation.

"Okay, then yes, I would appreciate it. When you get to the house, next to the front door, look to your left. The third brick from the bottom is loose. Pull it out and there should be a key under it."

"Okay, thanks."

She rubbed her hands on her sheet-covered thighs. "I hope they're going to let me out of here before too long. I need to get home to my children. My neighbors I'm sure didn't factor in overnight stays."

"But they came through for you when you needed it."

Her brow crinkled as though she hadn't thought of it quite like that before. "Yes, I suppose so."

"I think you have more friends than you might have been aware of."

"I don't know. Jacob says they're only offering to help so they can tell their friends they know the hijacker." She closed her eyes for a moment, then opened them with tears shimmering. "How is Jacob? When will he be able to come back home?"

"I'm not sure, but I would guess as soon as you're able to care for him." She hesitated. "We need the names of the friends your other kids are with. As long as you give permission for them to stay there and CPS clears them, they should be all right and can stay put until you're able to take them home."

"I . . . I don't know. I don't know if I should tell you that or not."

Kristine bit her lip, trying to choose her words carefully. "Look, they'll find them one way or another. If you cooperate and let CPS check in on them, things will go better for everyone. Especially the kids. You hear what I'm saying?"

The woman dropped her eyes and sniffed. Then nodded. "Yeah." She gave Kristine the names, and she sent the information on to Andrew and Nathan in a group text. They'd pass that to those who needed it. She looked up at Tabitha again. "The social worker brought Jacob by, didn't he?"

"No. I haven't seen him."

Rats.

Tabitha frowned harder. "Was he going to?"

"He said he was." She pulled her phone from her back pocket. "I'll check on him and see where he is. His name is Billy Freeman and he seemed like a decent man. Was very concerned about Jacob." Especially when the bullets were flying, but since Tabitha hadn't brought that up, she didn't see the need to add that to her worries. That would come soon enough. "The social worker promised to bring him here to see you."

Alarm widened the woman's eyes. "You don't think something's happened, do you?"

Kristine rose. "Excuse me while I find out." No more texting. She dialed Nathan's number and he answered on the second ring.

"Hey, what's up?"

Kristine filled him in.

"I'm sorry, what? He never took him?"

"No."

"Aw man. I thought he was one of the good ones."

"Can you check and see where Jacob is and what happened?"

"Of course. Give me a few minutes. I'll get back to you shortly."

"Thanks." She hung up and walked back into the room. "Agent Carlisle is checking."

Tabitha pulled at the tape on her IV. "I can't believe this. I've got to get out of here, get my kids, and get home. They're only keeping me here because that psychiatrist was coming by, but I can talk to him another time."

"But your oxygen levels . . . you may not be stable yet."

"I had some kind of weird reaction to the medicine. Yes, my oxygen kept going up and down, but I've been fine for the past few hours. My kids . . . they don't even know their father is dead and I don't want them to see it on the news." Sobs once more shook her thin frame and she dropped her chin to her chest.

Kristine crossed the room and placed a hand over hers. "Don't. Please. Let's find out what's going on before you leave against medical advice. You're right, your kids need you. And they need you healthy. In the meantime, you can call the friends that have your kids and ask them to make sure they don't see the news." It would give the woman something to do that would feel proactive for her.

Tabitha sucked in a breath and struggled to control her crying. It took her a minute, but she finally swiped the last tear. "Yes. Okay. That's a good idea. I can do that." She sent a beseeching look to Kristine. "But Jacob . . . in custody of CPS? I swore my kids would never know what it was like to be . . ." She shook her head, pressed her fingers to her eyes. "No, I don't want to leave them any longer with the people keeping them. I need to be with my children. I have to tell them their father is gone. I have to be the one to hold them when they cry."

Kristine slid an arm around Tabitha's shoulders. "I know. I understand. Just call one of them and have her call the others. Please. Give Agent Carlisle a few more minutes to find out about Jacob and I'll make sure you see him before you go to sleep tonight if at all possible. Then, as long as your friends check out, it's very possible Jacob can stay with one of them instead of going to an emergency foster placement."

"You think?"

"I mean, I can't promise, but I think it's a definite possibility. We can only find out if we ask."

Tabitha nodded, her eyes drooping. "I'm so tired, but one call. I can do that."

"Good."

She did, then dropped the phone beside her on the bed like it had taken every ounce of energy she had left.

"Rest," Kristine said. "I'll wake you when I know something."

"Okay." The woman was asleep as soon as her eyes shut.

Two minutes later, Kristine's phone rang. Andrew. She swiped the screen. "Hey."

"Nathan checked on Jacob and found out he ran away."

Kristine slipped out of the room, letting the door shut quietly behind her. "Details please?"

"I talked to Freeman and he said when he stopped at a red light, the kid took off. Apparently, when he got in the back seat, Jacob flipped off the child lock switch on the door and Freeman didn't see him do it. He's filed a report. Now it's a matter of hoping Jacob will show up."

"Why would Jacob do that when he was so desperate to see his mother?"

"Beats me. Maybe he didn't believe the social worker would take him to the hospital. He's not at the house. The crime scene people were still there, but officers went by to check anyway. No one has seen him."

"And as far as I can tell," Kristine said, "he's not here at the hospital. Tabitha told me she and Marcus grew up in the system. If Jacob's heard not-so-great stories about those years, he might be terrified to find himself in custody of the state."

"Yeah." Andrew's sigh reached her through the line, and she wished she could see his face, his kind eyes, feel his gentle hand on her shoulder as he offered comfort or a wise word . . .

"Okay, Tabitha's asleep for the moment," she said. "I'll fill her in, but she's going to insist on leaving. She'll want to look for Jacob herself. And honestly, I don't blame her. If it was my kid, I'd do the very same thing."

"I know. I get it. Try to dissuade her from that, though, if you can."

"Of course. She's so exhausted, she wouldn't get far anyway."

"Like I said, FBI and CSU are still at the house, but they're almost done. It's been searched up one side and down the other. Any and all papers, files, everything has been confiscated, so hopefully, there will be something in there to give us a clue who's behind the hijacking. In the meantime, I'm going by my parents' place, then I plan to meet my guy with the Serpentine Network connection. He might have some answers. I'll keep you updated."

"Good deal. I'm going to check on Tabitha and see if she knows where Jacob might go. She also wants me to go by the house to get some items for her." She hesitated. "She seemed to think the money would be at the house. That search warrant is still good for you, right?"

"Yes."

"And it includes the money, right?"

"Of course."

"Want to meet me there after your meeting? I mean, technically, I'm not allowed to do the search, but no reason I can't watch."

"I can do that. I'll text when I'm on the way, but it could be a couple of hours."

"Okay, I'll wait for your text, then see you when you get there."

"Talk soon."

They hung up, and Kristine took a deep breath and reentered the room to tell a woman who desperately didn't need more bad news that her son had disappeared.

ANDREW HUNG UP from the call to Kristine and made his way to his parents' bookstore, Pages & Prose. He hated that Jacob had run away, but there was nothing he could do about it at the moment. Officers were looking for him.

He had to focus on what he *could* do. And right now, that was talking to his parents about their decision to let Corey come live with them.

Temporarily. Because he just needed a place to stay, not money.

Right. Andrew hated to be so skeptical about a relative, but ten times bitten and all that . . .

He pulled into a parking space in front of the store and stepped out of the car. Movement to his left caught his attention, and he noticed a man in a hoodie standing on the curb across the street, hands in his pockets, watching him. Andrew couldn't make out his face, but he could feel his gaze.

Or was the guy debating about crossing the street to visit the bookstore? Or waiting on someone to join him?

Andrew stood a moment longer, just watching. A woman walked between them and the man turned to fall into step beside her. She said something to him and he laughed.

Andrew shook off the moment, twisted the knob, and pushed the door open. The little bell announced his arrival. He shut the door and sucked in a slow, deep breath. No matter how often they opened a new place in a new city, it always smelled the same. The smell he grew up on. And he had to admit, he never tired of it. The store was quiet, only a few customers browsed the aisles. Andrew found his father sitting on a stool behind the counter, reading a book.

He looked up and smiled. "Andrew. You should have called and let me know you were coming. I would have put a fresh pot of coffee on."

"That's what the Keurig is for."

His father grimaced. "Coffee in a plastic pod. I don't understand your generation." He walked around to give Andrew a hug.

"Instant gratification at its finest." Andrew patted his dad on the back, then nodded toward the stairs. "Mom upstairs?"

"She is. She wanted to throw a load of clothes in the washer and make the bed in the room Corey will be using. What's up?"

Corey. Ugh. "I had a few minutes before I have to meet someone and was hoping to catch you alone and talk to you about something."

A frown creased his father's forehead. "About what, Son?"

"You already mentioned him. Corey."

"Ah. Yes. I thought you might have more to say about the idea of him staying here."

They fixed their coffee and moved to the table behind the counter, where his father could keep an eye on the register but sit across from each other to chat. "What are your thoughts on that, Dad? What do you really think, because you and I both know Corey, and there's no way you can think this is a good idea."

"Well, I understand your concerns, of course, but I also understand your mother's need to help him."

Andrew nodded. "She explained. But his track record isn't the best. In fact, it's really bad."

"I know that."

Of course he did, but still . . . "And if he steals you blind?"

His father cocked his head at him. "You really think I'm not going to take precautions?"

Huh. Okay. "Like what?"

The man winked at him. "I'll sleep with my laptop under the mattress."

"Dad—"

"Son, let it go. This is a choice we're making in the hope of helping a young man who needs it." The door chimed and his father stood. "Now, let me get back to work and we'll chat when you come to dinner on Friday."

Friday. Right. Andrew stood. "All right. But just think about this? Promise me?"

"Of course." His dad hugged him and then Andrew found himself out on the sidewalk.

He shook his head and headed for his car. *Okay, God, here we are again. Back to this thorn in my side. How can Corey coming here be a good thing? I'm all for helping someone out, but if he takes advantage of Mom and Dad, you and I are going to have a lot to work on.* He paused. *Okay, a lot more than what we're already working on.* He sighed. *I know you've got this. Just help me* feel *it. Please?*

Again the sensation of being watched crept over him and he stopped to look around. Nothing seemed out of place or—

The guy in the hoodie was back. And looking in his direction. Andrew debated for a fraction of a second before heading across the street. He'd just ask him if he could help him with something. But the guy turned and walked away, vanishing before Andrew could reach him. For the next ten minutes, he looked for him, checking stores and restaurants.

Finally, he gave up but was tempted to get some security footage to see if he could get a look at the guy's face.

He checked his phone and found a message from Hank. He deciphered it and came up with *"Time changed to 10:00 PM to be safe. See u soon."*

SEVEN

Kristine had let Tabitha sleep for a little while. She'd texted her supervisor about the suspension, and he said lawyers were handling the discussion with the family and she was to stay out of it.

Of course she would, but she still wanted any updates available. Apparently, there were none.

So, she'd focus on doing what she could do without overstepping or being in the way. Lainie had stopped by and visited for a few minutes, and Kristine couldn't bring herself to tell her about the suspension. It nagged at her that she should trust her friends, but why burden them with it? They couldn't do anything about it.

But they could offer support, a little voice whispered.

She sighed and glanced at the time. The longer Kristine waited to wake the sleeping mother, the more trouble Jacob could get into.

She gave the woman's hand a light squeeze. Nothing. Slightly firmer pressure did the trick.

Tabitha's eyes fluttered opened and she yawned. "I fell asleep."

"Your body's been through a rough time, and emotionally . . . well, we all know our emotions can drain us."

"Jacob. What did you find out?"

Kristine hesitated a moment, then sighed. "There's no easy way to say this, but Jacob ran away from the social worker. The police are looking for him, but right now, we don't know where he is."

"What!" Tabitha shoved the sheet aside and swung her legs over the edge of the bed. "I've got to get out of here."

"Hang on a second and just think for me."

Tabitha paused. "Think what?"

"Where would he go? He seemed desperate to be with you. So why take off? Why would he do that?"

She blinked, then shook her head. "I don't know. It doesn't make sense. Unless . . ."

"Unless?"

"I mean, Marcus and I weren't big fans of the system. We talked openly about it and our dislike of it. We did say there were good people that truly wanted to help kids like us, but they were few and far between and we never stayed with many of them." She picked at the blanket. "He might not have believed the social worker would bring him here. Or he thought they'd put him into the system afterward. If he thought either of those things, then that's probably why he hasn't come here on his own."

Made sense. The kid was smart. "Do you know a safe place that he'd run to?"

"I . . ." She shook her head. "I don't know. Home? The church maybe? Although I can't really see that. He thinks everyone there is a hypocrite. I get it. Some are. But not all."

"Where's the church?"

"First Community. On Main Street."

Just a few blocks away. "All right. I can check and see if he's there somewhere." She stood. "If he comes here, will you let us know? At least then we'll know he's safe."

"Yes, of course."

"Thank you. I'm going to go get your stuff, okay?"

"Okay." She sighed, leaned her head back, and shut her eyes.

Kristine made her way out of the hospital and found that darkness was coming quickly. "Great." No wonder she was hungry. She hurried to her vehicle, opened the glove compartment, and found a protein bar. It would have to do for now.

Her phone pinged. Lainie.

Are you still at the hospital?

> No, on the way to First Community Church. I'm
> still looking for Jacob.

And frankly, some answers from the deceased Marcus Brown. He hadn't told them everything. She felt it in her bones. A quick search of the church didn't turn up the teen, so she headed to the Brown home.

When Kristine pulled to the curb, the poor house looked abandoned and forlorn in the shadows of the setting sun. She climbed out and found the key right where Tabitha said it would be. She started to insert the key but found the door cracked. "Huh." They must have left it open in the chaos of everything. "Weird." Or maybe Jacob had come home? She stepped inside to flip on the light.

Nothing. She'd get that taken care of later like she'd promised, but for now . . .

She pulled out her phone and activated the flashlight. Then hesitated. Searching the house in the dark might not be the most brilliant idea. She might miss something. Then again, if she didn't try, she may not get another opportunity. She shut the door behind her, pulled a pair of gloves she'd grabbed on her way out of the hospital from her pocket, and slid her hands into them.

She stood for a moment, thinking. She really should stay in her lane and wait on Andrew. Well, if she came across the money, she wouldn't touch it. She swung the light around. If she wanted to hide a bunch of cash, and make sure six kids and a wife couldn't find it, where would she put it? The ceiling? She found a broom in the small closet next to the washer and dryer, then panned the light over the surface while using the wooden handle to push gently on the overhead acoustic tiles.

It didn't take long to finish in the small space, so she moved to the den area to do the same and stopped. The small desk in the corner had been overturned, the drawers' contents scattered across the floor.

That combined with the cracked door worried her. But maybe in all the chaos with the paramedics and other people in the house, it had been an accident. She moved to the next room and looked inside. The boys' bedroom. Three twin beds and a small dresser against the wall. A few toys on the floor-to-ceiling shelves that lined the walls. She admired the creative storage ideas. She seriously doubted Marcus would hide the money in his kids' room, but she checked the ceiling anyway, then the overhead light. Sometimes people pulled the light down to hide stuff up behind it. It was a lot of trouble and included removing screws and the whole light fixture to get to the open space behind it, but . . .

Nothing. She even tried the shelving to see if it moved. Nope.

Kristine blew out a breath and moved into the room across the hall. The girls' room. Pink and purple covered the walls that could use another coat of paint, but again, the shelves around the perimeter. A few scattered toys and a lot of books. Nothing. Okay then. She'd do what she was sent here to do and let the FBI handle the rest like she was supposed to. *Sorry, Andrew, I tried.*

A sound from the master bedroom caught her attention.

Jacob?

The most likely answer. Could he be grabbing some things and planning to leave again? Or had one of the friends keeping the kids come to get something?

But there was no car out front.

She dialed 911 and listened for the call to connect, then stayed quiet while on the line. She turned the volume down as far as it would go in order to keep the dispatcher's voice from coming through.

Then she texted Andrew and Nathan.

> At the Brown home. Someone is inside. Not sure if it's Jacob. No car on the curb so could be him.

Andrew's text came through immediately.

Or it could be an intruder. Get out and wait for
backup.

She hesitated, then decided that might be wise. A loud crash from the bedroom had her backing toward the exit. Her foot snagged on the carpet runner and she stumbled, knocking against the wall.

"What the—" The voice came from the bedroom a split second before a figure appeared in the doorway. Hoodie, baseball cap pulled low over the ski mask that covered his face, dark clothes. She registered that just before he barreled out of the room and shoved past her.

"Hey!"

He kept going into the den, then the kitchen and out the side door. Kristine bolted after him.

The sirens sounded close, but not close enough. She raced after him. "Federal agent! Stop!" She figured it was a waste of breath, but at least she could say she identified herself as law enforcement.

He raced down the road, past the trailer park, and into another neighborhood. He zipped across someone's front yard and disappeared into the back. Kristine followed him, heart and feet pounding the same rhythm.

The sirens grew louder and she searched for the intruder, but it was too dark. With too many places to hide. The neighborhood had middle-class houses with well-kept yards. Trees and bushes lined the edges. He could be anywhere.

She stopped, panting a little from the mad dash, and listened, gripping her weapon, ready to face any threat. But all she heard was the commotion at the Brown home. She finally gave up and jogged back to the scene, badge plainly displayed, weapon tucked out of sight, empty hands at her sides. She didn't need to alarm anyone already on edge about a reported intruder.

Just as she reached the curb, Andrew pulled to a stop next to a cruiser. He climbed out and showed his badge. The tense officers relaxed a fraction. Andrew spotted her and hurried over to her and the officers now approaching. She told them about the intruder and pointed in the direction he disappeared.

"We'll search," the taller one said, "but he's probably long gone by now."

"I know."

They took off and she turned to Andrew.

"You okay?" he asked.

"I'm fine."

He tilted his head toward the house. "I don't suppose you looked for the money while you were getting Mrs. Brown's things."

"I plead the fifth. And you can't search for it either because CSU is gone and the intruder is a whole new case."

"Ah, but I had someone stop by the hospital to get written consent." He looked at his phone. "Yep. I'm good."

"Well, well. Mr. Prepared. That was fast."

"We're on a time crunch to figure this out." He frowned. "Although it seems like the crime scene unit would have found it if it was here."

"Seems like." She shrugged. "But the fact that I walked in on someone trashing the place says they think there's something worth looking for here too."

"Good point." Andrew nodded toward the house. "You wanna grab her stuff while I take another look?"

"Sure. Bring a flashlight if you have one. The power's off."

"Got one in the trunk, but let me make a call and see if I can get it turned back on." He connected with someone and two minutes later hung up. "It should be on shortly. Lead the way."

THE POWER WAS RESTORED almost immediately, thanks to his contact with the power company, but even with the help of Thomas Edison, his very thorough search of the rest of the house turned up nothing. Andrew led the way out into the single garage. Thunder rolled in the distance.

"That doesn't sound great," Kristine said behind him.

"Just the promise of a soggy night." And he really wanted to be home in his cozy little rental before the sky opened up. He hated storms. But business first.

To his left was a door that led to the backyard, a refrigerator against the wall next to it, and shelves and cabinets. "It's neat. Everything in its place."

"Maybe that will help you make short work of the search," she said.

Together, they scanned the area, with him moving items, opening containers, checking every nook and crevice they uncovered. The ceiling again, the floor, the walls. No secret compartment or hiding place. Nothing in the freezer.

Next, the attic.

Still nothing. Not even mice or any other kind of vermin. At least there was that to be thankful for.

Now he was sweating. A glance at his phone told him his time was running short. He was going to have to leave to meet Hank. He studied Kristine. A woman who'd captured and continued to hold his interest. He turned his attention back to the task at hand. Allowing her to distract him might cause him to miss something.

On the garage wall opposite the entrance to the house, there was a mounted organizer for yard work tools that held items like a rake, brooms, a spade, and a digging hoe. He nudged Kristine, who'd just closed a toolbox. "The shovel is missing."

She raised a brow. "Okay."

"Well, look at this place. It's in perfect order. Where's the shovel?"

"Maybe it broke? Someone borrowed it?"

"Yeah, of course. Maybe." He looked around. The outside lights were on. "I'm going to take a look around outside."

"You think he buried it."

"Yeah."

She followed him outside and he shivered in the cool night air while he scanned the backyard. He could see pretty well, thanks to the exterior lights.

"What are we looking for?" she asked.

"That. See it?"

"I do."

They walked together to the edge of the fence. The shovel was leaning into the corner of the fence and there was a hole in the ground next to it.

Kristine planted her hands on her hips. "Stating the obvious here—someone dug it up."

"Why do I think that someone is Jacob?"

"Or the guy who hired Marcus?" she asked. "Trying to get his money back now that Marcus is dead? But I don't know how he'd know it was here unless Marcus told him."

"Well, the only way to find out for sure is to locate them."

"Any ideas on how to do that?"

"A few." He glanced at his phone. "But I've got a meeting."

"What kind of meeting?"

"I'm not exactly sure. Guess I'll find out when I get there. My buddy who's undercover with the Serpentine Network reached out and wants to meet."

"Meet? In person? Is that safe?"

"Not by a long shot. He's been in the South Carolina branch of the organization, so it's a bit of a drive for him." He paused. "You want to come? You have to wait in the car and not let anyone see you, but it might be good for me to have backup."

"Sure, but what about Nathan?"

"He left earlier to go meet Jesslyn. I don't want to bother him. They need their time together."

She smiled. "You're a good friend."

"Nah, just collecting points for when it's my turn." He studied her, wondering when he'd work up the nerve to ask her out. Thunder boomed, a loud crack that made his ears ring. "Wow, sounds like the storm is going to be a doozy."

"I love storms."

"I'm sorry, what?"

She laughed. "I do. As long as I don't have to be out in them."

"Amen to that." Another chuckle escaped her and he cleared his throat. "So, you want to drop your car at the station? It's on the way."

"Sounds good. I'll meet you there."

Fifteen minutes later, her car was stashed at the station and she was buckled into his front seat. The rain was still holding off, but the thunder and lightning were still putting on quite the show. He shuddered and grimaced. Storms were not his favorite. It had been storming the night—

No. Don't go there.

"Tell me about your friend," she said once they were climbing the mountain toward Lake City Lake.

He didn't necessarily want to go there either—conversation-wise—but having her come along was his bright idea, so he probably owed her a response, not the vague brush-off he was considering. "Hank and I were partners for a little over a year. He and I were what you might call the golden boys of UC." He glanced at her from the corner of his eye and found her watching him. Intently. He cleared his throat. "Anyway, I was under for about three years, then got out about eighteen months ago. Hank stayed in."

"He's been undercover for over four years?"

Her shock echoed. He understood it. People had done it for longer, but it was still a long time. "Yeah. But that's his thing. He's divorced, no kids, and on a desperate mission to bring down gangs."

"Wow. So what happened in his past to spark that passion?"

He almost smiled. Of course she would link that to an incident in Hank's past. "Hank's younger brother, Glenn, got involved in a gang as a teen. He ended up a scapegoat and went to prison for a crime he didn't commit."

"But he took the rap."

"Yep. Hank's parents are pretty wealthy, so they were able to provide Glenn with a good lawyer. Then they got a private investigator involved, and in the end, eight months into the sentence, Glenn was finally cleared. His dad was there to pick him up the day he was released and the two of them were killed before Glenn even got in the car. Drive-by shooting by members of the Serpentine Network. Prison cameras caught the whole thing except it didn't reveal any faces. They had ski masks on."

She sucked in an audible breath. "Oh my. How awful. Were they ever caught?"

"No. The car was stolen, and in all the time he's been under, he can't find who ordered the hit—or who carried it out. It's possible those people are dead at this point. Gang members don't exactly have a long lifespan. But he stays to make a difference. To try and stop as much killing as possible. And if he finds who killed his dad and brother, then that would be icing on the cake."

"Wow. That's seriously tragic. And not to have any clues after all this time is terrible."

"Hank was gutted. Dropped out of law school and went to the police academy. That's where we met. Our paths crossed again at the FBI Academy. And one step at a time led us to going undercover together. The goal was for one of us to make it inside the Serpentine Network, but we both managed to get in."

"But you got out."

"I did." His turn came up before he had to try and figure out how to end the conversation, and he swung the SUV through a section of the trees, then followed a gravel path to a small parking area near the boat dock that was just ahead, waves lapping hard against the shore. He backed in, tires crunching, then stopped and cut the lights while leaving the engine running. No need for them to freeze while waiting. The moon shone bright in the sky. He handed her a pair of binoculars. "I don't know how well you can see in the dark, but keep an eye out, will you?"

"Sure."

He frowned. "Hank said he'd be in an older model black Buick Rendezvous." There weren't any other cars in sight. Not many people came to this part of the lake. One of the reasons he'd chosen it.

"Maybe he got held up."

"Yeah. We'll give him a few minutes." He glanced at his phone. "No text to cancel."

They fell silent and she made no move to talk. Instead, she had a distant look in her eyes, like she was thinking.

"You okay?"

She blinked and looked at him. "Yes. I'm fine."

"What's wrong?"

A laugh slipped from her. "Just . . ." She shrugged. "I was thinking about something Tabitha said at the hospital. We talked a little about how life can really throw you a curveball, but you just have to find the strength to keep going." She bit her lip.

"What's your curveball?"

"I've been suspended for the moment. The family of the woman who was stabbed on the plane is making accusations that the air marshal was negligent."

He gaped, then shut his mouth. "When did you find that out?"

"A bit ago."

"And you didn't think to share?"

"I guess I just needed to process it. But everyone will be called in to give their account, so I might as well let you know it's coming. My boss doesn't think it will take long to clear it all up, but the fact that it's even happening is . . . depressing. We work so hard trying to keep people safe and they just . . . don't get it. Or appreciate it. Some days it gets to me."

He reached for her hand and held it, her palm warm but callused in a few spots. "I'm sorry, Kristine. You did everything by the book and you did it right. I don't think you have anything to worry about."

"I'm not terribly worried. Concerned and frustrated with the whole thing, but . . ." She shrugged.

"Thanks for telling me."

"Sure."

He paused while seconds ticked past. "My cousin wants to move in with my parents." He almost bit his tongue in half. Why had he blurted that out? "Sorry, I didn't mean to change the subject and make it about me."

"Please, change the subject. I don't mind a bit. From your tone, I'm guessing your cousin moving in is not a good thing?"

"No. It's a terrible thing." The only good thing was sitting next to her in a car in the dark. Other than that, all he had going on at the moment were bad things. Like memories being churned up at the thought of seeing Hank in person for the first time in a year and a half. And Corey's arrival? Yeah, he didn't have time to deal with that. But he would.

"I'm sorry. Legit terrible? Or terrible because . . ."

"Corey's an addict."

"Oh. Legit terrible then. But he must have convinced them he's changed? Off drugs?"

He shrugged. "Looks like he has. Only God knows for sure."

"You're worried."

"Of course. I know his history. And you and I both know how well addicts can play people. Manipulate their family and friends into believing—" He tapped his thumb on the steering wheel. "Sorry, I'm trying to figure out how to convince them I think they're making a big mistake and will regret trusting him without making them angry with me. I don't want to . . . alienate them, I guess is the word."

"Ohhh, that's a tough one. But would they really hold your thoughts against you?"

He shot her a small smile. "No. But it might make things tense when Corey moves in. I'm praying about it. A lot."

"Well, that's good. God can use all kinds of situations."

"He can. I just wish he'd choose a different one."

"Oh, I don't know about that. You never know what that might entail."

He chuckled. "Okay, you have a point." He glanced at his phone again. Where was Hank?

"Maybe something happened and he's not able to get here or get word to you," she said.

"It's very possible." It was scary how well she read him. "I think that's what I'm worried about the most."

Kristine shifted toward him. "You think he's in trouble."

He flicked a glance at her. "I do."

"And you're trying to figure out a way to check on him without possibly putting him in danger should there be another reason besides trouble for his delay?"

Did he have his thoughts printed on his forehead? "He's got about a two-hour trip one way, so I'm still trying to figure out why he wants to meet in person. He never leaves the gang for long periods of time, so for him to be willing to travel this far . . ."

"He's taking a big risk."

He shook his head. "A stinking phone call is a big risk. This . . . this is on a whole other level. I do know he's got a good reason."

"You think he's got something major on the hijacking? Something he doesn't want to pass along through a phone call or a text?"

"It's possible. I wish I knew."

They fell silent. "One other possibility is that his cover's been blown and he's running."

"I thought of that." Andrew stepped out of the car to watch the road.

Still dark. No headlights. No text. No Hank. He climbed back into the car. Kristine had leaned her head against the window and closed her eyes. She didn't open them when he slid into the driver's seat. He checked on Jacob and so far no one had seen the kid. He passed the news on to Kristine.

Fifteen minutes later, he sighed.

"I'm sorry, Andrew," she said, her voice soft. "Maybe he'll text you to reschedule."

"Yeah, maybe—"

Headlights cut across his car and Kristine jerked into a sitting position, her hand going to her weapon.

The lights shut off and a man stepped out of the vehicle. A man he recognized. His adrenaline slowed. "That's him," Andrew said. "Stay here, okay?"

"Sure."

He got out and shut the door, wondering what was going on with his friend. "Hank."

Hank wrapped him in a hug and held on. "Andrew," Hank finally said, "boy, am I glad to see you."

Andrew returned the man hug and stepped back. Hank had aged in the last eighteen months. His beard needed a trim and his hair was pulled back in a short ponytail. Blue eyes met his and Andrew's heart clenched at the weariness in them. "Talk to me."

"I walked away."

"Sorry, what?"

"I walked away. I didn't think I could do it, but I had to if I want to live. I asked one too many questions about who killed my dad and Glenn, and things were getting itchy. This morning when I walked out of my apartment, two SN members were in a car across the street watching me. I didn't let on that I knew they were there, but they followed me all the way to the restaurant I always stop at in the morning to grab my biscuit and coffee. Then back in my car to ride my route." Riding his route, getting information, looking like a drug dealer, and more. "They were still following me," he said. "I've been under long enough to know they were just waiting for the moment they could strike, so I did some zigging and zagging, lost them, ditched my phone, scanned my car for any tracking devices, and came here."

Well, the tossed phone explained the lack of communication. "I know that was hard, man, but you did the right thing. We all have to know when it's time to call it quits." His underlying meaning wasn't lost on his friend, who gave him a sad smile.

"Yeah," Hank said. "I know. I'm still not sure I wasn't followed. I just need to lay low for a while." He ran a hand over his scruffy beard and head. "Once I shave and clean up, no one will recognize me. Ending up dead is not on my to-do list this week."

"Glad to hear it."

"Two more things."

"Yeah?"

"One, Showbiz is still after you."

"That's not news."

"No, I mean he's got people all over the country looking for you. He's widened the search. He's even put a bounty on your head."

Andrew sighed. "I'm sorry for his son's death. I even feel guilty about it, to be honest." Not like Isaac Mason's death. That was different. So very different.

"Wasn't your fault."

"Indirectly it was. But he won't find me. I look completely different, he doesn't know my name, and while he might have people looking for me, I'm not too worried about them finding me. What's the second thing?"

The man scrubbed a hand over his jaw and closed his eyes for a moment. "I didn't learn who killed my dad and Glenn, but I did find out that their deaths may have been partly my fault, and I need your help to figure out how to deal with that."

EIGHT

Silence.

Andrew obviously didn't know what to say, but Kristine had a feeling there was more to the story. And no, she didn't feel one bit of guilt at eavesdropping through her open window. It had been stuffy in the car. She'd needed air.

Eh, not really true. The heat was blowing so she could have simply turned that off or switched it to air, but she wanted to hear what was said.

". . . gonna explain what you mean by that?" Andrew was asking.

"Yeah, but not here. I'm still processing what I learned. Let me think on it a bit more."

"All right. You can stay with me for a while. I'm in an Airbnb with a spare room. You can use it for now."

"No, I'll figure something out. Staying with you isn't safe, I mean for you."

"I think I can handle it. Here's a new phone."

"Thanks. I'll forward my old number to it."

"Is that smart?"

"It is the way I'll do it."

"All right then. Ditch your car and hop in. After we drop Kristine at her car, we'll talk."

After a brief hesitation, Hank pocketed the phone and said, "I just picked up this vehicle after I ran. None of the SN goons know it. I think it's safe to drive it."

"Fine, then follow me."

"Okay. I can't think of another alternative except to get a hotel room."

Raindrops plopped on the windshield, but she left the window down for the moment.

"Lead the way." Hank's voice was rough, tired. "No need to stand here and get wet. I'll be right behind you."

Kristine's phone buzzed and she watched the text from her father banner across her screen.

I had some business in town. Stopped by the townhome and found you're not home. You okay?

She rubbed her eyes and sighed, then tapped,

Fine, Dad. Talk later.

He gave her a thumbs-up emoji and let it drop. She relaxed a fraction. That wasn't so bad. If that was the way he handled all their interactions, she wouldn't get so annoyed with him.

Her brother's words played in her mind like they did several times a day. *"Walk away from him, Kris. He's too controlling. You give him an inch, he'll take ten miles."* And just like she did several times a day, she shoved them away.

Honor your father and mother.

Those words echoed too.

But where was the line? At what point did she . . . *could* she . . . walk away from him and not look back? Physically, she might be able to do it. Emotionally? Not yet. Because of her mother. It was her fault her father was alone now. Her fault . . .

The door opened and Andrew slid into the seat, jerking her from her thoughts. He glanced at her window and quirked a smile.

She grimaced. "Busted. Sorry. I'm nosy. In my defense, if it had been a deeply personal conversation, I would have rolled it up."

"It's fine. You saved me from having to repeat the conversation."

He put the car in gear and drove back up the little gravel road to the main turnoff. Lake City Lake faded into the background and they began to wind their way back down the mountain.

Kristine couldn't see the drop-off to her right, but she'd driven the road enough to know it was there. It reminded her of a friend who'd died. "You know, we haven't been to Bolin's since Brenda's death." Brenda had been mostly Steph's friend. James's sister had been caught up in helping Detective Tate Cooper, the man who was now her husband, find Brenda's killer. He'd been connected to Bolin's—the ecotourism hot spot in Lake City. "The owner, Cherry Bolin, has been struggling to make ends meet after all the bad press."

"I heard about all of that."

"Once this is all over, we should go up there and have fun. Support the place." She glanced in the side mirror to see Hank's headlights staying with them.

"Zip-lining?" he asked.

"Or river rafting. Do some glamping. They have some nice cabins, firepits, the works."

He laughed. "I heard about that glamping stuff too. You guys seriously don't do tents?"

She wrinkled her nose at him. "You do?"

A hard slam into the back of his vehicle cut his laugh off and threw them against the seat belts, then back. Kristine cried out and tossed a look at Andrew. "What . . . ?" Seeing him fighting the steering wheel, she twisted in the seat to see Hank disappear over the edge. "Hank went down the mountain!"

"He hit us, but someone hit him."

"Yes, and he's coming back for another!"

No sooner were the words out of her mouth than he slammed on the brakes. The second impact was harder than the first and sent them skidding toward the edge of the road. Kristine clung to the door handle while the seat belt bit into her shoulder.

The vehicle roared past them and around the next curve. The squeal of tires on the slick road faded and Andrew's car jerked to a stop.

"We have to help Hank!" Kristine scrambled for the door and pushed it open, looked down into a black void, and sucked in a breath. A hand grabbed her bicep and kept her in the seat. His headlights illuminated the drop-off and she was right over it. "Andrew?"

"Yeah, shut the door and hang on a sec."

She did so and he backed up the SUV. Once she was certain it was safe, she shoved out of the vehicle, ignoring the chilly downpour. "We have to get to Hank."

Andrew stood next to her, rain drenching him. "I know." He looked at his phone. "I don't have a signal, Kristine."

She checked her phone. "Me either. You don't happen to have that new satellite emergency thingy on your phone, do you?"

"Nope. My phone is too old."

"Yeah, same here. Great. I'm getting a new phone as soon as we get out of this."

"Whoever ran us off the road knew this was a dead zone." Kristine led the way to where Hank's car had disappeared and spotted it about twenty feet down, trapped between an outcropping on the side of the mountain and a tree. "Hank!"

No answer. She scanned the area. "We're going to have to go to him."

"Yep. Someone must have followed him in spite of what he believed." He shook his head. "All right. I'm going down. You want to wait here?"

The drop-off was sloped enough she thought she could make it. "No, you might need help."

An engine purred in the distance and Andrew froze.

She snagged his gaze. "You think he's coming back? Or someone who could be help?"

"I don't know and I don't think we should find out. Hang on a sec." He ran to his vehicle, opened the rear door, and pulled out a backpack, then hurried back to her. "All right, let's go."

"Medical supplies?"

"Yeah. And more."

The engine grew louder as she stepped off the shoulder and started making her way down. Andrew stayed behind her. It was a slippery journey, and the rain came down harder, almost blinding her. She swiped her eyes and kept going. When she finally reached the car, she looked inside. Hank was out cold, facedown against the airbag. She reached through the shattered driver's window and felt for a pulse. It thudded strong beneath her fingers and she let out a breath of relief.

"He's alive."

"Thank God. Let's get him out of there."

A loud crack cut through the sound of the rain, and a spark shot off the hood of the vehicle.

"Someone's shooting at us!" Andrew's shout reached her at the same moment his hand clamped around her arm and pulled them to the ground. Wet soaked her jeans, chilling her, but adrenaline pumped and fear spiked. Then her training kicked in and she ignored the urge to run. Hank needed their help.

Andrew rose to his knees, and she did the same. He opened the driver's door, which added a bit more protection from the shooter's location. Two more pops sounded and the bullets bounced off the car.

"Can you get him?" Andrew asked. His breath whispered across her cheek, a brief moment of warmth in the cold she was now feeling in every pore of her body.

"I think so. I don't want to hurt his neck if—"

Another bullet shattered the cracked windshield, sending glass throughout the interior.

"Don't have time to worry about his neck," Andrew said. "The guy is coming down." He pulled his weapon and popped off a shot, sending the attacker ducking behind a nearby tree before Hank shifted, catching her attention. His head rolled toward her. Maybe his neck was fine.

Andrew growled. "Stupid rain is messing up my aim."

Hopefully it was messing with the other guy's too. "Hank's coming around," she said. She turned back to the dazed man. He had a gash on his forehead and who knew what other injuries. "Hank, come on. We've got to go. Can you walk?"

"What? Um . . . yeah."

"Someone's shooting at us." She glanced up the embankment. "Or they were. But we have to be careful. They might start up again."

He blinked at her and his eyes finally focused. "They found me."

"Seems like it." Andrew looked around. "We could stay here and see who runs out of bullets first, but I don't want to take a chance he's got more firepower than we do. So, come on."

Andrew grabbed his buddy's arm and hauled him out of the vehicle. "Hang on to me. Kristine, lead the way."

"I have no idea where I'm going."

"Doesn't matter as long as it's away from the bullets."

He had a point.

She slipped a shoulder under Hank's armpit and wrapped an arm around his waist. He sucked in a harsh breath at her tough grip. Something else was hurting besides his head, but they needed to go. "I'll help. You think he's really going to come after us? Especially now that he knows there's at least one weapon between us?" She had her gun as well but wouldn't pull it out until she needed to use it.

A shot rang out once more and Kristine flinched. "Never mind. Let's move."

Andrew let go of Hank, turned, and fired back. "Stay down," he said. "Keep the car between us and the shooter. There are plenty of trees to use as cover if we can get to them."

Kristine looked around. And finally recognized where she was. "Down or up?" It was a ways down through a sparsely wooded area with a wounded man who most likely needed a hospital. But from where they were, up would be even harder. Down it was, then across to a flatter hike back toward the lake.

Two more pops that Andrew answered with his own weapon again. "He keeps coming. He doesn't seem to care that I can shoot back."

"That's seven bullets for him," Kristine said. "I've got Hank. You cover us and let me get him down to that flat area. We'll be wide open for a short time. Once we're there, we can walk until we find a place to climb and head back to the lake. There are houses there. With phones."

"Got it. Go."

Kristine got a better grip on the groggy Hank who was, thankfully, able to support most of his own weight, and started down, stepping carefully. She didn't want to lose her footing and send them both tumbling down the steep embankment. She glanced back to see Andrew a few feet behind her, moving sideways, weapon still in his right hand. While she paused to find her next step, she shot another look back over her shoulder and caught movement about twenty yards up.

"You see him?" she asked.

"Got him. Federal agent! Drop your weapon!"

Andrew's shout earned two more bullets whizzing in their direction. Kristine flinched. That was too close for comfort. Unfortunately, the guy was a good shot for someone moving and shooting at the same time. In the pouring rain. It wasn't as easy as the movies made it look. Andrew popped off two more rounds. She glanced over her shoulder. The guy had found cover once more.

She pulled Hank down next to a tree. He dropped to sit, back against the trunk, knees bent, body shivering. Hard. Shock? Pain? The weather? Probably a combination of all three. The rain still came down, but it wasn't the deluge it had been just a few minutes ago. "Hang on, Hank."

"I-I'm hanging." His teeth chattered, then he let out a low groan and bent away from her to lose whatever had been in his stomach. Then he leaned back, head against the tree. "S-sorry."

"Don't worry about it. I'm sure you have a concussion."

"Yeah. Feels like it."

Andrew joined them. "The shooter is hunkered down for the moment." He frowned at Hank. "You don't look so good, buddy." ·

"I've been shot before. This ain't near as bad."

"I'm pretty sure I know where we are," Kristine said. "Lake City Lake is that way." She pointed up and to the left, back the way they'd come. "Based on how far we drove before the guy struck, we're probably about two miles from James and Lainie's house. If we can get there, we can call for help. They keep a satellite phone in case the reception is wonky."

Andrew peered around the tree. A crack sounded and he jerked back. "I don't think we have a choice. He's going to keep coming. I don't want to waste any more bullets on him." He helped Hank to his feet. "Let's go, my friend."

"Not sure I can make it, Ross. Head is spinning and legs are weak."

"You'll make it if I have to carry you."

"Sorry about all this. I shouldn't have . . ." The man visibly gathered his strength and stepped forward. "I got it. I'm good."

Since Andrew was doing the heavy work in holding Hank upright, Kristine removed her weapon. "Go down to the flat area, and then we can head up on an easier slope," she said. "It's my turn. Hurry from tree to tree."

Andrew hesitated, looked like he wanted to protest, but she drilled him with a hard gaze, and he finally nodded, tightened his grip around Hank, and started up.

ANDREW WAS CONCERNED about Hank. He also worried they were all going to wind up with a bullet in them, but he kept going because he had no choice. And besides, he was cold, and movement was the only way to keep his blood flowing. Thunder rumbled overhead and lightning flashed. He said a quiet prayer that no one would get struck by lightning—and that he wouldn't freak out in the storm. He wasn't necessarily afraid of storms, but he'd admit to an intense dislike.

In answer to his breathed prayer, lightning held off through the open area. They made it down to flatter ground, still no shots coming their way, and Andrew pulled Hank to the tree line. Hurrying from tree to tree, they climbed upward, aiming for the road Kristine said would take them back to Lake City Lake. A flash of lightning lit up the area a second before the clap of thunder shook the earth.

The shooter's gun barked again, and this time pain sliced along Andrew's upper right shoulder. He cried out and nearly let go of Hank.

"Andrew!" Kristine's terror for him came through in her shout.

"I'm all right! That's eleven bullets."

Kristine's weapon answered in kind, and he turned to see the guy drop back with a harsh yell. Then rise and fire four pops close together.

Then silence.

He was either reloading or injured and down for the count. With each step, Hank hung heavier in Andrew's grip, and now Andrew's shoulder felt like someone had taken a blow torch to it.

Kristine hurried to him, slipped, and went down hard on her hip.

"Whoa!" He wanted to reach for her but didn't want to drop a very quiet Hank. "You okay?" he asked her.

She grimaced and popped back up, aiming her weapon behind them. "Fine. Nothing hurt except my dignity."

The shooter remained quiet. "Glock 19?" Andrew asked.

"Maybe. I counted fifteen bullets."

"Could be reloading." He wanted to turn around and go after the guy, but Hank . . .

"There's a path somewhere just ahead," Kristine said. "I've walked it with Lainie and the others. It runs parallel to the road."

"I'm watching for it. Hank, talk to me. How are you doing? Can you go another little bit?"

"I'm a Marine, you moron. I'll go as long as I have to."

The words were said without heat and Andrew almost smiled. "Semper Fi, my man."

"Semper Fi. Now shut up. Talking hurts." Hank pressed a hand to his left side and ground out the words that ended on a groan.

Andrew's smile faded. His shoulder hurt too, but complaining about it was a waste of breath.

Minutes passed where the only sounds were the rain, their steps, and harsh breathing.

Kristine caught up to him and pointed to a break in the trees. "Through there. I'm fairly sure that leads to the walking path around the lake."

"That's a three-mile trek."

"Yeah, but we're going right at the fork and James and Lainie's place will only be another half a mile. And the good thing is, I know the door code to get in if they're not there."

"Perfect." He just hoped Hank could hold out that long. Yes, the man had been a Marine, but a body could only take so much.

He checked behind them.

Nothing. He glanced at Kristine. "You think you hit him?"

"I know I did. Not sure how bad, though." She shuddered and rain dripped from her hair to slide down her face. "How bad are *you* hit?"

"A graze." He shivered as well, feeling the cold to his bones while his shoulder was now throbbing a painful beat. But hope stirred. He recognized the area now and picked up the pace, hoping Hank would be all right. The man uttered a low groan that sounded more like a growl, but he followed Andrew's lead and walked faster.

It seemed like an eternity passed before the house came into view, and miraculously, Hank was still on his feet. Sort of. "Not too much farther," Andrew said.

"I'm fine. Can go another mile or two if we need it," Hank mumbled.

"No need for that, Iron Man."

"Dude, please, not Iron Man. He died in the end, remember?"

"Oops, right. Sorry. Captain America?"

"That's better, I suppose."

Incredibly enough, despite the circumstances, Andrew bit off a smile. He'd missed his friend. After the . . . incident . . . Andrew had pretty much cut the man out of his life, ignoring Hank's attempts to reconnect. It was just too painful. Guilt was a strong emotion that he'd become very successful at ignoring. But right now, it was rearing its ugly head, demanding attention. With extra effort, Andrew shoved it aside. He had other things to worry about at the moment.

Kristine hurried ahead of them, still clutching her gun, gaze intent on the area around them. She was in full protector mode, and quite honestly, it was a sight to behold. She was magnificent.

Hank stumbled and Andrew grabbed him with a short silent order to himself to pay attention. Knowing Kristine was being so vigilant allowed him not to beat himself up about his momentary lapse.

Two minutes later, they were inside with the door locked. "There's a first aid kit in the bathroom," she said. "In the linen closet, second shelf from the bottom."

"Thanks." Andrew maneuvered Hank to the hall bathroom while Kristine made a beeline to the kitchen to look for the sat phone.

Hank lowered himself to the toilet with a groan and dropped his chin to his chest. His shudders had turned into the shakes. "Sorry, man, I might need to lay down for a minute."

"Can you let me help you get out of those wet clothes?"

Hank lifted his head and shot him a perturbed look. "I got it if you can find me something to put on."

Andrew raised a brow, thinking his friend was optimistic about his abilities right now. "You're shaking too hard to do much."

"I got it." The words were low but firm.

"Fine, but if you pass out on me and hit your head again, I'm not going to be happy with you."

Hank simply stared at him.

Andrew rolled his eyes and slipped out of the bathroom. Maybe all that stubbornness would get the man through the next few painful minutes. His throbbing arm reminded him he needed the first aid kit too. But he'd let Hank do what he needed. In the meantime, he forced himself to walk into the master bedroom. It felt like such an invasion of his friends' privacy, but he knew if they were aware of the situation, they'd insist he do exactly what he was doing.

First, he used the master bath to examine his wound. Surprisingly, it didn't look too bad. Stung like nobody's business, but a couple of Band-Aids and he'd be fine. It took him three minutes to find two pairs of sweatpants, T-shirts, socks, a Panthers sweatshirt, and a hoodie. Clothes for both of them. He carried Hank's set back to the bathroom and knocked. "Found some clothes. Give me yours and I'll toss them in the dryer."

The door opened and a hand appeared with wet clothes dangling from it. Andrew took them. "You need any help?" he asked.

"No."

Well, all right then. He gave the dry items to Hank, then said, "Help yourself to the first aid kit."

"Will do. Then I'll bring it out to you."

"Thanks. I also have my backpack with supplies if you need them."

A hand appeared and he put the pack into it. The door shut once more.

Andrew put the wet clothes in the dryer, then stepped into the kitchen as Kristine entered, a towel wrapped around her saturated head. "Are there any more towels?" he asked.

"Yeah. Several. In the guest bathroom. Want me to take a look at that shoulder?"

"It's just a graze."

"Nevertheless, bet it hurts like crazy."

"A bit."

She studied him a moment, then motioned down the hall. "Help yourself to the guest bathroom while I borrow some of Lainie's clothes. She's so little, I'm not sure if hers will fit me, but I'm going to look. Anything's better than wearing this stuff."

"Agreed. Did you call James or Lainie? Local law enforcement? An ambulance for Hank?"

"No to all of the above. I can't find the satellite phone."

He blinked. "No way."

"Yep. They always have it on the counter and it's not here. They take it when they go camping or hiking or whatever, so they probably have it with them." She sighed. "Did anyone mention them going anywhere? They may have decided to take a little trip since we couldn't go to the Keys."

"Not to me."

"Me either." She pulled at her wet shirt and grimaced. "I'm going to change while I think about the next step."

"I'll be thinking too."

Kristine disappeared down the hall and into the bedroom he'd just come from. Seconds later, Hank came out of the hall bath, walked into the den, and eased onto the sofa, favoring his left side. He had a bandage on his head and his face was pale.

Andrew sat across from him in the recliner. "How are you feeling?"

"Like I was in a car wreck."

"Cute."

"But a little more human now that I'm warmed up. I hope your friends don't mind, but I took a shower and found the Motrin. Waiting for it to kick in shortly." He pressed a hand to his eyes, then dropped it to look at Andrew. "Sorry I brought this to you. Seems like trouble has found a way to track me no matter where I wind up." His eyes flickered. "I never should have come here."

"Stop. Don't do that. I'm glad you came if you're in trouble."

"Oh, I'm in trouble all right. We both probably are now that we've reconnected."

"I know. I'm sorry, man. This is on me." Again. Guilt surged and he pressed his palms to his eyes. How did he deal with this? Hopefully better than the last time he'd been the cause of someone's pain. Someone's death. He'd been proven not to be responsible for an innocent man's death, but it didn't help when he *felt* responsible.

Andrew walked to the window to look out. The rain still fell, but it was more of a drizzle at this point. He went from window to window, checking for any sign the shooter had managed to follow them, but all was still at the moment. He turned back to Hank. "What did you mean, you might be responsible for Glenn's and your dad's deaths?"

Hank's features darkened, then he sighed. "After Glenn went to prison, I got involved in the SN trying to figure out how things went so wrong, why Glenn would cop to a crime he didn't commit. I made it clear I wasn't happy with his choices, and I guess I made some enemies. Someone in the gang, someone new—I don't know where he came from—alluded to that just before I had to take off. He said something kind of cryptic like 'When you ignore subtle messages, sometimes you have to be slapped in the face to get your attention.' I think he meant someone took out Glenn and Dad as a way to send me a message."

"Wow."

"I'll be looking into that after this mess is all over. Wherever I am."

"What do you mean wherever you are?"

He shrugged. "Just thinking out loud. All that aside, I did some more investigating into the hijacking. Asked a few questions and all that."

"Is that what tipped them off?"

"No, I don't think so. But can't say for sure. We had it playing on the news. I couldn't ask about the tat since that isn't public knowledge, but everyone else seemed to be as surprised as I was about the incident."

"Hmm." Andrew rubbed his chin. "Did you find anything else out?"

"Nothing concrete. But I have to say, I don't think your guy was a member of the SN. No one had heard of him."

Andrew frowned. "That's so weird. I don't get it. Why would the person who hired him force him to get that tattoo?"

"To throw shade on the gang? Maybe it's someone who has a beef with the gang? Or a beef with Brown?"

"Any of the above is possible."

A lull fell between them, and Andrew thought Hank might be drifting back off. But the man roused and eyed him. "How have you been since . . . you know."

Andrew suppressed a flinch. Yeah, he knew. "I've been fi—" No, he wouldn't lie. "It's been hard. I dream about it sometimes. Not every night, but enough that I can't seem to move on."

"You shut me out. Even after the civil suit and everything."

The mild accusation stung, but he couldn't refute it. "Yeah, I did. I didn't do it on purpose, I just had to deal with that in my own way." He looked down at his hands. "You were a great partner and a phenomenal friend. I regret how I pushed you away and I've wanted the chance to apologize."

"No need for all that. You were grieving."

"True, but that was the time I needed my friends and family most, and I should have leaned into that instead of running away from it."

"Why did you?"

Andrew swallowed hard. "I suppose because I was . . . am . . . ashamed."

Hank raised his right brow. "Ashamed of what?"

"An innocent man died partly because of me, and I still don't know how to wrap my head around it. I wake up a lot of nights in a cold sweat because I'm trying to save him and he's . . . just gone. He literally disappears in my dreams. As though to mock me and my failure."

"Come on, man, you weren't to blame."

"That civil suit was rough. I honestly wasn't sure it was going to go the way it did. A man died while in our custody. I was there and I—"

"—was not responsible."

"I know, but his family was devastated. I still see his mother's eyes glaring at me, blaming me. His brother too."

"You know as well as I do that when something like that happens, people need to place blame. Whether it's deserved or not."

He did know that, but it didn't help much.

Kristine chose that moment to join them, and Andrew snapped

his lips shut on the response he'd been about to make. He *was* to blame and no one would convince him otherwise. And someone like Kristine deserved so much better than him. He swallowed and tried to ignore her loveliness but found it impossible.

She'd dried her hair and pulled it back into her signature ponytail. She'd also found a pair of plaid sleep pants that stopped mid-calf and an oversized sweatshirt. She carried her wet clothes into the laundry room off the kitchen. Andrew grabbed his and tossed them in with Kristine's. "You feeling okay?" he asked her.

"Yep. Just concerned about your friend."

"I am too."

"How's your shoulder?"

"Fine. Just gouged the skin a bit."

"Want me to stitch you up?"

"No need for stitches. It's okay. I'll be right back. Gonna check on Hank."

Andrew moved to the open area of the kitchen to see Hank sleeping.

"Andrew?"

Kristine's tense voice returned him to her side. "What?"

She pointed out the kitchen window. "That."

A car was coming down the road, slow and intentional. Looking for them?

NINE

Headlights cut through the rain and swiped across the kitchen window. When the car pulled into the drive that would take the driver down the side of the house to the garage, the external lights came on once more and she recognized the vehicle.

She blew out a low breath and wilted against the sink. James was home. Oh, thank God. She wasn't sure she had it in her for another fight to live right now. "You better go meet him at the garage door and let him know all is well so he doesn't shoot us. And assure him that the squatters will be moving on soon."

"Will do." Andrew crossed the kitchen and opened the door.

She heard the sounds of the garage door rolling up and the car entering. The engine cut off and the two men walked back into the house.

James eyed her with concern. "Tell me what's going on."

"Your sat phone's not here." She couldn't help the slight accusation in her tone.

"No, I have it with me. Lainie and I were going camping, but the rain kind of changed the plan. She decided to work the night shift and save the time off. I was working too and then decided to come home, get in my favorite recliner, and sleep for a few hours."

"Sorry to ruin that plan," Kristine said. "We've been on the run from a guy we believe is a member of the Serpentine Network sent to kill the man on your couch."

"I have a man on my couch?"

"Wearing your clothes, no less," Andrew said. "His name is Hank Gallagher. He and I were undercover together when I was in the gang unit, and he was checking into the SN for me, trying to see if they were behind the hijacking. His cover was compromised and he came to me for help, but it looks like someone followed him and tried to kill him. Kristine and I got caught up in the crossfire."

"Hank's car is down the side of the mountain," Kristine said. "Once we got him out, we had to run. In the rain. To your house . . ."

". . . to get the sat phone that wasn't here," Andrew finished for her.

"Do I need to get it?" James asked.

Andrew grimaced. "Yeah. We need to call it all in."

"I winged him," Kristine said, "so we'll need to check the hospitals in case he seeks treatment there. I doubt he will, but . . ." She shrugged.

"Got it."

"And we're going to need a ride to the hospital," Andrew said. "Hank needs to be checked out and probably admitted. He's got a head wound, most likely a concussion since he was out cold for a while. He's a Marine, so I've got no idea what other injuries he could be hiding."

James nodded. "Get him and we'll drop him at the hospital and get someone to the wreck site."

Kristine gave a mental groan. It was going to be a very long night. She checked the clock. Make that *longer* night.

Thankfully, the drive to the hospital was uneventful. Hank didn't even put up much of a fuss when Andrew woke him and told him he was going.

"He's in pain," she murmured once Hank was settled into his hospital room for the duration.

"He *was*. Think the drugs are starting to kick in."

Andrew had been right. His friend had a concussion. It was mild, but nevertheless, they wanted to keep an eye on him. He also had a broken rib.

"He pressed his side a few times, but never indicated the pain was severe," Andrew said.

"His headache probably overshadowed it."

Andrew grunted. "No, he just didn't say anything. We had to move and he knew it."

She rubbed her face. They'd both called their supervisors, and a crime scene unit was heading to the area of the wreck and shootout. Apparently reports had come in from neighbors about shots fired and local officers were already there.

Violent Crimes would be the investigating agents in the incident, but Kristine would be keeping an ear to the ground to see how that played out. No doubt Andrew and Hank felt the same.

She and Andrew had filled out the paperwork and given their statements to the agents as well as to James and Cole. Thankfully, she and Andrew wouldn't be out of action too long. Since no one had been injured—that they could find—after the shooting review, everything would be handled by the local field office in conjunction with the Lake City Police Department. Andrew could return to investigating the hijacking case, and she could finish out her vacation-slash-suspension-days while being updated on the case via Andrew and Nathan. But for now, Kristine just wanted to go home and crash. Unfortunately, there was more work to do.

Well, for the guys.

She could go home at any point now that she'd done everything in line with reporting a firearms discharge in the line of duty, but she really didn't want to leave until they were done here.

"What are you going to do about keeping an eye on Hank?" she asked. "The shooter probably called in reinforcements after realizing everyone survived the crash. They could be headed this way even as we speak."

"He'll need protection for as long as he's in the hospital for sure," James said. "And probably when he leaves."

Andrew nodded. "Already got the hospital covered. Hank's room and the rest of this place to make sure no innocents get caught in a crossfire." His eyes flashed and his jaw hardened for a moment before he blinked it away. "An agent should be here shortly. Hospital security is on his room until the agent arrives. Hank should be released sometime tomorrow, assuming all goes well the rest of the night."

"Okay," she said, "we need to get the cars. Mine's at the station and Andrew's is still on the side of the road."

"They won't be done with mine for a while," Andrew said. "The Bureau will provide one until mine's released."

It took another hour to get Andrew's rental delivered, along with burgers, fries, and shakes for everyone.

After downing the food, Kristine was done. She nudged Andrew. "Will you take me to get my car? I need sleep."

"Of course. We all could do with some sleep. Let me check on Hank one more time and then we can go."

Once they were in his rental, she buckled up and leaned her head back against the cushion. "It's been a day."

"A doozy for sure."

He started the engine and they headed toward the station in silence. She was too tired to consider the quiet awkward. Finally, he pulled into the lot and parked next to her car.

She reached for the handle. "Thanks for the ride."

"Sure. See you tomorrow?" He glanced at the clock. "I mean later today?"

"Absolutely. I want to stay involved as long as I can. I know the FBI will handle the incident we just survived and want to stay in the loop on that, of course. But the hijacking? That's my main interest. Please keep me as up to date as you can."

"We'll make it happen."

"Thanks, Andrew."

He reached for her hand and gripped her fingers. "Kristine . . ."

She stopped and turned to look at him. He let go and raised his hand like he wanted to touch her face and she stilled. Her phone buzzed and his hand dropped, destroying whatever moment there might have been. She suppressed a groan and tried to get her pulse under control while she grabbed her phone from her pocket and looked at the screen. "My dad's been calling and texting nonstop. I'd better get home and deal with this." She forced herself to look into his eyes and then had to swallow hard at the expression she didn't dare try to decipher there. "I, um . . . I'll catch up with you later."

He looked like he wanted to say something else, but just nodded. She climbed out with a wave, got into her car, and headed home, her pulse still racing. And now she was going to talk to her father, which always shot her blood pressure up and spiked her adrenaline. But it was four in the morning. Should she really call him? She debated until she pulled into her driveway, then decided why not? One text said to call him immediately. It was an emergency. She mentally rolled her eyes. His emergencies were never truly emergencies, but she dialed his number anyway.

He answered halfway through the first ring. "Kristine." The relief in his voice triggered a frown.

"Yes."

"Emily's been in an accident."

ANDREW SLEPT until nearly ten. He could have taken the day off while Nathan continued with the hijacking investigation, but hanging around his rental did nothing to excite him. Everyone except Kristine had gone back to work to save their days after their vacation plans had been so rudely nixed. And that was fine with him. He'd rather work anyway.

Especially if he could use it as an excuse to see Kristine.

And since that's where his thoughts went, he decided he really needed to either ask her out or just forget about her, because all his lectures to himself about how he shouldn't get romantically involved with someone never seemed to take root when it came to her.

He checked in on the search for Jacob Brown and learned no one had seen the boy. Which worried him. Then again, if Jacob had the cash, he might be just fine. The problem was . . . did anyone else know he had it?

But someone else could have dug up that money. If the money had indeed been there.

Andrew had a strong feeling it had.

He climbed in the car and headed to see Hank at the hospital. The man hadn't answered his text asking how he was this morning.

He found the room and knocked.

"Come in."

When he stepped inside, he found Hank dressed and shoving his wallet and the new phone that had been retrieved from the wrecked car into his pockets—very carefully.

"What are you doing?" Andrew asked.

"Leaving."

"You sure that's a good idea?"

"I've got to get out of here before someone gets hurt because of me. I'm just surprised it was quiet last night."

"Maybe the guard on the door deterred any kind of attack?"

"Maybe, but I doubt it."

"So you've been discharged?"

"Sort of."

"You're going AWOL?"

"I think it's AMA here."

Andrew rolled his eyes. "You do realize insurance might not pay if you do that."

"I'll get permission."

"Right. Come on then. Let's get you officially released. I'll take you back to my place and get you comfortable. Stay put."

Andrew worked out the release with the doctor, then returned to collect his friend. Hank rose from the bed, stopped, then lowered himself back onto it, his face a shade paler than when Andrew walked in. "Just give me a minute."

"Dude. Stay here."

"I can't." His friend met his gaze. "Every minute I'm here puts everyone in this hospital in danger. They'll send someone. It's just a matter of time."

He wasn't wrong.

"All right, let's—"

A knock on the door stopped him. Hank froze, then relaxed a fraction. "You wanna get that?"

"Sure."

Andrew opened the door to find a pale-looking Lainie on the other side. She'd been crying. "Hey." He frowned. "What's wrong?"

She ran her fingers under her eyes, cleaning up the smudged mascara. "I saw you come in. Did Kristine call or text you?"

"No, why?"

"She's here, down in the surgery waiting room. Her sister was in an accident yesterday and is critical."

A punch to his gut wouldn't have hurt more. "Oh no. Second floor, right?"

"Yeah. Her father is with her and her brother is on the way from New York. I think her aunt Wendy is coming as soon as she can get here from Virginia."

"Thanks, Lainie. The others know?"

"James does. He's passing the word along. I didn't want to send out a text, you know?"

"Of course." He turned back to Hank. "Tim Jackson is the agent outside your room. He can take you to the Airbnb and stay with you while I hang here with Kristine. That okay with you?"

"Sure, man. Give Kristine my best."

Andrew nodded, then followed Lainie to the surgery waiting room, where Kristine sat in an uncomfortable chair with her head tilted back against the wall. A man who must have been her father sat next to her, eyes on the television hanging from the ceiling in the corner and playing silently with captions.

Andrew stood for a moment, hating to wake her. She obviously hadn't been to bed yet. Before he could decide whether to walk away or sit or what, Kristine stirred and opened her eyes. Her father had yet to turn his attention away from the screen.

Kristine blinked and sat up straight. "Andrew? Lainie?" She stood. "Hey."

"Hey, I was visiting Hank, and Lainie told me you were here. I'm so sorry. What happened?"

"She shouldn't have been with them, that's what," her father said. "I warned her, but she didn't listen. Now look what's happened. I need some air." He rose to his feet and stomped out of the waiting room.

Kristine blew out a low breath and rubbed her face. "Sorry about that."

"It's okay. He's hurting."

"He's . . . something all right," Kristine said. "Emily was heading to the airport for a red-eye flight with her friends, Dana and Tia, when they wrecked. The driver, Dana, ran a red light, lost control, and drove into a convenience store. I didn't know until several hours later."

Andrew blinked. "How awful."

"It's bad," she whispered. "Dana's in a medically induced coma, Emily's been out of surgery for about an hour and we're waiting for a room in ICU, and . . ." She pulled in a deep breath, then cleared her throat. "Tia died a few minutes ago."

Lainie gasped. "No."

"Dana's parents are here somewhere and Tia's haven't been located yet."

"I'm so sorry," Andrew murmured. "Have you gotten any sleep at all?"

She laughed. A sound without humor. "No. But as soon as Emily gets into a room, I'll try to grab a few hours in the sleeper chair next to her."

"Okay, well, just let me know if you need anything."

"Of course. Thank you."

"I'm going to finish the rest of my shift," Lainie said, "but I'll check in on you before I leave."

Kristine gave her friend a hug and Lainie disappeared out the door.

She motioned for Andrew to have a seat. He did, taking in her appearance. Even after the night she had, being shot at and on the run didn't take away from her attractiveness. With her hair in a messy ponytail, face pale, and worry lines around her eyes, she still exuded a strength he envied. His phone buzzed and he glanced at it. A text from Hank.

Where are you? I need to talk to you. I just remembered something.

In the surgery waiting room. Will meet you at the side exit near the cafeteria? Don't think you should go out the main door.

See you there in 5.

Andrew told Kristine and she nodded. "I'm going to stay here until I can see Emily."

"Of course. Text me if you need anything."

"I will. Thank you, Andrew." She studied him a moment longer, then gave him a small smile. "I hope when all of this is over, we can have our vacation at the beach. I have a feeling we're all going to need it."

"I'm counting on it." More than she knew. Maybe by then he'd be ready for romance and everything that came with caring for someone. He wasn't ready to use the L-word yet. All he knew was that every time he thought about the future, Kristine was in it. He just didn't know how that was going to work. Or *if* it was going to. But he thought he wanted it to.

Just as Andrew was turning to leave, her father walked back into the waiting room holding two cups of coffee. He passed one to Kristine, then looked at Andrew. "Oh, sorry. I should have asked if you wanted something."

"That's all right, sir." He held his hand out for a shake. "I'm Andrew Ross. Nice to meet you. Sorry it's under these circumstances."

"Greg Duncan. Likewise." He nodded to Kristine. "Any word?"

"No."

The man sighed and tears came to his eyes. He blinked them away and lowered himself into the same seat he'd been in earlier.

Andrew reached for Kristine's hand almost without thinking and gave it a quick squeeze before he let go. "I'll be praying for Emily and Dana."

"Thank you," she whispered.

He left before he was tempted to keep Hank waiting longer and made his way to the door. Footsteps followed him and he turned to get a look at a man in a black hoodie, head ducked, hands in the front pockets of his baggy jeans. Andrew stopped and the guy passed him, but he sure did look like the dude who'd been watching him outside his parents' bookstore.

He started to ask him if he was following him, but the guy knocked on a patient room, then slipped inside.

Andrew shook off the paranoia and hurried to find Hank. The man was just inside the door talking to Tim Jackson and Sherry Hyatt, the agents assigned to protect him.

Hank looked up and walked toward him. Carefully. He never raised a hand to his broken rib, though, and Andrew almost shook his head. Once a Marine, always a Marine. The other two agents stayed back to give them some privacy but were close enough if needed.

"What'd you forget?" Andrew asked.

"I started thinking about it. You remember I said the television was on and the news report came on about the hijacking?"

"Yeah."

"I wasn't really paying attention then, but after I talked to you, I started asking questions. One of the guys, Hopper is the only name I know him by, asked me why I was so interested in the hijacking. I just shrugged and said it was weird. He said I should focus on what was important and leave stuff that's none of my business alone."

"You think he knew Marcus Brown?"

"He didn't come out and say that and I didn't want to push too hard, but he didn't like me asking questions."

"But he could know something about the hijacking?"

Hank sighed. "I suppose it's possible. Or I'm reaching and seeing things that aren't there. But it wasn't too long after that I felt like I needed to get out of Dodge."

"Good job listening to your gut."

"Then again, he's never liked me, so it could have just been his way of showing how tough he was. Who knows?"

"All right. We'll get an agent in that area to pick him up and do some questioning."

Hank nodded. "Thanks for letting me crash at your place."

"Meet you there."

"Okay." He and the agents walked toward the exit with Andrew right behind them.

"Andrew! Wait!"

He turned to see James, Cole, Jesslyn, and Kenzie heading toward them. "Hank, hold up a second, would you? I want to introduce you to a few people if you feel like it."

"Sure."

He made the introductions, then Kenzie said, "We came to be with Kristine. Have you heard anything about Emily?"

"It's not good." He told them what he knew.

Kenzie frowned and nodded. "We won't keep you."

"Where's Nathan?" Andrew asked. "I haven't talked to him in the last hour or so."

"Investigating the hijacking," Jesslyn said. "He said to call him when you got a moment."

"I'll do that as soon as I'm in the car."

The others said their goodbyes and headed for the elevator. Andrew said a quick prayer for Kristine, her sister, and Dana as he, Hank, and the agents headed toward the exit once more.

Hank's phone rang and he looked at the screen. "I need to take this. You mind?"

One of the agents nodded.

Hank swiped the screen and listened. Once again, his face went pale. "All right. Explain. In detail, please."

TEN

Kristine was watching her sister and praying when Emily opened her eyes.

"Hi," Kristine whispered. A tear slid down Emily's temple, wrenching Kristine's heart from her chest. "It's okay, Em, rest. Sleep and heal. You're going to be fine."

Moments later Emily slept again, her breathing a reassuring rhythm. Her face was black and blue where she'd hit her head, but the docs said there was no swelling on her brain, miraculously enough. She'd still need a lot of healing after the surgeries she'd been through.

Kristine glanced at her phone. A text from her flight instructor, Mac Adams, wanting to know when she planned to schedule her next solo flight. She needed a minimum of ten hours' solo flight time. She grimaced and ignored the text. After her last solo attempt—the one she hadn't told anyone about—she was terrified to try again.

She'd gone up, a healthy mix of excitement and fear thrumming through her veins. Mostly excitement. She'd been ready to go, taxied down the runway, and taken off. And then the engine cut out on her. She was certain she was going to die, and the memory of those few minutes of sheer terror, of letting God know she was ready if he was, was stamped in her mind. The fear hadn't really been for her, but of leaving Ethan and Emily without a buffer between them and their father. *Please take care of them, God.* That was the prayer she uttered before the engine caught, sputtered, then caught again. With her instructor's calm but tense voice echoing in her ears, she managed to land the plane. It was a rough landing, but she'd walked away. And now, she didn't know how she'd manage to go up again alone.

She walked out into the hall and found her father. He was leaning against the wall, eyes closed, head tilted upward. She placed a hand on his arm and he jerked to attention. "Sorry," she said, "I didn't mean to startle you."

"It's okay. How's she doing?"

"She woke up for a second, then slipped back under. She knew I was there."

"Good. Good." He raked a hand over his head. "I was on the way back and saw you in there. I decided to let you have your time and wait out here."

"Oh. Well . . . thanks." Maybe?

His nostrils flared. "I can't believe this happened. First you with the hijacking, now her with the wreck . . . I may have a nervous breakdown. I can't believe she would do this to me."

Of course he would make it all about him. She bit her lip on the words she wouldn't allow herself to utter. "Well, why don't we just focus on helping her heal? And grieve. Remember, one of those friends died."

"You didn't tell her that, did you?"

She gaped at him. "Of course not!"

"Right. Sorry. Good."

Kristine sucked in a calming breath. "Why don't you go home for a few hours and get some sleep? I'll stay with her and doze in the little chair." His face would probably not be the one Emily wanted to see when she was able to stay awake a little longer. And goodness knows, she didn't need their father saying anything upsetting to her. Like blaming her for not listening to him and being in the car in the first place.

He frowned. "No, I think I'll stay here."

"Suit yourself." Kristine returned to the room and checked on her sleeping sister once more. The nurse walked in to do the same. A loud growl from Kristine's stomach raised the woman's eyebrows, and Kristine held up a hand. "No need to say anything. I'm going to grab something to eat." She looked back at her sister. "What if she wakes up, though?"

"I'm going to be here for a few minutes. If she wakes, I'll tell her you'll be right back."

Kristine nodded. "Deal."

She left the room, noting her father was gone, and made her way down to the main floor where smells from the cafeteria grew stronger. At the sight of Andrew she stopped while her heart did a little happy dance. He was with two other agents and Hank, who had a phone pressed to his ear. She decided her stomach could just hold on a minute and headed toward them. Hank hung up and pushed his way out of the hospital. The agents and Andrew followed.

Kristine stopped, disappointed that he left before she could get his attention. She snorted and shook her head. She was acting like a lovesick teen. She spun on her heel and headed to the cafeteria, grabbed her food, and made her way back to her sister's room. Her father hadn't come back yet. Emily was still sleeping. Kristine's phone buzzed with a text from her aunt Wendy, her mother's sister.

I've been delayed. Will be there as soon as I can.

Kristine tapped back.

No worries. I'm here and so is Dad. Somewhere. Ethan is on the way.

I've talked to Ethan. Think he's having travel problems too.

Just be careful.

Will do. Love you, kiddo.

They were all "kiddo" to their aunt. She glanced at her watch. Visitors in the ICU were limited to thirty-minute increments. She'd stay until she was kicked out.

She texted Andrew.

Everything okay with you and Hank? I saw you guys on my way to the cafeteria, but didn't want to interrupt. Hank looked upset.

She waited for the little dots to tell her he was responding. It took a minute, but they finally showed up.

We're as okay as we can be. Hank learned someone from the gang turned up dead. It's someone he'd been pumping for information and had gotten pretty tight with. He's shaken, but handling it.

He thinks the guy's dead because of him?

Yes. The guy was supposed to keep an eye on him. He believes that because Hank disappeared on that guy's watch, he was killed. So he's blaming himself.

Oh my. I'm sorry.

I am too. He's sad, but dealing. Going to get him settled. Check in and let me know how Emily's doing. I'm praying.

Thank you.

She reread the messages once more and said a prayer for Hank. She didn't envy those who went undercover. It was a hard, risky, dangerous job. But someone had to do it. And in spite of her father's insistence that her job was going to get her killed one day, her flights were *mostly* boring.

And that was the way she liked it.

HOURS AFTER HIS LAST TEXT with Kristine, Andrew lay in the strange bed in the unfamiliar house in a city that was starting to feel more like home than the one his house was located in. It didn't help that his wound throbbed a bit. Enough to be annoying, not enough to make him want to get up and take anything.

He couldn't help wondering how Kristine was doing and if she needed anything. Hank was in his guest room and seemed to be settled, although he admittedly was still shaken about the call from the UC officer. The guy who'd died wasn't a true friend, and he and Hank had clashed on more than one occasion, but Hank hadn't wanted him dead, and definitely not because he'd run. Andrew tried to put a face to the name, but he couldn't remember the guy.

He rolled over and punched the pillow while he let his eyes roam the room.

This was ridiculous. He sighed. He was wide awake. Why did he bother to even try sleeping? He'd never been able to nap, not unless he was absolutely exhausted. Which he wasn't. He was simply tired.

He threw the covers off, pulled on sweats and a T-shirt, then walked into the den to take his laptop from the charger and sit at the kitchen table.

He typed in *Marcus Brown*, opened another tab, and typed *Tabitha Brown*, then *Colleen Pearson*.

He'd asked other agents to look into what Hank had told him about the guy named Hopper, but so far nothing had come in about that.

One thing Jacob had said echoed in the back of his head. The restaurant his father would use if he was going to meet someone. The same place he took his kids on the weekend.

Mike's. The café on South Main. And the look on Jacob's face when he mentioned it.

He pulled up the notes and saw that two agents had already been there and talked to the staff. Yes, Marcus Brown was in there all the time. No, they didn't know who he might have met with to arrange a hijacking. Everyone was shocked that the family man would do such a thing. And there was no helpful security footage.

Andrew leaned back and blew out a low sigh. Now what? There *had* to be something. He texted Nathan.

> I want to go by Mike's. Wanna meet me there?

Sure. What for?

> Just to check it out. If Brown was going there on a regular basis, I want to see what he saw, feel the atmosphere, etc. Maybe talk to the workers once more.

All of them were tracked down and questioned.

> I know.

Okay, sure, I'll be there in 15. At Mike's not your place.

Andrew sent him a thumbs-up emoji, rose, and got dressed in work clothes. He checked on Hank, who was out cold in the guest bed, then texted the agents on the house that he was leaving. He beat the after-church lunch rush to the café. Only a few tables were occupied, and he spotted Nathan seated at the bar. Andrew nodded to his partner. "How's it going?" he asked.

"Nothing new. You?"

"Same."

"What bugs you about this place?"

"Jacob."

Nathan raised a brow. "Okay."

Andrew shrugged. "I don't know. Just something about his expression when he mentioned the place. Like it was . . . longing."

"Longing."

"Yeah . . . you know, like when you look at Jesslyn." He smirked.

Nathan narrowed his eyes. "You really want to go there? Because I could bring up Kristine and your puppy-dog eyes."

Andrew snorted, ignoring the heat climbing into his neck. "Dude . . ."

"Yes?"

"Okay, fine." He looked around, taking in the scene. Two diners in their mid-twenties across the restaurant next to the big picture window. A table full of college-aged kids probably from the nearby Lake City University. The young girl in the booth in the corner who had a book open, an empty plate and half-filled glass of tea in front of her. He paused. She was awfully young to be by herself, but she didn't look distressed. He'd ask a worker about her before he left. There could be a hundred reasons for her being there, but he still wanted to make sure it was a legit and safe one.

He slid onto the seat next to Nathan. The waiter pulled a device from his pocket and stepped up to them. "I'm Trevor. I'll be waiting on you today. What can I get you?"

Andrew closed the menu. "Lemonade and the burger plate, with onions, please."

"Same," Nathan said. "But no onions."

The guy tapped the order in and headed for the drink machine.

"Figured we'd eat while we were here," Andrew said. "It's almost lunchtime and I'm hungry."

"I can always eat a burger. And they're amazing here. Fresh, hand-pattied, cooked juicy and just right." He paused. "Now I might eat two."

Andrew laughed.

Trevor returned with chilled glasses of lemonade some might think better suited to a hot summer day, but Andrew didn't care about the temperature outside. He took a swig and sighed. "I'll be back just for this," he told Nathan.

Nathan laughed. "You've never been here?"

"Nope. You?"

"A couple of times. Jesslyn introduced me to the place."

"Nice."

"Yeah, but she doesn't let me get the onions if I plan on kissing her."

"Are you planning on kissing her?"

"First chance I get."

Andrew chuckled. Maybe one day he'd be leaving onions off his burger too. One could hope.

Trevor returned with silverware and napkins. Andrew subtly showed his badge to the guy. "Do you mind if I ask you a few questions?"

The young man sighed. "Sure, but I don't have anything new to add to what I already told the other agents."

"You know Marcus Brown?"

"Of course. Everyone knows him. He was a regular. And I guess everyone *really* knows him now after the whole hijacking thing." He wiped down the counter near them and tucked the rag into his back pocket. "And that's exactly what I told the others who came in asking."

"No cameras with any footage?"

He shook his head. "Everything resets after twenty-four hours and Marcus hadn't been in for at least a week."

"No cameras across the street either," Nathan said.

"Order up!"

Trevor grabbed the two plates from the kitchen window and placed them in front of him and Nathan. "Ketchup?"

"And mustard," Andrew said.

Once they had the burgers ready, Andrew took a bite, swallowed, and vowed he'd be back.

Trevor refilled the lemonade, and Andrew tilted his head at the girl in the booth. "Who's that?"

"Ginny's daughter. Ginny is one of our cooks here. The kid's

name's Cheyenne but everyone calls her Chey. She was being bul-
lied at school, so Ginny took her out and homeschools her now."

"While working full-time?"

He shrugged. "She's a single mom. They make it work. They live in
a small apartment out back, so Chey comes and goes as she pleases.
And at least Ginny knows where she is."

Not his business. People did what they had to do.

"Hey," Trevor said, "I just thought of this. She's good friends with
Jacob, Marcus's son. The kid would come in after school all the time
and they'd be thick as thieves." He shrugged. "Haven't seen him for
a few days, but before his dad decided to hijack a plane, he was in
here all the time."

Andrew straightened. "Well, that's good news. Do you mind asking Ginny if we can talk to Chey?" They could work around parental
permission, but it was always easier if they could get it.

"Sure. I'll send her over when you guys finish eating."

"Thanks."

It didn't take long to devour the rest of the food and get a lemonade to go. A woman stepped out of the back and walked over to
them. "Hi, I'm Ginny. I hear you want to speak to my girl."

"Yes, ma'am, if that's all right. You're welcome to listen in, of course."

She waved a hand. "I've gotta keep cooking. Chey'll fill me in on
what you got to say."

"Before we talk to her," Nathan said, "do you mind telling us what
you know about Marcus Brown?"

"Check the notes of the other dude that was here. He wrote it all
down and I ain't got anything else to add."

"Right." Nathan nodded. "Thanks."

She leaned over the counter. "Hey, Chey?"

The girl looked up from her book with a frown. "What?"

"It's ma'am."

"Right."

"These nice gentlemen need to talk to you for a minute. You be
polite and cooperate."

130

"Whatever."

The woman rolled her eyes and sighed, then shot a look to Nathan and Andrew. "She won't stand up to bullies, but she'll defy me like no one's business. Help yourself, boys. I wish you luck."

Andrew held in a grimace and looked at Nathan. "Maybe one of us would be a little less intimidating?"

"Yeah. I'll slide into the booth behind you and listen."

"Perfect."

Andrew walked over to the young girl, who eyed him with a wary expression. "What?"

"Do you mind if I sit?" He showed her his badge. "I'm a federal agent, but I'm also a friend of Jacob's and I'd like to ask you a couple of questions if that's all right with you."

Her brows rose at the mention of Jacob and she nodded. "Fine. Is Jacob okay?"

"Well, that's what we're trying to find out." Andrew settled across from her in the booth and folded his hands on the table. "I hear you're homeschooled?"

"Yes." She mimicked his position, linking her fingers in front of her, forearms resting on the edge of the table.

"But you know Jacob from school?"

"Yes."

Well, she was a talkative one, wasn't she?

He cleared his throat. "You know Jacob's missing."

Her eyes flickered and her jaw tightened. "I heard."

"Can you tell me where you think he might have run to?"

"No."

"Can't or won't?"

"Can't." She frowned. "He was supposed to meet me here yesterday, but he never showed. After all his father did . . ." She shrugged. "I guess he just needed some space."

"You're here a lot?"

"All the time. I live here. Well, not here, but close by. I use the internet to do online school while Mom works, so it's not really homeschooling. I'm still enrolled in the public school. Mom just thinks saying she's homeschooling me makes her sound like a better mother. She's not."

At least her answers were getting longer. "Does she ever hit you?"

Chey sighed and shook her head. "No, she doesn't abuse me. She's just . . . her. Always controlling, never letting me do what I want to do." She looked up at him through thick lashes. "I know I have it better than a lot of kids. I just give her a hard time." A flicker of shame crossed her features before she looked away.

"Most kids your age do."

She shrugged. "She lets me have a phone, so I guess she's not all bad."

"I'd say not." He paused, and she studied him with her dark eyes. She was a pretty girl who'd probably turn into a beautiful woman. Her mother's controlling was probably related to that fact more than anything. "Did you ever see Jacob's dad?"

"Sure. All the time."

"And did you ever see him meeting with anyone?"

She tilted her head. "Maybe. Why?"

"Because we don't think Jacob's dad wanted to hijack that plane. We think someone forced him to. So, if we could find that person, we could help clear some of that up and make Jacob feel a little better about his dad."

"Oh." She sat silent, looking at her hands. "I don't think I can help you."

Andrew wasn't so sure. "Look, Chey, Jacob could be in trouble. Like big trouble. We just want to help him." If Jacob had the money, it wouldn't take long for the guy who wanted it back to start looking for him too.

"Jacob can take care of himself," she said. "He's really smart and he and his dad went camping a lot."

"Out in the woods?"

"Maybe."

"If you had to pick a place to go look for Jacob right now, where would you go?"

She sighed and twisted her mouth in thought. "He likes books. He might hang out in the library during the day. I don't know about at night."

"That's helpful."

She hesitated. "I . . . might have something on my phone that could help you find the man Mr. Brown met with a few days ago."

Andrew stilled. "Like what?"

"I was bored and was taking pictures. Even some video. Mr. Brown and that guy are in it. The angle's probably not very good and I don't know if it'll help you find him or not, but if it helps Jacob or his dad, I'll give it to you."

ELEVEN

Kristine blinked and shifted on the chair. She'd managed to fall asleep and her phone said she'd been out for three hours. Wow. She needed it, sure, but hadn't expected to basically pass out. She was surprised the nurse had let her stay. Then again, it wasn't like she was tiring out the patient. She stood and stretched out the kinks, grabbed her half-full water bottle, and chugged the rest of the contents.

Then returned to her seat to pull out her phone and check messages.

She had a long text from Andrew—obviously voice-texted—about meeting a young girl named Chey who had given them a little clue about Marcus Brown. She couldn't wait to hear about that one and texted him that very thing.

She moved on to emails. Then paused. Her father hadn't texted. Weird. Not that she really wanted him to, but still . . . the silence was disconcerting. Should she text him?

She sighed and tapped the screen when a sound from the bed froze her.

Emily. Kristine walked to her sister's side and gripped her hand in a gentle squeeze. Emily's eyes stayed closed, but she squeezed back. "Hey, little sis, you want to wake up?"

Emily's eyes fluttered a few times, then opened and connected with Kristine's. She grunted, and Kristine wet a cloth in the sink and held it to Emily's lips. A faint nod was her thanks. Then Emily cleared her throat. "What . . . ," she whispered, her voice hoarse.

"Your throat's probably sore. They had to take you to surgery to remove your gallbladder, fix your broken leg, and put your left hand back together."

Emily lifted her casted left hand, let out a low groan, and lowered it gently back to her side. "Dana? Tia?"

Oh boy. "What happened to the car? Why did you wreck?"

"Brakes," she whispered.

"The brakes went out?"

"Yeah." She winced. "Hurts."

"Hang on, I'll call someone."

The nurse entered. "What can I do for you, hon?"

Kristine smiled at the endearment and racked her brain for the woman's name, then shot a subtle glance at the whiteboard on the wall. Naomi. "She woke up a minute ago and said 'hurts' so I called you."

Naomi looked at her computer and clicked a few keys. "I can up her morphine dose a bit and I'll let the doctor know." She patted Emily's arm and her sister stirred and moaned. Naomi nodded. "Oh yes, we'll take care of that right now."

Once she was done, Kristine waited, but Emily didn't stir again and Kristine wasn't about to wake her back up. The longer she could put off telling her about Tia, the better.

Naomi left with the promise to be back shortly.

Her phone buzzed with an incoming call. Her supervisor. She walked over to the window and swiped the screen. "Hello?"

"Hi, Kristine, I thought I'd update you. How are you doing?"

"Well, concerned about the accusations, but honestly, that's moved down the list of things to worry about right now. I'm at the hospital with my sister. She was in a car accident."

"Oh no. I'm so sorry to hear that."

She pressed her fingers to her eyelids. "Thank you." She filled him in on the details, then asked, "What's the update?"

"OPR is still investigating, trying to determine if any misconduct occurred."

"Okay."

"They'll be ready to talk to you soon."

"Just let me know. I'll be at the hospital a lot, so they know where to find me. I can even come to the office if necessary."

"It's looking like you're going to be in the clear, though."

Relief swept through her. "Thank you, sir."

She hung up, then tapped a text to Andrew.

> What's your next move?

Headed to see if we can track down the missing Jacob at the Lake City Library—the South Main branch. He likes to read according to his young friend here. How's Emily?

> She woke up briefly. Long enough to say the brakes failed on the car.

Uh oh. So sorry. She's going to be okay, tho, right?

> Looks like it, but they're watching her closely. Keep me updated on if you find Jacob. I can't believe he's managed to stay hidden this long.

I'm starting to wonder if someone's helping him. Trying not to imagine the worst.

Not imagining the worst was almost impossible. She sent him a heart emoji and then froze. What? Wait! Why had she sent *that*? No, no, no. Now he would think . . . what?

She let out an audible groan and lowered her head to her palm. Great. Why was she so awkward when it came to that kind of thing? Should she say she didn't mean the heart emoji, that she'd hit the wrong one trying to send the thumbs-up?

No. Absolutely not. She certainly wasn't going to stoop to *lying*. She'd just let it be and pray he ignored it too. No sense in bringing attention to it. Right?

Naomi popped back in and checked Emily's vitals and IV bag. "Anything you need, Ms. Duncan?"

"Kristine, please. You're going to be seeing a lot of me until Em's moved out of here."

The pretty woman smiled. "Kristine. Sorry it has to be under these circumstances, but I'm pleased to meet you. You know your time here is up, right?"

"Yes, I know."

"Okay then. She's going to be sleeping for a while with the extra meds. Why don't you go home, freshen up, and get some food? I'll keep an eye on her and let you know if anything changes."

Kristine nodded, then rose to write her and her father's phone numbers on the whiteboard. "Just send a text to me first and I'll get here as fast as I can. My dad and Em don't get along very well, so I'm not sure . . ." She shrugged.

"I'll take care of it."

"Thanks, Naomi."

"Of course."

She slipped out and Kristine blew out a low breath. The nurse was right. She should go home and take a shower, change clothes, and grab some food.

And then check in with Andrew and Nathan again.

The elevator door opened and her father stepped out, met her gaze, then looked away. "How is she?"

"She's sleeping. You should go home and get some sleep. Or go to my place and crash for a while. Use the key with my permission."

"I should stay."

"No, you really shouldn't. Naomi's keeping an eye on her. She just got some fresh meds, so Emily's not waking up anytime soon. Go home."

His eyes flashed, but he nodded. "Fine. You know, if she had just listened to me when I told her not to go, this wouldn't have happened."

"Dad, please. Just stop. Emily is a grown woman. You've got to stop smothering her and trying to control her."

He waved a hand, dismissing the topic. Because he didn't want to hear it. She sighed. Why did she even try?

"Where are you going?" he asked.

"Ethan'll be here soon. I'll be back when he gets here or Emily wakes up. For now, I'm heading home to take care of me so I can help take care of her."

"We still need to talk about you joining my company, Kristine. I need you."

She blinked. And stared. "I honestly don't even know what to say to you right now. I'll be back." She walked past the elevator and headed for the stairs, her mind whirling at her father's behavior. Emily was in the ICU and he was pressuring her to join his PI firm? Was he that clueless or was it some kind of coping mechanism? She hoped it was the latter, because it was bizarre and she didn't have time to figure it out right now.

ANDREW STOOD OUTSIDE the Lake City Public Library and looked at the video Chey had shared with him. He'd sent it to Nathan as well as the analyst, who was running it through facial recognition. Unfortunately they didn't have a hit yet. And might not get one. The man Brown had met with had been seated in profile to Cheyenne but wore a shirt with some kind of logo on the left shoulder. The analyst would be working on that as well.

His phone buzzed with a text from Kristine.

Emily is sedated for now and she has a great nurse
who told me to get lost in a very nice way. So
on the way home to grab a shower and change

clothes, etc. Let me know if there's anything I can do to help.

> Glad Emily's doing okay. You should probably grab some more sleep while you can.

Might do that too. So nothing I can do right now?

> Not at the moment.

Talk later then.

A pang of disappointment hit him. He should have made something up. Maybe he'd run by there before he went home. Just to make sure she was okay. And say what? *I wanted to see you?* Hmm. Maybe not.

Andrew glanced at the parking lot looking for Nathan and spotted a black truck backed into the corner space in the rear of the lot. He only noticed it because he thought he remembered seeing it behind him on the way over. He looked closer, but the driver's seat was empty. He was being paranoid.

Nathan chose that moment to turn into the parking lot.

Together they walked into the library. "I'll go right, you go left," Andrew said.

"Check the study rooms."

"And the bathroom."

It didn't take long to cover the entire building open to the public, with no sign of Jacob. Andrew walked to the desk, and the young man behind it looked up. "Help you find something?"

He showed him Jacob's picture. "You know him?"

"Sure. He's in here all the time. Loves the science fiction section."

"When's the last time you saw him?"

"Before his dad hijacked the plane."

Ouch. "Okay. Do you mind if we take a look in all the employees-only places?"

"Why?"

"We're looking for Jacob and want to make sure he's not hiding here."

The guy frowned. "Huh. I doubt he would be there, but there are some good hiding spots in the back. Help yourself."

"Thanks."

Ten minutes later, Andrew and Nathan met at the front door. "He's not here," Nathan said.

"Nope." Andrew scanned the parking lot. He couldn't help it. The truck was gone.

He texted Tim Jackson, one of the agents guarding Hank.

> How's everything there?

Quiet.

> Good. Thanks. Headed to the office. Let me know if you need anything.

Will do.

For the next few hours, Nathan and Andrew worked on the case of the hijacking. He looked up other hijackings over the past twenty years and printed them out. There weren't that many, but he was curious to know if any had been instigated by the Serpentine Network. He took a short break and checked in with Chief Badami, who said they'd found the spent shells at the scene of the accident, which were now with forensics. The shells not matching his or Kristine's weapon were from a Glock 19 as they'd suspected.

Finally, the fatigue kicked in and he looked over at Nathan. "I'm going home."

"It's about time. This is your day off, remember?"

"Right. See you later."

Andrew grabbed a couple of pizzas from the Brick Oven Pizza Factory on his way home—well, as home as an Airbnb could be. But he liked the house. It was something like what he'd buy if he was going to stay in Lake City.

The home was perched on a mountain slope and had a rustic elegance feel to it. The exterior, constructed of wood and stone, blended into the natural surroundings. His favorite part of the house was the large windows offering panoramic views. The back deck was perfect for enjoying an early morning cup of coffee or just watching the sunset after a long day of investigation and chasing bad guys.

And it was a perfect safe house for Hank.

When he got there, one of the Bureau vehicles was gone. He frowned and walked inside to find Tim and Hank playing cards at the kitchen table.

"Where'd Sherry go?" He set the pizzas on the counter.

"She had a little family emergency," Tim said. "Her son fell and broke his wrist."

"Ouch."

"Yeah. But it's been quiet. Hank had himself a good nap but said television hurt his head, so . . . cards."

Hank stood and walked to the refrigerator to grab a Coke. "Got some steaks for the grill. Corn on the cob and baked potatoes."

"You went to the grocery store?" Andrew couldn't help the slight note of disapproval in his voice. "You're supposed to be hiding and healing, remember?"

His friend shrugged. "I can't sit here all day doing nothing. I'll go stir-crazy. Cooking steaks? Now that I can do. Besides, Tim and Sherry are great. We just looked like three friends shopping for dinner."

Andrew refused to argue with him. The man had killers after him and pulled this kind of stunt. He sighed. He was a grown man who made his choices. He'd just have to live with any consequences. And pray for no collateral damage.

Hank frowned. "Seriously, man, we watched our six the whole time. No one was watching."

Tim shook his head. "We dressed him up in a disguise. A really good one. We were fine."

Hank's frown deepened. "Honestly, I'm a little confused at how quiet it's been. This isn't like the SN."

It wasn't. But it also wasn't wise to be out in public when someone was trying to kill you.

Andrew let it go. They were all professionals. If they were confident in that little outing, then fine. He ate two slices of pizza before shoving the leftovers into the fridge and decided to grab a few more hours of sleep. First, he checked in with Kristine.

> How are you?

Tired. You?

> The same.

Anything new?

> No, Jacob wasn't there and no one has seen him. I might go back and talk to his friend Chey and see if she has any other ideas.

That sounds good. My aunt Wendy just got here. She's Mom's sister. She's going to be helping with Emily even though she and my dad can't stand each other. That's another thing Jess and I have in common. Her aunt couldn't stand her father either.

> Ouch. But still, that'll help having her there, right?

Guess we'll see. Probably. I came back to the hospital to wait for Wendy. There's no sense in us both being here, so I think if I can spell Wendy every so often, I can still *not* help with the investigation. You know what I mean?

I got you. Let's talk in the morning and make a
plan for the day.

Sounds good. I'm going home now, will come back
early in the morning to check on Emily, then be
free to NOT help.

Haha. Understood. Later.

Later.

No heart emoji this time.

Well, that was disappointing.

He must have fallen asleep faster than he'd thought he would, because he was almost surprised when he woke. The house was dark. Quiet.

And yet . . .

Something had disturbed his sleep.

Or maybe he'd just had enough rest and his body was ready to get up?

A buzz next to his bed startled him. Ah, the phone. He forgot he'd left it on vibrate. Four in the morning. All righty then. The text was from Kristine.

I can't sleep. I hope you have your phone on silent,
but on the off chance that you're awake, feel free
to text me.

I'm awake. Want some leftover pizza?

He hit send before he could delete it, then wondered what had possessed him to ask her that.

If you're serious, I can bring cheesecake.

He blinked. Okay, he *really* liked her.

I hate to ask you to get out at this time of

morning. I can come to you. You might want to go
back to bed once you're up for a while.

Haha. Cute. After so many years flying, my
circadian rhythm is permanently damaged.
I don't mind coming there.

Andrew chuckled.

I'm fine with you coming over.

Okay, send me the address.

He did so.

Hey, that's not too far from me. Ten minutes
max. See ya in a bit.

A low hum caught his attention and he lifted his eyes from his
phone to listen. As though that would help.

Coming from outside? Maybe.

He threw the covers off, pulled on a T-shirt, then a sweatshirt,
and shoved his feet into his sneakers, all in under five seconds. He
walked to the window and listened.

Nothing.

He frowned and left the bedroom to step into the combination
dining area and great room. The back deck was off that and the
kitchen was to his right. The other two bedrooms and bath were
straight across from him.

The living space was empty. "Tim?" Andrew glanced at his watch.
The agent could be walking the perimeter of the house, checking
for weak areas.

He sniffed. Gas?

He strode into the kitchen, started to flip the light on, and froze.
Flipping a light switch when he thought he smelled gas might not
be the smartest move. Instead, he tapped the flashlight app on his

phone and the strong beam lit up the area. He crossed to the gas stove and found all the burners off.

Okay then. The basement? He looked back over his shoulder. And where was Tim? He walked to Hank's room and pushed the door open. If the man felt good enough to go grocery shopping, he could help him out. "Pssst!"

Hank's eyes opened and his hand slid to his weapon on the end table. "What is it?"

"Not sure, but we're going to investigate. I smell gas, so no flipping light switches. You good?"

"Right behind you." His phone light added to Andrew's helped brighten the area. "Where's Tim?" he asked.

"I was hoping you'd know that."

"I was catching up on years of lost sleep. Sorry."

Andrew didn't blame him. They walked back through the great room, then into the kitchen. "Basement?"

Hank nodded and opened the door. Gas hit them in the face and Andrew gasped and shut the door. "We've got to get out."

"He's waiting to pick me off," Hank said, "but yeah, this place could definitely blow. We're going to have to take our chances."

"Grab your wallet and anything else you can fit in your pockets, and we'll go out the master bedroom window."

"Dude, that's a two-story drop."

"If we go out any normal exit, someone could be waiting. We'd be sitting ducks. We have to do the unexpected. There's a fire escape ladder in the master closet."

"Then let's go."

Hank took off toward his room, and Andrew headed toward the master bedroom and grabbed his wallet, badge, and weapon too. Then the ladder. He was worried about Tim, but he wasn't in the house, so getting out was priority number one. Then they'd look for the agent.

Hank had come in and opened the window. A cool breeze blew in and they both breathed deep of the refreshing air. Then Andrew connected the ladder to the window frame and threw the rest of it out.

He looked at Hank. "I'll go first. This is going to hurt your rib going down. And whatever you do, don't look down. Your head isn't exactly steady." He'd text Kristine as soon as they were free of the house and the gas. She didn't need to walk into this situation.

"I got this, Ross, just go. I'm sure it's not going to feel great on your arm either."

He had a point. Andrew climbed out and down as fast as he could, ignoring the fire shooting through his shoulder. He got to the bottom and tripped over something.

A body.

He knelt next to the man and shone his phone light in his face. "Tim." With a gash on his forehead. "Tim's down here. Be careful."

The ladder rattled and Hank was halfway down. "What happened?"

"Don't know." He held the ladder still for Hank, who stepped off the bottom rung with a grunt. "Tim's out cold, but he's still breathing." And he still needed to text Kristine not to come. He grabbed his phone and sent her the text.

> Stay away from the house. In the middle of a situation.

"Well, we can't leave him here. If the house blows, it'll fry him."

"Yeah." And Hank couldn't help carry the man. Andrew wasn't sure he could either, but he was going to have to try. Tim groaned and Andrew helped him to his feet. "Good timing."

"My head is going to explode," Tim muttered.

"What happened to you?"

"I'll tell you when I figure it out."

"No time to talk about it now anyway. Head down the hill away from the house. It's full of gas and we don't want to be anywhere near it if something sparks." He held on to Tim on one side and

Hank did the same on the other, even though the action had to be torture for his broken rib. They headed toward the hill not nearly as fast as he would have liked. The sound of a car pulling into the drive froze him for a brief second. "Oh no."

Kristine.

TWELVE

Kristine climbed out of her car and pulled out her phone to text Andrew that she was there, not wanting to knock or ring the bell in case Hank was sleeping. And where was Tim, the—

"Kristine!"

She spun to see Andrew and Hank rush toward her from the area behind the house. "Hey, what are you—"

Gunshots rang out and they all hit the ground. Kristine rolled next to her car and sucked in a breath while she drew her weapon. Hadn't they just done this?

Andrew and Hank dropped next to her.

"You guys good?" she asked.

"Yeah," Hank muttered. "I guess. I don't have any bullet holes, so that's a positive."

"How'd they find you?" she asked.

"Who knows?"

She hadn't led them here, had she? What a horrible thought. "When did all this start?"

"Shortly after we texted. They didn't follow you."

He was a mind reader. Freaky. "Okay, so now what?"

"I've already called backup," Hank said. "Just waiting on them to get here."

Andrew peered around the vehicle and pulled back. "Then we just either need to hold this dude off—"

The next crack of the weapon sent the bullet through the window of the house. And the next. Then the next.

"What's he doing?" Kristine asked.

Andrew shifted, his brows pulled tight, then realization dawned. "He doesn't know we're out here. The house is full of gas and he's trying to hit something metal to spark it and make the house explode. Run for the back! There's a hill down the side that will offer some protection. Tim should be there waiting."

They took off as the gun popped one more time. Twice. And again. They rounded the side and scrambled for the hill Andrew pointed out. The explosion rocked the air and sent the three of them to the ground, hands over their ears, heads ducked.

Sirens screamed over the roar of the flames, and blue and red lights bounced onto the scene. Kristine's ears rang and her heart pounded. She rolled over to look at the damage, and the house was burning hard. If someone had been inside, they would be dead. Even her Bucar was burning. The gunshots had come from the street above and to the left of the blazing home. "Should we go after him?"

Andrew dug a finger in his ear. "I'm not sure, but I thought I heard a motorcycle speed off."

"You did," Tim said, dropping beside her. She flinched.

With the explosion and the ringing in her ears, she'd missed his approach and the motorcycle leaving. But still, something niggled at her.

She gripped her weapon and looked in the direction she thought the bullets may have come from. But the shadows were too dark, even with the law enforcement vehicles lighting up the night.

She moved closer to the guys. "Does any of this feel off to you?"

Hank snorted. "Like all of it?"

"No, I mean, since when do gang members sneak into houses and tamper with gas lines—I'm assuming that's what happened—

and then stand outside and shoot bullets hoping to make the house blow? I mean I'm just guessing, but that's sure what it looked like to me."

"Yeah, me too," Andrew said.

Hank frowned. "You have a point. That's not gang work. At least not any kind of gang work I've ever heard of. But what else could it be?"

"No idea," Kristine said.

"Come on," Andrew said. "Let's get up there and give our statements. Hopefully all the lights and people have scared him off."

Hank nodded. "And the dogs will be going after him. They'll have a better chance of catching him than we will." A chopper roared in the distance and they looked up to see the spotlight sweep toward them. "And then there's that."

Kristine gripped her weapon. "Good. That means no one will be shooting at us. I'm tired of being shot at, personally."

"Ditto," Andrew muttered.

She followed him, Tim, and Hank back up the hill, well away from the fire and toward the flashing lights. They were still careful, watching the dark spaces. "Just because you heard a motorcycle doesn't mean it was his," she said.

"Maybe not." He frowned as though thinking of something else.

"What?" she asked.

He shook his head. "Not sure. It'll come to me." He stopped. "And it just did. Something woke me up out of a sound sleep. I think it was a drone."

"A drone?" Kristine asked.

"Yeah. And those bullets were coming hard and fast, but it didn't sound like an automatic weapon. I think he used a drone to shoot up the house. That's why he didn't know we were outside when he started shooting. He was too far away to see us."

Hank shrugged. "It's a good theory."

When they made it to the top of the hill, Nathan rushed to meet them. "You guys okay? What happened?"

"Someone found Hank," Andrew said. "At least that's what it looks like."

Nathan blinked. "How?"

"Not sure. Tim needs an ambulance and a hospital visit. He's probably got a concussion."

Tim slipped out of Andrew's helping grasp and made his way over to the nearest car to lean against it. Then slid to the ground and put his head in his hands.

"Ambulance should almost be here. I called one just in case."

Kristine's phone buzzed and she glanced at the screen. A text from the night nurse, Leanna.

> Naomi gave me instructions, so I'm texting according to those. I know it's late—or early—but Emily is asking for you and your brother just got here. Your aunt is here as well.

"I've got to go to the hospital, guys. I'll give my statement and take off—" At Andrew's look, she froze. "Except I don't have a car, right?" Last she'd seen it, it had been on fire. She looked in that direction. Firehoses still rained waterfalls on it.

"I'll drive you as soon as we can get away," Andrew said. He paused and grimaced. "Except the car was in the garage so . . . I'm probably going to need a new car too." Another pause. "Did Tim's car survive? As long as the keys didn't blow up, we can use his."

She pulled her phone from her pocket. "You check with him. I'll call the Bureau." She eyed him. "If you keep destroying federal vehicles, they're going to start docking your pay."

"Ha! They should give us hazard pay and be grateful."

She smirked. "Yeah, let's go with that one."

He sighed. "I have some stuff at my parents' house, but I'm not going to wake them at this time of night." He looked at Nathan. "I don't suppose Hank and I could borrow some clothes?"

"Hank's too skinny to wear my stuff. My jeans would fall off him. You could hit James up again for something for him. But you might be able to wear some of mine. We'll figure it out. Let's rendezvous at James and Lainie's. I'll let them know we're coming."

"Poor James and Lainie," Kristine said, "getting invaded once again."

"They'll be mad if we don't."

He wasn't wrong. Andrew went to grab the keys from Tim, who was now in the care of paramedics, and Kristine raked a hand over her head and texted Ethan she would be there shortly.

As long as she didn't have to outrun any more explosions. Or bullets.

She left that last part off the text and stuck her phone in her pocket, said a prayer for Emily, and went to join Andrew in the borrowed Bureau vehicle.

IT TOOK THE NEXT SEVERAL HOURS to finish everything that needed to be done.

And now, after a few hours of sleep at James and Lainie's house, Andrew was ready to fight back. He hated that Hank was a target, and it seemed whoever was after him didn't care if innocent people got in the way. Now everyone but Kristine—who'd gone to be with her sister—sat in James and Lainie's den discussing their next options. Kenzie and Cole had insisted on being a part of the discussion, but so far, they hadn't said much. Cole, who sat on the end of the couch, his big body sprawled, legs crossed at the ankles, looked more thoughtful than anything. Kenzie sat next to him, her dark eyes taking in everything, right elbow on her knee, chin resting on a fist. Cole had brought Andrew the keys to an older model sedan that belonged to the Bureau. At least his personal vehicle was safely ensconced behind his parents' bookstore.

Hank, dressed in James's jeans, Panthers sweatshirt, socks, and his own shoes, paced in the kitchen away from the windows. Andrew was confident that they hadn't been followed to the lake house, but still, his nerves twitched. And obviously Hank's did too. Andrew was still dressed in his sleep pants, T-shirt, and shoes. James had loaned him another hoodie. He was going to have to replace the man's wardrobe at this rate.

"Okay," Hank said, walking into the den but keeping a wall at his back. "Here's what we're going to do. I'm going to be the bait and you're going to have my back. Then once we have whoever's trying to kill me in custody, I'm going to disappear. Because if I don't, no one in my life will be safe. Including me."

For a minute no one said anything, then protests erupted.

Hank held up a hand and everyone fell silent. "Look, I realize you don't know me. And honestly, it's humbling that you would care so much about my fate. I can't say thanks enough, but I've got to do this. It's the only way to stop this guy."

Andrew studied his friend and former partner. "All right. Let's figure this out. What do you have in mind?"

"We use a safe house. Something up in the mountains, away from everything—everyone who could get hurt. The only issue is making sure he knows where I am and where I'm going."

"You'll have to appear in public," James said.

Hank nodded. "That's the tricky part. How do I do that without putting other people in harm's way?"

"Think about who you're talking to. We can do this if we do it right. We keep you surrounded," Nathan said. "A big ole group of us."

"Then when we leave—wherever—the grocery store or something?" Hank said. "Andrew, Cole, and I can take off up the mountain to the safe house with James here bringing up the rear. Hopefully our guy will follow."

Kenzie frowned. "It sounds too easy."

"One can hope, right?" James said.

Cole shifted and cleared his throat. "We have to try. This guy is getting bolder by the hour. We have to stop him before he succeeds. This is what we've trained for. This is what we do. So let's do it and protect one of our own."

Hank nodded, relief on his strained features. He was hurting and probably needed pain meds and to lie down.

"All right," Andrew said, "let's get this hashed out and sent up the food chain for approval." Lake City PD and the FBI were about to become partners once more.

THIRTEEN

Kristine sat in the chair next to Emily's bed. Aunt Wendy had hugged her and excused herself to get a few hours of sleep. Emily had stirred a few times but had yet to fully wake again, thanks to the powerful meds pumping through her small frame. That was the one thing that gave Kristine comfort. Emily wasn't in pain, physically or emotionally. Yet. She just prayed her sister could heal a little more physically before she had to tell her about Tia.

The door opened and Ethan entered, took a look at his wounded twin in the bed, and ran a hand over his bloodshot eyes. He'd driven all night, and as far as she knew, he hadn't slept in a really long time. He had to be exhausted. But he nodded to Emily. "How is she?"

"The same. Why don't you go to my place? I'll give you the key and you can make yourself at home. It's a three-bedroom town house. Use the bed that's made. Although, Dad was there for a while yesterday, so all the beds might be made at this point."

He shot her an amused look through his weariness. "You still don't make your bed?"

"Leftover teenage rebellion. Dad can't punish me for it anymore."

The amusement faded. "Yeah. He was such a tyrant."

"He was. Still is in a lot of ways. I used to think we had it good because he never hit us. Not like some kids. But I didn't realize the extent of the emotional abuse until I was an adult. Talking to Jesslyn about her own father's manipulative nature was a big help. For some reason it helps to know I'm not alone." Jesslyn's father, mother, and two younger sisters had been killed when she was seven, but her aunt had fed Jesslyn information about her father's character and personality over a period of time, allowing her to fully understand her childhood flashes of memories. Thankfully, in the end, before he died, he'd been a changed man.

Unfortunately, Kristine wasn't sure that was possible for her father. Then again, God could do miracles. She was still praying for one.

Ethan sighed. "I'm just glad I'm not around him much anymore."

"Have you seen him?"

"Yes, briefly. Outside the room. He started going on and on about how she shouldn't have been with her friends, that this never would have happened if she'd just listened to him, yada yada." He grimaced. "I just can't win with him. You know that. I finally walked off before I got to visit Emily. I was just waiting for him to go before I came back."

Ouch. "I know. I'm sorry. I just keep praying for him. Otherwise I wouldn't be able to deal with him either."

He studied her with narrowed eyes. "You know, I never was real big on the whole church thing, but because you seem so . . . I don't know . . . peaceful about everything, I figured I'd give it a try."

Kristine blinked. Peaceful? Her? She stared at Ethan. "Really?"

"Well, yeah. I mean . . . I don't know. You just seem to roll with everything without batting an eye. And then with Dad . . . I'd never be able to deal with him like you do."

She closed her eyes and thought about it. Then nodded. "Yeah, okay. I guess there is a peace that's come with acknowledging our father is never going to win the Father of the Year award."

"At the church where I've been going, there's a guy there. A man in his forties, I guess. He's got the wife, two kids, and three dogs. Lives in a nice house in the burbs, et cetera. He's an accountant by day but a spiritual warrior and mentor after hours." Ethan laughed. "Well, probably all the time, but I only see him at church. He's about five ten and a hundred fifty soaking wet. Doesn't look like he could fight anybody and win. And then there's a guy who's a Navy SEAL. I mean, you can picture him. In the best shape ever, buff, with tats and a look that would intimidate just about anyone who crosses his path. But man, he loves God." He shook his head. "Seeing them worship together in the same place just did something for me. It was powerful in a way I can't really explain. I don't know why, but I needed to see that it didn't matter what your outward appearance was. What mattered is what's on the inside. And the cool thing? They're not shy or ashamed of telling me they're praying for me. I mean, I never even asked them to, and they just came up to me—on two separate occasions—and told me so. I figure that might be God trying to get my attention."

Kristine stared. She'd never heard him talk this much. Especially not about spiritual matters. And he probably related much better to the accountant than he did the SEAL. Maybe it was the exhaustion loosening his tongue. "Wow. This is recent, right?"

"Yes. Just over the past couple of months." He rubbed his eyes. "And I know I need to forgive Dad and move past all of our childhood pain, but I'm not there yet."

She stood and hugged him. "I'm so proud of you, Ethan. And I fully believe that you'll get there. That's my prayer for you. That you can forgive and move on and be the man God is calling you to be." But what about her? Had she forgiven and moved on? The sharp squeeze in the vicinity of her heart had her wincing.

"You know," she said, "when Mom was alive, she was the spiritual head of the family, not him. And I get it. It's what a lot of women have to do these days if they want to raise kids who love the Lord." She waved a hand. "All that to say, you didn't exactly have a role model as to what a godly man looked like. I'm so glad you have at least two now."

"Me too."

"If Aunt Wendy hadn't spent a lot of time with us after Mom died," she said, "I'm not sure where I'd be spiritually."

"Yeah, I didn't pay much attention to her."

"This is one of the most interesting conversations I've eavesdropped on in a while," Emily said, her words slow and slurred, but she was awake.

Kristine stepped over to her and gripped her hand. "Welcome back, little sis."

Her eyes landed on Ethan and tears began to drip down her temples. "Hey, li'l bro."

"Only by three minutes."

It was familiar banter and Kristine soaked it up. Emily looked at her and turned serious. "Thank you for being here."

"Where else would I be?"

"On a plane?"

"Seriously?"

Emily's hand squeezed. "You're always here for us, Kris. I don't know what we'd do without you." She swallowed hard.

"Well, let's hope we never have to find out."

"I was laying here thinking while y'all were talking and realized I don't think we've ever said thank you."

"Come on, Em, thank you for what?"

"For everything. After Mom died, you took over."

"Aunt Wendy took over."

"No," Ethan said, "she's right. You did."

Kristine frowned. "I did?"

"Yes." He laughed. "You were there for every game, every parent-teacher conference, every broken heart. You, Kris, not Dad or Aunt Wendy, although I'll give her credit for trying. But she had her own life. You gave up yours for us. Tried to help us not miss Mom so much." He shrugged, and Kristine wasn't sure what to say or do.

Other than turn into a sopping, crying mess. And that wasn't happening. Much. She pulled in a ragged breath. "Well, I just . . . I mean—" She sniffed. "I don't know what to say."

Emily squeezed again. "You don't have to say anything. Just know that we appreciate it. There aren't enough words to express that, and I'm sorry I haven't told you that before." She swiped a tear. "Almost dying makes you look at things a little different—and say things you've thought but never actually said. Now, I've said it."

"Thanks, Em. I'd do it all over again if I had to." She had to change the subject before the knot in her throat strangled her.

Emily shot a frown at Kristine. "I've been scared to ask and you haven't brought it up, but I have to know. How are Dana and Tia?"

Kristine worked hard not to let her ragged emotions show on her face, but she must have failed because Emily's drugged gaze sharpened.

"Tell me."

She had no choice. "Dana's recovering like you, but Tia didn't make it, sweetie. I'm so terribly sorry." No sense in dragging it out.

Emily gasped, then tears flooded her eyes and poured over her temples. Kristine grabbed the box of tissues and did her best to catch the grief, wishing she could mop it up as easy as the liquid. She didn't say a word, just let her sister cry. Then realized she was crying with her. Again. She used a few of the tissues for herself. "I'm so sorry, Em."

The sobs continued for a few more very long seconds before her sister hiccupped and caught her breath. "I can't believe it," she whispered. "It doesn't seem possible."

"I know." She leaned her head against Emily's, and Ethan walked to the bed to grip his sister's hand. She lost track of how long they stayed that way, but Kristine finally pulled back and asked, "How's your pain level?"

Emily sniffed and pressed the fingers of her good hand to her eyes. "Not too bad," she finally said. "But I'm not worried about that. Poor Tia . . ."

The door opened and their father stepped into the room. When his eyes landed on Emily, he smiled. "Finally. You're awake. I've been so worried, baby."

Emily looked at Kristine. "My pain level just spiked. I need more drugs."

Before she could respond, someone knocked, and a nurse let herself in the open door. "Hi there. I'm Leanna, and Naomi terrifies me. She's still here covering until lunchtime. If she learns of the crowd back here, I'm toast. I'm sorry, but one of you needs to go." The words were direct, but her eyes and tone were kind.

"I'm not leaving Emily," their father said. "I'll be right here."

Emily blinked. "But—"

"And I'll be here too," Ethan stated with a hard look at the man they all felt like they needed to team up against.

Kristine looked at Leanna. "I'll go," she said. Reluctantly, but she did have work to do. "Text me if you need me."

"Perfect," Leanna said. "You can come back in a little while. Now that she's awake, we don't want to tire her out with visits that are too long. She needs to rest."

"Agreed."

She kissed Emily's cheek, hugged her brother, nodded to her father, and slipped out of the room with Leanna.

The nurse patted her shoulder. "I'll watch out for her. Now that she's awake, Naomi and I will be more strict about the rules. I'll kick them out in thirty minutes."

On impulse, Kristine hugged the woman. "You're the best. Tell Naomi she is too and I owe her a big hug."

"Thank you. Yes I am. You can put that on my evaluation. Naomi's too."

Kristine laughed and headed for the elevator, checking her phone as she walked. She had about fifteen text messages. One was confirmation that her rental had been delivered with directions how to find it in the lot. Thank goodness. No more Uber for her. The other messages were on the loop, letting her know that everyone was at James and Lainie's house and updating her on their conversation.

And then a private message from Andrew, who wanted to know

if she'd go shopping with him, then to dinner if she wasn't too tired. Today.

She froze, reading the message four times. Was he asking her out on a date?

HAD HE REALLY ASKED HER to go shopping and then to dinner with him? He verified he'd typed those words and actually sent them.

Yep. He had. An hour ago.

Should he specify it wasn't a date? Just two friends hanging out? No. He shouldn't.

Why not?

Because deep down he wanted it to be a date.

But not if she didn't.

He closed his eyes and huffed. He was a grown man. This should not be so difficult. But Kristine was special.

And intimidating, if he was honest. But definitely special. He didn't want to blow it.

"Andrew?"

He opened his eyes and found everyone in the room looking at him. "Oh. Sorry. I was thinking about something." Agonizing about a stupid text.

"More like a *someone*," Nathan muttered for Andrew's ears only.

Andrew shot his partner a dark look and Nathan looked away with a grin.

"So, are we good with the plan?" Hank asked.

"I'm not sure I'm good with it," Kenzie said, "but I'll be close by to offer any medical assistance should any—hopefully not—be needed."

Andrew tapped the update in his phone to Kristine. Three seconds later, his phone buzzed.

I'm here.

His heart did that weird thing it did whenever he was about to be in her presence. It really needed to stop doing that.

She knocked, then opened the door, stepped inside, walked over to the only seat available, and sat next to Andrew. "Hey," she said in response to the greetings. "Fill me in on what I missed." She looked at her phone. "The last I heard, there was some kind of plan where Hank was going to be bait and draw out whoever is after him."

"That's basically it," Hank said. "And these guys are going to be my rescue squad should I need it."

"Okay, then. What can I do?"

"How's Emily?" Kenzie asked.

"She was awake and tolerating our father's presence. Ethan is there to be the buffer or referee or whatever. They'll text me if I need to come back." She rubbed a hand down her face and frowned. "I'm in for helping with the plan, but don't you think it's going to be obvious that we're trying to set him up?"

"We'll just have to be not obvious," Hank said. "I think I know what to do. There's a gun store in town, right?"

Andrew leaned forward. "Yes."

"Then you and I'll go there. I'll go in, make a purchase while you stay outside looking like you're standing guard. I'll come out and then we'll head to the safe house in the mountains." He shook his head. "I just have a feeling he'll strike at night at the safe house—and he'll probably bring friends. It's what I would do."

"All right. We'll make sure we have SWAT on standby," James said with a glance at Cole, who nodded.

"How soon can we do this?" Hank asked.

Cole pulled his feet in and leaned forward to match Kenzie's pose. "I think we can get it all together in two days. The hardest part will be getting the place, but I'll find something. Then I'll take the team up there to scope it out and see what kind of setup we need."

"Perfect," Andrew said. "James, do you and Lainie mind if we use your home for a hideout over the next couple of days? I can run to my parents' and grab some stuff, but I'm going to need to go shopping.

I'll get some things for Hank while I'm out. Kristine's going to help me, right?" She actually hadn't answered his text.

She froze for a split second, then nodded. "Sure."

Andrew wanted to kick himself. Or have someone else do it. He shouldn't have put her on the spot. "I mean if you have time. If you need to be with Emily, I understand."

"No, she's okay right now. I'll check in, of course, but unless there's some kind of emergency, I should be good."

She hadn't taken the out he'd offered her.

His hopes rose. "Okay, great. I need to run by the bank, then we can get this done. Lainie, text me anything you need me to pick up for the next couple of days."

"I'll do that," she said.

Andrew looked at Kristine. "I know you just got here, but you ready?"

She stood. "Ready when you are."

FOURTEEN

Kristine hadn't thought going shopping with a guy could be so fun. But they hit two stores in downtown Lake City and a café for a to-go coffee, then headed to his parents' bookstore. Pages & Prose was a quaint store that held the delicious and unique smell of books. She stepped over the threshold and breathed deep. "This place is amazing," she said.

He smiled. "And they'll make a bundle when they sell it."

"They're going to sell?"

"When they're ready to move on. My parents are nomads at heart. Come on, I'll give you the tour."

It didn't take long. By the time he finished, a man in his early sixties who *had* to be Andrew's father came out of the back. He was tall with broad shoulders, had Andrew's green eyes and the same small dimple in his left cheek. He looked strong, capable, and curious.

"Andrew," the man said, "good to see you." He turned his attention to Kristine. "I'm Christopher Ross. And who is this lovely lady?"

Kristine held out a hand. "I'm Kristine Duncan. So nice to meet you."

"And you. So what brings you two by?"

"I need some stuff that I stored here," Andrew said. "There was an incident at the Airbnb where I was staying and I need to replace a few things."

Shock held the man still for a moment. "Wait a minute. I think I saw that on the news. That was your Airbnb?"

"It was."

Mr. Ross's eyes narrowed. "Good grief, Son, what are you entangled in to have someone come after you like that?"

"It's not me. It's a friend. And we're all fine, so that's what matters, right?"

The man grunted. "If you say so. Your mother's out with some church ladies who've pulled her into their friend group, so just go on up and get what you need. I'll entertain Ms. Duncan."

"Kristine, please," she said.

"And I'm Christopher. My wife's name is Mel."

Andrew touched her shoulder. "I'll be right back."

"Take your time."

He hurried through the shop, and she heard his footfalls going up a set of stairs.

"So, how did you and Andrew meet?" Christopher asked.

"Through mutual friends, but he's working a case that we both have a vested interest in."

"I see. Andrew's a good man. I raised him right."

"I can tell."

"Good." He grinned. "I like you."

After a few minutes of small talk, Andrew's return footsteps sounded. He appeared with a small suitcase a little larger than a carry-on. "I'll bring this back when I'm done with it."

"That's fine."

Andrew patted his father on the back, stepped back, then turned to Kristine. "You ready?"

She smiled. "Whenever you are."

She walked to the door, and Andrew's father met her there to take her hand in a light squeeze. "It was wonderful to meet you, Kristine. I hope I get to see more of you in the future."

"That would be lovely."

Andrew joined her. "Sorry to pop in and run, Dad, but we've got to go."

"We'll still see you on Friday, yes?"

"I'll be here." He hugged the man and patted his shoulder. "Give Mom a hug for me."

"Happy to do so."

And then Andrew was ushering her out the door.

Back in the car, she turned to him. "Your dad is great."

"He really is." He tilted his head. "Dinner at Mike's?"

"Mike's? Sure, I'll never turn down one of their burgers. They have awesome cheesecake too."

"I figured the cheesecake would come into play. And how is it I seem to be the only person in town who didn't know about that place?"

"You don't live here, Andrew. It's okay."

"Still . . ."

She laughed and he pulled away from the curb.

The restaurant was just two blocks away, and soon they were seated at the table, lemonades in front of them. His gaze swept the room.

"You looking for something?" she asked.

"Some*one*."

"Who?"

"Chey."

"Oh, Jacob's friend."

"Yep."

"Still no word about him, huh?"

"No. Unfortunately. His mother went home from the hospital yesterday morning. I've been wanting to go by and see her but have been a little busy trying to stay alive and keep Hank that way too."

Kristine groaned. "I should have gone by to see her. She probably feels like we've abandoned her."

He grimaced. "I know. I'll see if someone can stop by her house and check on her."

"No," she said. "How about you and I do that. Let's take some food from here and go see them."

"Seriously?"

"Sure. James, Cole, Kenzie, and others from the SWAT team do it occasionally when they come across a family or someone in need. No reason we can't do the same. They could use it."

He nodded, a look in his eyes she couldn't fully interpret but thought it looked a whole lot like respect. "All right. Yeah, that's a good idea."

"I have another idea."

"What's that?"

"I'm thinking about the hijacking." She shrugged. "I know you guys are still investigating."

"Mostly waiting for reports to come back, but yeah. What are you thinking?"

"Have you looked at past hijackings to see if there's anything similar to this one? You know, like someone being forced to carry out a hijacking or someone who was forced to get a tattoo beforehand, or . . . whatever. And I don't mean just in Lake City, because I think my mother's was the only one. Like ever."

"That's right. And yes, we've looked into them nationwide. Why?"

"Any hits?" she asked.

"Not really. We're still looking at them, but do you have something else on your mind?"

"Maybe. I want to look at something first. Something I've never looked at before."

"What's that?"

"The hijacking that killed my mother."

ANDREW BLINKED. "You've never looked at it before?"

"No."

"Why not?"

"Because my dad discouraged it, mostly. He was adamant that looking at it would just cause pain and heartache. He even refused to let us turn the television on because he didn't want the constant reminder blaring in our home. And while I don't agree with him about much, that one I kind of did. I just didn't want to relive it. It was horrible enough when it happened. That was as a teen. Later, as an adult, when I could look at it, I was afraid to."

"Afraid?"

"Afraid I'd become even more obsessed. I mean, I became an air marshal because of her. In honor of her. To possibly help other families not lose loved ones to hijackings." She shook her head. "Her hijacker went down with the plane. No one's really sure what happened. The black box was never found, so no answers there, and I was just secretly concerned that if I started looking for answers that might not be 'findable,' for lack of a better word, I'd never be able to be at peace."

"But?"

She gave a short laugh. "But Jesslyn. Seeing how finding answers about her family's deaths, finding the person responsible for them, helped her so much, I wonder if I shouldn't try to do the same. It could backfire, of course, but then again, it could end well too."

"Makes sense."

She studied him. "Does it?"

"Yeah. It does. I can get the report for you if you want."

"I have access to it."

"I know. Just thought it might be easier if I did it."

A slight smile curved her lips. "It might be at that." Her eyes flickered with something else. Something she wasn't sharing. Then it faded and she said, "Sure. You can get it for me. Thanks."

A young man walked out of the kitchen area and into the dining room, sweeper in hand. "That's Trevor," Andrew said.

"Who?"

"The guy who waited on Nathan and me last time. Hey, Trevor."

The guy stopped and looked at Andrew with a frown. "Yeah?"

"I don't know if you remember—"

"Oh yeah, burgers and lemonade guys. I remember you." He eyed Kristine with an appreciative look. "But your partner's looks sure have improved."

Kristine gave a barely audible snort, then coughed to cover it up. Andrew smirked, then asked, "Where's your friend Chey?"

Trevor leaned on the handle of the sweeper and shrugged. "Dunno. Guess she's got other things to entertain her."

"Yeah? Like what?"

He hesitated. "You know that kid you were asking about? Jacob Brown?"

Kristine straightened and Andrew nodded. "Yes."

"I think I saw her with him out behind the restaurant. She was giving him food. I mean I think it was him but can't be a hundred percent sure. I tried to look on the footage, but he had his head covered and kept his face turned away."

"He knows the cameras are there," Kristine said.

"I almost called you guys but wanted to be sure it was him. Then he was gone and I haven't seen him since. I've been watching for him, though. He's probably like a stray cat. Feed it and it'll come back."

Andrew wasn't sure he liked the analogy but kept his mouth shut, because while it was kind of offensive, it was possibly accurate. "So you're saying Chey most likely knows where he is."

"Maybe. I asked her about the kid this morning and she shrugged me off. Told me to mind my own business, that I obviously needed meds because I was hallucinating." He shrugged. "I wasn't hallucinating, but I can't promise it was Jacob either. Could have been another friend, but she was so secretive, it made me wonder."

Made Andrew wonder too. "When did you see them together?"

"This morning, right before I asked her about him."

"Well, at least we know it's likely he's alive," Kristine murmured.

"You still have my card?" Andrew asked Trevor.

"Yeah. Got a picture of it on my phone."

"Okay. Good. Call or text me when Chey comes in again, will you?

Or if you catch her giving food away. Don't stop her or call her out on it, just call me, please?"

"Yeah, okay. I can do that."

"You're a good kid, Trevor."

He flushed. "I try. Most of the time anyway."

Kristine laughed and Andrew smiled. "Now," Andrew said, "can you pack us up a dozen burger plates and the chicken finger catering tray? We'll take that to go."

"Sure thing. Let me go put the order in."

Once they had the order packaged and in the back seat of the Bucar, Andrew aimed the vehicle toward the Brown house.

"I just had a thought," Kristine said.

"What if they're not home?"

She blinked. "Yeah."

He chuckled. "It occurred to me too. Well, we'll have enough food to feed everyone at James and Lainie's."

"True." She paused. "You don't think we should have found Cheyenne and asked her about Jacob?"

He pursed his lips. "Normally I would say yes, but just from meeting her, she's a good liar. Or a skilled actress. She's not going to tell us anything if we ask. We're going to have to catch them together. What do you think about an early morning stakeout?"

"You read my mind once again."

He pulled to the Browns' curb and parked. One vehicle was in the garage. "Think she might be home."

"All right," Kristine said, "let's do this."

FIFTEEN

Before Kristine could even ring the bell, the door opened and a young boy around the age of seven stared up at them with wide eyes. "Mom! Someone's here!"

Tabitha, barefoot and dressed in black leggings and an oversized T-shirt, appeared and pulled her son away from them. "Go finish coloring, Ollie." The child scampered away, and she eyed the bags in their hands with a raised brow. "Hi."

"I hope you don't mind us bringing food."

"Um . . . no, not at all." She glanced over her shoulder and sighed, then opened the door.

Kristine and Andrew stepped inside the immaculate kitchen and set the bags on the table. "I guess we should have called," Kristine said, "but it was a spur-of-the-moment thing."

"It's fine. Kids, come on in here if you're hungry. Some friends brought Mike's burgers."

A stampede came from the back of the house and the den area. The kids surrounded the table, eyes wide. Tabitha distributed the food, then tilted her head toward the den. Andrew and Kristine followed her into the now empty-of-kids room. She took in the new recliner in the den, the new coffee table and end tables, new board games stacked on the built-in shelves, and an Xbox hooked up to the new flat-screen television.

She met Andrew's gaze, noted his raised brows, and bit her lip on the first words that wanted to roll off her tongue. Instead, she pretended not to notice the new items.

"What's all this for?" Tabitha asked.

"We just felt like doing something for you. We wanted you to know we haven't abandoned you."

"Well, we're doing okay. You didn't need to." She hesitated and looked around the room, her expression uncomfortable but borderline defiant. Then she sighed. "Thank you. It's been a rough few days."

"Tabitha," Andrew said, his voice low, "where's Jacob?"

She frowned. "Why are you asking me? You're the ones who lost him."

"He ran," Kristine said, "and you never asked us if we had any word about him." She waved a hand at the room. "And this? Jacob has the money, doesn't he?"

"He didn't buy anything I didn't need." Her gaze flicked to the Xbox. "Except maybe that, but Marcus and I'd been saving to get that for the kids for Christmas." She tightened her shoulders and lifted her chin. "We needed Christmas to come a little early this year."

Kristine sighed. "Where is he?"

"Why does it matter? He's safe."

"Then why doesn't he come home?"

She rubbed her palms on her leggings. "He's afraid he'll be in trouble for running away, but I told him I talked to the psychiatrist at the hospital and he cleared me. The overdose was an accident. My church family has stepped up and is helping."

"Or . . . he doesn't want to give the money back?" Andrew asked.

The woman bit her lip and nodded. "I think that's probably part of it. Will we have to? I mean, part of me feels guilty about all of this, but another part of me feels like it somehow allows Marcus to give us what he wanted." She held up a hand. "I'm not saying I agree with what he did, but if we have to give the money back, then it feels like he died in vain." Tears dripped down her cheeks.

"He has to give the money back," Andrew said. "That money is evidence in a crime that's not solved yet. It needs to be examined, to see if it can be determined where it came from."

"How are you going to figure that out?" Tabitha asked. "It was cash. In small bills." Her voice cracked on the last word. "Jacob doesn't want me to get in trouble. He won't give it to me and he won't tell me where he is."

"But you probably have a suspicion?" Kristine asked. The noise from the kitchen was rising quickly and Tabitha hurried to defuse whatever argument had been sparked.

The kids settled and she returned to the den. "Maybe," she said in answer to the last question. "He likes the library. He likes Mike's. And he likes the church, whether he'll admit it or not." She shook her head. "I don't know. And honestly, I'm not sure I should tell you if I did."

"If you know where he is and don't tell the authorities," Kristine said, her voice soft, "you're obstructing an investigation and could go to jail. Then where would your kids be?"

Tears welled and she swiped them away. "Right. Well, I guess it's a good thing I don't know where he is, isn't it?"

Loud voices once more from the table sent a flash of desperation across the mother's face. She walked back into the kitchen, and they followed her. "Brian, Ella, if you don't stop arguing, you can go to bed without any dessert." The kids hushed and Tabitha walked to the cabinet, pulled down a canister, and opened it.

Kristine tensed. "Tabitha?"

"Some of the money is in here. Jacob left it in the mailbox. I haven't spent a dime of it." She pulled out a pile of cash encased in a Ziploc bag and held it out to Kristine, who sidestepped and motioned for Andrew to take over. This was potential evidence that might be needed for a trial, should they ever catch the person behind it all.

"Do you have another bag you can drop it into?" Andrew asked.

Without a word, Tabitha went to the pantry and pulled out a grocery bag, dropped the money into it, and once again held it out. "I couldn't spend it," she said. "I just couldn't. I wanted to, but I couldn't."

Andrew took it. "Thank you. And I'm glad you couldn't spend it. It shows a lot about your character."

"But not Jacob's."

"He's a kid," Kristine said. "This will be a learning experience for him." Hopefully.

Tabitha motioned them outside. Once they were on the porch, she asked, "Is Jacob going to be in trouble?"

"I think if you could convince him to stop spending the money and turn it in," Andrew said, "the DA can probably be persuaded to go easy on him."

"I don't see him. I never see him. He never comes inside if he even comes here at all. He always has the things delivered."

"Okay, well, if you can help us find him, that's the best thing you can do for him. Convince the other kids that if they see him, they need to tell you. No matter what Jacob tells them to do." Andrew gave her a card. "Please."

She nodded and a crash came from inside. She swiped a tear and yanked the door open to tend to her kids.

"That poor woman," Kristine said.

"Yeah. Come on. Nothing else we can do here. I'll get someone to sit on the house and see if Jacob shows. He might be coming by and she just doesn't know it."

Kristine followed Andrew to the car and climbed in while he made the call. She checked her phone and had a message from her aunt Wendy.

> Everything is fine here. Ethan finally left to get
> some rest. Emily is sleeping. Your father is nowhere
> to be found. Naomi is a godsend. All is good.

Kristine hearted the message and rubbed her eyes.

Andrew looked at her after he hung up. "I've got some news for you."

"What's that?"

"You know those hijacking cases we pulled to see if there are any similarities to Brown's circumstances?"

"Yes."

"We went beyond hijacking. We looked at criminal incidents from airports in Asheville, Lake City, Raleigh-Durham, Greenville, Spartanburg, Charlotte, and Atlanta over the last thirty years. Your mother's was one of them, of course."

Kristine stilled, wondering why she wasn't surprised that her mother's hijacked plane had something in common with Marcus Brown. "Well, it makes sense. There haven't exactly been that many hijackings. What? Two or three actual attempts? A small handful that were stopped before anyone even knew what was planned?"

"Yeah."

"So, what did you find?"

"There were two that we wanted to look at. Your mother's and one that involved a disgruntled FedEx worker in 1994. I gave them a cursory scan, but we want to take a harder look at them. You want to join us and look at your mother's?"

"I guess I do." She pulled in a deep breath. She could do this, right? Her father's voice filled her head. *"Leave it alone. Don't go there. Don't put those images in your head. You need to remember your mother the way she was the last time you saw her."*

Kristine flinched at her own thoughts. The problem was the last time she saw her mother was after she'd told her she hated her.

ANDREW WAS IN A HOTEL for the night. Hank was with James and Lainie. Hopefully they'd all get some rest.

Thankfully, this hotel room was a suite with a full kitchen, separate bedroom, and a workspace. Most importantly, it had a full-sized coffee maker. Its decanter was now closing in on empty. He, Nathan, and Kristine sat at the table with laptops open and the two case files in the middle.

Andrew hadn't really been hungry, but Nathan had claimed starvation, so he and Kristine ordered and consumed most of a pizza. They'd just finished going through the first case from three years ago. A young man had gotten angry at one of the flight attendants and used her uniform scarf to practically strangle her. Then he demanded that the plane be flown to a different location. There'd been no marshal on that flight, but an off-duty police officer had taken the man down and held him until the plane landed.

Nathan leaned back. "That wasn't a premeditated hijacking like ours was. I don't see any similarities here. What made this one stand out?"

"The fact that he wanted the plane to go to a certain place but didn't know what he'd do when he landed. Brown said something real similar. Could be just a coincidence. What about you, Kristine? Anything you want to add?"

"No." Her gaze was on the other unopened file.

The one that was patiently waiting for review.

The one that held all the information she said she hadn't looked at.

He had a hard time understanding that one. If it had been him, he would have been reading as soon as he had access to the information.

But not her.

Andrew eyed her. She looked a little pale, but the firm set of her jaw said she was ready to get down to business. He passed her the file, and she pulled in a breath and flipped it open. He watched her read. She was still, with only her hand moving to flip to the next page. She read to the end without stopping, then turned the stack of papers upright so page one was facing her once more.

Finally, she looked up, eyes wide, face even more pale than when she started.

"Kristine?"

"Did you read this?"

"I glanced at it, but no, not in depth or detail. Why?"

Nathan leaned forward and frowned. "What do you see in there?"

She blew out a low breath. "I think the guy who hired Marcus Brown was behind my mother's hijacking as well."

Nathan blinked and jerked back. "What?"

Andrew raised both brows. "Huh?" He shook himself. "What makes you say that?"

"Look." She flipped the file around. "Look at the details. Mom's hijacking was sixteen years ago. I was sixteen at the time. It says here that passengers who called 911 reported a man with 'some kind of homemade knife' was threatening to start killing people." She went quiet, then said in a low voice, "He said he had to or they would kill his family." She looked up. "Who does that sound like?"

Andrew shot a look at Nathan, then back to Kristine. The three of them blinked at one another for a full five seconds. "I have to say, you've got my interest," Nathan said.

Andrew nodded. "Same."

"I don't believe this," she muttered. "How could I not have ever looked at this?"

"Don't beat yourself up too bad," Andrew said. "Who wants to read a blow-by-blow recap of a loved one's death?"

She sat back and rubbed her face. "I don't know. I didn't want to know what her last moments were like. Filled with terror and probably replaying—" She blew out a sigh and blinked away a few tears, then shook her head.

"Replaying what?" Nathan asked.

"Nothing." She stood and shoved her hands into the back pockets of her jeans. "What kind of daughter does that make me? I defied my father at every turn and yet, on this . . . I just let him have his way. I caved. I didn't know these details. That the hijacker who went down with the plane wasn't the only person responsible. I didn't know that he was threatened just like Marcus Brown. I didn't know any of that. Not until this very moment. How could I not know that?"

Andrew leaned forward. "Maybe you weren't ready to hear the details. Not that anyone is ever *ready* for that, but you know what I mean. I can understand a father wanting to protect his children from that kind of thing."

"That's probably part of it, I'm sure. But the truth was, it was easier to try to forget. To block it and not have to think about it because thinking about it would have driven me mad." She tossed up her hands, then planted them on her hips. "It still might." She returned to her seat at the table and snagged another piece of pizza. "Who was the hijacker's family?"

Andrew took the file. "Well, his name was Devon Bell. He was married to Allison Bell and they have four children."

"But what else?" she asked.

"He died in the crash, so they couldn't question him, obviously, but the report says it was the cell phone video footage that clued them in to the fact that he wasn't working alone. Back then, there wasn't a lot of video, but there was *some*. And some phones were recovered and the information retrieved." He continued to read, summarizing. "Before the plane went down, passengers were calling their families and sending goodbye videos. And other videos with instructions to deliver the footage to the police. We haven't had a chance to watch what little there was, but it might help figure out the connection." He paused. "I just don't know if you should watch it."

"I don't know if I should either, to be honest." She lowered her gaze to the report once more. "It's . . . I just . . . I don't know what to think. My brain is spinning, but I'm going to try and make sense when I voice this because it almost seems too absurd to even say out loud, but if it's the same person responsible for both hijackings, then the other glaring connection is me and my mother. Does that mean my mother was the target all along sixteen years ago?"

Andrew rubbed his lips while another thought popped into his head. "And does it mean you were the target this time?"

"But . . . why?"

"Who knew you were going to be on that flight?" Andrew asked.

She scoffed. "Everyone."

SIXTEEN

It was two in the morning now and they were all drooping. Kristine hadn't wanted to give up trying to find more links between the two incidents. They'd printed both manifests and had analysts working on finding any connection between everyone on the two planes.

"This is going to take forever," Kristine said.

"Yeah," Andrew said. "Why don't I follow you home so you can get some rest."

"That's really sweet, but no need for you to go out. My home is five minutes away."

He smiled. "Exactly. I don't mind making sure you get there safe." The smile faded. "Because if someone tried to crash your plane, then who knows what else is going on? I'd feel better if you'd let me do this."

"It was your plane too." He pursed his lips and eyed her silently. She sighed. "But it wasn't your mother. True."

"I didn't say that."

"You didn't have to." Had he known where she lived and taken this hotel because of it? Or was she giving herself too much credit and reading into his expression things that weren't there?

Probably the latter. She nodded goodbye to Nathan and they all climbed into their respective vehicles.

She was home within five minutes, but she had to admit she watched her mirrors the whole way. Andrew stayed with her, which kind of pleased her and annoyed her at the same time. Pleased in that he cared enough to do so and annoyed that he felt he needed to. But someone had tried to crash a plane. *Her* plane. And whoever that was, he—or she—wouldn't let a little thing like an FBI agent derail him.

But why go to all that trouble? Why not just hire a sniper to take her out? Morbid, yes, but so much easier.

It didn't make sense. Could it be someone she'd thrown off a flight wanting to get even? A relative of someone, indignant and angry on behalf of their family member? But if it was connected to her mother, then the connection was way deeper and didn't have anything to do with a passenger.

She just didn't see how it could be a huge coincidence that her mother's plane had been hijacked and now hers.

No way.

But who? And why?

The questions continued to swirl, but she was out of time to think about them at the moment. She pulled into her parking spot and climbed out, wondering if he was out there in the dark, watching. Okay, she was glad Andrew was there.

A shiver slithered up her spine and she walked over to him. "To-morrow morning?" She paused and looked at her phone. "I mean in four hours? Meet you at Mike's?"

"Want me to swing by and pick you up?"

Kristine hesitated, then nodded. "Sure, that's fine. See you in a few."

He started to get out of his car, but she spun and hurried to her townhome. A glance over her shoulder just gave her a view of the dark night, parking lot lights, and unidentifiable shadows. Andrew was there, though, still watching, standing next to the driver's side, arm on top of the window, face set in a frown. What was that all about?

She almost asked him, but they were both exhausted and needed what little sleep they could get. A conversation could wait. She waved and unlocked her door, stepped inside, and twisted the lock behind her.

She called the nurse's station to check on Emily and was assured her sister was asleep and not in pain. Emily had asked for her phone the last time she'd been awake, so that was a good sign. She'd be transferred to a regular room sometime tomorrow . . . or rather today.

Relief swept through her at all the good news. Now if they could just find who hired the hijacker, the connection between the two incidents, and Jacob, of course, then all would be well.

After double-checking her locks and windows, she glanced at her laptop, picked it up, and carried it into her room. After washing her hair and brushing her teeth, she climbed into bed, set her alarm, and pulled the laptop in front of her.

A loud buzzing woke her. She blinked and blinked again. Her phone read 5:30 a.m. A groan slipped out before she could stop it. But she stretched and grabbed her laptop from the edge of the bed before it could hit the floor. So much for working last night.

Twenty minutes later, she was climbing in Andrew's passenger seat. "Morning."

He grunted his greeting.

She smirked. "Exactly."

"This kid better show up. I don't have the energy for this early morning stuff." He aimed the Bucar toward Mike's.

"You're an FBI agent. You can't tell me early mornings aren't a regular part of your existence."

"They are, but I've never gotten used to it or liked it. I try to catch the bad guys in the afternoons or at night."

She laughed. "Cute."

"How did you sleep?"

"Like a rock."

"Really? No nightmares from everything that's happened over the last few days?"

"Not last night. I was too tired, I think. My brain just shut off. I'm actually not sure it's flipped back on yet. You?"

"One nightmare." He frowned. "But it had nothing to do with the hijacking or being shot at or being chased in the pouring rain—or watching an innocent man get killed in a holding cell."

"Okay." She glanced at him. "What?"

"Nothing. The nightmare was that my cousin Corey moved in with my parents."

"Oh. Wow. That's really bothering you."

"It is. I'm worried for them. And all my prayers seem to be hitting a brick wall."

"They're not, Andrew. Truly."

"I know that in my head." He tapped his chest. "This is a little harder to convince."

"I know that feeling."

He fell silent and she did too, checking her phone and finding a text from her father. She ignored it. Andrew turned onto a side street that led around to the back of the restaurant and parked. They had a perfect view of the door that led to the kitchen.

It was shut tight and no one was hanging around, looking like they were waiting on someone. She bit off a sigh. "Where's Nathan? He too good for early morning duty?"

"Naw, he had something to do with Jesslyn a little later. I told him I was fine doing this alone. Well, with you, but not with you, right?"

"Of course. I'm just keeping you company."

"I appreciate it."

"You're welcome. Now go back to the innocent man getting killed in the holding cell, will you?"

He flinched. "I'd rather not."

"Hmm. Okay then."

Silence fell and Kristine yawned, shut her eyes, and leaned back against the headrest.

"Or maybe I'd rather," he said after several minutes.

"That's okay too." She didn't open her eyes and look at him. If he was hesitant to talk about something, having her watching him might make it harder.

He cleared his throat. "I don't talk about it much."

"I gathered."

"In fact, I don't know why I want to now."

"You don't have to."

"I know." He paused. "Are you going to keep your eyes closed?"

"Would you prefer I open them?"

He snorted. "Maybe not."

"I'm listening."

A sigh slipped from him and he stayed silent. She wondered if he changed his mind. Again.

"Okay," he finally said, "so you know Hank and I were undercover for a long time with the Serpentine Network."

"Yes."

"We'd been under forever, trying like crazy to get the evidence we needed to cut the head of the snake off."

"I see what you did there."

He laughed, the sound indicating he might be relaxing a fraction. "Anyway, we could have taken down the organization underlings at pretty much any point. We had so much evidence against *them*. But we never could get the evidence we needed to nail the leader. We called him the phantom because we never saw him. Ever. But he went by the name Showbiz. So we weighed our options and decided to stay and keep working to find out who he was. He had a tight crew. Only two people that he trusted without question. I was trying to be the third."

"And?"

"And it almost worked. His son trusted me, but I needed his father. I needed to get close. When I couldn't do that, I turned to his son. The guy was jumpy and an addict, but for some reason, he thought he could trust me, so I used that. I was trying to take it slow, but my SAC at the time, well, he was impatient. He needed something good to happen so he could look like he was competent."

"Let me guess. He wasn't."

"No. He was put in that position because of who his father was golfing buddies with. Among other people."

"Ouch."

"Anyway, the Serpentine Network has that signature jacket they all like to wear."

"Black with red trim and a green snake around the neck."

"Yeah." He paused and let out an audible breath.

Kristine snuck a quick peek. He had his hands on the steering wheel and his knuckles were white. She reached out and placed her left hand on top of his right one. He glanced at her and turned his hand so they were palm to palm, fingers laced. She swallowed hard.

Whoa. She closed her eyes again, wanting to encourage him to keep going, but couldn't get the words past the tightness in her throat. His touch just did something to her insides. It drew her to him like an almost inaudible whisper in the dark. One where you wanted to know what was said, but weren't sure you should get that close. He could hurt her. Not physically. He'd never do that. But emotionally? Oh yeah. "The jacket. What about it?"

His hand tightened around hers, then released it. "I'll have to finish this later. Look who just showed up."

She opened her eyes and turned to see a figure in a dirty hoodie, hands jammed in the front pockets of his jeans, walking toward the door. As soon as the guy knocked, Andrew and Kristine slipped out of the car and made their way toward him. No sense in calling out just yet and giving the guy a chance to run.

They closed in behind him and then Andrew said, "Hello, Jacob."

THE KID SPUN FAST and Andrew held up a hand in warning. "Keep your hands where I can see them."

Jacob's hands shot into the air and he stared at them with wide, scared eyes. "Don't shoot me."

"No one's going to shoot you," Kristine said.

"Do you have any weapons on you?" Andrew asked.

"N-no. Nothing. I swear. Not even my pocketknife."

"Can I pat you down?"

"Yeah. Sure." Jacob held his hands out to his sides.

Andrew shot a look at Kristine, who nodded. She'd cover him.

The door opened just as Andrew finished with Jacob, and Chey stood there gaping. She snapped her mouth shut and glowered. "You need to leave him alone."

"Relax, Chey," Andrew said. "We just want to talk to him." He nodded to the restaurant. "Wanna do this in there or come with me to the station?"

Jacob swallowed hard and Andrew's compassion meter kicked up a notch. The kid was terrified. "I-I'll do whatever you want me to do," he said.

"Okay, then let's go inside and talk."

"Can Chey stay with me?"

"Sure." Maybe if Jacob didn't want to talk, Chey would be scared enough to do so for him.

Once the four of them were seated in a booth in the very back of the restaurant, Andrew looked the boy in the eye. "We know you dug up the money your dad buried. I need you to turn in whatever money is left, and I need you to do it ASAP."

He flinched and frowned. "And if I don't?"

"You'll be arrested. That money is the fruit of a serious crime. You can't keep it."

Jacob went white. He picked at a fingernail. "My dad told me where it was the day before the hijacking. I asked him where he got the money, but he just said he'd taken a major gamble that paid off and I was the only one who knew where the money was. If something happened to him, I was to use it to take care of Mom and the kids."

Andrew eyed him. "What else did he say? Why didn't he want your mom knowing about it?"

"He said if she knew about it or spent it, she would probably get in trouble with the law, but I was a kid, so I'd be fine." He raked a shaky hand over his head. "I didn't know why he thought she'd be in trouble because of his gamble, but I didn't ask. Anyway, I was just trying to do what he told me to do."

"I get it, but now so do you. You going to cooperate and return the rest of the money or make this difficult?" *Please cooperate.*

Jacob shot a glance at Chey, who gave him a subtle nod. The teen sighed. "Okay. I'll give it back. I wasn't trying to steal or do anything wrong. I just wanted to help make my mom's life easier, do what my dad told me to do. I promise."

"Then if you cooperate, you should be fine."

"Do we have to give back the stuff I bought with the cash? I mean, I don't think I can get that money back."

"No, probably not. As long as we get the rest of it, everything should be all right."

"Fine. I'll give it back." He dropped his gaze to the table and shivered.

"Let me buy you a good meal and then you can take us to get it."

Jacob nodded, and Chey, who had been silent through the whole exchange, sighed. "I told you, Jacob."

"I know." He glanced at Andrew. "She told me I needed to turn the money in, but I thought since Dad basically died for it, I should do some good with it." He squirmed in his seat. "I . . . uh . . . paid for two kids in the youth group to go to camp this summer. And I paid someone to help mow Mrs. Crabtree's lawn for a year. Her husband died a few weeks ago and I overheard her say she didn't know how she was going to keep up with the house, much less the lawn. And some other stuff like that."

"I see." Andrew's heart went out to the teen. "You're a good young man, Jacob. Your heart's in the right place. I don't ever want that to change, okay?"

Jacob's shoulders relaxed a fraction and he gave a quick nod. Kristine's approving gaze straightened Andrew's spine. He liked that look from her aimed at him.

"Where's the money?"

"Not far."

They ordered breakfast and forty-five minutes later, Andrew and Kristine stood in Chey's apartment bedroom behind the café. Jacob had stashed the money with Chey, who'd stuck it under her mattress. She shrugged at Andrew's raised brow. "It's a cliché for a reason. No one looks there anymore, right?"

"I will from now on," he muttered.

His phone buzzed. Nathan.

Call me when you get a chance. Nothing urgent.

Once he and Kristine were back in the car, he called Nathan, who answered on the first ring. "What's up?" Andrew asked.

"The team going through all of the hijacking cell phone footage from our flight found something interesting."

"What?"

"The guy, Erik Leary? The passenger in 29C? The one we cleared? He had two phones."

"Okay. Explain?"

"Some of the footage showed him talking on a phone while the hijacking was going on. No big deal. A lot of people were on their phones calling loved ones or 911 while everything was going down. But then he's on a different phone a short time later."

"But why?"

"Exactly. You up for a visit?"

"Absolutely. When?"

"Now?"

"I'm on the way." He'd explain about Jacob and the money later. "Kristine's with me."

"Well, she'll have to hang back on this one."

Kristine nodded her understanding. "No problem." He hung up and aimed the Bucar toward Mr. Leary's home.

He pulled to the curb about the same time Nathan did. Andrew scoped the area with interest . . . and dread. "It's empty," he said.

"Yep." Nathan ran a hand over his head. "Looks like it."

"Unbelievable. He was clean. Squeaky clean. What did we miss?"

"Could be something else. He could have a very valid reason for having two phones. You have two. I have two."

"Right. True."

"But why not mention it?" Nathan asked. "We specifically asked him about multiple devices. He said he had a laptop, an iPad, and a phone. Singular."

"Yeah." Andrew sighed. "I'll write up the affidavit for the search warrant and call in a favor to get a rush on it. Then we can get the crime scene unit down here and let them go through it, but I'm guessing they won't find anything."

"One can hope." Nathan shook his head. "I'll work on the passports. Make sure they're flagged and see if they've been used recently." He grabbed his phone, and Kristine shoved her hands into her pockets, then leaned back against the car.

Andrew made the call and looked at Kristine. "You want me to take you to the hospital so you can be with Emily? This is going to take me a while."

"No, I'll catch an Uber."

He frowned. "I don't think that's a very good idea."

"I'll be fine." She pulled out her phone and started to make the call, and he placed his hand over hers.

"Really," he said. "I want to take you. Nathan can hold down the fort here until I get back."

She hesitated, a light pink staining her cheeks, then shrugged. "All right. You can finish telling me your story."

He frowned. "Story?"

"About the innocent man who died in the holding cell."

Oh. That story.

Maybe he should let her catch that Uber.

SEVENTEEN

Kristine could tell he didn't want to talk about it. At least that's what he was apparently telling himself. But he'd opened up the topic, so there was something inside him that wanted to spill whatever it was he'd kept such a tight lid on. He'd told her the first part and mentioned something about an innocent man dying on his watch but hadn't offered the details. She wanted the details if it wouldn't traumatize him to tell her. And from his reaction to her asking, it very well might just do that.

The drive to the hospital would be about twenty minutes. She'd let him make the call as to whether or not he'd—

"Okay, fine," he said, tapping the wheel. "I started, might as well finish it. Hank and I were undercover, as I said before. I had made friends with the leader's son and asked him to meet privately. I had video evidence of him torturing a rival gang member and was going to try and turn him against his father for less prison time. I knew the two didn't get along very well and thought he might be willing to save his own hide by giving me his father."

"And?"

"Someone followed him. Neither of us realized it until too late and he shouted, 'Traitor,' shot Showbiz's son in the head, and disappeared. I couldn't take a chance on going back under at that point.

My cover was busted. He was dead before he hit the ground. Hank said the guy filled Showbiz in and told him I was the one who shot his son." He scowled. "I didn't, but I feel like I got him killed anyway."

"You didn't know he was going to be followed."

"I should have expected it. Showbiz has a lot of the members followed, but I'd never known him to have his son followed." His eyes clouded, then he shook his head. "Anyway, about a month after that, Hank slipped us info about a deal going down at one of the empty buildings in the warehouse district. It was so cliché, it wasn't even funny. I'm a firm believer that every empty warehouse should be searched at least once a week because nothing good ever happens in such a place. Really, it was just bad. But there were guns and drugs that we could take off the street, so we set it all up." He drove, his eyes on the road. She kept hers bouncing between the mirror and his face.

"Set up the sting?"

"Right. Hank was determined this was going to bring out the top man because it was such a big cash deal. The warehouse was for sale. Big sign, everyone knew it. What we didn't know was that someone was coming to see it that night. We didn't find that out until later. So, when the sting went down, the Realtor and his client got swept up in the mess."

"Oh my. Bet that wasn't good."

"To say the least. In our defense the Realtor had a jacket on that looked so much like the ones the Serpentines used that if you weren't looking close, you'd never realize it was a different one. Anyway, by the time everything was sorted, the Realtor and his client were in separate holding cells. The client was loud and combative, yelling that we didn't understand, that he was going to sue the department, but you know how it is. Everyone protests their innocence. Everyone is going to sue. It's just par for the course. The Realtor was quiet and reserved. Now, I realize he was scared—terrified, really. He was in with a gang member—"

"What?"

"I know. I know. And there are no excuses, but nevertheless, it was crazy that night. Everything that could go wrong did. By the time the sting was over, the holding cells were packed. We were out of room and had to group them together. Members of the same gang went together. Others were kept separate. And we thought the Realtor was a member of the same gang as the guy in the cell, so putting them together shouldn't have been a problem."

"Only it was."

"Yep. It wasn't too long afterward that I could tell something was off. The Realtor started saying the same thing as his client, and there was no way they could overhear each other. It dawned on me that they might not be blowing smoke. That there could have been a real screwup. I was going to let him out and talk to him. And then . . . for some reason we still don't know, this gang member attacked the innocent Realtor. I was twenty feet away and ran for the cell to get in there, but I—" He shuddered and focused on driving for a moment while Kristine waited, dreading what he was going to say next. Which was nothing until he pulled into the police parking spot at the hospital.

She looked at him. "You weren't in time."

"No. It wouldn't have mattered anyway. I didn't have a key. I was yelling for one of the local officers to get it open, but he just wasn't fast enough. No one could get a clear shot the way he was situated and with the other prisoners in there blocking a shot . . . and the truth is, even if I did have a key, it wouldn't have been fast enough. I know that now, but it still . . ." His hands clenched around the wheel, then released. "The gang member snapped the Realtor's neck like it was a toothpick."

Nausea swirled for a moment and she swallowed hard. "I'm so sorry."

"The family filed a civil suit, but we were cleared of any wrongdoing, as were the others involved and . . ."

"And?"

"And I don't talk about it. Ever. To anyone."

She wanted to ask, why her? Why now? Instead she bit her lip, then leaned over the console to wrap him in an awkward hug. He shifted and returned it, burying his face in the side of her neck for a long moment. After a few seconds, he pulled back slightly and looked into her eyes. Silent. Staring. She refused to break contact and let him look, wondering what he was hoping to find. Finally, he cupped her cheek and she caught her breath, thinking he was going to kiss her.

Instead he touched her lips with his thumb and shook his head. "Not here."

She blinked. "What?"

"The first time I kiss you is not going to be in the front of a Bucar."

"The first time you—" She chuckled. Then laughed. He wanted to kiss her. And planned to do so more than once.

He frowned. "What's so funny?"

"You." Her laughter faded. "But not funny in a mean or weird way. I like it."

"Good. Because I do want to kiss you. It's just that Cole told me something a while back that stuck with me. He said he waited for the perfect moment to kiss Kenzie, and I thought that was somehow . . . right."

She smiled. "Kenzie told me that too. She said it made it super special." She touched his cheek and decided, since she was being honest, she'd just lay it all out there. "Kissing means something to me, Andrew. I haven't had a lot of relationships in my life. I think that's why Jesslyn and I are so close. She hasn't either." She shrugged. "I've dated a few people, even thought I might marry one of them before he decided he wanted the benefits of marriage without the ceremony—and he didn't want me to have anything to do with my dad. Who, in his defense, was being incredibly obnoxious and controlling. But, still, it hurt. And scared me off getting close to someone. But you're different."

"How so?"

She shook her head. "I honestly don't know if I can explain it. I think it's mostly because I admire you. Have a lot of respect for you.

It attracts me to you." Not to mention his rugged good looks and killer smile, but she wasn't about to say that. At least not yet. Maybe later. After their first kiss. She sucked in a breath and sat back. "You're dangerous for me. I don't want to get hurt again."

"I don't know anyone who does." He paused. "And since you're being so open and vulnerable, I'll say that I feel the same way. I have baggage that I'm not sure is fair to inflict on someone else."

She shot him a small smile. "Who doesn't?" She looked away, wondering if she should say more.

"What?" he asked.

"Nothing. You need to go. Nathan's waiting on you."

"He can wait a few more minutes. Tell me."

"Matt broke up with me because . . . well, for a lot of reasons, I suppose, but you want to know what the biggie was?"

"Because he's an idiot?"

She snickered, then sobered. "No. Well, yes, there's that, but no. And it wasn't solely because I refused to sleep with him before we were married either, although I do think it played a role in everything. It really was because of my dad."

"I know you've mentioned he's a bit of a helicopter parent, but is there more?"

"Yeah. A lot more, and Matt couldn't deal with my dad's constant showing up, calling, and texting. And I honestly didn't blame him."

"I haven't really noticed that."

"I haven't let you." She paused and frowned. "And it does seem like it's been a lot less since Emily's accident. He's distracted right now, but once she's back on her feet and living her life again, I feel sure his annoying behavior will start up again."

"Have you talked to him about this?"

"Yes. Bluntly. He listens, apologizes, and then all is well for a while. Then he reverts back to his old behaviors. I try to understand. He's lonely. Still talks about missing my mom." She gave a light shrug. "I wish he'd start dating, but he says no way, that my mother was the only one for him."

"Your dad wouldn't scare me away."

"Hmm. Well, I'm not sure we need to find that out." She pushed the car door open and stepped out. "Go see what you can find at Leary's house. We'll talk later."

"Kristine . . ." He sighed. "Yeah. Okay."

She made her way into the hospital, watching Andrew's reflection in the window. He waited until she was safely inside before he pulled away.

And now she needed to go visit with her sister, check on her father, and see where Ethan and Aunt Wendy were. Sometimes family was hard. But they were hers and she loved them. Still, sometimes when family was hard, running away was attractive.

She grimaced and shoved the thoughts from her head. She'd never run away from anything in her life. She sure wouldn't start now.

ANDREW COULDN'T PUT THE CONVERSATION with Kristine out of his head. Of course. But he made a valiant effort as he wound his way back to Erik Leary's home. He voice-texted Nathan to let him know he was on the way. He glanced in the rearview mirror and noticed the black SUV that had been behind him since he'd left the hospital.

He slowed to see what the vehicle would do. It passed him at the next opportunity and he shook his head. He was acting paranoid. Maybe not without good reason, but still . . .

The white car that had been behind the black SUV stayed back a good distance.

At the four-way stop, he came to a full stop.

And the white car behind him slammed into him. The airbag deployed and hit him in the face. Pain radiated from his right cheek and down into his neck.

The driver's door opened. "Dude, I'm so sorry. Are you okay?"

Andrew took a second to take inventory and decided other than a little whiplash and a whole lot of flowing adrenaline, he was relatively unhurt. "Yeah, I think so."

He turned to face the reckless driver, only to find himself staring into the barrel of a gun. "I was going to just kill you," the man said, "but I decided to have some fun first. Get out."

"What?"

"Out!"

Andrew ordered his brain to kick into gear. He debated whether he should reach for his own gun when the barrel of his attacker's weapon rested against his temple. "What do you want?"

"You dead. Eventually. But we have some business to take care of first."

"Why?"

"Because—" A pause. "No, I think I'll let you figure it out."

"Figure what out?"

"Get out of the car."

Andrew obeyed only because it meant the guy had to move back, shifting the weapon from pressing against his head to merely aiming at it.

Sirens sounded in the distance, and for a split second, his attacker was distracted.

Andrew punched up his arm against the other guy's forearm and the weapon spun out of his grasp. His curses rang out over the sirens getting closer.

The attacker dove for the gun and Andrew tackled him, his still healing shoulder from the gun battle in the woods protesting the move. He ignored it, ducked under a swing from the guy, and threw his own punch that glanced off a cheekbone.

The man let out a low grunt, shot to his feet, and ran for the white car with the crumpled hood. Andrew went after him, but the world tilted and he slipped and fell to his knees. By the time the dizziness passed, the car had disappeared. Andrew rolled into a sitting position as two police vehicles roared to a stop. He stayed seated, forearms resting on his knees. Okay, maybe the jolt from being rear-ended had shaken him up more than he thought. It was surprising how hard a little car hitting an SUV felt. But the total unexpectedness of it had caught him completely off guard.

Footsteps poured toward him and he looked up. He didn't recognize the officers who hurried his way, hands on their weapons. "Are you all right?" the nearest one called.

"Yeah. I think so. Can one of you go after that white car you must have just passed? I need him in custody."

The one nearest his car waved that he had it, hopped back in his vehicle, and took off in the direction Andrew indicated. The other officer called in an ambulance. Andrew held his head and tried to process. Someone wanted him dead.

Him. But why? Had Showbiz found him? Seemed like a logical assumption. And yet . . .

First the hijacking that looked to be targeting Kristine, then someone going after Hank, and now this. So, were they wrong and the hijacking had been aimed at *him*? But the connection to her mother's incident refuted that. Maybe? Or had the Serpentine Network put it together that he was helping protect Hank and decided to come after *him* to get to Hank? Or was there something else he was missing? Probably. But what?

The world had gone mad. That was clearly the only explanation possible. Or Showbiz had found him.

The other officer returned the same time the ambulance came screaming up the road. Andrew groaned, his head starting to hurt. He texted Nathan the very short version of what had happened and said he'd be at the hospital. He didn't think he needed to go but knew his supervisor would insist, so Andrew wouldn't bother protesting.

Besides, Kristine was there.

Nathan's text said he was on the way to the hospital and wanted a full report.

Andrew agreed, but they were going to have to make this fast. He and the others needed to get to the safe house to ensure they had everything set up for tomorrow.

"How'd you guys get here so fast?" he asked when the officer stood in front of him.

"Neighbor in the house about twenty yards from the stop sign heard the crash and just called 911. Said he's done it before and figured he'd better call and play it safe just in case someone was hurt. The fire station was right around the corner. My wife's a firefighter and we stop there for lunch a few times a week. Today was one of those times."

"I'm thankful."

Thirty minutes later, he sat in the emergency room while Nathan paced next to the bed. Back and forth, back and—

"Dude," Andrew said, "please sit down."

Nathan sighed and sat. A knock on the door raised Andrew's hopes. Jesslyn walked in and Andrew's hopes hit the floor. Nathan's did not. His face lit up and he walked over to kiss his wife and give her a hug. "What are you doing here?"

"Heard about the wreck over the airwaves."

Another knock. "Come in."

Kristine stepped inside, her frown intense, eyes narrowed. "Hey, guys." Her gaze sought his. "Are you all right? I heard about what happened. I had to come see for myself that you were okay."

"I'm all right. Got a little shaken up, but overall, I'm fine." She'd come to check on him. She was worried. All of a sudden he felt better. Not that he wanted her to worry, but he was glad she cared enough to do so.

Shut up. He did his best to turn off his internal monologue. Kristine cared enough to come see him. That was all that mattered.

Lainie and James and Cole and Kenzie showed up next, bringing Hank with them.

"What are you doing here?" Andrew asked Hank.

"Glad to see you too." He shrugged. "Figured this would make more sense to draw someone out. Looks like they've connected you to me so we're moving up the timetable on everything." He looked at Cole and the others. "As soon as I walk out of this hospital, I'm heading up the mountain."

Andrew glared. "Not without me, you're not."

A small smile curved his friend's lips. "I figured you'd say that. We went by your hotel and packed you a bag."

"When?"

Hank frowned. "What?"

"When did you go by and pack a bag?"

"Probably an hour before you got creamed," Hank said, his voice low. "I was going to see if you'd come with me, counted on you saying yes, and knowing your go bag was destroyed when the Airbnb exploded, went to your hotel room and grabbed your stuff. You think somehow the gang put it together?"

Andrew pressed a palm to his aching head. "The thought occurred to me, but I don't know. Maybe. If they had someone watching the hotel." He sighed. "Which they probably did, so they decided to take me out of the picture."

Hank frowned and shook his head. "No way, man. We were real careful, not wanting to lead them to you."

"And yet, here we are," Andrew muttered.

They all exchanged glances and he sighed. "It's okay, guys, truly. I'm not hurt, just sore. No concussion. Thankfully, my shoulder wound is fine. I probably need a chiropractor and a good massage, but I'll live. So let's do this."

"We'll finish getting it set up," Nathan said. "Stay here until I give you the green light. I think at this point, it's stupid to put you and Hank together in the same car. Let's divide you up, make it look like we're trying to protect you by delivering you separately to a safe house."

"*Trying* to protect them?" Kristine asked.

"You know what I mean."

"We'll do what we're trained to do," Kenzie said. "Keep them safe just like we would anyone else."

Nathan frowned. "Exactly. That's what I meant."

"I know," Kenzie said with a small grin. "Just giving you a hard time. Wouldn't want you to feel left out of the group, you being the newbie to this little community."

Kristine chuckled and Cole snorted.

Nathan rolled his eyes. "Thanks, but I'm not the newbie anymore. Hank is."

She looked at Hank, who'd raised his brows. "Okay, I guess that's true," she said. "Welcome to the crew, Hank."

Hank smiled. "Thanks?"

"They're a good group," Andrew said. "Just be warned, once you're in, there's no way out."

"Only because no one ever wants out," Kenzie said with a light punch to Andrew's shoulder.

"On that note, we need to get out of here before we're *kicked* out," Cole said. "Andrew, sit tight for a bit. Your FBI buddies are trying to track down Leary and find who just tried to kill you. Until they do, we're going to work on finding whoever is after Hank."

"That works for me."

"Good. I'll be back to get you. For now, come on, Hank. Let's get this done."

"On it," the man said and headed for the door.

They left and quiet descended. Kristine stood by the window, arms crossed, looking at Andrew through her lashes. "How do you really feel?"

He shrugged with the shoulder that didn't hurt. "Like I said, a little beat up, but nothing that will slow me down."

"I want to be there. At the safe house."

"You can't."

"I know. I just want you to know that I want to be there. And would if I was allowed." She walked over and hugged him. Gently. Oh so gently. "You scared me."

He closed his eyes and breathed deep, touched by her concern. "I'm okay, Kristine. Really." He could stay like this, in her arms, for much longer than the moment would probably last.

She nodded and pulled back. Yep. Way longer. He studied her and frowned. She'd been worried about him, yes, but there was something else bugging her. "What is it?" he asked.

She pursed her lips. "What?"

"What's bothering you? Besides all this?"

Surprise flared in her eyes and she opened her mouth to speak, then snapped it shut. "Hmm. You read me that easy?"

"Trust me. It's not necessarily easy. I'm just looking."

"It's not important right now. I'm not making this about me." She gave a small dismissive laugh.

"You're not. I am. Please. I don't want to think about me right now. Do me a favor and tell me."

"Well, when you put it that way . . ."

"You're stalling."

She sighed and pursed her lips. "Fine. I haven't signed up again for a solo flight and I've been trying to figure out why. I couldn't put my finger on it until Emily just told me something that made everything click."

"What'd she say?"

"Without using the words, she basically said I liked to play it safe. I haven't told her or Ethan or even my dad about my lessons, so we weren't talking about that, but the conversation led me to connect the dots for this. Solo flying wouldn't be playing it safe."

"Since when have you ever played it safe?"

She shot him a sad smile. "You'd be surprised."

"Come on. Being an air marshal isn't exactly playing it safe."

"Well, it's not like you guys. On the front lines fighting crimes, going undercover with gangs, handling hostage situations, being on SWAT and whatnot. I handle drunks and the occasional ragey flier. Discounting most recent events that have nothing to do with my job, I've never been shot at or even had to draw my weapon. So . . . yeah, I've mostly played it safe because I've been able to. I mean, my father would disagree, but nevertheless, it's true."

"Okay, when you put it like that, but still . . ."

"Yeah."

"And you've trained, worked hard to get your license, done everything you're supposed to do to fly solo. Safely. People do it every day. Why do you say that's not playing it safe?"

"One of the reasons, I think, is because if something happens and I crash and die, then it would be something I did to myself—and my family. The hijacking situation, being chased by gang members and getting shot at, is something that was done *to* me. That's pretty much out of my control other than fighting back. This solo flying thing, though? I can control that and it's something that could take me away from people who love me. Who've made it very clear they still need me. And I think that's why I'm so hesitant. Which is weird, because when I'm with my instructor, Mac, I don't even think about all that. Much."

"Do you enjoy flying?"

She smiled. "Yeah, I love it." And frowned. "I just . . ." Her smile vanished and she bit her lip. "I had a bad experience. Went up for my first flight and the engine went out on me."

He gasped. "What happened?"

"It was a glitch in the engine. I obviously managed to get it started again and land safely, but now, I want to hurl every time I think about flying solo. I think about what could have happened. I think about Emily and Ethan and even my dad and the effect it would have on them."

"I can see why you'd be a little hesitant about going up again." He fell quiet, then said, "Maybe if you talked to Emily and Ethan about it, it would help settle that?"

She studied him. "Maybe. Or maybe it would completely freak them out. They're supportive of what I do. At least when I work, I have two highly qualified pilots flying the plane. I'm not sure Emily and Ethan would like the whole solo flying thing. I know how my father would feel."

"I'm sorry, Kristine. That's tough. I get what you're saying, but maybe by talking it all out with them—" His phone pinged. "We'll have to continue this another time. We've got the green light."

EIGHTEEN

Kristine's phone rang just as she reached Emily's room. It was Cole. She swiped the screen and stood outside the door. "Hey, Cole, what's up?"

"There's no easy way to tell you this, but I've been monitoring the investigation on Emily's car wreck."

Kristine frowned and stilled. "Okay. And?"

"The brakes were tampered with."

Weak-kneed took on a whole new meaning as she leaned against the wall to stay upright. "Dana was driving. It was her car."

"The detectives are looking into her background to see if anyone has a grudge or if there's a disgruntled boyfriend, but so far nothing's turning up suspicious."

"Right." She ran a hand over her head, then pressed her fingers against her eyes. "I'm at the hospital with Emily. Let me talk to her and see what she has to say."

"Tate and his new partner are on the way to question her. They need an official statement."

"Of course. All right."

"Just wanted you to know."

"Thanks. I appreciate the heads-up." They said their goodbyes, and she walked into Emily's room to find her sitting up in bed eating a bowl of something that was probably supposed to be orange Jell-O. Or trying to eat. With her left hand in a cast up to her elbow, she was struggling. She was alone and Kristine was glad. She wanted some time with her sister without anyone else listening, because this wasn't going to be an easy conversation. Seemed to be all she had lately. Difficult conversations. "Want some help with that?"

Emily looked up and pushed the cup aside. "No. I managed to get all I wanted. I'd rather have cherry."

"I'll let Naomi or Leanna know. They'll make it happen."

"Thanks. So how's Andrew?" Kristine had explained his situation in as few words as possible when she'd gotten the call from Nathan about the wreck. As she ran out of Emily's room to head to the emergency room, she'd promised to come back with news as soon as possible.

"He's fine. A little rattled, but thankfully, fine."

"And someone hit him?"

"Yes. On purpose."

Emily's eyes went wide. "Wow, who'd he make mad?"

"Not him, someone he used to work with. We suspect they went after Andrew to get to this other guy. Thankfully, someone saw the accident and called it in and the other guy ran off." The long-winded explanation was just a way to avoid what she really needed to say. "Anyway, I can't believe you feel good enough to sit up and eat something."

"I don't, really, but if I want to get out of here, I need to."

Kristine frowned. "You've had a rough time, Em. No need to rush it. And where are Ethan and Aunt Wendy?"

"They left. Dad was getting on Ethan's nerves, and I think Aunt Wendy needed a break too. I asked everyone to leave and give me some space." She chewed her bottom lip. "Is that mean?"

"No. Not at all. Do you know where they went?"

"No, Ethan just said he was going to cool off, Aunt Wendy said she was going to make some phone calls, and Dad said he was going to chill in the cafeteria." Emily picked at the sheet, then looked up to meet Kristine's eyes. "What's wrong with him anyway?"

"What do you mean?"

"He's being so . . . nice. It's unnerving. I think that's why Ethan had to leave. It was driving him nuts that he couldn't figure out the angle."

Kristine laughed. "Well, I imagine Dad's feeling grateful you're still alive but realizes how close he—we—came to losing you. Maybe he's just, I don't know, filled with regrets? Maybe he wants to make amends with you?"

Emily studied her, the bruises on her face still clear, although changing colors as they healed. "Hmm. Maybe." She scowled. "I doubt it, but guess time will tell."

It didn't take much to tire Emily out, and Kristine needed to ask her about Dana before her sister decided to take a nap. "Hey, change of subject. Detective Tate Cooper's on his way here to talk to you about *your* wreck."

"Okay. I'm not sure what I can tell him. One minute we were laughing and excited about getting on the ship and the next Dana was screaming she couldn't stop the car. And then I woke up here." A tear slipped down Emily's cheek and she brushed it away.

"Was Dana dating anyone?"

"Yeah, Brody McGill. He won't leave her side until she's released." She grabbed a tissue from the box on the end table and blew her nose. "Is she awake yet?"

"No, she hasn't regained consciousness yet. You don't have a brain injury. She does. They're keeping her in a medically induced coma."

Emily frowned. "I didn't think she was hurt that bad. Or at least not worse than me."

"She didn't have any broken bones, just the hard knock on the head."

"Wow."

"So, Brody and Dana," Kristine said. "Any bad feelings between them?"

"What?" Emily frowned. "No way. He was actually going to fly into the Bahamas and ask her to marry him on the beach. Then we were going to have an engagement celebration right there at the resort." She bit her lip and more tears spilled.

"Oh. Wow."

"Yeah." She sniffed. "Why are you asking?"

Kristine rubbed her eyes and sighed. She struggled for the words and finally found them. "Someone tampered with the brakes on her car."

Emily's eyes narrowed and she shook her head. "That can't be right."

"It's right."

"So, you're saying someone *wanted* us to crash?"

"That's what it looks like. Tate's going to ask if you know who."

"B-but I don't. I can't even fathom it. No way. That's crazy."

Kristine hated upsetting her sister, but the questions had to be asked. "Think about it, hon, okay? I know you don't want to think it's possible someone may have gone that far to hurt your friend, but we have to consider the possibility. The facts don't lie, Em. Someone messed with the brakes. The question is, who?"

They fell silent for a few minutes while Emily processed the information.

Kristine was about to offer to leave her alone when Emily sighed. "I don't want to talk about that. Let's talk about our father. So you really think Dad's being nice because he has regrets?"

"I do." Kristine let her change the topic. "It's the only thing I can think of anyway. I recommend you enjoy it while it lasts."

"Hmm. Right." She glanced at the door. "I don't know how long he planned to chill in the cafeteria, but if he's still there, I'd love a frozen lemonade." She snagged her phone. "I'll text him and ask him to get me one."

"No need," Kristine said. "I'll get it for you. I need to make a call, so I'll do that while I walk down there. Tate should be here soon too."

Emily hesitated, then set her phone back down. "Thanks. And I don't know what good it'll do for Tate. The answers won't change."

"Well, sometimes different people can ask the same question a different way, sparking a different thought. So, just go with it, okay?"

She sighed. "Fine. You know more than I do about this kind of thing."

"Great. I'll be back with your frozen lemonade soon."

"Thanks."

Kristine left the room and headed toward the elevator that would take her down to the cafeteria on the first floor. She'd been spending way too much time in this place, as she already knew she was going to get the lemonade for Emily and a chocolate milkshake for herself.

She pulled her phone out and dialed Andrew. When it went to voicemail, she hung up, stepped off the elevator, and turned right, passed the hallway that led to X-ray, and stopped. Backed up and gaped. A man had her father shoved up against the wall, forearm against his throat. "Hey! Let him go!"

The man spun away and shoved through the exit door behind him. Her father grabbed his throat and sagged against the wall.

Kristine raced over to him and grabbed his arm. "Dad!"

"I'm okay," he croaked. "I'm okay." He crossed the hall and dropped onto a bench, breathing hard, pain registering on his pale face.

She grabbed her phone and dialed 911, reported the incident, and was assured hospital security was on it. Then she turned back to her father. "Are you sure you're all right? Let's get you to see a doctor."

"No, no, I'm good, but honestly, people will do anything in broad daylight these days."

"What did he want?"

"My wallet."

"And you didn't recognize him?"

"What? No. He just came up to me and shoved me against the wall and demanded my wallet. Then you shouted and he ran. That's the gist of it right there."

"Unbelievable."

"Tell me about it."

Hospital security arrived, along with two other officers who took their statements. The whole time she was talking to them, something nagged at her. She hadn't gotten a good look at her dad's attacker, but he reminded her of someone. And it finally hit her who.

Her phone rang. It was Andrew. She looked at the officers who were just finishing up with her dad. "I've got to take this." She shifted her gaze to her father. "After I finish this call, I'll get Emily the frozen lemonade she wanted. Why don't you go up and rest for a bit once you're done here?"

"I think I'd rather go home."

"You can't drive after what just happened. I'll drive you home. We'll take your car and I'll figure out how to get back later."

He started to protest and she held up a hand. "Please. No arguing with me on this, okay?"

"Okay. Fine." He nodded. "Let's finish up here, take Emily her lemonade, then you can take me home."

"Good plan."

She stepped out of hearing range of her father and the officers and swiped the screen.

"Hey," she said.

"Hey, I'm sorry I missed your call, but I was on the phone with my SAC."

"I was just calling to see how things were going, but now I have another reason."

"What's that?"

"My dad was just attacked in the hospital and I think I recognized his attacker."

"What! Who?"

"Erik Leary."

ANDREW STRAIGHTENED from his slouched position in the safe house recliner and stood. "Erik Leary? You're sure?"

Nathan's head snapped up at the mention of Leary's name. Andrew put her on speakerphone as Cole took a seat.

"Yeah, maybe. I didn't get a good look at him before he bolted, but he should be on the security footage."

Andrew rubbed his chin and sighed while he thought. "Okay, obviously there's some kind of connection with Leary and the hijacking. And you said yourself, it could be related to your mother's."

"So Leary is coming after my family now?" Kristine said. "Was he responsible for my mother's hijacking?" She sighed. "That doesn't seem possible. He's not old enough. He's what, thirty-two?"

"Yeah."

"So it's not him. But also, why would he be on a plane that he knew could possibly go down? Again, that doesn't seem likely. He didn't seem like he was ready to end it. And for what? Money? Then where is it?" She finished that last question on a rush of breath. "Sorry, I just have lots of thoughts. Unfortunately, I have no answers."

Andrew frowned. "What if we need to look at this from a different perspective?"

"Okay. Like?"

"So, from all the information gathered, it looks like we weren't supposed to crash. Let's assume the plane was supposed to land somewhere safe. Why would someone want to hijack a plane that we're all on, most specifically *you* were on, if we're going to speculate that the same person who hijacked your mom's plane didn't actually want it to crash as well, but something went wrong and the plane went down?"

She went quiet. "Okay. Can you explain your reasoning?"

Andrew rubbed a hand down his face. "Could it have been a distraction from something else?"

"Like what?" Kristine asked.

"No idea. What was going down at the same time?" Andrew walked to the desk in the corner of the room and rummaged. "I need a pen and paper." Once he had what he needed, he returned to his seat and began writing while thinking out loud. "Okay, since our crime board is at the station, let's do this the old-fashioned way. One, the person behind the hijacker chose someone who didn't have a whole lot to lose if he failed, but a lot to gain for his family if he succeeded. Any connection between Marcus Brown and Kristine's mom, Rachel Duncan?" He drew two stick figures and labeled them, then drew a line between them with a question mark over it.

"None," Nathan said. "His background barrel has been emptied and scraped. There's nothing there. Same with the wife, Tabitha. Nothing connects her to Kristine's family in any way. And Jacob's father told him where the money was the day before the hijacking."

"But who was in their house that night?" Kristine asked. "That wasn't Jacob, it was a man. Could it have been the person who paid Marcus, then decided to come back for the money?"

"That's my guess," Andrew said. "Two, the connection between the Serpentine Network and Marcus."

"Nonexistent," Hank said. "That tat was just a red herring. But whoever hired Marcus was either familiar with the gang or re-searched it so he could give Brown a picture of what to get. But that's easy enough."

"Right. Three, what's the connection between Marcus Brown and Erik Leary?"

"It looks like the person who hired Brown also hired Leary," Na-than said, "but the dots aren't connecting as to who knows both of them. They run—ran—in totally different circles. Brown was barely scraping by financially and was in terrible health. Leary was well-to-do, decent credit, no obvious need for cash or any reason to risk his life to get it."

"Unless he was blackmailed," Kristine said. "Hold on a sec." Mur-mured voices filtered through the line, but Andrew couldn't catch the words. "Dad wants to go home, so I'm going to take him."

"You need anything?"

"No thanks. Hang on once more while I get him settled." More rustling, then the slamming of a car door. "Okay, I'll call back when I can talk without being overheard."

"Sounds good."

She hung up and Andrew turned to Nathan and Cole. "We're on pause for the moment. Anyone need something to drink? A Coke? Water?"

"Water," Cole said.

"I'm good," Nathan said.

Andrew grabbed the drinks from the fridge. They continued to discuss the case while they waited on Kristine's call.

Finally, his phone rang and he grabbed it and put it on speaker. "Pick up where we left off at blackmail," he said.

"Okay, I have a few minutes. He wanted a burger to take home for later so he's inside McDonald's to get it. And before you think I'm a terrible daughter, I offered to go in and get it for him, but he told me to quit treating him like he was helpless."

"Dads," Andrew huffed.

"Right? Anyway, I can talk while he's in there, but I don't want him to overhear anything so if I go quiet, you know why."

"Got it."

Cole waved at him.

"And Cole has his hand raised. Yes, Cole? You have something for the class?" The bit of humor brought a snicker through the line from her, and he smiled.

"I do," Cole said. "Say someone blackmailed him. But with what? You just said there's nothing in his past."

"Nothing that showed up."

"True. But again. Who?"

Andrew drew a big question mark on Leary's face, then another one on the word blackmail. "We have a lot of question marks on here."

"And why did he attack your dad in the hospital?" Cole asked Kristine. "He said Leary wanted his wallet. What would he need that for?"

Kristine gave a sigh and Andrew heard the frustration loud and clear. She wanted to talk. "None of this makes any sense," she said.

"No, it doesn't," he said. "Look, we have a whole force still working the hijacking. We'll figure it out soon." They had to. "We can keep thinking on that, but for the moment, until new information comes in, we're kind of at a dead end." He blew out a low breath. "What do you say we pivot to focus on catching who's trying to kill Hank?"

"Do you think this guy knows where the safe house is?" she asked.

Andrew turned the speaker off and waved to the others that the conversation with them was over. Nathan grunted and headed for the kitchen, pulling his phone out probably to call Jesslyn. Cole and Kenzie headed to their stations, where they would be watching from various windows. Outside the perimeter, the rest of the Lake City SWAT team and more officers were backing them up. "It's hard to say. We made an effort to cover our tracks so as to throw off suspicion that we're luring him into a trap, but not so careful that he couldn't find us. All that to say, if he knows we're here, he doesn't appear to be in any hurry to do anything about it."

"Just be careful. Please?"

"Definitely."

"Okay, Dad's coming. Gotta run. I'll let you go. I'll figure out how to get home later. Keep me updated, will you?"

He didn't like her not having a plan to get home, but he didn't get a say. "Of course."

They said their goodbyes, and Andrew hung up, wishing he could keep her on the phone longer or do something to help her, but for now, they were in different places with different things to do. He paused. There was one thing he could do. "Hey, Nathan, what's Jesslyn doing?"

"Working, why?"

"Think she could take a couple of hours off?"

"Probably. Again, why?"

He explained the situation and Nathan called Jesslyn. She told him she had time to go pick up Kristine.

With that settled, he rose and walked to the window. At their elevation, a light snow had started to fall, but the Weather Channel didn't predict anything more than a couple of inches. Although if the temperature kept dropping, it could make the roads treacherous.

But for now, with all the security, it was the safest place Hank could be. He thought about asking Kristine to come too, but if the Serpentine Network decided to strike harder than they anticipated, the safe house might not be quite so safe. Though she was a trained federal agent—she knew how to fight back.

Time ticked by while they went back to their speculation and tossing out ideas for which way the hijacking investigation should go. About an hour later his phone buzzed with an incoming call. His father. He swiped the screen. "Hey, Dad, what's up?"

"We've been robbed."

"You've been what?" Surely he'd misheard.

"We've been robbed, Andrew."

He stood, heart thudding. "Are you all right?"

Cole and the others stopped talking and looked at him, brows raised, silent questions in their eyes.

"I think so," his father said. "I walked in and he shoved me as he rushed out. I hit my head on the doorframe, but I'm okay. Can you come?"

He wanted to say he'd be there as fast as possible, but . . .

No, his father was hurt. And he'd asked Andrew to come. He needed to go.

"Hold on one sec, Dad." He told the others what had happened, and they voiced their concern.

"Go, man," Cole said.

"Thanks. He wants me to come, but I feel like I should stay here." So torn.

Cole shook his head. "Go. We'll be right behind you as soon as we make sure the coverage here is taken care of."

"Yeah. Okay." Into the phone, he said, "I'll be there as fast as I can, but I'm about an hour away." It would take him at least forty-five minutes to wind down the mountain and another fifteen to twenty to get to the bookstore.

"It's fine," his father said. "The police are here and we'll be okay, but I wanted to let you know. Take your time, please. Don't rush." A pause. "But I really am glad you're coming. I think your mother needs to see you."

"Right. Not rushing. I'll be there soon."

The others offered support and love as he hurried out of the house, and he waved his thanks.

His parents had been traumatized and he needed to find out why. And who needed to pay for it.

NINETEEN

Kristine made sure her father was settled at home while Ethan stayed with Emily. Their brother was going to have to return to New York early the next morning, so he wanted as much time as possible with his injured sister before he had to leave.

Her father lived an hour from Lake City, but she had felt like she should drive him home and make sure he was as okay as he insisted he was. She ordered groceries to be delivered just as he came out of the hall bathroom, scrubbing a hand down his face. "You gonna stay here tonight?"

"No. Just long enough to make sure you're all right."

"I'm fine. Wouldn't mind the company, though."

She wasn't staying. No way, no how. She'd better start making calls soon to get a ride home. She'd pay for an Uber if she had to. But first . . . "Can we talk about Emily's friends?"

He stilled, then raised a brow. "What about them?"

"You said they were bad news. What made you say that?"

"*Now* you want to know?"

She just kept her gaze steady on his. He finally shrugged and settled into the recliner opposite the television. "That Tia girl was kicked out of high school for cheating on one of her finals. She had to get her GED."

"Okay, so?"

"So, that goes to character."

"And yet she graduated college with Emily at the top of their class. People can make mistakes and still be good people. And not only that, people can change."

"And that Dana girl. The one in the coma? She was arrested for drugs in school. For using and dealing. She got off with a slap on her wrist because her daddy is a senator. Rich, entitled brat."

Kristine could only stare at her father. But in the back of her mind, she was sorting through reasons someone would want to kill Dana. Reasons related to drugs? "Is she still involved in that?"

He shrugged. "Beats me. That's why I didn't want Em hanging around her." His eyes darkened into storm clouds. "But she didn't listen and now look where we are."

Kristine bit off a sigh. He always thought he was right. Even when it was clear to anyone else that he wasn't. "Let that go for a minute, will you? Did you find anything else out that would indicate Dana had someone who wanted to see her dead?"

"What? Why?"

"She's a senator's daughter. That in itself might make her a target."

He blinked. "Yeah. Maybe."

"And someone tampered with her brakes."

He snorted. "Well, there you go. Do you need any more proof?"

"Dad, she's in a coma. Someone tried to kill her. This whole thing is being investigated as an attempted murder. If you have any information that you can share as to who could have done this, you need to give it to the detectives."

He sighed and raked a hand over his head. "Fine. I'll dig up all my notes and files and take those to the police first thing in the morning. Happy?"

"Yes. Thank you. And one other thing. Do you mind if I look at Mom's stuff in the attic?"

He frowned. "What? Where did that come from? You've never shown any interest in that stuff before."

"I know. Now I'm interested."

"Why?"

"Does it matter?"

"Yeah. It matters. Why stir up old memories that are better left buried?"

"Because she was my mother. I need to do this. For me."

He studied her, eyes the exact same shade of gray as hers. But somehow different. What was it that she was seeing now that she'd never noticed before? Something . . . lacking. He shrugged and looked away. "I don't think I have that stuff anymore. I probably gave it to charity."

"Dad!" She blinked. "Why would you do that?"

He slammed a hand on the arm of the chair. "Because she loved her job more than she loved us and I didn't need the reminders!"

"Well, she was my mom and I wanted her stuff! Emily and Ethan might have wanted something too. You should have asked." She pulled in a ragged breath. *Don't yell. Stay calm.* She forced her fist to relax. "I can't believe you did that."

"It was just stuff. You didn't need it and neither did Emily or Ethan. And it was just reminders."

"What do you mean, she loved her job more than she loved us?"

"Nothing. I shouldn't have said that." He rubbed his head. "I'm tired."

Drop it or push it? With him? It was better to wait if she wanted answers. As much as it pained her, she dropped the subject. "Yeah. Okay. I'm sorry I yelled." She didn't want to leave with angry words between them. She turned toward the kitchen.

"Hey, Krissy?"

"Yes?" She turned back to meet his gaze. His eyes were soft and filled with . . . love? Maybe? She wasn't sure. But wanted to believe it.

"Thank you for everything. I'm . . . sorry about your mom's stuff. I guess I should have asked if you guys wanted it."

"Yeah, you should have, but it's done and we'll just move on."

Right. Move on. She went to the kitchen to get some space and set her phone on the counter. The doorbell rang. "I'll get it, Dad."

She opened the door and gasped, placing a hand over her racing heart. "Jesslyn! What are you doing here?"

"Besides giving you a heart attack? Giving you a ride home. I'm guessing you didn't see my texts that I was on the way?"

Kristine grabbed her phone from the counter and looked. Three texts and two calls. And her phone was on silent. She sighed. "No, I didn't, but thanks. That helps so much. I appreciate it."

"And I have another bit of news," Jesslyn said, eyes on her screen.

"What?"

"Nathan just texted that Andrew's parents' store was robbed. He's on the way to them now."

She gaped, then snapped her mouth shut. "Oh no. Are they all right?"

"Yeah." Jesslyn glanced at her phone again. "The guy was there when they got home and shoved Andrew's dad. He hit his head but is okay. So, Andrew is going to be dealing with that for a while."

"I'll text him and let him know I'm here if he needs anything." She stepped back, relieved that she could leave ASAP. "I'm more than ready to go. Come in a sec while I tell my dad I'm leaving."

Jesslyn stepped inside and Kristine set her phone back on the counter to grab two water bottles from the fridge. She passed one to Jesslyn. "For the road."

"Perfect."

Kristine said a quick goodbye to her dad, who was dozing in the recliner, then grabbed her coat off the back of the kitchen chair. They headed toward Jesslyn's car, and Kristine reached for her phone only to remember she'd left it on the counter. "Ugh. I left my phone. I'll be right back."

She hurried back to the porch, pulled out the hidden spare key, and let herself in.

And stopped. Her father stood in profile near the refrigerator, one of the cabinet drawers open while he read something on the paper he held. At her entrance, he shoved the paper in the drawer, slammed it, then spun to face her.

"You think about knocking?" He glowered at her.

"Uh, sorry, Dad, left my phone." She snagged it and stuck it into her back pocket.

"Right. Knock next time."

"Sure thing. See you later. Call if you need anything."

Kristine almost confronted him about whatever it was he was hiding but decided she didn't want to know. She left again and this time made it to the car, slipping into the passenger seat. "Thanks again," she said, pulling out her phone to text Andrew.

Jesslyn smiled. "I didn't mind the drive. It gave me some time to think about things."

"Like?"

"Change."

"You say that with a note of regret in your voice. Everything okay with you and Nathan?"

"Yes, for the most part. You know the Bureau is going to assign him somewhere and I'm going to have to follow."

"Yeah, I know." The Bureau had a habit of doing that. But Jesslyn knew that when she agreed to marry the man. "You don't want to go?"

"Oh, I do! Yes, of course. I'll be fine. My biggest regret? Leaving the youth center." She laughed. "How silly is that?"

"Not silly at all." Jesslyn had opened a youth center in honor of her parents. "You've poured a lot of blood, sweat, and tears into that place. Not to mention money. It's a huge success and so many parents have come to rely on it as a safe place for their kids to go."

"I know. And I love it. I also love Nathan, so . . ." She blew out a sigh. "God will work it out. I have faith in that, so I'm not stressing too hard."

"But a little?"

"Yeah. A little."

"You know the one thing you haven't said you'll miss?"

"What's that?"

"Your job as deputy fire marshal."

"No, I guess I haven't."

"It'll work out. God has a way of doing that."

"I know. You're right. I just wish he'd give me a little more advance notice about things."

Kristine laughed. "Well, just keep bugging him until he does."

"Yeah, I'm good at that."

The rest of the ride home went smoothly, even though she kept an eye on her mirror. She couldn't help notice Jesslyn doing the same thing. Her mind kept going to Andrew, though. "Should we go by the bookstore?" she asked.

"No, Andrew's there. He'll keep us updated and let us know if we can do anything."

"Okay. I don't want to be in the way or make him feel like he has to pull his attention away from his parents for any reason. I'll wait for him to text or call me."

But goodness, it was hard to do that.

ANDREW PULLED TO A STOP at his parents' home-slash-bookstore and hurled himself out of the vehicle and up the three porch steps to the front door. Other officers had already arrived, but he flashed his badge and made his way inside to find his mother wrapped in his father's arms, sitting on the couch in the reading corner. Both of his parents looked worn and pale. Older than their sixty years.

"Sorry it took me so long. Tell me everything." He pulled up a chair from the card table and planted it in front of them.

"Oh Andrew," his mother said, "it was just awful. Your father and I had gone to get some food, and when we came back, the door was open and the cash register had been broken into and the displays knocked over . . ." She sniffed and swiped at the stream of tears sliding down her cheeks. "And he came rushing down the stairs and out the door, pushing your father . . ."

A sob slipped out and Andrew wanted to smash the man's face. Doing his best to keep his emotions in check, he said, "It's okay, Mom. I'm here. I'll take care of this. Are your cameras working?"

"Yes, of course, but all you can see is a person wearing a mask. We already looked."

"That's okay, I want a copy anyway."

"Sure." His father nodded, then rubbed his temples, careful not to touch the wounded place.

"Let me get you some Motrin for that headache."

He ran up to their apartment and found the medicine and two water bottles.

Once he had them taken care of, he walked over to James, who'd arrived seconds after Andrew had walked through the door. "Thanks for taking this. There's no one I'd rather have on this case than you and Cole."

"We've got it covered, I promise."

"I know. Thanks. Although I'll admit I feel torn, because you guys should probably be with Hank."

"He's got so much coverage, he's probably suffocating," Cole said. "Kenzie will let us know if we're needed. Right now, we're here for you. Jesslyn is with Kristine."

"Thanks. Good." He glanced at his phone. "She texted me. I need to answer." He tapped a reply that he appreciated her offer and he'd be in touch when he had more information.

"We'll grab the security footage," Cole said, "and see what the analyst can come up with."

Andrew started to rejoin his parents when he noticed them deep in a whispered but fervent conversation. Then his father stood to pace in front of the couch while his mother sat staring at her hands. Andrew frowned and went to place a hand on his father's bicep. The man stopped but wouldn't meet his eyes.

"Dad? What is it?" he asked. "What are you not telling me?"

"Nothing, Son. It's just . . ." He looked at his wife and sighed. "Nothing."

"That's not true," his mother said. "It is something and I can't ask you to keep it from Andrew." She stood and pressed her fingers to her lips. "Corey came by today asking for money."

"What? I thought you said he was coming Friday."

"We thought so too, but he came today and said he was in debt to some bad people and needed the money today or they were going to kill him."

"Did you give it to him?"

"No." His father shook his head. "I refused."

"What did he say? Was he angry?"

His mother laughed, a short sound without humor. "No. I wouldn't say he was angry. Desperate, but sad too. He just shook his head and said we were his last hope." She lifted her chin. "But I agreed with your father. We couldn't give him the money. I told him to go to you and ask for your help. We explained to him that the only way out of all his problems was to face them, not continue to pay the people who keep adding more and more to the total he owes them. He'll never be free of them at that rate."

"So," Andrew said, "it's possible he came back and did this."

"No," his mother said. "I don't believe so. That's why I didn't want to even mention him. Corey would never do this. We got him a hotel room at the Lake City Inn for three nights until we can figure something out."

"What about the man's build? How tall would you say he was?"

His dad's eyes slid away. Then he sighed and shook his head. "Maybe around six feet or so. Slender, not real bulky, but he was fast. I still don't think it was Corey."

But it was a description that *could* match him.

Andrew scrubbed a hand down his cheek. "All right. I need you to tell all of this to Cole and James. I'll be back in a little while."

"Where are you going?"

"To take care of something. But I'll be back. Hopefully with some answers."

"Andrew—"

His mother's call didn't stop him. He headed for his vehicle. It only took him ten minutes to reach his destination and another five to get the room number of his cousin. Room 206.

He bypassed the elevator and took the stairs, found the room and pounded on the door. "Corey? It's me, Andrew. Open up."

Silence.

He banged again. "Corey! I said open up."

The lock finally clicked and the door opened. Corey stood there, blinking and rubbing sleep from his eyes. He was dressed in knit shorts and a T-shirt and was barefoot. "What in blazes are you doing, Andrew? I finally felt safe enough to fall asleep and you go waking me up. Thanks a ton."

Andrew pushed inside the room. Corey backed up, his sleepy, bleary gaze on Andrew's face. Andrew let his anger bubble to the surface. "Where were you three hours ago?"

"Right here. Asleep. Why?"

Could it be true? He let his gaze roam the room. King bed, desk, chair with a pair of jeans and a sweatshirt hanging on the back, closet. He walked to the closet and opened it.

"Hey, what are you doing?"

No clothes. None.

He walked to the dresser and opened the drawers. No clothes.

So, unless he ditched the ski mask, it wasn't Corey who'd broken into his parents' store. He turned. "I might owe you an apology, but I'm not sure yet."

"Huh? Okay. What?" Corey blinked and ran a hand down his face. "Wanna tell me what this is all about?"

"Someone broke into Mom and Dad's store and robbed it."

His cousin's eyes widened. "And you think it was me?" He snorted and sighed, then dropped to sit on the bed. "Of course you do."

Andrew gestured to the closet and dresser. "You ran with the clothes on your back."

"Yep. I had a visit from my bookie's hurt men—"

"Who?"

"Sorry. My name for them. You know, like hit men, but hurt men. The guys who come to beat you up because they think that's going to make you pay back the money you owe faster."

"Enforcers."

"Right. Enforcers. Hurt men."

Yeah. That had never made sense to him either. "Corey . . ."

"They demanded money. I don't have it. I gambled it all away instead of spending it on drugs."

"Because that's better?"

"No. I'm clean, though, Andrew. I had a good job. Was doing really good. And then I got laid off. I tried finding more work, but no one wants to hire an ex-con. So, I was down to my last two hundred bucks with no sight of any more coming in. I was going to work my last day and then come here, but I ran out of time." He shrugged. "I mean, if I hadn't gambled it, I would have snorted it. And I didn't want to go back there. I've done a lot of lousy things in my life, but I didn't break into the store. I'd never do that."

Andrew pulled on every ounce of patience he could muster. "If it wasn't you, then it was probably the guys after you, and you led them straight to my parents!" He jabbed a finger in Corey's chest.

His cousin winced and jumped off the bed. "I'm sorry! I didn't know what else to do or where to go!" He paced to the window.

Thankfully, he'd had the sense to close the curtains, but Andrew said, "You might want to stay away from the window."

Corey moved to the corner of the room. Then he raked a hand over his head. "They didn't follow me to the bookstore. I was careful. Paranoid. Looking over my shoulder every minute. No, it wasn't me."

"So, it's just a coincidence?"

"It has to be."

Andrew scoffed and shook his head, then stomped to the door and grabbed the handle. "Stay away from my parents until you get this mess cleaned up."

"How?" Corey asked. "How do I clean it up when I can't pay them off?"

His cousin sounded so lost and so miserable that Andrew stopped and dropped his chin to his chest. *Don't do it, don't do it. Don't you dare.*

"Who do you owe money to?"

Corey bit his lip and shrugged. Mumbled something.

"What?"

"Bobby Bigfoot!"

Andrew wanted to bang his head on the door attached to the handle he should have pushed ten seconds ago. "Dude . . ."

"I know. I'm an idiot."

"To put it mildly." Bobby Bigfoot was one of the most feared organized crime bosses on the planet. He was ruthless, evil even. A man no one wanted to cross. Including a lot of those in law enforcement. You sure didn't want him knowing your name. Andrew sent up prayers for patience and wisdom. And this time paused to listen. It was a short pause, but something shifted inside him. Compassion. *Thank you, God.* He sighed and turned back to Corey. "Fine. I'll help you. On one condition."

"What?"

"You have to be a CI."

Corey huffed out a harsh laugh. "You mean be a snitch."

"Yeah. It's the only way."

"But how? He doesn't trust me. He wants to kill me."

"We can fix that. When you show up with double what you owe him, he'll want to know where you got the money."

"I want to know where I got the money."

"You're going to kill someone to get it."

Corey's eyes bugged and Andrew almost smiled. "Not really, but we can make it look like you did. Then you're going to convince him you're the master of mansion home invasions and he wants you on his team. That you've learned your lesson and you're going to make it up to him if he'll give you the chance."

"But what if he doesn't? What if he decides to shoot me right there on the spot? I saw him do it to another dude and I don't want him feeding me the next bullet."

Andrew stilled. "You saw him shoot someone?"

"Yeah. Right between the eyes. It was awful." He shuddered. "One minute he was begging for his life and the next, his brains were scattered on the back wall. Truly the most horrible thing I've ever seen in my life. I have nightmares about it."

"Okay, new plan."

"What kind of new plan?"

"I need to make some phone calls."

For the next two hours, he worked on the plan, got everything set up, then closed his eyes, took a deep breath, and turned to his cousin, who'd been stretched out on the bed watching game shows. "Listen up."

Corey muted the television and sat up. "What?"

"Here's the deal. The FBI is going to protect you for now. They have to be sure they have a solid case. You'll need to tell them everything, help them build this case so they can establish that the person you saw murdered disappeared without a trace. You understand what I'm telling you?"

"Yes," Corey muttered. "And after that?"

"Well, not so much after that, but while they're establishing all of that, they'll also be questioning you about Bobby Bigfoot and his associates, any other crimes like gambling, extortion, burglaries, truck hijackings, and so on, along with any other potential witnesses to those crimes."

"Um . . . that sounds like a lot."

"It is. You can cooperate or die. It's pretty much your choice." He really wanted the man to cooperate.

Corey held his hands up in surrender. "I'm in, Andrew, because in spite of what you think, I *don't* have a choice. I want to live, and if this is what I have to do to make that happen, then I'm in."

Andrew narrowed his eyes and studied him. Yes, he was all in. Andrew relaxed a fraction. This might work out well for all of them. "Okay, perfect. Also, during all of that, the application will be filed for WITSEC, and US Marshals will review it and determine your suitability for the program and that you understand and agree to all the terms that will be outlined and explained to you."

He rubbed his jaw. "So, they could deny it? The application?"

"They could, but honestly, if you give them everything you have and are forthcoming with all the information, then I don't think they will. Bobby Bigfoot is a bad dude and they know it."

"Right."

"So you're good with this?"

"Yeah."

Andrew hesitated, then pulled Corey in for a hug. "I want this to work for you, man."

Corey stepped back, tears in his eyes. "I'm sorry for everything, Andrew. But I appreciate you helping me." He hesitated. "Why are you?"

"Because God told me to."

"Oh."

"And you better put forth some effort to get to know him because you need him."

"Maybe I'll find a church wherever I land."

"You do that." And he'd stay in touch too. There were ways even in WITSEC that he could communicate with his cousin. It would help him not feel so cut off.

Once the two FBI agents arrived, Andrew greeted them and turned his cousin over to them. Then he walked out of Corey's hotel room, exhausted, but satisfied with the plan they had in place.

Andrew reached his car, heard a footfall behind him, and spun.

Scented liquid hit him in the face and he gasped. Breathed in the distinct smell of chloroform and stumbled to lean against the car. Darkness closed in and he let himself sink to the ground, not wanting to fall and risk hitting his head.

A man leaned in. "Now, the fun begins."

TWENTY

Kristine rolled out of bed at the first hint of sunrise. She'd spent all night tossing and turning about several things. Her father, for one. So many thoughts and questions that the only way she could turn those off was to switch to wondering why Andrew hadn't returned her texts and a call. So, she called Nathan, who answered on the first ring.

"Hey," he said. "Um, good morning."

"Sorry if I woke you, but what's up with Andrew? I've texted him five times, called once, and left a voice message, and am getting no response. Frankly, I'm a little worried."

"Yeah. So, his parents' store got broken into last night, and Cole and James were handling that while I stayed with other agents to keep an eye on Hank. I haven't heard from him either. Fell asleep waiting for him to respond."

She knew about the store. That was the whole reason she wanted to talk to him. Or at least a big part of it. The other part was she just wanted to hear from him. "That's not like him."

"No, it's not, but he's dealing with a lot right now. It might take him some time to respond."

Kristine sighed. "Fine. I'll give him a couple more hours in case he got to bed late, then I'm finding him to see if he needs help."

"We can all do that."

"Good. Thanks. Talk to you a little later."

She hung up and considered calling her boss and begging to be put to work. On a flight to anywhere in spite of the suspension. But since that would just be a waste of time, she debated another idea. She wanted to know what her father was hiding. She texted him and asked him to call when he woke up.

Her phone buzzed with a text.

> I'm not sleeping. I'm on a case in Charlotte. Be back later tonight.

> You sure you feel up to that?

> I'm fine. Talk later.

Kristine raised a brow at her screen and pursed her lips. All righty then. She considered plan B and decided she would go with that. And not feel one iota of guilt. Her father was hiding something, and she needed to know what it was.

She grabbed her keys and texted Nathan.

> I've got to run a quick errand to Asheville. Text me if you hear from Andrew, please? And any movement at the safe house?

> Will do and not yet.

Kristine hurried to her car, climbed in, and made the hour trip to Asheville without incident, even though her nerves were strung tight and she watched her mirrors. But she made it to her father's house and let herself in using the well-hidden key.

She went straight to the drawer he'd shut so fast yesterday and opened it. Nothing. Well, of course not. She shut the drawer. Next stop, his office. She walked into the back bedroom and noted how neat he kept it. His camera was gone, but if he was on a case, he'd have it with him.

She sat at the desk and opened the first drawer. Bingo.

A lone piece of paper that looked like it had been handled quite a bit had been placed on top. A letter from her mother. Her heart stuttered at the realization.

She snapped a picture of it, then started reading.

Dear Greg,

The fight last night was the last straw. We can't keep on this way. We're a terrible example to the kids of what marriage should be—

She stopped and sucked in a trembling breath. No, she didn't want to read this here. She couldn't. She'd read it later in the privacy of her home, where she could cry or kick something if she needed to.

And besides, she was still worried about Andrew and wanted to touch base with him.

But first, she made her way to the attic and searched until she found the stack of boxes she was looking for.

So, he hadn't thrown them out. A wave of anger swept over her. She grabbed the first one and hauled it to her car, then went back for the others. By the time she was done, she was sweaty and breathing hard. The chilly air outside felt good and a sense of peace washed over her. She had what was left of her mother's things and could go through them at her leisure. Which would be fast, because she couldn't help but wonder if there was a clue somewhere in there about the person behind the hijacking that had killed her.

Despite her desire to read her mother's letter, she drove straight to the bookstore and found the Rosses cleaning up. When Mr. Ross spotted her, he set his broom aside and came to greet her. "Kristine, good to see you. How are you?"

"That's my question for you." She looked past him to the woman who had to be Mrs. Ross. She was wearing an apron and putting books back on the shelf.

Mr. Ross introduced them and his wife smiled. "We're okay.

Thankful it's just stuff that was damaged and nothing more than a bump on the head that will heal. Could have been a lot worse."

"Yes. For sure. Is Andrew here?"

"No, we haven't seen him this morning. I called him a couple of times and it went straight to voicemail."

Now that was alarming. "Wait a minute, he's not here?"

"No. I thought he might show up but figured he caught a case or something that he couldn't get away from."

"But he'd call. At least communicate that, right?"

"Well, yes, I would think so."

Something was wrong. Something was terribly wrong.

ANDREW'S HEAD POUNDED and his stomach churned. Nausea was never a welcome visitor. He lay still, praying for it to pass. Finally, after several deep breaths, he kept everything in place. Then he opened his eyes and the blurry room came into focus.

This was *not* his hotel room.

And his hands were double zip-tied in front of him. *Oh boy. Okay. Think, Ross, think.* But his brain was a scrambled mess at the moment. He focused on the zip ties. Breaking two would be a challenge, and to do that he was going to need more strength than he currently had. He struggled to a sitting position and waited once more for the nausea to pass. More deep breathing and finally everything settled.

Two facts. He was in a bedroom on a bed, and his hands were bound in front of him.

Why was he in a bedroom? And *whose* bedroom was it? And how long had he been out? And how was he going to get out of the zip ties?

A flicker of a memory danced across his mind and he frowned. He'd confronted Corey, gone out to his car, and . . .

And what? Had Corey done this?

No . . .

The spray in the face.

It was coming back to him.

The guy behind him had sprayed him with something that knocked him out.

And brought him here.

He lifted his bound wrists and rubbed a hand over his chin, then looked for his phone. Gone, of course. His head ached something fierce and he tuned in to the raging thirst clawing at him. The bathroom was across the room, and that meant he had to ignore the headache and other physical discomfort and make the effort to get off the mattress. The thirst forced him to move. He swung his legs over the side and stood, weakness invading him, and he almost dropped back down to let the darkness dancing in front of his vision take him under again. He hesitated, panting, searching for the strength to move, then stand. His dry mouth and burning throat sent him stumbling to the sink. He twisted the faucet and was relieved when water poured into the basin. He tilted his head to drink until he was satisfied. Feeling much better, he turned the water off and stood still for a moment, thinking.

He needed a weapon. He scoured the bathroom.

Nothing. Even the toilet seat and tank lids had been removed. There was no glass shower door to break. No shower curtain rod. He might be able to dismantle the sink parts and use one of the pipes, but that would take time he wasn't sure he had.

So . . . nothing. He stepped back into the bedroom. There was a mattress but no boxspring. And no window to break and use the glass as a weapon—or a tool to cut the zip ties. He frowned. This wasn't an ordinary bedroom. Someone had planned this pretty meticulously. He looked up. There was a light, but it was built into the ceiling with some kind of protective cover over it. Could he break it? Maybe. If he could reach it. But even standing on the mattress, he wouldn't be tall enough to even touch it.

There was one possibility. A built-in wooden desk with no drawers. He could probably bust up the desk, but that would make a lot of noise, and he'd rather not alert his captor to the fact that he was awake and moving. He walked to the bedroom door.

Somehow he didn't think he was going out that way, but he tried the knob, shocked when it turned under his palm. He hesitated. He was able to move freely about the room. The door was unlocked. Which meant his captor wanted him to come out.

All righty then.

With an overabundance of caution, he pulled the door open and stepped into the hall, then followed it into a spacious kitchen. He tried the door and found it locked. And no way to unlock it from the inside. Oookay. Weird. There was a den off to the left, so he aimed his steps that way.

"'Bout time you woke up. Was starting to wonder if I gave you too much juice."

Andrew stilled and focused on the man in the recliner aiming a gun at him. Dirty blond hair, narrowed green eyes. Some would probably say he was a handsome man. But the hate in his eyes was chilling. "Who are you and why have you brought me here?"

"You'll figure it out in a minute when we go make a visit to the one person in my life who loved me."

Loved. He narrowed his eyes. His captor looked familiar, but he couldn't place him. Wait a minute. "You were watching me from the street outside my parents' place."

"Yes. It came in handy to know who they were and what they mean to you. You look like you're a close-knit family."

It made him sick that this man had spied on his parents, knew where they lived, knew what they looked like. Knew way too much. He hoped he hid his revulsion, because he had a feeling that would only please the man. "Helpful how?"

"To know you'd come running if they were in trouble."

"You broke into their store?"

"I did. And like I figured, you came running."

Which enabled him to follow Andrew to Corey's place. He'd fallen right into a trap he'd never seen coming. "What's your name?"

The man rose. The gun never wavered. "You can call me Ty."

Ty. Ty. Ty . . . ?

Nothing in Andrew's memory database pinged recognition. "Ty what?"

"Like I said, you'll figure it out. Go out the front door and walk up the hill. There's a path, you can't miss it. Don't try any funny business. Hands tied up or not, I don't trust you."

Andrew held his hands up like any good captive. "I need a coat."

"It's not going to matter in the end. Go."

So he planned to kill him. Shocking. He walked toward the door. As soon as Andrew stepped outside, he was hit by the isolation—and the biting cold. Snow drifted down from the gray sky and had been for a while, according to the white ground.

Did his captor plan to put a bullet in him or leave him out in the cold to freeze to death? Neither option was particularly appealing, but for the moment, Andrew did as the man said. The temps here were fifteen to twenty degrees cooler than where he'd started his day yesterday, which meant they were far up in the mountains. He just wasn't quite sure where, but he had a feeling even if he had his phone on him, he wouldn't have a signal.

Thankful for the heavy sweatshirt layered over a long-sleeved shirt, his jeans, and Bureau-issued boots, he might have a chance if he wound up stuck in the elements. Assuming he could get his hands free. Because he sure didn't plan on sticking around to let this guy kill him.

For now, he walked up the hill with self-defense moves rolling through his mind. He could turn and kick the gun away and take the guy down, but at the moment, he wanted answers. And the only way to get those was to let this scene play out.

"First grave on the right," Ty said from behind him.

Grave?

Andrew walked up to it, his boots crunching snow and the gravel beneath it, and read the name on the upright headstone. *Isaac Mason. Beloved brother and best friend. Taken too soon. Rest easy and know that you will be avenged.*

Isaac Mason. The Realtor who'd died in the cell on Andrew's watch.

"You've been after me?"

"Yep. Shot at you, chased you through the pouring rain and forced you off the road—along with that dude who was in the way—blew up your house, and so on."

"That was you. After me." He had to repeat it just to make sure.

"You deaf? I said yes."

A pause as he fought to keep his balance on the uneven ground. "So, all this time, you weren't after Hank?"

"Who's Hank?"

The air left Andrew's lungs as the light bulb turned on and everything became clear. They'd never considered Andrew was the actual target. "Why'd you shoot up Marcus Brown's house? What's your relationship to him?"

"Don't know what you're talking about." Ty aimed the weapon at Andrew. "Get the rope."

Andrew didn't have time to ponder the denial of shooting up the Brown home. "What?"

"In front of the headstone. Brush the snow off and get the rope."

So that's why his hands were tied in front of him and not behind his back. Ty wanted him to hold the weapon that was supposed to kill him.

Without taking his eyes from Ty, he had to use both hands to swipe. He refused to flinch at the icy chill that came with putting his bare hands in the snow, but when his fingers came into contact with a frozen coil of rope, the ice spread to his blood.

He pulled it up from its snowy grave. A noose. "What am I supposed to do with this?" He was determined to keep the man talking while he figured a way out. His hands were blocks of ice at that point and shivers had set in.

Ty smiled. A smile as cold as the snow. "My brother had his neck snapped like a twig. You're going to experience the same thing. That tree right there is going to be your final resting place."

Andrew didn't bother to look. "You could have killed me when you had me unconscious and unable to fight back. Why not just string me up then?"

The man snorted. "Where's the enjoyment in that?" His eyes narrowed. "I want you to know what's coming. The feel of the noose in your hands, the walk to the tree, watching me as I kick the ladder out from under you. Feel the terror that my poor brother felt that day. In the end, you'll die the same way he did."

Andrew's stomach twisted. Did he really think Andrew would make it that easy for him? "Ty, I had no way to know Isaac wasn't part of that gang. He had on a jacket that was almost an exact match."

"Did he tell you he wasn't involved?"

"Of course he did. So did half the people we arrested that night."

"I watched the footage of what happened to him," Ty said. "I saw him begging for help, for someone to get him out of there. And everyone just ignored him."

He wasn't completely wrong. Andrew had ignored him and all the others shouting for release. But something in the man's voice had finally registered. A tone. The terror. Something. And he'd started to go to him when the other gang member had grabbed him. "I tried to get to him. I didn't have a key. I couldn't get in."

"You were there. Standing at the door. Just watching."

"I was yelling at the guy to let your brother go."

"Liar. You were egging him on."

"No, I wasn't. I tried to save him."

"All your protests amount for nothing. You testified to the same thing. And while no one else could see your lies, I can."

"So that's why you singled me out? Picked me out of all the agents involved in that sting that day?"

"You were the one who put him in that cell. I saw that footage too. When you put someone in a cell where they can't protect themselves, it's your job to do so."

Again, he wasn't wrong.

And Andrew needed to figure out a way to escape. Fast. "How do you plan to get that noose around my neck? Or me up swinging from the tree?" A glimmer of an idea for escape was forming.

"Easy," Ty said. "I shoot you somewhere that doesn't kill you, then hang you."

He lifted the weapon and Andrew dove. The bullet whistled past his ear and Ty yelled when he realized he'd missed. Using both hands, Andrew picked up a handful of gravel and whipped it toward Ty. The man screamed again when the little missiles pelted his face. Using his hands as one unit, Andrew slammed them against the man's arm and the gun tumbled to the ground. The injured Ty recovered faster than Andrew had calculated, and a hard fist slammed into Andrew's gut, knocking the wind out of him. He stumbled back, gasped for air, and dodged Ty's attempt to grab him.

"You're not getting out of this alive," the man said.

"We'll see about that," Andrew finally managed to croak out and swung his leg in a roundhouse kick that caught Ty in the knee. He howled and went down.

Andrew scanned the ground for the gun but couldn't spot it. Ty pulled a knife and Andrew decided it was time to run.

TWENTY-ONE

It hadn't taken Kristine long to alert the others to Andrew's disappearing act. At first, they weren't too worried, but after numerous attempts to get in touch with him with no luck, Cole, James, and Nathan agreed to look for him while others stayed with Hank.

They were all now back at Andrew's parents' bookstore getting the security footage to see if they could tell which way he went when he left the store.

"Here it is," Mr. Ross said.

He clicked a few keys and they watched Andrew drive away. West.

Mrs. Ross stood, arms crossed, watching everything, blinking back tears. "You think he's really in trouble, don't you?"

Kristine went to the woman. "We're not sure, but the fact that he's not answering his phone and it's going straight to voicemail is worrisome."

"Agreed. He always gets back to us as soon as he can." She paced to the back of the store, then returned to where they were gathered around the computer. "He was angry about the break-in and would have gone to see Corey, I feel sure. I think you need to check with him."

Cole and James exchanged a glance.

"Corey?" Nathan asked.

238

"My nephew. I think . . ." She looked at her husband. "*We* think that Andrew suspects that Corey is the one who broke into the store."

"Did he?"

She shook her head. "I don't believe he would do it, but Andrew's never thought much of Corey or trusted him. With good reason. It's possible he went to confront him."

"Do you know where to find him?" Nathan asked.

She nodded, wrote something on a pad of paper, ripped off the top piece, and handed it to Kristine. "We put him up at this hotel. He was going to start staying with us on Friday, but I didn't have the room ready yet."

"He said some people were going to kill him," Mr. Ross said, "if we didn't give him the money to pay them back, but we couldn't give him what he was asking for."

Mrs. Ross linked her fingers in front of her.

Kristine waved the paper at the guys. "Let's go talk to Corey."

It took them fifteen minutes to get to the small hotel on the edge of town and note Andrew's car wasn't in the parking lot. It took them five more minutes to identify themselves to the FBI agent on Corey's door. They were obviously just getting ready to leave. Nathan shook the man's hand after the guy inspected Nathan's badge. "We just need to talk to him for a few minutes before you leave."

"Sure." He motioned Corey to the door.

"We're friends of Andrew, Corey," James said. "Your aunt and uncle told us where to find you. Call them and verify it if you need to."

"No, it's okay. What do you want?"

"Andrew was here, right?" James asked.

"Yes."

Cole leaned in. "You know where he went when he left?"

"Home, I assume. I don't know. Why?"

"He didn't say?"

"No." Corey frowned. "What's wrong?"

Nathan rubbed a hand down his chin. "He's missing."

"What are you talking about? Missing?"

"Meaning no one's heard from him since he left here and we need to find him," Nathan said. "And we need your help to do it." He raked a hand over his head and turned, but Kristine heard him mutter, "And that's terrifying."

Kristine had had enough. "I'm going to see if there's footage."

She left them with Corey and the agents and found the manager, who was in her mid-fifties, soft-spoken, and kind. Her name badge read Helen. When Kristine explained the situation and requested the security footage from the previous night, she gasped. "Yes, of course. Give me just a minute to pull it up."

Seconds later, they watched Andrew walk to his car. A figure came into view but had his back to the camera. He approached Andrew from behind and, when Andrew turned, sprayed something into his face. Andrew staggered. Before he could do anything else, the figure shoved him into the driver's seat, ran around to the other side, and pulled him into the passenger seat. And still, she couldn't get a look at his face.

"Whoa," Helen said, "that doesn't look good."

"It doesn't. Can you send that to me?" At least it proved Corey wasn't involved in the snatch. Unless he somehow managed to get word to the guy that Andrew was there and when he left. Which didn't seem highly possible since Andrew's visit was completely un-planned.

"Wait a minute," Helen said. "There might be more. He shoves him into his car and drives off, but let's go here to the other camera." Her fingers flew over the keyboard and she found them leaving. An-drew's car turned right out of the parking lot. Toward the mountains.

"Okay, that's his Bucar. They can track it. Maybe."

She texted Nathan and he answered right back.

Probably not.

Rats. "Can you send someone that footage?" she asked Helen.

"Sure. What email address?"

Kristine had the footage sent to Nathan, Cole, and James. Then stopped. "How did he get here?"

"What?"

"The guy who grabbed Andrew. Andrew wasn't planning on coming here. One more thing. Can you pull up the footage of the front door for the two hours preceding Andrew's arrival? Then run it on fast forward until I tell you to stop."

"All right."

Cole came into sight on the camera live feed monitoring the lobby, and she stepped out of the back office to wave for him to join her. "James and Nathan are still with Corey," he said. "The guy's a little messed up. We're going to help him, though."

"Good." Kristine motioned to Helen. "This is our new BFF, Helen. Helen, this is Cole."

"I got the file," Cole said. "Thank you." He nodded to the screen. "What else are we looking for?"

"How the guy got here. We know what he was wearing. It was a navy blue hoodie and he had a beanie under the hood. I want to see if someone dropped him off or what."

"We'll check the back cameras too," Helen said. "I can do that over there on that computer if you want to look on this one. It'll go faster that way."

"You're the best," Kristine said. She motioned to Cole. "I'll let you do the honors."

Helen shifted to the other computer and Cole moved into her seat. Kristine found herself bouncing between the two.

"He was watching Andrew. I'm guessing he even followed him here." She texted Nathan.

Come to the lobby, will you?

He arrived seconds later.

"Can you use your resources to trace every plate in the parking lot?"

"Of course, but unless we have a face to match the driver to, it's not going to help much."

"I have an idea about that too." She dialed Andrew's father and he answered mid first ring. "Hi, Mr. Ross, this is Kristine. Can you look at your street footage around the time of the robbery and take note of all the cars there? Every make, model, and plate you can find."

"Sure. I can do that."

"Great, text them to this number when you're done."

She hung up. "The guy got here somehow. The first thought is he left his car in the lot when he grabbed Andrew. The second thought is that he parked down the street somewhere, so we might need to cover those cars as well."

Cole pulled his phone from his pocket. "I'm going to pull in some manpower."

Minutes ticked past and Helen shook her head. "No one matching his description got out of a car at the entrance. But look at this."

She played a section of the footage where a man came from around the edge of the bushes, head down, hoodie up. And beanie on his head. "That's him."

Thirty minutes later, her phone pinged with a text from Andrew's father with a list of plates. She looked at Helen. "Give me what you've got so far."

"Printing now."

The printer whirred behind her, and she snatched the sheet from it and started going through the list.

And came up empty.

Deflated, she flopped back. "Rats."

"You know," Helen said, "there are two other hotels near here. Maybe he parked at one and walked over?"

"Yes." Kristine straightened. "It makes sense the direction he came from. Maybe he did." Assuming he hadn't already come back for the vehicle. But they had to try. She got on the phone with the other hotels, requesting the same information on all the cars in their parking lot.

It didn't take long to get it. With a prayer on her lips, she started comparing the first one while Nathan worked on the second one. Cole and James hovered. Helen excused herself to help someone at the front desk.

"There! I found it. The plate at the hotel next door is the same as one of the plates Andrew's father sent." She looked up, met Nathan's gaze, then Cole's. "We were right."

"You were," Nathan said. "So who does it belong to?"

"Whoever it was, he followed Andrew from the store. He knew Andrew was going to be there and waited for him to leave. Followed him here and then grabbed him."

"Which means the robbery was just a ploy to get Andrew to the location?" Nathan asked.

Kristine hesitated. "Could Andrew have been the target all along, and we just assumed it was Hank because of how everything played out?"

"I'd say that's a really good theory." Nathan looked up from his phone. "The plate belongs to someone named Isaac Mason."

ANDREW HAD RUN HARD. So had Ty. While Andrew had desperation on his side, Ty had rage and a knowledge of these woods. Andrew had no idea how much time had passed, as Ty had taken his smartwatch from him as well as his phone. But according to the sun, he'd say at least two hours, possibly more.

He was cold, but not frozen. Tired, but not wiped out. His hands were cold, but not numb. Ty had left the zip ties loose enough not to cut the circulation off.

Moving kept his blood pumping. He'd even broken out in a sweat as he'd walked, then run, then backtracked in his own steps to throw off Ty. He wouldn't fool the man forever, but he hoped he was buying himself some time. He was going downhill, looking for any route with tracks or disturbed snow. He saw bear tracks, deer, and more.

He did *not* see his attacker. But Andrew knew better than to pretend the man wasn't following. He had no idea where he was location-wise, but so far there'd been no sign of civilization.

With a glance over his shoulder, he continued his trek, maneuvering his hands up under his sweatshirt. A flash of movement to his left swung him around in time to see a blade arc toward him. He threw up his arms to block the plunge, his left forearm slamming against Ty's. It knocked his aim off, but the blade sliced Andrew's rib as it went down. Fire licked against his side and he hissed even while he swept a kick against Ty's nearest ankle. The man yelled and hit the ground. The knife skittered away from him like the gun had earlier.

Andrew dove for the knife, closed his hands around the hilt, blade up and facing him. A quick jerk of his wrists pulled the blade up to slice through the zip ties. A hard slam into his back knocked him sideways and he lost the knife.

Ty's harsh breaths were close, practically in Andrew's ear, and he swung an elbow back to catch the man in the side of the head. Ty grunted and fell back while Andrew's cold hands fumbled for the knife once again. But Ty rolled, quick as a blink, and pulled out a garrote, thin but strong. He wrapped the wire around his gloved hands, pulling it tight with a twisted snarl. Did this man have no end of weapons?

The sharp wire was meant to cut into Andrew's skin, leaving deep, painful wounds as the pressure increased. Knowing the man expected him to run again, he charged forward and slammed into Ty. Ty lost his grip on the wire with his left hand, and Andrew shot out his own hand to grab the man's right wrist. The wire dangled. Still a threat.

Ty kicked out and reared forward, shoving Andrew off him. Andrew lost his grip and his footing. He went down with a grunt but rolled in time to miss the kick aimed at his head.

Summoning his last reserves of strength, he pushed back hard, sending Ty stumbling. He used the moment to dart down the hill and throw himself behind the nearest tree trunk. Ty was pushing himself up, favoring his battered knee. Andrew's lungs burned and his vision blurred, but escape was the only thing on his mind.

Breathing heavily, Andrew took off again, climbing over tree trunks, desperately searching for a hiding place.

Or a weapon.

He chose the nearest hill and started up it. Just as he reached the top of the hill, something clamped around his ankle, pulling him to his knees, his jeans soaking in the wet snow. Ty had recovered faster than expected. Andrew rolled and kicked out with his free foot to connect with Ty's head.

The man screamed and fell, rolled, and came up with another knife. Smaller than the first one. Andrew lurched to his feet just as Ty slashed at him and caught his bicep. Andrew cried out and reared back. His fingers grasped for something. Anything. Closed around a solid piece of wood about the thickness of a baseball bat.

Ty stood over him, grinning, the knife in one hand, wire in the other. "No more games, Ross. This is the end for you."

He lifted the knife and brought it down toward Andrew's throat. Andrew swung the wood into the man's fist clutching the hilt and knocked it sideways. Ty yelped as the weapon flew through the air and hit the ground, disappearing into a snow drift.

A chopper sounded above, getting closer by the second. Ty whirled to face him and Andrew lurched to his feet. They were both breathing hard. Andrew had about one more swing in him. He gripped the wood like the bat it resembled. "Stop it, man. It's over! That chopper's up there for me!"

Ty let out a bloodcurdling scream and catapulted himself toward Andrew. A crack sounded just before the wood connected with Ty's skull. The man went down like a rock.

Andrew leaned over, gulping air. He went to his knees, all his wounds now screaming. The chopper landed in the clearing close enough that the wind from the blades chilled him to the bone. He crawled to Ty, who lay still. Unmoving. And with a bullet in the middle of his forehead. Andrew wilted, freezing, shaking, adrenaline ebbing now that he was safe.

Safe. Would he ever take that for granted again?

"Andrew!"

His partner's cry reached him over the noise, but he didn't have the breath to respond.

Kenzie reached him first and knelt next to him. "I see blood. Where is it coming from?"

"Not sure. Rib and arm, I think." He shuddered.

"I need a warming blanket over here!"

Seconds later, Kristine was there and dropping a blanket over him. "You scared us."

Nathan and other agents swarmed Ty Mason, who was very obviously dead. Another blanket appeared and was placed over the man.

"How'd you find me?" he asked.

"It's a long story," Kenzie said. "We'll tell you on the way to the hospital."

Nathan looked down at Ty's body. "It's going to take a while for the ME to get here."

Kenzie looked up. "Well, Andrew needs to get to a hospital and get warmed up. It's not subzero temps out here but still cold enough for some hypothermia. Plus he's lost quite a bit of blood."

Andrew closed his eyes. He had no more strength to fight the darkness sweeping over him. He decided to go with it, secure in the knowledge that his friends wouldn't let him die.

TWENTY-TWO

The Life Flight ride to get Andrew to the hospital had been intense, with paramedics working to patch him up and raise his body temperature. Now, he was ensconced in a room, out of any immediate danger to his life. The nurse said she didn't expect him to wake anytime soon thanks to the drugs, so Kristine made her way to Emily's room, where she found her with their aunt. "Hey, sis. Hey, Aunt Wendy."

Emily smiled. "Hey. What's up? You look . . . rough."

"Ha. Thanks. It's been a day."

"Tell me about it?"

Kristine gave her an abbreviated version, ending with Andrew's trip to the hospital.

Her aunt blinked. "Goodness, that sounds terrifying."

"It was." Just the condensed version was enough to make her sister pale, which was why she'd left out the more horrifying details.

"Wait," Emily said, "he's hurt?"

"Yes, but he's going to be okay." *Thank you, God.*

"You like him a lot, don't you?" Emily asked.

Kristine's heart pounded an extra beat. "Yes. I like him an awful lot."

"Then you need to be with him. Make sure you're there when he wakes up."

"I'll go back in a minute. Is Dad here?"

Her sister frowned. Then scowled. "No. I don't know where he is. He's insisting I come live with him after I'm discharged, but I just can't do it, Kris. I won't."

"I've already offered to have her come stay with me," Aunt Wendy said. "But don't tell your father yet. Just agree with him for the moment. We'll work out the details later."

Kristine eyed her aunt. It wasn't often she showed her dislike for the man. "I agree," she said. "Don't say anything to him yet."

Emily's frown deepened. "All right. I'll play along, but I don't like it."

"I just think it's best," Aunt Wendy said. "He's been in a strange mood ever since your accident. I know he's worried, but he's still all broody and moody."

He really was.

"Okay, well, text me if he shows up." His lack of communication lately was . . . weird. Kristine wasn't really interested in talking to him, but at the same time, she wanted to know where he was and what he was doing.

"Go," Emily said. "Aunt Wendy is here. I'll be fine."

So, Kristine went and found Andrew still sleeping. She sat by his bed and opened the picture app on her phone to read her mother's letter, only to be interrupted by a knock on the door. She opened it and slipped into the hallway to find Hank. Everyone else had gone back to their respective jobs with strict orders for her to text when Andrew was awake.

"Hey," she said. "Andrew's still sleeping. What's up?"

"How is he?"

"He's okay. He passed out at the scene from blood loss and everything else, but he's surprisingly really good. Just needs some time and rest to regain his strength."

"Good. I'm glad. He and I've had some crazy times together."

"Yeah, he told me about some of them."

"I'm glad he can talk about that with you."

"I am too."

He scrunched his beanie hat in his hands and pulled in a deep breath, then let it out. "Anyway, I just came by to tell Andrew thanks for everything." He shook his head. "I can't believe the guy was after Andrew and the gang has no idea where I am. It's kind of mind-blowing."

"No kidding. So what will you do now?"

"They want me to go back under."

"How are you going to explain your disappearing act?"

"I'll leave that to the bigwigs, but they'll come up with something airtight."

The door opened and Andrew stood there, fully dressed although a bit pale. "Ready to go?"

"You can go back to bed, dude," Hank said. "I'll come in there and talk to you."

Andrew hesitated, then nodded. "I wouldn't mind at least sitting down."

Once they were all comfortable with Andrew back on the bed, Hank in the window seat, and Kristine in the chair, she sent a text to the others that Andrew was up. And dressed.

Hank leaned in, hands clasped between his knees. "It was you he was after all along."

"Yep. We figured that out the hard way, but at least we now know." He rubbed his eyes. "How'd you know where to find me? I don't think anyone's answered that one yet."

Hank motioned to Kristine. "She figured it out. Found the plate that matched the car. Nathan did a little research and came up with an Isaac Mason. As soon as he said that name, I knew who had you. From there, we tracked Tyler Mason to his property in the mountains. He and Isaac were close. Ty graduated college, had a good job, but when he lost Isaac, it changed him."

"So, he hunted me down to get his revenge."

Hank nodded. "Yeah, something like that."

"It's unbelievable, the timing on everything. All of the attacks . . . we thought those were directed at you. If you hadn't shown up when you did, it would have been pretty clear who he was after."

"But why shoot at you at Brown's house?" Kristine asked. "I don't see him as being a lousy shot. He missed on purpose?"

"Well, that's the weird thing. He said that wasn't him."

"Not him?" She frowned. "Who else could it be?"

"I don't know. I'd say he was lying, but he admitted to everything else. Why lie about that?"

"Weird. Maybe he just wanted to mess with your head."

Andrew looked doubtful but shrugged, then winced. "Maybe. I don't know."

"Well, he's not going to hurt anyone ever again," she said. "Let's be thankful for that." And she was, but it still bothered her.

"Amen," he whispered.

With her mother's letter on the phone burning a hole in her hand, Kristine couldn't stand it any longer. She rose. "I'll give you guys time to say your goodbyes while I take care of something."

Andrew frowned at her. "Everything okay?"

"Yes, sure." She waved her phone at him. "Just need to look at something."

"Okay."

She stepped out of the room and debated whether this was the best place to read the letter but honestly didn't want to wait any longer. Reading it in the privacy of her home wasn't an option if she wanted to do it anytime soon. She made her way to the waiting room on Emily's floor and found a seat in the corner. She opened the letter and started reading.

Dear Greg,

The fight last night was the last straw. We can't keep on this way. We're a terrible example to the kids of what marriage should be and we need to get help. Or we need to go our separate ways. Like I told you last month, I've already talked to a divorce attorney, but don't want to take that route if you'll agree to counseling. I'm still waiting for you to agree. I won't wait much longer. Please be prepared to talk when I get back from today's flight.

Kristine said some really ugly things to me and I know she will regret them once she calms down. Please tell her that I understand. I forgive her. All is well. Tell her that I didn't take this flight because of what she said. I'm taking it because you and I need the distance. That being said, please let her know I expect her to apologize when I get back. And give her the letter I left her. I couldn't leave without at least reaching out to her.

Kristine gasped. Why had her father never told her about this last message from her mother? And what letter had her mother left? A slow rage started to build and she sucked it back. Not yet. She had to finish reading.

I'm so concerned about this continued controlling behavior you're exhibiting.

Right, Mom?

We've talked about this. It was there when we got married, but over the past few years, it's really gotten, ironically enough, out of control. No one can live up to your expectations and you're suffocating the life out of me and our kids. It's got to stop. Either get help—and I'll go with you—or we're done. I hate to leave town on this note. Part of me thinks it's not fair, but talking to your face isn't getting results, so I'm trying this way.

Please, let's figure out a plan to work on this together.

You have three days to think about it. Tell your kids you love them and mean it. Tell them I love them too. I do love you, Greg, I just can't live this way any longer. And won't.

Xoxo,
Rachel

Tears dripped off her chin and she read the message again. Over and over. Especially the part about her mother not taking that flight because of what Kristine had said. All these years, she'd blamed herself for her mother going on that flight she hadn't been scheduled to take, the one she'd volunteered for. Because her parents needed distance. And her father knew how she blamed herself and said nothing. *He knew!*

Because it was easier to control someone who blamed themself for killing your loved one.

"Unbelievable." Rage washed over her like a tsunami.

After the sixth read through, she tucked the phone into her back pocket, swiped her hands across her face, and gathered her composure. Her aunt was with Emily. She had no idea where her father was, and she had to calm down before she confronted him with this.

And she had her mother's boxes to go through. She needed to do that ASAP because there was no telling what else she might find in one of them. Hopefully the missing letter. She texted the group and let them know she was headed home and bolted from the hospital.

Once she had the boxes in front of her, she started going through the first one. It held her father's old cases. She counted. Only thirty-five total. "There's no way these are all of his cases," she murmured aloud. So what were they? She started going through them one by one and stopped when she came across some familiar names. "Oh, Dad, what have you done?" She read through each one, her heart dropping with every word. Then she pushed the files aside and dug more, coming up with another folder—this one a map with coordinates and blueprints of a home. But whose home? And why did her dad have this? She kept on, looking for the one thing she really wanted. The letter from her mother. And came up empty. But now she had so many suspicions that she didn't know which one to chase first.

ANDREW WAS TIRED. After everything he'd been through, he was just plain exhausted. But he wanted to see Kristine. Thankfully, someone had managed to retrieve his phone and watch so he was able to get her text saying she was fine but had some personal things to attend to. He hoped she didn't mind him barging in, but he had some personal things to attend to as well. Like asking her if there was any way she'd consider going out with him. He'd shared the whole sordid story of his role in an innocent man's death and she hadn't run away screaming. Maybe there was hope.

He made his way to her townhome and knocked.

It took her a minute, but she opened the door and he took in her ragged appearance. Dark circles under her eyes and tear-stained cheeks. He frowned, stepped inside, shut the door, and pulled her into a hug. His side and shoulder protested, but he ignored them. "Did you sleep at all?"

"Off and on in between boxes. Oh, Andrew, I just . . ."

"Tell me," he said.

"I can't," she whispered.

"I told you my past," he said, "terrified you'd think less of me." Scared to death she'd walk away. But she hadn't. "Tell me."

She sniffed and led him to the couch. "I've been carrying a burden ever since my mother died. The day before she left for her final flight, I told her I hated her, that she was a horrible mother and that I wished she'd just stay gone. Later I learned she'd taken a flight—one she hadn't planned to be on—and I assumed it was because of what I said to her."

"Oh man, Kristine, how awful for you. I'm so sorry."

"She tried to talk to me before she headed to the airport, and I refused to come out of my room. It was a Saturday. She was supposed to be back Wednesday. We'd had our fair share of arguments before, but with this one I was particularly cruel."

"Why?"

"Because I wanted to go out with a boy and my dad said no. I wanted her to convince him to say yes. And she refused. She said this time she agreed with my father." She shot him a wry look. "I was stunned because they never agreed on anything. Turns out my dad had arrested him the week before for drunk driving. He didn't want to tell me that, because that boy's daddy had managed to do some fancy talking, paid a hefty fine, and got the charges dropped. Dad told Mom, of course, but Dad knew I was going to see this kid at school and didn't want it known that he was the one who told me. I found out through the high school rumor mill."

"That's tough."

"Unfortunately, I never got a chance to tell her I understood. I found out Wednesday at school and she died that day on the flight home."

His hand rubbed her back. "I don't even know what to say."

"There aren't any words, so you don't have to try to find them. But here's the kicker. My mom wrote my dad a note and told him to tell me that she knew I didn't mean what I said and she forgave me. Turns out she took that flight to give *them* some space, not because of what I said. He didn't tell me. And she left me a letter. One that he was supposed to give me and didn't." She threw her hands in the air. "How could he not tell me? How could he keep that from me?"

"I agree, that's awful. Why would he do that?"

She sighed. "This is going to sound terrible, but I suspect it's because a kid who's racked with guilt is easier to control than one who knows her mom didn't die hating her. I haven't asked him yet, though. That's on the agenda for later today. When I can do it without screaming at him—or killing him." She shook her head and bit her lip. "I thought all these years that she died thinking I hated her. But she didn't." She passed him the phone. "Here. Read it."

He did, then passed the device back to her. "Wow."

"She didn't hate me, Andrew. She really didn't."

"Of course not. All parents know that they're going to argue with their bratty teens and the teens are going to say things they don't mean. It's in the parenting handbook."

She gave a low laugh and swiped a stray tear. "Yeah, I guess so."

He waved a hand at the mess of papers spread across her kitchen table, on the floor, and over her coffee table. "What's all this?"

"Stuff my dad had in his attic. I was hoping he had something on my mom's hijacking case but haven't come across anything." She reached for a stack of papers and handed them to him. "Found these, though."

He read the top of the first page. "Divorce papers."

"Yeah."

"Ouch."

"Very much ouch."

"They're not signed."

"No. She said basically that she was going to come home, give him one last chance, and if he didn't agree to go to counseling, she must have had these ready."

He sighed. "I'm sorry, Kristine."

"I am too." She pushed her phone toward him again. "Take a look at this picture. The map is too zoomed in to get a good location visually, but I think these are coordinates." She swiped to another picture. "These are blueprints. It looks like it's a house, but the longitude and latitude don't show anything but ocean. I may just not be able to blow it up big enough on my phone. It's somewhere off the coast of the Outer Banks, though. I tried googling it and didn't get much with that. And Google Earth just shows something that looks like an island."

"Weird."

"I thought so." She sighed. "And there's more."

"What?"

"I'm not sure. I don't want to make any accusations until I know for sure."

"Accusations about what?"

"It . . . I . . . I'll tell you soon. For now, I need to go see him and ask him about everything, because I'm just not sure." She shook her head. "I have no idea who this man I've called Dad is. Like no idea."

"Want some company?"

"No. I have one more box to go through, but I'll take it with me. I want to visit my mother's grave before it gets dark, then I'll head over to see my father to confront him with everything and see what he has to say about it all."

He hesitated. "Then at least let me go to your mother's grave with you?"

This time it was she who paused, then gave a slow nod. "Yeah, I'd like that, but I need to have a conversation with her, so don't think that's weird, okay?"

"Not at all. I won't even listen. I'll just be there if you need me. Come on, I'll follow you, then you can go to your dad's."

Thirty minutes later, she sat on her mother's grave, fingers tracing the letters of her mother's name. *Rachel M. Duncan. Mother and Wife. Missed forever. Loved for eternity.*

Andrew stood about five yards away, giving her the privacy she so obviously wanted. He had to look away, the scene almost too much for his heart to handle. When he looked back, she was on her knees, arms wrapped around her middle, forehead touching the headstone, tears dripping into the snow. Her shoulders shook with silent sobs. And he couldn't stay away another second. He went to her and wrapped her in his arms.

And heard her whispering.

"I'm sorry, Mom. I love you. I miss you. I need you. But mostly I'm sorry, Mom. So very sorry. I'm apologizing like you wanted me to. I wish I could take it all back. I'm so sorry."

"She knows, Kristine. She knows."

"I'm sorry, Mom," she said again, then turned her face into his chest and wept.

He had no idea how much time passed while he held her, but she finally stirred, kept her face turned from his, and used her mittens to wipe her face. She sniffed, and he dug a napkin from his coat pocket. "It's clean. I think."

She gave a strangled laugh and blew her nose, then tucked the wad into her own pocket. "Thanks."

"You okay?"

"Yeah." She looked up. "Sorry you had to witness that."

"It's okay. I'm glad I was here."

She smiled. "I am too." The smile slipped from her lips and she said, "Now I have to go see my dad."

"I can come with you to that too."

"No. Thanks for the offer, but this is something I have to do myself."

He didn't like it but could see she was serious. Resolute. She was going to face this demon by herself. Fight this battle alone. He nodded. "Okay, but I want to pray with you before you go."

"I'd love that."

TWENTY-THREE

Kristine sat in her car in her father's driveway and sucked down a shaky breath while her knuckles turned white with her grip on the steering wheel. Was she really going to do this? All the evidence ran through her head in a matter of seconds. Circumstantial evidence, but it all added up. The names cinched it for her. It was the only way everything made sense. Yes, she had a few questions, but those didn't matter in the grand scheme of things.

She knew what she knew.

Even if she didn't want to know it.

She glanced at the stack of folders on the seat beside her. Her father's cases. She'd gone through the last box after her breakdown on her mother's grave and now knew the connection between Marcus Brown, Erik Leary, Colleen Pearson, and the man who hijacked her mother's plane. She knew the person behind her own plane's hijacking. At least she thought she did.

What would happen if she was completely wrong?

She'd ruin everything.

Say words she could never take back. Again.

She wasn't wrong. She wanted to be, but she wasn't.

Was she?

She looked at the park across the street. The one her dad used to take her, Emily, and Ethan to when they were little. When he and her mom got along and loved each other. When they'd laughed and planned and looked at one another with love instead of the sadness and disappointment she'd come to recognize in her mother's eyes. The anger and . . . madness? . . . in her father's.

Years in the past that seemed like yesterday. The park was empty today thanks to the cold and the gray clouds that threatened rain, but those sunny spring days were forever etched in her memory as some of her favorite times. She should tell Andrew to come, be here. But she couldn't tell anyone her suspicions, because there was that small percentage she might be wrong.

She opened the car door, then shut it. Then grabbed the files from the passenger seat, opened the door again, and stepped out. She had to do this. *Oh please, God, tell me I'm doing the right thing. Give me the right words. Don't let me say something I'll regret.*

With that prayer whispering from her lips on repeat, she walked through the two-car garage, past her father's pickup truck and his car, up to the back door of her childhood home, and twisted the knob to step inside the kitchen. She inhaled. Sometimes she imagined she could still smell her mom and the light flowery perfume she used to wear.

This was dumb. She turned to leave and her shoes squeaked on the floor.

"Who's there?" her father called from down the hall.

Too late to change her mind now. "It's just me, Dad."

She hesitated, then pulled her phone from her pocket.

"Krissy? I'm in my office."

"Coming."

She sent a text to Andrew.

> If what I suspect is true, it might be better if you're here.

What do you suspect?

That my dad was behind both hijackings.

She waited.

I'm on the way. Don't do anything until I get there.

Don't call anyone or tell anyone. Not yet. I could be wrong.

K, it's too dangerous if you're right. It's not safe to confront him.

It's too late. He knows I'm here.

"Krissy? What are you waiting on?"

From the tone of his voice, he hadn't discovered she'd taken the boxes from the attic. She walked through the kitchen to the back of the house where his office was and found him sitting at his big oak desk, laptop open, camera next to him. He looked up. "What are you doing here?"

Kristine swallowed. "It was you, wasn't it?" *Please look like you don't know what I'm asking.*

He stilled and his face lost all expression. "What are you talking about?"

He knew.

"I said some things to Mom before her last flight, which makes me hesitant to ask what I feel like I need to ask."

"Quit talking in riddles. Spit it out."

"Fine. You paid someone to hijack Mom's plane, didn't you? You paid Marcus Brown to hijack mine but bought off Erik Leary to make sure the plane didn't actually crash, because in some weird way, you do love me and don't really want to see me dead, you just want to control me. It was you." She tossed the files on his desk. "You came across these men in your cases. Tabitha Brown thought her husband was cheating because of all of his doctor appointments that he was hiding from her. Erik Leary's boss was considering promoting him,

260

but someone he worked with reported the man had a gambling problem and you proved he did, then paid him to make sure *my* plane *didn't* crash. If it looked like it was going to, he was to rush in and save the day. Be a hero. That's what you put in your notes. And Mom's plane. You hired her hijacker to throw a scare into her, but one of the flight attendants panicked when he held a makeshift knife to her throat and she punched in the code to the cockpit. That's the story all of the text messages and phone calls from the passengers managed to put together. No one knows what happened after that because they never found the black box."

He simply watched her.

"Well?" She threw her hands in the air. "Don't just sit there. Tell me I'm wrong. Deny it and explain all this away. Please," she whispered. "Tell me I've got it all wrong."

"But you don't," he said. "I'm actually impressed you figured it all out."

For a moment, she couldn't speak. Couldn't move. Couldn't breathe. He was so calm about it all. Too calm. So she would have to be as well. "I have questions."

"Ask them."

"How did Tabitha Brown pay for your services? She didn't know it, but they had medical bills and not a penny extra to their name. Where did she get the money?"

"She was a charity case. She came to me and asked me what I charged, told me her story. I did a little investigating, planning to blackmail Brown with his cheating, only to find out he was dying. I promised her he wasn't cheating and that he would tell her everything in due time."

"Only you made him an offer he couldn't refuse instead."

"Yep."

"And Erik Leary? How did you meet him?"

Her father actually rolled his eyes. "We became acquainted when I had to buddy up to him to prove he had a gambling problem. Caught him on video. His boss wasn't happy and Leary was nose-diving toward broke. He was only there to keep the plane from crashing. He wasn't supposed to intervene unless the cockpit was breached."

"And how was he supposed to intervene? He's not law enforcement or trained to stop a hijacker."

"He's a martial arts expert. He assured me he could take care of any situation that arose. I had to believe him because I couldn't have the plane crash. That couldn't happen again. I made that clear."

"Wait a minute. Nothing came back on his credit report. No huge debts, he had money in his account, and so on. Nothing was flagged."

Her father snorted. "Of course not. The people he was gambling with don't exactly leave records for the police to find. Nevertheless, he was getting to the point that he was going to have to sell his house. He couldn't clean out his bank account without his wife catching on. He came to me for work. Asking for a job. He'd been in the military and could do surveillance. He needed a big payout. And he needed it fast. I realized he'd be perfect for what I needed. Again, just took a phone call."

"I . . . I . . ." She pulled in a ragged breath and tried to form her thoughts. "So why did he attack you at the hospital? I assume you lied and he wasn't after your wallet."

"Not a complete lie. He did want money. I just didn't have it in my wallet. I'd already paid him some, but he wanted more. I was in the middle of promising I'd get him some just to get him to leave when you showed up. Not that I was actually going to pay the man, but I was trying to buy some time. I would have gotten rid of him later, the thief."

Gotten rid of him? As in *kill* him? She had a sick feeling that's exactly what he meant. She wasn't about to ask, but he'd already killed her mother and a plane full of people, so what would one more dead person matter? "How did he know it was you?"

He rubbed his chin. "He recognized me from when I buddied up to him during the investigation I was conducting for his boss. The one that lost him the promotion. In the end, he was happy to take my money for a seat on the plane and try to provide a distraction so you'd mess up—be accused of negligence or something—and lose your job. But Leary didn't really hold up his end of the bargain with that, did he? No, I had to go and convince that woman's family she should sue you because she got hurt."

She gaped. Her brain was going to short-circuit any moment now. "Wait a minute. You're behind my suspension? What good does me being suspended do?"

"Hopefully give you time to see I was right. That you needed to find something safe, something that kept you at home. On the ground." He rubbed a hand down his cheek. "I was just doing this for you, Kristine. I only have your best interests at heart."

"You have no heart," she whispered.

He scowled and she bit down hard on the words she wanted to fling at him. "One more question. Why did you kill my mother?" The words came out on a choked sob, but she refused to let the tears fall. She could cry later.

"I didn't want to kill her. That wasn't the plan. But . . ." He stopped and breathed deeply through his nose. "She was going to leave me." His voice was surprisingly neutral. Soft. Deadly? "She was going to take you kids away from me."

"No. She wouldn't have. Not if you would have agreed to counseling."

He almost looked taken aback, then realization dawned. "You found the letter."

"Yeah."

He nodded and stood. "You took me by surprise when you came back in after leaving the other day. I overreacted." He frowned. "I don't do that very often. Nevertheless, I should have hidden it better, but I didn't take you for a snoop."

"I learned from one of the best."

He ignored her dig. "How long have you had it?"

"For just about a day."

"Ah. You came in when I was working a case."

"Yes. I also found all the boxes of Mom's that you said you tossed.

Made me wonder what else I'll find once I finish going through those. I did find something interesting. You have some property off the Outer Banks?"

"You shouldn't go looking in places you have no business snooping into." His eyes darkened, and for a moment, she was glad she brought her gun. If he'd been willing to kill her mother, would he kill her too? She shoved the terrifying thought away. He glanced down, then back, the black look gone. "You want to know everything, I see."

Did she? "I . . . yes. Including what you did with the letter she left for me."

"I burned it."

Her heart squeezed. Had he really? Or was he lying again?

"I found the divorce papers," he said. "About two months before that flight. One she wasn't even supposed to be on. I didn't think she'd have the guts to actually go see a lawyer and have papers drawn up, but she proved me wrong." He shrugged. "I couldn't let that happen."

"So you planned a *hijacking*?" Who did that? Who planned *two*? Her father, apparently.

He huffed. "It wasn't supposed to go down that way. Yours went exactly like it was supposed to. Pretty much."

"*Mine?*" He waved a hand as though everything was of no consequence and she let it go. It wouldn't make any sense to belabor the point. "Tell me about Mom's."

He shook his head. "She wasn't supposed to die. She was *never* supposed to die. None of them were. I was just losing control and needed her to come to her senses and realize that she was supposed to stay home with you kids and stop traipsing around the world on a stupid plane. When I found the divorce papers, I lost it. Started planning right then and there. I knew there would be a flight coming up and had everything ready so all I had to do was make a phone call. I came up with the perfect plan and found the right person to help me carry it through. It was just a matter of timing." He swallowed hard. "Then two months later, we had that fight, she left the letter and took that last-minute flight"—he frowned—"and I made the call."

Kristine gaped. Then snapped her mouth shut. "I . . . I almost can't even compute what I'm hearing. You loved Mom." A pause. "Didn't you?"

"Of course. Why do you think I was doing whatever it took to keep her home?"

"That's . . . that's not love. That's obsession or wanting to control, but that's definitely not love." She hesitated. "Do you even know what love is?"

He sighed and scrubbed a hand down his cheek. "Of course I do. I love you kids. Which is why I'm always checking up on you and making sure you stay safe. Doing whatever it takes to keep you that way!"

"But . . . a hijacking!" She blinked, wondering if he was a psychopath. It almost sounded like it. Which meant she could be in some serious danger. She wanted to scoff at the thought but couldn't. And she still had questions. "That was you in the Brown home, wasn't it?"

He nodded. "I went looking for the money. He wasn't supposed to say a word about being hired to do that job. Idiot. So, I wanted my money back. Couldn't find it, though. Then you showed up and I had to get out of there before you . . ." He shrugged.

"Before I recognized you." She fell silent and simply let her brain spin. "And the tattoo you told Marcus Brown to get? What was that?"

"Just a way to confuse things. Throw the investigation off." He smiled. "And it worked."

Kristine rubbed her eyes, thinking about how she was going to get away from him. She didn't really see him letting her leave. Not with everything she knew. He could deny it, of course, but a simple investigation into him would most likely unearth the evidence needed to put him away for a long time.

"And I did love your mother," he said. "Very much."

Love her or want to control her? "Where did you meet Mom?" she asked.

"On a flight. You know that."

"Exactly. Doing something she loved doing. Why would you want to take that away from her?"

"Because she was supposed to love me more! *Us* more."

Psychopath was becoming more of a possibility. Or at least antisocial personality disorder. "So you argued. And when you found the divorce papers, you decided to kill her. Along with all those innocent people on the plane with her." She was going to puke.

"No. No, no, no. It wasn't supposed to be like that. I don't know what happened, but he was never supposed to get into the cockpit."

"But he did. And the plane crashed. And they all died. Because of you."

He narrowed his eyes. "No, not because of me. Because of *her*. If she'd just done what I told her, none of that would have happened."

Kristine froze as those words echoed in her mind. Where had she heard him say that before?

With Emily. In the hospital.

Now she knew the answer to her earlier question. He'd kill her without blinking.

She backed up and his gaze sharpened.

"I have to go," she said. "Andrew and the others are expecting me. I need to process all of this. Think about things I almost can't even understand."

He stepped around from behind his desk, gun in his hand. He aimed it at her. "No, I don't think you're going anywhere. You've disobeyed me over and over and over with no consequences. But now there has to be some and I know exactly what those are. You've just moved the timetable up a little bit."

Kristine spun and ran, pulling her phone from her pocket. Something slammed into her right shoulder and a sharp pain radiated from the hit, sending her to her knees next to the kitchen door.

Her muscles went sluggish. She'd been hit with a drug, not a bullet. Which meant time was short.

She shoved the phone into her sock and hiking boot and pulled her pants leg over it.

Everything slowed.

Her father appeared in front of her and she had no way to fight him. Now she just wanted to sleep.

"Come on, Krissy-girl. Time for us to fly the friendly skies."

"Wha—?"

He laughed. "Don't worry. I'm going to take care of you. Very good care of you. So good you'll never have to worry about anything ever again. And I'll never be lonely again. Emily is next." He raked a hand down his face and blew out a sigh. "Thank goodness she didn't die in that wreck. I never meant for her to be hurt, you know. That idiot Dana was going way too fast." The familiar anger tinged with the mental instability that had always been there flared in his eyes, and Kristine wanted to weep. "But that's neither here nor there. It's water under the bridge. Then it will be Ethan's turn. I'll have to figure out how to get him incapacitated. Shouldn't be too hard. At least he's extended his stay and isn't leaving so quickly."

"No . . ." Why did her voice echo in her head? "He left yesterday." Didn't he?

He picked her up, carried her to his car, and slid her in the back seat. Then patted her down. "Where's your phone?"

"Car . . ." She struggled to sit upright, but it was like fighting quicksand.

"Then it can stay there. Be a good girl and stay put until I get back. I have to hide your vehicle." He pulled back and shut the door.

The darkness was swirling, just beyond her reach. It took every ounce of concentration, but she managed to get her phone and type a message to Andrew. The driver's door opened and she hit send before her fingers lost strength, and she closed her eyes. The last thing she heard was the device bouncing on the floorboard.

ANDREW COULDN'T DO IT. He couldn't let her handle this by herself. Whatever this was. But she'd obviously lost sleep over it and was having a tough time dealing with it. He'd told her he was on the way to her father's, and she wasn't answering his texts.

He tapped the wheel while he drove. So why wouldn't she respond? Unless she'd been right and her father had—

His phone pinged. Kristine sharing her location.

> 911 help follow me Dad bad hired hijacker.
> Drugged me. Don't call follo—

What kind of message was that?

A desperate cry for help for sure. She was in trouble and the last place she'd been was her father's. Her father had hired the hijacker? Could that possibly be what she meant?

He pulled over and sent a group text to everyone. It was faster than calling.

> Kristine's in trouble. She went to see her dad, but I got this text.

He copied and pasted it.

> Someone tell me what this means.

She was in trouble. He knew it in his gut. Andrew read the message again. *Follow me.* He could do that. He knew exactly where she was and the little dot was moving toward Lake City, so Andrew simply watched it. When it turned off the main road about ten miles from his location, he made a U-turn and headed after her.

He called Nathan, who answered on the first ring. "I'm following her. She sent me a location ping on her phone and I'm headed after her."

"Can you tell what the destination is?"

"Not yet, but they're on the outskirts of Lake City. What's there?"

"Um, a couple of restaurants, housing developments, a few commercial properties, the airport, and . . . I don't know. Keep following her and reporting in your location. I'll head in that direction too."

"I'll just do the same thing she did and ping you my location. You can follow me while I'm following her."

"Perfect."

Andrew did his best to close in on the vehicle containing Kristine, but it was in a hurry and going fast. And then it stopped at the airport and he was still about seven minutes out.

He pressed the gas.

A lot could happen in seven minutes.

TWENTY-FOUR

Kristine groaned. Where was the train that hit her? Twice. Her head was going to explode if she didn't find some Motrin. But she couldn't seem to move.

The roar of an engine reached her. She knew that sound. A plane. Wait. What? How—

Her father.

She was in one of the reclining seats and lying on her side. She tried to sit up, but the nausea was intense. "Gonna be sick," she mumbled just in case anyone was listening.

"Bathroom's right behind you."

She lay for a moment trying not to heave. There was no way she could get up and make it to the bathroom.

A cold cloth settled across her throat, then a second one on her forehead and that helped. Her stomach settled slightly.

"There's a bowl next to you if you need it, but I recommend making it to the bathroom."

She blinked and the ceiling came into focus. Yep, definitely a plane.

She didn't answer. Didn't move. And thankfully, didn't hurl. The feeling passed, but she was desperately thirsty. As though he read her mind, he pressed a bottle of water into her hand. She drank in sips, making sure the liquid was going to stay put. It did and now she wanted to close her eyes and go back to sleep.

But since she seriously believed her father was going to kill her, that wasn't happening. She just needed to figure out what the plan was, and if he was going to kill her, why was she on a plane? Was he going to drop her out of the aircraft with a faulty parachute so her death could be ruled an accident?

But talking required more effort than she had at the moment, so she stayed silent.

One other thing registered. They weren't moving.

She was on a plane, but they were still on the ground.

Biting off a groan, she turned her aching head to look out the window. It was dark outside. They were on the tarmac. The engine was running but the pilot wasn't in the seat.

Kristine rolled her head once more to see her father sitting in the chair across from her, reading his iPad like he was sitting at the local café with all the time in the world on his hands. "Where are we going?"

"To my own little hideaway where we can live out the rest of our days in peace."

Okay, she was done talking. She had to figure out a way to get off this plane. The steps were down, the gun wasn't in sight, so she could just walk off, right?

She started to stand and something clanked. She pulled with her right foot and found she was chained to the table post. Long enough to reach the bathroom behind her, but she wasn't going anywhere else until he let her or she managed to get out of the shackle around her ankle. "You're sick," she whispered.

He raised a brow. "We'll have to work on your manners."

"Dad, you seriously can't think you'll get away with this."

"I will. And as soon as Emily's released from the hospital, she'll be joining you. And eventually Ethan."

"How can you afford all this?"

"Easy. Your mother's life insurance paid out two million, and I made some wise investments over the past few years. I live simply but comfortably. And you will too." He set aside his iPad and leaned toward her. "The island is very nice. I've built a home there where you'll have your own private suite. It's filled with books and games and various ways to entertain yourself. And when Emily and Ethan get there, it will be even better. We'll be a happy family once more."

He was living in some twisted fantasy world, and she hadn't recognized how much he needed help.

He glanced at his watch. "Vinny should be here soon and we'll be on our way."

"People will look for me."

"I'm sure, but they won't find you. Especially since your phone is now smashed to bits in the men's bathroom with no way to still track you."

His icy certainty chilled her to the bone. "Dad, you were a cop. You arrested people for kidnapping and other bad stuff. Do you not see that you're doing the exact same thing you put people in prison for?"

He grunted. "It's not the same at all. I'm simply protecting my kids from a world gone mad."

"No, by doing this, you're a *part* of that world gone mad. Please, it's not too late to stop this and get help."

He slapped a hand on the table. "Shut up. You say one more thing like that and I'll assume you're past the point of redemption." He pulled out his phone and tapped the screen. "Stupid pilot," he muttered. "What's taking him so long?"

She sat back. There was no reasoning with him. None. And that was downright terrifying. So, since she couldn't talk sense into him and she had no idea if Andrew had gotten her message, she had to find a way to get off this plane before it took off.

ANDREW PULLED INTO the small airport's parking lot and ran inside the hangar. There was one plane on the tarmac, engine running.

A man hurried toward it and Andrew guessed he was the pilot. He went after him, using his badge to get past security. "Hey, hold up a second," he called to the pilot.

The man glanced back, his eyes went wide, and he broke into a jog to hit the steps. Andrew ran as fast as he could and managed to jump onto the bottom step just as it started to retract into the plane. He bolted up them, stumbled, and fell into the plane with a grunt.

"Andrew!"

Kristine's cry mobilized him and he rolled to his knees, only to freeze when he found himself facing the barrel end of a gun. The hand attached to the weapon belonged to Kristine's father. The pilot stood at the entrance to the cockpit gawking at both of them.

"What do you think you're doing?" her father demanded.

Andrew rose to his feet, hands held so the man could see them. "I wasn't sure at first. It's crystal clear now."

The man gestured with the gun. "Sit down, and if you make me mad, I'll shoot Kristine."

Andrew walked into the cabin and took the seat next to Kristine. Her body heat soaked into him and he gazed at her. "Got your message. Backup's on the way." He made sure to speak loud enough that her father heard. Andrew looked out the window to see blue lights flashing in the darkness. Talk about perfect timing. His hand itched to go for his gun.

Greg saw the approaching law enforcement and looked at the pilot. "This is your fault. You took too long to get us going! Get this thing in the air. Now."

"But—"

"Do it or I shoot one of them. Understand? And if that doesn't work, I'll make sure you're dead before I'm caught. But if you get me to Norfolk safely, I'll make sure there's a bonus in it for you."

The pilot didn't say another word. He went to the cockpit and took his seat, put his headphones on, and started taxiing. Seconds later, they were in the air.

Greg looked at Andrew and Kristine. "Now, we have about an hour and fifteen minutes to figure out how this is going to play out." He looked at Andrew. "Give me your weapon and don't play dumb. Give it to me or Kristine will suffer."

Andrew slid his gun across the table to the man, who took it and shoved it into his waistband. Then he sighed and frowned. "I don't think having you along will be beneficial to what I need to happen with my children, so you'll have to be disposed of."

Andrew blinked. "Disposed of. Like I'm not a living, breathing human? Like I'm the trash you need to take out?"

"No, of course not. It's all regrettable, of course, but you know too much, and you and I both know that you're going to do whatever it takes to bring me in."

"What if I said a life with Kristine was worth more than putting you away?"

Greg paused, tilted his head as though he didn't quite know what to make of that question. "You mean if I let you two live, you'll forget about all of this? That I was in part responsible for an entire planeload of deaths? And almost was again?"

Andrew shot a look at Kristine, and white lines around her mouth told him how hard she was biting her tongue. Andrew searched for words while realization dawned for Greg.

"Oh, you didn't know." He shot an approving look at Kristine. "You didn't tell him. Interesting."

"Only because I didn't have a chance," she shot back.

The approval darkened, but he stilled, listened, then scowled. "We're going down. Why are we descending?" His yell reverberated off the cabin walls and he turned slightly so he could still keep Andrew and Kristine in his line of sight, but hollered to the pilot, "What are you doing?" He glanced out the window and cursed. "We're going the wrong way! Don't you dare land this plane back in Lake City!"

"I've been ordered to do so, sir."

"No!" He slid out of the seat and aimed his gun at the pilot. "I'd rather be dead than face prison!" He pulled the trigger just as Andrew launched himself at him. Greg turned the weapon back toward Andrew, but it was too late. Andrew moved in, close enough to hit the man in the Adam's apple with the palm of his hand. Greg gagged, lost his grip on the gun, and clutched his throat.

Andrew whipped out his cuffs and handcuffed the man to the seat leg. He could stay on the floor.

"Andrew, get me loose. Now!"

Kristine's frantic cry whipped him around. "What?"

"Never mind. Go hit the autopilot switch or we're going to crash!"

It registered that they were going down pretty fast. He ran to the pilot, who was slumped over the controls, blood pouring from a wound in his back. "Where is it?"

"I don't know! I'm not familiar with this—"

"Found it." He flipped the switch and the plane slowed, then leveled out. He checked the pilot and found a pulse. The man was just unconscious. He'd hit his head on the window when the bullet slammed into him. He pulled him out of the seat and into the cabin, where he laid him on the floor. Then he treated the wound as best he could, packing it with one of the blankets in the overhead bin.

"Hang on, buddy, we'll get you help as soon as possible." He returned to Kristine. "You're going to have to fly this plane."

TWENTY-FIVE

Kristine nodded, her face white. "That's already occurred to me, but you're going to have to get me loose first."

He paused. "I could shoot it off, but I don't want to risk another bullet. There's an axe on board somewhere. Where do I find it?"

"Cockpit. Look for the toolbox." She moved next to her glaring father, who'd regained his breath, and started checking his pockets. He fought her with his free hand and she punched him in the temple.

He flinched back and went still, his shock evident.

She stared at him. "Move again and no one will blame me if I go find a knife and slit your throat." She wouldn't do that, of course, but wanted him to believe she would. He stayed still, jaw tight, bruise forming where her fist had connected. Her hand throbbed and she honestly didn't care. Her left hand closed around his key ring. "Never mind. Found the key."

In seconds, she was loose and had the ankle cuff around her father's leg. No sense in taking any chances. Then she went to the cockpit and slid into the pilot's seat. She put the headphones on and connected with the control tower. Nausea swirled once more in her empty stomach. She looked back at Andrew. "And this is why you always have two pilots on board."

"This plane doesn't require it."

"I know."

"And besides, there are two pilots. You and the wounded guy. We need to get him to a hospital as soon as possible."

"If he would wake up, that would be a lot easier."

"You can do this."

Kristine pulled in a steadying breath and nodded. "Right." Her heart pounded and she gripped the control stick. "Right. And I'll have someone talking me down too. Okay, here we go." The hum of the engine was steady. That was good, but the sky pressed down on her. At least the gray clouds hadn't released their bounty. "Please, God, don't let it rain."

"Amen," Andrew whispered.

She turned her attention to the mic while Andrew checked on the pilot and her suspiciously silent father. *Ignore them. Andrew's got them covered.*

She wiped her sweaty palms on her jeans and returned her hands to the stick. The altimeter was spinning too fast and the horizon seemed a little bouncy, but they were still in the air. Her mind flashed to her lessons. Her instructor's voice in her ear. *"Keep your wings level. Trust your instruments and stay calm."* Right. Stay calm. No problem.

She spoke into the headset. "Control, this is N763Delta. Pilot has been shot and is unconscious. Two other passengers on board in addition to myself. I do have some training but am going to need help landing this craft."

The silence that followed was an eternity, with her heart still pounding out a frantic rhythm in her ears.

Finally, the radio crackled. "N763Delta, this is Lake City Control. We're here. Stay calm and we'll get you on the ground safely. What's your current altitude?"

Kristine glanced at the altimeter. "Five thousand feet. And falling. I'm going down too fast."

"Glad you recognize that. We need to reduce your speed. Ease back on the stick."

She obeyed and let out another breath of relief when the plane responded like it was supposed to. She glanced at Andrew, and he gave her a thumbs-up. He looked like she was getting ready to pull up to the nearest restaurant and let him out to get a table. Calm, cool, and completely confident that she could do this.

"Done."

"Good. We've got you on the radar. You're doing great. Nice and level. Line up with the runway you should be seeing in just a few seconds."

The ground was close and getting closer, but she'd done this before. Not with this aircraft, but it was all the same. Her training finally kicked in and she spotted the runway.

The first raindrop hit the windshield and she tensed. "No, God, please."

"You're doing great," the voice said. "You're perfectly lined up with the runway. All you have to do is guide her in."

Right. Easy peasy.

She squinted through the windshield and turned on the wipers. "Coming in," she said. "Reducing altitude to two thousand feet, soon to be a thousand."

"Perfect."

A scuffling sound made her glance back, and she saw Andrew lifting the pilot. "I'm going to get this guy into a seat and buckled," he said.

"Yeah. Do that."

He did so and Kristine heard him say, "Hang in there. We're real close to getting you help."

The runway grew larger. She could do this. Three ambulances, firetrucks, and law enforcement were on the side of the strip, ready to bolt into action as soon as she brought the plane to a stop.

"You got this," Andrew said. He slid into the seat beside her and buckled his seat belt.

Her father was still shackled and lay on the floor. If something happened, he would be safe enough.

"All right, at five hundred feet cut power and flare the plane."

"Got it."

The plane dipped lower, the runway rushing up to meet her. In her hyperalert state, she was aware of every sound, every vibration in the controls. Her world had shrunk to the strip of concrete in front of her.

"Five hundred feet," she said. "Here we go." She pulled back and the plane began to glide. The runway was right there. She kept her movements steady and sure.

"Flaring now," she said. The rain came down harder, but she had this. Exhilaration flared too.

"Excellent. I was just getting ready to tell you to do that."

She pulled back, the nose lifted, and the wheels touched the ground with a soft thud, bounced, then settled. She guided the plane down the runway while her pulse pounded and tears clouded her vision. The wipers cleared the way and she came to a gentle stop.

For a moment, everything was silent, then Andrew was there, unbuckling her and pulling her out of the seat. "You did it, Kristine. You really did it."

She looked up and smiled. "I did. I really did." She pulled the curtain of the cockpit closed, wanting complete and total privacy at the moment. She was so full of conflicting feelings. Gratitude they were alive. Utter grief at her father's betrayal and the kind of man he was. But one thing she was sure of was Andrew, and she wanted more. "This may be a wildly inappropriate thing to ask right now, but I just—" She closed her eyes, opened them. "Can you kiss me now?" For some reason, she just needed him to. She needed the connection, the reassurance that everything was going to be all right. That she and her siblings would heal.

He narrowed his eyes, the tender expression saying he understood, and leaned over to cover her lips with his. The kiss lasted a full minute and still wasn't long enough. She clung to him, a sweet warmth flooding her and hope blossoming in the vicinity of her heart. The banging on the side of the plane pulled them apart and she gazed up at him. "This is so counting as my first solo flight."

IT TOOK THE NEXT SEVERAL HOURS to get everything sorted. The pilot was at the hospital. He'd lost a lot of blood, but at least he was alive.

Kristine was still talking with one of the special agents assigned to their case—she'd been kidnapped whether she wanted to admit it or not—and Andrew had filled in the other one. He now stood in the hallway of the local police station waiting for her to come out of the interrogation room. They'd been questioned separately, which was protocol. But now all he wanted was to wrap her in a tight hug and possibly kiss her again.

Make that definitely kiss her again. And hold her for a million years. There was no denying his feelings at this point, even if he wasn't quite sure how he got here after battling them for so long. Battling and losing. Wishy-washy was the term for it. He didn't want to be wishy-washy any longer. He wanted to leave the past where it belonged—in the past. He had a future, and it was time to look toward it instead of over his shoulder.

"Andrew?"

He lifted his head to see Nathan making his way toward him. Hank walked behind him.

Andrew straightened and went to hug his friends, who were more like brothers. "Dude," Hank said, his voice gruff. "Thought you were a goner there for a while."

"I never doubted all would work out well." Okay, maybe there'd been a moment or two, but . . . "Kristine is still telling her story. We can find a seat that allows me to watch for her."

"At the end of the hallway," Nathan said. "We can pull a table over. Gonna have to make more room for the rest of the crew on their way here."

Once they were seated with Andrew facing the hallway, he looked at Hank. "Thought you were leaving."

"I was, but I'm still on the group text and all these messages were coming in about all the drama going down, so I couldn't just take off quite so fast."

"Thanks, man," Andrew said. "And you get to stay on the loop if you want."

"I'd like that, but probably not a good idea."

"Yeah, I know. I'll get another burner so we can stay in touch."

"Perfect."

Kenzie walked through the double glass doors on the other side of the security wall, followed by Jesslyn, Lainie, Tate, and Steph. Once they were cleared to enter the main area, they made their way to the table.

"Don't think we're all going to fit here," Lainie said. Cole and James were still with Kristine's father and would probably be tied up with him for a while. His lawyer had met them at the station.

The door opened and Kristine stepped out, spotted them at the end of the hallway, and headed toward them. She looked wiped out and Andrew looked at the others. "Rendezvous later?"

They took the hint, and even though some had just arrived, they gave Kristine their supportive hugs and disappeared, leaving Andrew to pull her close and breathe in the scent that was all her.

"I want a shower and a bed. And some food."

"In that order or . . . ?"

"Food on the way to the hospital."

"To tell Emily and Ethan before they see the news?"

"Exactly."

"How's your dad?"

"I don't know. I can't think about him at the moment."

"Want some company?"

"Yes." She turned into him, rested her cheek on his chest, and hugged him tight. "Thank you, Andrew."

"Absolutely."

"On a happier note, my supervisor texted while I was giving my statement and said that I've been found not guilty of any kind of misconduct on the flight. He said many passengers spoke on my behalf and the video footage supported it all. My suspension has been lifted and I can go back to work as soon as I'm ready."

"I'm so glad."

"Me too." She paused. "I don't think I'll be ready for a couple of days."

"I think that's understandable."

The ride to the hospital was silent, and Andrew figured she was running different conversation scenarios through her head about how to explain everything to Emily. In the end, she'd probably say something entirely different. They made their way to Emily's room.

Andrew stopped at the door. "Want me to wait out here?"

"No, come on in. It's okay. You were there. You can answer any questions I might not be able to."

"After you then."

They knocked and entered to find Emily, Ethan, and their aunt Wendy playing a game of cards. The television was off, thank goodness.

Emily took one look at Kristine and said, "What's wrong?"

"You guys are up late."

"I couldn't sleep," Emily said, "so I figured no one else should either." She frowned. "Now, what is it? I can see something's going on."

Kristine sighed. "Ethan, I'm glad you and Aunt Wendy are still here." She nodded to Emily. "You're right. There's something I need to tell you before you see it on the news, and it's going to be hard to hear. But just know that we're in this together and we'll get through it together."

Emily and Ethan exchanged a glance and Aunt Wendy frowned.

"What is it?" Emily asked.

For the next thirty minutes, Kristine talked and Emily, Ethan, and their aunt sat in stunned silence punctuated with tears and shocked gasps.

After several rounds of hugs and two boxes of tissues, Emily fell asleep, and Andrew and Kristine found themselves back out in the hall. He took her hand. "Wanna get some coffee at the all-night diner around the corner?"

She yawned. "Okay, as long as it's decaf, although I don't think a gallon of the caffeinated stuff will stop me from sleeping."

"I won't keep you long."

She curved her hand into the crook of his elbow. "I don't mind. I like being with you."

He pulled away and wrapped his arm around her shoulder to tuck her close. "And I like being with you." He stopped walking and turned her toward him. "More than I even know how to express. I was terrified to tell you about what happened to Isaac Mason. But you didn't push me away. You offered me comfort. When my parents' place was broken into by Tyler Mason to get me out in the open so he could follow me, you were there to help. You came looking for me—"

"Just like you came looking for me," she said, "when I desperately needed someone to find me."

"We make a good team, Kristine. If you're willing, I want to see where this leads. The truth is, I've not been interested in anyone like I am you. I haven't let myself. Being undercover and falling in love don't mix well."

"I'd think not."

They hurried to the car and soon found themselves outside the diner.

"I'm not going back under," he said, his hand on the door.

"And that makes me glad. I know there's a need for it and someone has to do it, but I'm not gonna lie, I'm glad it's not going to be you."

"And I had a chance to plead some with God. About you. About the future. About everything. I think he's brought us through this, to this point in time, for a reason. I want to investigate that further."

She stood on tiptoe and lightly brushed her lips with his. "That's one investigation I intend to be fully involved in."

He grinned, then the wind whipped across the back of his neck and he shivered. "And I want to finish this in the warmth of the diner."

She laughed and they hurried to find a booth in the back that offered a modicum of privacy. She slid across and he slipped in beside her.

They ordered and she yawned again. Remorse hit him. "Aw, Kristine, I should take you home and let you get some sleep."

"No, no. I'm fine. I'd rather be here with you. All I'll dream about is crashing a plane."

"But you landed it. Beautifully, I might add."

"I know, but I was terrified I'd crash, so I'll dream I crashed it."

He shook his head, then reached for her hands. "Are you okay? Tell me what I can do."

She sighed and bit her lip, then blinked back tears. "No, I'm not okay," she said, "but being with you makes me a lot more okay than I would be if you weren't with me."

"Then I wouldn't want to be anywhere else. But there's something else going on. What is it?"

"I still haven't found my mom's letter to me. Dad said he burned it. Maybe he really did."

"I'm so sorry."

She shrugged. "I would love to have it, of course, but seeing the one she wrote my dad is comfort enough. I'm grateful for it."

"You've been through every single paper in the house?"

"Pretty much." She smiled. "I'm going to be okay, Andrew. In time."

"I know. I believe so too. And time is one thing we both have. As long as God allows anyway."

"I'm okay with that. Now change the subject, please."

"Sure. Where do you want to go on our first date?"

"Second," she said with a laugh. "Because I don't have my wallet with me so you're going to have to buy my dinner. And I want cheesecake."

"Cheesecake. Of course. Two slices?"

She sighed and batted her lashes at him. "I may love you."

His heart stuttered, but he simply smiled. "That's the plan." He leaned down and kissed her, long and sweet and solid.

She blew out a low breath when he lifted his head. "Honestly, that's about got cheesecake beat."

"About?"

She shrugged and snuggled closer. "You'll just need to keep working on it."

He laughed. "Happy to oblige."

TWENTY-SIX

TWO AND A HALF MONTHS LATER
NEW YEAR'S EVE

Kristine, Jesslyn, Lainie, and Steph stood around a glowing Kenzie and helped her get her bridal veil pinned to her upswept hair. Once it was finished, they stepped back, and Kristine swallowed a rush of tears at her friend's beauty.

Kenzie's ninety-eight-year-old Grandma Betsy sat in the plush wingback chair overseeing everything, her aged hands resting on the top of her cane. Tears sparkled in her eyes. "Darling, I don't think I've seen a more stunning bride."

Kenzie went to her grandmother and carefully knelt in front of the woman. "You did when you looked in the mirror all those years ago. Trust me. I saw your wedding pictures."

Grandma Betsy laughed, a lovely, light chuckle that Kristine wanted to lean into. "I was sure a looker in those days." She sighed. "I miss my George every day, but what a reunion it's going to be in heaven one day. Probably pretty soon too."

"Not too soon, please," Kristine said. "We like having you here." She hoped the woman would still be around for her wedding, because she just plain wanted her there. Betsy winked at her and Kristine leaned over to give her hand a gentle squeeze.

Kenzie rose, pulled in a deep breath, and let it out slowly. "It's about time, don't you think?"

Kristine and the others gathered around her with Grandma Betsy in the middle. "Ready for a prayer?"

"Yes. Always."

One by one, they each said a short but heartfelt prayer for Kenzie and Cole, and Kristine finished with, "Lord, you're in the business of doing amazing work, and the fact that you brought Kenzie and Cole together proves you're still in the miracle business as well." Everyone chuckled. "Seriously, we pray for this day when they pledge their love before you and friends and family. May they always keep their eyes on you, depending on you to lead them wherever you would have them be. And to always put the other before themselves. Hold them tight, and thank you for letting us be a part of their lives and this very special day. Amen."

"Amen," the others echoed.

They made their way to the sanctuary of the newly built Lake City Community Church. It had been the target of an arson, but the church body had come together to rebuild and were now stronger than ever. She followed the bridal party to the back of the church with Kenzie in the lead. Kenzie's father wheeled his wheelchair over to her and then stood.

Kenzie gasped. "Dad?"

"I've been working on this since your engagement. I can make it down the aisle without falling but will have to sit down after I hand you off."

Kristine bit her lip on a smile. Leave it to Mr. King to use a football term.

Kenzie laughed and swiped a tear. "That's perfect. The most wonderful wedding gift a girl could get." Kenzie's brothers gathered around her and gave her one last hug before lining up next to the bridesmaid they'd escort.

For a moment, Kristine grieved that her father wouldn't walk her down the aisle. That he wasn't going to be a part of her life or her children's lives. That the legacy he left wasn't honorable or good. Then she lifted her chin. It might not be what she wanted, but she could use it to teach her children what not to do. She and her husband would teach them to have integrity and be honorable, God-fearing, God-loving people. If her father would repent and express remorse for his actions, she'd find a way to be a part of his life. All she could do was work on forgiving him so she didn't become bitter and filled with a hate that was never far away. But that was a choice. And she was choosing to be free of him and his hold on her life.

Andrew stepped up beside her. He was a handsome man on any given day, but today he took her breath away. The good thing was, she had a very good idea of who the father of her children would be and wasn't worried one bit about how they'd turn out.

He leaned over. "You're stunning, Kristine Duncan. You take my breath away."

She smirked. "Glad to know it's mutual."

He grinned and she took his arm. The music started, and when it was their turn, they headed down the aisle together side by side. Cole stood at the altar, his eyes riveted on the back of the church, searching for the woman he loved. Kristine smiled. The next time she walked down the aisle, she planned to be in a white dress with Andrew waiting for her. The thought thrilled her, pushing away any sadness that might want to intrude with thoughts of her father. At the front of the church, she took her place on the second step and turned. The doors opened once more, and Kenzie, on her father's arm, took the first steps toward a new life.

Thirty minutes later, they were downstairs in the large room for the reception, and Andrew pulled Kristine aside, tilted her chin, and kissed her.

She blinked up at him. "You know I never mind you kissing me, but what was that for?"

"I love you, Kristine. And I'm not just saying that because of where we are or that I've been swept up in all of the wedding excitement. As we were going through this weekend with the bachelor party and all the wedding stuff, I kept watching Cole and he was so chill. He was completely confident and excited for this day. No doubts. No nerves. Just some impatience for the day to get here."

"Kenzie's been the same."

"And it made me think about everything that's happened, that I could have so easily lost out on what's important. That I don't want fear of getting hurt to rule me. Right now everything is working out and that's great. Mom and Dad are happy, Corey's heading into the witness protection program and going to testify against a really bad guy the FBI has been after for a long time, my brothers are doing great. Life is good. I even checked on Tabitha Brown and her kids, and they've been adopted by their church community and everyone is thriving. But I know that's not a guarantee there won't be hard times in the future. *Time* isn't guaranteed. All we have is what's in front of us. A limited amount of time on this earth. And I'm ready to spend it with you." He cleared his throat. "So, that's where I am with how I feel about you. No doubts. No nerves. Just impatience to tell you that I love you."

She swallowed back the tears that were surfacing, so touched by his honesty and vulnerability that she almost didn't have room in her heart to feel it, but she didn't hesitate in her response. "I love you too, Andrew. Everything you said, I feel the same."

He nodded and blinked away the tears that had appeared for a brief moment. "Good. That's really good."

She grinned. "I'll love you even more if you take me over to the dessert table."

"They have cheesecake?"

"Five different kinds."

"You're going to try them all, aren't you?"

"Absolutely. And so are you."

He kissed her again. "Okay then, let's go."

Yep, he loved her. She gazed up at him. And she loved him. Right now, in this moment, all was right in her world and she sent up a prayer of gratitude to the one who made it all possible.

Read on for a sneak peek
at the first book in
Lynette Eason's new series.

Available Summer 2026.

ONE

FBI Special Agent Collin Sullivan gripped the wheel and glanced in the rearview mirror once more. The silver sedan was still there, following at a discreet distance, but it was enough to set his teeth on edge.

His partner, Piper Whitaker, sat in the passenger seat, her jaw set, brow furrowed. She shot him a quick glance. "You see it too?"

"Yeah."

"See what?" Ollie Callahan, a fourteen-year-old foster child and murder witness, had hearing like a bat. Sully thought she was asleep. "The car behind us?"

No sense in lying. "Yes. You recognize it?"

"I can't really see it very well. It's too far back." She gazed out the rear window.

"Turn around," Sully said. "Don't let him know you've seen him."

"Oh. Sorry." She faced front again and lowered her gaze to her hands, but not before he caught the sheen of tears in her eyes.

Remorse kicked him. "It's okay. I could have prefaced my question with 'Don't turn around.'" The teen was a good kid, as far as he could tell. She'd just been in the wrong place at the wrong time. And it was his and Piper's responsibility to make sure nothing happened to her.

Like death.

A bullet pinged off the back bumper. Ollie screamed and flattened herself against the seat, her seat belt still around her. Piper pulled her weapon and rolled her window down while Sully pressed the gas, the digital speedometer inching up past sixty, then seventy. Tennessee's frigid temperatures whooshed through the window. The poor heater had been fighting a losing battle almost since he'd cranked the vehicle at six o'clock this morning.

"There's two of them now," Piper said. "Black SUV coming up on the left. Silver sedan hanging back on the right. Passenger of the SUV is the one who fired the weapon."

"Hold on."

Sully pressed the accelerator, and the engine roared as they wound through the rolling farmland dotted with patches of dense woods. The Smoky Mountains loomed in the distance. He glanced back at Ollie. She lay still on the seat, quiet as a mouse.

The road narrowed. Weathered fence posts whipped past. Barren cornfields offered no cover or escape. His hands tightened on the wheel while his brain searched for options.

Broken Chains Ranch was less than ten miles ahead, but they'd never make it before their pursuers caught them. And besides, he didn't want to lead the bad guys right to his cousin's doorstep.

Another shot took out the side mirror.

Ollie screamed but stayed put.

Piper took careful aim and fired.

Missed.

Sully winced. She was a good shot, but trying to hit a target in this situation was difficult.

Ollie whimpered, and his heart clenched for the child. No kid should have to witness and go through what she had unintentionally found herself in the middle of. "Ollie, hang in there, hon."

"I'm hanging, Sully." Her voice shook. She was terrified, of course, but she was also one of the bravest people he'd ever met. He needed to tell her that as soon as they got out of this mess.

The black SUV surged forward, right on their tail, then pulled up beside them. Piper gasped. "Is he positioning for a PIT maneuver?"

Sure looked like it to him.

With impact imminent, Sully accelerated and steered slightly toward the shoulder of the road.

When the hit came, his SUV spun, but because of his countermeasures, he was able to gain control after a 360 that left him slightly dizzy. Somehow he was still on the road and heading in the direction of the ranch with the black SUV falling behind them.

"What just happened?" Piper shouted.

"I don't know, I'm just grateful we're still in one piece."

The wind from the open window whipped around them, and Sully's mind raced. They couldn't outrun them much longer. Whoever *they* were, *they* had fast cars. And knew how to execute PIT maneuvers.

That worried him. He glanced in the rearview mirror once more. "We passed an old barn a while back. With the overgrown access road."

"Yeah," Piper said, "I saw it. About a quarter of a mile back."

"I'm going to go for that. I have an idea."

"What?"

"Hang on." He slowed and did a quick U-turn. The sedan shot past with a squeal of brakes.

"I don't know about this, Sully," Piper said. "They could split up and cut us off."

"Maybe. Or they'll just follow us."

"What are you thinking?"

"Flash-bangs are in the back, right?"

"Yes."

"Then I've got a plan."

"All right, then. Let me know my part when it's time."

Ollie sat up, and her slender fingers pressed into his shoulder. "Sully—"

"Not now, kiddo. Get back down and stay there, okay?"

She did as he said. "I'm scared."

"I am too, but we're going to fight our way out of this and be just fine. Got it?"

"Sure." Her dubious tone conveyed what she really thought.

But she didn't know everything that was going through Sully's head right now, which was the mantra that he could not fail. *Would not fail.*

Not this time.

Please, God, let this work.

The black SUV edged closer once more, but Sully was ready. He had one chance to get this right. Movement caught his attention—the second vehicle had dropped back.

He glanced at Piper. "As soon as I stop, I'll pop the back. You grab the bag and hightail it back into the passenger's seat."

"Got it." She rolled the window up, cutting off the bone-chilling wind.

Sully sucked in a breath, said a quick prayer, and cranked the wheel hard left.

Gravel sprayed as he whipped the SUV onto the overgrown access road. Tree branches slapped against the hood, leaves and twigs snapped and sprayed across the windshield.

Nothing like leaving a trail a blind man could follow.

The abandoned barn loomed ahead, the weathered boards having seen better days. But it would do for what he needed.

Piper looked back. "Splitting up like I thought they would."

"It's okay." He pressed the accelerator and aimed for the barn's gaping doors. He slammed on the brakes and spun the wheel hard once more. The SUV slid sideways into the barn in a shower of dirt and rotted wood.

Piper was already out of the vehicle as he popped the hatch.

Less than five seconds later, she was back in her seat. She shoved the go bag on the floor and snagged a flash-bang. "Ready."

"Here he comes," Sully said.

"And the sedan?"

"Don't know." He frowned. "Hands over your ears and close your eyes, Ollie. Got it?"

"Yes!"

He nodded to Piper, who waited. Seconds ticked past and the black SUV roared into sight. It slammed to a stop and Piper tossed the weapon under the vehicle. She yanked her door shut, ducked her head, and clamped her hands over her ears.

Sully did the same.

The bang and flash came. He'd expected it, but it was jarring all the same.

He didn't wait for the dust to settle. He threw the vehicle into reverse and shot through the back wall of the barn. The wood came down, thumping and bouncing off the car. He threw the vehicle in drive and pressed the gas, aiming for the long dirt drive.

"The sedan!"

Piper's cry alerted him to the vehicle coming down the drive, spitting dirt in its path. They were now nose to nose.

"Sully!"

"He won't crash into me."

"Then I'm worried about you crashing into him!"

Almost on cue, the driver swerved. He fumbled with the wheel, fishtailing, then rammed into an old, rusted tractor.

"Go!" Piper's urgency fueled his own, and he accelerated toward the road, taking the path he'd created on his mad dash to the barn.

"Ollie! You okay?"

"I'm okay," she said, sounding a bit breathless.

Sully allowed a moment of relief to sweep over him. And gratitude. They were safe. For now.

However, relaxing wasn't an option. He swept his gaze between the mirrors, looking for movement, any sign that their pursuers were still on their tail somewhere. Piper did the same. She was a good partner, and he was glad she had his back. "We bought some time," he said, "but they're not done. They'll regroup, replan, and come back."

Piper shot him a tight smile. "Let's hope Maya's security is as good as she says it is."

"It is. David and I helped her come up with it." David Sinclair, Maya's head of security at the ranch, was also one of Sully's childhood buddies. The man had been looking for something different and approached Sully about any job recommendations. He'd sent the guy to Maya, and she'd hired him a few months ago. "David and Maya discussed us using the ranch as a safe house," he said. "And they agreed Ollie would be safe there. She's got top-notch tech out there in the middle of nowhere."

"Well then, that makes me feel so much better. Security by David and Sully. What could go wrong?"

A soft chuckle came from the back seat, and he found a smile curving his own lips. He enjoyed sparring with Piper, and apparently Ollie liked it too. She sat up and met his gaze in the rearview mirror. "Will they find us at the ranch?"

"I can't promise they won't, but I *can* promise that the ranch is a special place with special people, and you'll be as safe as possible there."

She nodded, and he sent up another silent prayer. *Please, God, let us be safe there.*

THE ROAR OF THE ENGINE COMING UP the dirt driveway caught Elena Thompson's attention. She was outside the barn with four of the ranch's occupants—Gina Delaney, Frank Boggs, Adam Andrews, and Nick St. James—teaching them how to make a solar still. A simple enough process with only a few materials needed, but it was something none of them had ever seen before, so she had a captive audience.

The SUV sped along with purpose, dust flying behind it.

Maya Sullivan Price, the owner of the Broken Chains Ranch and good friend to Elena, joined her in watching the approach.

"Who's that?" Elena asked.

"My cousin."

"Oh yes. We've met. Mr. FBI Special Agent Collin Sullivan."

"Sully to most. Pain in the neck to others," Maya murmured.

Elena laughed. "Who's with him?"

Maya pulled Elena to the side, out of hearing range of the others. "I'm just letting you in on this because I have permission. He has his new partner, Piper Whitaker, and a young girl who witnessed a murder with him. Her name is Olivia Callahan."

Elena's laughter faded. "Oh, how terrible."

"Yeah. Sully and David used to work together in some capacity at the Bureau. David and I talked about it and agreed to let them hide out here until the trial." She waved her phone. "Sully called and said they were attacked on the way but managed to get away."

"Attacked! By whom?"

"The people who want his protectee dead, I would assume."

"Poor girl."

"She's a foster kid. Been in and out of the system almost as long as she's been alive."

The words kicked Elena in the gut. "Life can be so unfair." Maya's dark eyes glistened with a compassion that Elena knew was reflected in her own gaze. "But," Elena said, "if she's coming here, we'll take care of her."

"We?"

"Yep." She gave a decisive nod. "We."

Maya hugged her and looked back at the others, who continued to work on the project in front of them. "I don't want them to know or worry about this. I hesitated to say yes when Sully asked if he could bring her here. But David and Sully felt like this was the best place for her." She shrugged. "I'm still not sure, to be honest. The ranch is supposed to be a place of calm and healing, not a hideout for people on the run. But the girl . . ." She chewed her bottom lip. "I had a hard time saying no to this one. Sully sounded a bit desperate."

"There is no way to say no to that," Elena said. She glanced at Frank. "You should let Frank in on it. He was special ops and is completely trustworthy in spite of his gruff voice and scruffy appearance." His black beard curved around his chin and his bushy brows could use a good trim, but he had the kindest heart of anyone Elena had ever met.

"Maybe. I'll have to run that by Sully. Right now, all anyone knows is that my cousin, his sister—also my cousin—and her daughter are coming to visit."

"Right."

Maya bit her lip. "I pray I'm making the right decision," she said, her voice low and soft.

"You've said over and over that you want this ranch to be a refuge. A place of restoration. Well, there you go. If that little girl has seen a murder, she's going to need us to be her village."

Maya's worry faded from her features. "I knew you'd say that. With your certification in wilderness therapy and trauma counseling, it may be you who'll be able to help Ollie the most."

"I'm happy to help her any way I can, you know that, but Rachel is here too. She's the trained counselor." Rachel Evans, their art therapist, was a former military chaplain. She'd had her own counseling practice in town until Maya talked her into moving it to the ranch.

"We'll just see what she needs, then make the judgment as to who can help her the most."

"That works." Elena nodded to Adam. "He was in the system a few years, and from what little he's shared, I can tell you it's not a fun place to be. In some ways I think his wounds from that are worse than the ones he got in combat." She shot a pointed look at his titanium leg attached to what remained of his thigh.

"Yeah," Maya whispered.

And then there was no more time to chat. The SUV pulled to a stop in front of the house, about fifty yards away from the barn.

"All right," Maya said. "I'm going to get everyone settled."

"I'm right behind you," Elena said.

"Thanks. They need to meet everyone as soon as possible so they can be familiar with who belongs here."

And so they could also know if someone *didn't* belong.

Elena dismissed her class with promises to finish the project in their next session, then followed Maya to the main house. She let her gaze scan the area behind it in the direction of the mountains that hid . . . a lot.

"You okay?" Maya asked.

"Yes, why?"

"You've seemed a bit preoccupied lately."

Elena shrugged. "I just saw someone in town the other day who reminded me of my childhood."

"Your childhood? With the cult?"

A snort slipped out. "Preppers."

"Cult."

She wasn't convinced they were an actual cult, but she wasn't convinced they weren't either. So . . . "Okay, whatever. But yeah."

"Who?"

She sighed. "It doesn't matter. It was just a glimpse. I'm probably seeing things. Let's focus on your company."

"Fine, but you're spilling the tea later."

Elena should have known better than to try to hide anything from the person who knew her best.

The main house was a ranch that spanned about five thousand square feet. Elena lived in the lower-level apartment while Maya and her husband, Gideon, had the top space. Elena's small living area, complete with two bedrooms, a den, and a tiny kitchen, was all she needed—and more. She was the only worker who lived in the big home, and she paid a modicum of rent because she didn't feel right mooching off her friend.

Although, to hear Maya tell it, Elena was the one doing the favor.

The tall man who'd just exited the vehicle was Collin Sullivan. Sully. Elena had met him a few times over the past six months she'd been there. And Maya had told her all about the cousin she adored, so she felt like she knew him. Maybe. He favored Maya in looks. Dark hair, dark eyes, deeply tanned skin even in November. Five o'clock shadow. A couple of inches over six feet.

He caught her staring and held her gaze, a hint of amusement coloring his eyes. "Hi."

Busted. "Hi. Good to see you again." Thankfully, her voice was steady, no hint of her weirdly rapid pulse. And with her turtleneck and hoodie on, there was no way for him to see the heat climbing into her neck. Hopefully it would stop before it reached her cheeks.

"You too," he said.

The back door opened, and he turned his attention to the teenager climbing out.

The witness. Poor girl.

The front passenger door opened, and a woman with pretty features that were set in a hard expression emerged. Her eyes scanned the area, then swept back to the house.

Maya went to Sully and hugged her cousin. "Welcome. We'll get you all set up. I've got a four-bedroom cabin available that's not too far from the house, but secluded so you can easily see if anyone approaches. It's set pretty close to the lake and has an updated security system. It's called Serenity."

Sully nodded. "That sounds perfect."

Maya smiled. "Let's hope it can live up to its name."

"Definitely. I can't thank you enough for being willing to take us in at the last minute like this. Our last two places were compromised, and we've been running out of options."

Elena raised a brow. "Sounds like you're trusting someone you shouldn't."

His gaze collided with hers, and it was like a physical impact smack in her gut. She swallowed. Weird.

"I don't want to think it," he said, "but can't say it hasn't crossed my mind." He gestured to the tall woman still standing by the car. "Everyone, this is Piper Whitaker, my partner, aka my sister and cousin to Maya." Piper was only about three inches shorter than Sully. And she was very pretty. The woman nodded and offered a small smile. "And this brave young lady," Sully continued, "is Olivia—better known as Ollie—Callahan, my 'niece.'" He air quoted the last word.

302

Once the introductions were made, Maya held out a key to Elena. "Do you mind showing them the cabin and giving them the code to the alarm system as well as the door code? I have a phone call I need to make."

Elena took the key and curled her fingers around it, letting the jagged edges dig into her skin and keep her grounded. Now wasn't the time to be mooning over Collin Sullivan. Not that there was ever a good time for that.

Focus.

"Of course," she said, forcing a smile. "Happy to do it. Let me grab a golf cart and I'll lead you out there." She could ride with them and walk back but figured this way would be easier.

And hopefully would offer her a moment to disconnect that weird attraction arcing between her and Sully.

Pushing the man to the back of her mind, she hurried to the building next to the barn and snagged the keys from the wall. The ranch owned six golf carts, and she hopped into the one nearest the door. She pulled out of the building, noted the three refugees all tucked into the SUV, and motioned for them to follow her.

They fell in behind her, and within ninety seconds, she pulled into the small horseshoe-shaped dirt drive. The cabin was the biggest one on the property and most would call it a house, but all the structures around the lake and up the hill into the woods were known as cabins.

She unlocked the door with the code and waited for them to grab their things. Ollie, who still hadn't said a word, clutched her small rolling carry-on and stepped inside. Elena met her gaze and offered her a reassuring smile. The girl's lips never twitched.

Elena drew in a breath and motioned to the area in front of her. "The layout is the kitchen, dining area, then the great room in one big open area, which you can see from here. To the right are two bedrooms. On the basement level there are two more bedrooms. You access the stairs through the great room. I think Ollie should have that bedroom next to the stairs. It's safest and there's no door leading out to the porch."

"Perfect." Sully nodded to Piper. "Why don't you get Ollie settled.

I'll be fine with whatever—even the couch at night so we can all be on the same floor. In the meantime, I'm going to check over the security system."

Piper nodded and led Ollie through the kitchen and dining area, then made a right and disappeared into the hallway. The agent had placed herself between the far windows and Ollie. Smart. But something about her movements seemed off. Stiff, like she was . . . mad? Worried? "She doesn't agree that this is the best place for Ollie?" she asked Sully.

He quirked a small smile. "I'm impressed. And annoyed. How'd you guess?"

Elena shrugged. "Body language. Some people are easier to read than others. Why would you be annoyed?"

"Because you read her that easily."

"Oh." She smiled and nodded to the wall in the kitchen. "The security panel's over here." He followed her. "You'll find it in good shape." She tilted her head at him. "Or did you do this one too?"

"No, I didn't."

"Oh, well, Maya must have taken direction from what you did with her home, because this one has the motion sensors, infrared cameras, and more."

"Good to know."

She stilled. He was right behind her. And she hadn't heard him approach.

"You seem to know a lot about the security setup," he said, taking a step back and giving her some breathing room.

She cleared her throat. "Let's just say I learned at a very young age how to spot weakness in a perimeter." Her tone was light. Her memories were not. "Maya knows I have relevant experience, and she's smart enough to put that to good use."

She reached for the panel, but Sully's hand shot out, catching her wrist. Her pulse flared and she tensed. "What are you doing?"

"You have blood on—there."

"What?" She looked down. Then opened her hand. Thanks to the key she still gripped, a small, jagged trail of blood had traveled from her palm to her sleeve. She'd squeezed the little piece of metal too tight. "Oh, for crying— It's nothing." She pulled away, uncomfortable with his powers of observation—and how much she liked the feel of his hand on hers. She cleared her throat. "This is the panel. Obviously. I should probably . . . um . . . go do . . . something. Like clean up the blood and change my shirt."

Wow. Awkward much? Heat climbed into her neck for the second time that day. She passed the key to him. "That's for the door in case the code doesn't work. I don't expect that to happen, but at least you're prepared."

"And you're prepared in every way, aren't you?"

At his observation, she blinked, then shot him a small smile. She grabbed a paper towel and pressed it to the minor wound. She turned to leave and stopped when she spotted Ollie in the doorway, eyes now on Elena's bloodstained sleeve. Something flickered in her expression. Recognition? Understanding?

"You've hurt yourself," Ollie said. "It's your way to stay focused, not let yourself think about other things, isn't it?"

Elena's breath caught and Sully went still. "Um—I didn't mean to. It was an accident." But she *did* have her coping mechanisms. Not that she needed to air that dirty laundry.

"Sometimes," Ollie said, "I add numbers up in my head. Hard numbers. It helps clear my mind of everything else and makes stuff fade into the background."

Elena walked to the teen who'd seen too much. Who'd learned too young how to cope with those things. "I could teach you other ways," she said. "Maybe not better, but possibly. If you wanted. I mean, if it's okay with Sully and Piper . . . er . . . Agent Whitaker."

Ollie's eyes widened, and Piper, who'd stepped up behind the girl, made a sound that might have been a protest. Then she said, "Piper's fine."

Sully's quiet "thank you" made Elena realize she might have crossed a line she wasn't aware was there. Maybe she shouldn't have made the offer to Ollie without clearing it with Sully and Piper. Well, whatever. She'd let them figure it out and then tell her what to do.

She straightened, nodded to the others, and headed out the door. She was halfway to the golf cart, desperately trying to keep past memories, feelings, and fears at bay, when she heard footsteps behind her.

"Elena, wait."

She looked back to see Sully gaining on her. She tried to push the memories of her family's compound from her head. Along with everything she'd been programmed to believe—and later had to unlearn. She took a steadying breath. "Yes?" Thank goodness the word came out low and calm.

He stopped next to her, eyes kind. Concerned. Compassionate. "You mentioned some ways to help Ollie. Did someone teach them to you?"

She huffed. "That's what you want to know?"

He shrugged. "Yes."

"Then no. No one taught me. I had to figure a lot of things out alone." She met his gaze. "But that's why I'm here now. So others don't have to do the same."

"I see."

"Do you?" He probably did, and that made her want to squirm. "I've got stuff to take care of," she said. "A class to finish tomorrow, so I need to make sure I'm prepared." She was, but it never hurt to double-check. "Talk to you later."

After parking the golf cart, she hurried into the barn, where her students had put all the pieces of the still. Just being in the barn and planning what she was going to do tomorrow grounded her. She had a solar still to finish building so she could demonstrate how it purified water. Simple. Practical. And one more tool in her belt of those kinds of survival skills.

The other kinds—the ones Ollie needed—would come later. For now, she just had to ignore the way Mr. Big Shot FBI Special Agent Collin Sullivan seemed to see right through her carefully constructed walls.

And pray she hadn't made a huge mistake by giving him a glimpse of what lay behind them.

ACKNOWLEDGMENTS

Writing this book has been a journey that would not have been possible without the support and contributions of many remarkable people who I owe so much to.

First and foremost, thank you to Jesus. Without him, none of this would be possible.

Next, I would like to express my deepest gratitude to Andrea Doering, Barb Barnes, and Jessica English, whose guidance, insight, and patience—sooooo much patience—helped shape this work in countless ways. Barb, you still can't ever fully retire. I'm not ready to stop writing yet. ☺

I am profoundly grateful to retired FBI Special Agent Dru Wells, who always gives me the most help in getting my law enforcement accurate.

Special thanks go to the Beta readers, whose excellent editorial catches helped make sure the book shines.

And as always, I owe a debt of gratitude to everyone at Revell. This book, and all books with my name on them, are a result of amazing teamwork by incredibly talented individuals. Thank you, Revell!

I can't say enough thank-yous to Tamela Hancock Murray for

helping make all of my publishing dreams come true. You're the most wonderful agent and friend and I love you bunches!

This book would not exist without the unwavering support of my family. To Jack, Lauryn, and Will, thank you for your endless encouragement, understanding during long writing sessions, and belief in me always.

Finally, to Jack—your love, patience, and support always get me through to the end even when I want to go kick some cabinets and throw my laptop in the trash. This book is as much yours as it is mine.

Lynette Eason is the *USA Today* bestselling author of *Double Take*, *Target Acquired*, and *Serial Burn*, as well as the Extreme Measures, Danger Never Sleeps, Blue Justice, Women of Justice, Deadly Reunions, Hidden Identity, and Elite Guardians series. She is the winner of three ACFW Carol Awards, the Selah Award, and the Inspirational Reader's Choice Award, among others. She is a graduate of the University of South Carolina and has a master's degree in education from Converse College. Eason lives in South Carolina with her husband. They have two adult children. Learn more at LynetteEason.com.

Connect with
LYNETTE

Sign up for Lynette Eason's newsletter to stay in touch
on new books, giveaways, and events.

LYNETTEEASON.COM